TRAVELING THE OUTLAW TRAIL

The few good guys—the stubborn roadrunners and hundredplussers who're still hanging around—are avoiding me. I don't even go out on the highway anymore. My wheels are just not fast enough. Now that Cora's given up on me, there doesn't seem to be any sense in staying around this tar-patch and performing my loner number anymore.

Well, let them shove it.

Let them all shove it.

I'm taking my wheels and going on down the road, heading west, across the great plains and through the mountains, where the fields are greener and so, I'm told, are the punk kids and cops . . .

A Set of Wheels

ROBERT THURSTON

B®

BERKLEY BOOKS, NEW YORK

Portions of this novel first appeared in
substantially different versions in *Cosmos* magazine
and in *Clarion*, an anthology edited
by Robin Scott Wilson.

A SET OF WHEELS

A Berkley Book / published by arrangement with
the author

PRINTING HISTORY
Berkley edition / February 1983

—

ISBN: 0-425-05820-4

In memory of

JOAN KATHLEEN THURSTON
(1942-1980)

And for
JASON GARETH THURSTON

PART I

1

GOT to have wheels. No other out, no other escape from this. Lincoln Rockwell X says he can get me a car. Only catch, I got to go to the ghetto for it. Some catch, a catch of nine-tails. I might get wheels all right, but I might drive out dead. Still—if I don't do anything about it now, I'll be wrinkled and greybearded when I can.

The shit's on the wall, Lincoln Rockwell X told me. And you can have it for the taking.

It's a good car? I asked him.

He gave me his oh-you-sucker! grin.

I sell what I can get. It's my market nowadays. I take the money, you take the consequences. The shit's on the wall, man. Many, many tickle. What you going to do?

I don't know, frankly.

Well, frankly gets you no capital gains. I'll see you around.

No, wait!

You buying?

I'm thinking.

You go ahead and think, but I'm not sticking around.

But—

I want slow, I can buy me a pet snail. When you're through thinking, contact me. You know where to find me, man.

He left. That was two hours ago. I'm still thinking.

Hell.

Shit.

Got to have wheels, got to have, got to.

I'll never get a safedry license anyhow. You got to be the son of a safedry. They'll shove you this crap about safedry's high life expectancy, just to hide what's true, that it's all kissass games. My father's screwed me royal. He's a known traffic vile. I been turned down now seventeen times for a learner's permit. Bureau clerks laugh among themselves when I come in.

Got to have, got to.

I want to have wheels, okay, I go to the ghetto. Today.

Dad's come home. Used to be, he'd look in on me. Now he just heads straight for the kitchen and the altar where he keeps his bottles. He looks like hell these days, like he's been studying winos from old movies. He's got this crooked dazed grin, these sleepy dazed eyes, thrown away ragdoll hair. His body is shrinking. Looking at him, I see strange new anatomical curves and twists almost every day.

I try sneaking off from the kitchen doorway. No good. He's known I'm there all the time. Nothing much escapes his attention. Maybe he's acting this wino part after all. Maybe he's gone back to showbiz and he's got this job playing a whacked-out wino. He's just been preparing a role, watching other winos, pretending to be one of them just to get their moves down pat. Drinking special tea, made to look like wine by adding food coloring to water, then placing it in old bottles. Sure, he's been practicing the role for five years.

Hello son, he says. Son o' mine.

Sounds like his tongue's swollen to three times its normal size, instead of its usual two.

I love you, son.

You're aces with me too, pops.

My old Andy Hardy/Leo Gorcey routine, he loves it.

I saw your mommy today.

His weak voice can't support the kind of irony he's trying to give it. He says irony was his forte on stage and in his one supporting part in a monster movie. He made me watch that movie once. All I remember is that, on our ancient television set, his hair looked like it was dyed lavender. He didn't like me pointing that out. I learned a lot about actorish irony from him, some of it gets me exactly what I want. But no wonder he's so whacko. Visiting my mother is the sort of blunder that started him on this five-year binge in the first place.

How is mumsy? Haven't seen her for weeks. She seems to've overcome her addiction to the telephone, too.

She's more beautiful than ever. She just returned from one of those Swiss beauty treatments. Harold sent her.

Harold is the moderately well-to-do man that Mom is either keeping company with or married to. She sometimes pretends one, sometimes the other. Harold's not so bad, only moderately well-to-do bad. Biggest thing I have against him, he won't buy me a set of good wheels. He lets me drive his, though. That's his liberal concession. But only on the safe dull streets of the guarded and patrolled neighborhood where he and Mom live. What little I know about driving—and it's damn little since he won't let his precious Pontiac go over 40 mph—I get from Harold. I got so tired of his screaming every time the speedometer needle hit 41 mph that I stopped paying duty visits, even turned down his offers to go out for a spin the last few times I did go there. Mom wants me to like Harold. He's not so bad. She could do worse. With *her* track record, she's lucky Harold ever wanted her.

Mom went to Switzerland *really*? I say, figuring Dad to be on one of his more imaginative binges. I can't picture Harold brushing the moths away from his wallet to provide the small fortune it costs to cross the old and oily Atlantic these days. Anyway, he's got no power, no influence, so there's no way he could wangle all those permits that'd allow Mom to leave the country and cross the Alps.

Of course not to Switzerland *really*, Dad says. All I said was Swiss beauty treatment. You can get one downtown so long as you're willing to lie in a coffin for two weeks.

Oh, should have—how's she look, Mom?

I told you, beautiful. Don't you ever listen? I love you, son.

Gets so lately I hardly even notice his drunken jumps from one thought to another.

Ah, I think you're the bee's knees, pops.

Allow me to give you a piece of advice, fatherly wisdom, son.

Oh, shit, here it comes! Even though I know he's acquired about as much wisdom as there is sediment at the bottom of one of his wine bottles—which is to say, none, since there's *no* sediment at the bottom of the kind of rotgut vintage he puts away—I say to him:

Shoot, Dad, I'm all ears.

Which is better than your mother who is all mouth.

God, I wish I didn't have to chuckle politely at cheap-shot lines like that. I'm itching to flee the kitchen, get out of the house, rendezvous with Lincoln Rockwell X. Dad straightens himself up to full slouch and intones:

As you travel through this life, brother, whatever be your goal, keep your eye upon the doughnut and not upon the hole.

Shit, he hasn't been this blotto since—since when? Since the last time he dropped in on Mom.

That verse was a part of my youth. Painted on a side wall of display window, bakery—my old neighborhood, my old hometown, wherever that was. The bakery, whole town, demolished long ago. Nice little bakery, owned by a German family. Every Lent they made fastnacht keuchls. Flat doughnut, granulated sugar, sometimes powdered, hate powdered—

What about the verse? I say. Have to interrupt dear old Dad when he starts wandering like that, especially when I got to get the hell out of here. Lincoln Rockwell X, as he so often says, lets no cooling gather around his heels.

The verse. Used to see it almost every day, in my youth. Keep your eye upon the doughnut and not upon the hole. I thought it must be all about doughnuts.

Would you like me to pick up a dozen crullers while I'm out?

Doughnuts they make now are glutinous poison. A jelly doughnut today is like red-colored vaseline enclosed in chewable rubber cement. But the doughnuts of my day—well, you'll never know that, son. Your eyes are chrome. What was I saying? The doughnut. Finally I reached the age where I could appreciate homily. Let me live in a house by the side of the road, watch the race of men go by, the men who are good and the men who are bad—forgotten rest of it, I think.

Maybe if it had been about pastry. . . .

Homily. Homely folk wisdom. Keep your eye on the doughnut, keep your eye on what is real, substantial, pragmatic. And not upon the hole—emptiness, sin, the insubstantial, the—

You might not believe this, but I really figured that out when I first heard the verse.

He recoils. I add a perfunctory pops, trying to put a smidgen of Andy Hardy into it, but it's too late in the sentence. He's hurt and I'm sorry, really sorry, and feeling sorry is what he wanted from me in the first place. And I'm sorry about that, too.

Practicality of doughnut versus irrationality of hole, he says.

His continuing on the subject is now defiant. Good solid Americana, pursue the American dream, it is achievable, it is as real as the doughnut. Optimism. That's what built this country, optimism. Henry Ford, that great old Jewbaiting optimist. Fisk, Gould, Carnegie, all of them optimists. Rockefeller. All my schoolbooks told me they were optimists, farseeing men who believed in the potential of this country. Optimistically. Theodore Delano Roosevelt, optimist, warmonger, elephant-hunting cripple. Kept his eye on the doughnut, yessirree. Why—

I'm not much interested in American history, pops.

Yes, I recall your grades. But that's okay. Now I don't much believe in American history, son, or homily. My advice to you, forget the doughnut. Keep your eye upon the hole and not upon the doughnut. That's my—the truth, shadowy and ragged. Do you understand what I am saying, son?

I understand. Better than you could ever guess.

Perhaps you do. I often think that odd intelligent things go on behind those chrome eyes.

He seems to be nodding out. I edge back toward the door.

Exactly like yours, your mother's eyes, he mumbles. Hers . . . sterling silver, not chrome . . . all the same, isn't it?

The old bastard, he's always got to add insults about mother. I charge out the door, not waiting to see if he's asleep yet or not.

Busclerk, bastard, turns me down. Won't even discuss with me. No seats available, he says. The buses are to be utilized by those whose trips have a useful purpose, he says. The old party line. Only bastards with jobs, with errands relating to jobs, with special cards affirming that the trip is a necessary one, sons of bitches who got an in with somebody and who know who the hell to pay off and can ride themselves without having to put up with bastard busclerks who know exactly how many free seats they got available and how much they'll take from you to suddenly discover just where immediate seating exists. Well, I can't give the bastard a cent. What money I got, I got to keep clear—to pay Lincoln Rockwell X, to get gas for the wheels he's keeping for me. So I turn away from the bastard busclerk without even telling him where to get off.

Have to walk crosstown. Terrific. I always enjoy sauntering along the sidewalks, feeling my shoulder muscles tighten at the gunning of each car coming up behind me. Not many cars out today. Three or four carloads of punk safedrys out cruising. They shout insults at me, but I remain detached, try to look like I'm just a safedry out slumming the sidewalks. Can't offer to fight them because I'm alone. I tried partnering a few times, and running with gangs, but it never worked out. Only bastards ever wanted to partner with me were fuckers so dumb they embarrassed the hell out of me. Only gangs that'd have me had no guts and you were safer being alone as running with them. So I stay alone, pay no attention to the high-voiced bastard who quick rolls his window down (he's probably got push-button controls, the stupid asshole), quick shouts lookit the dogshit on legs, and quick rolls the window back up again. Crummy bastards, they drive through the streets, their windows locked tight when they're not throwing out challenges, when they're not throwing out rocks, their bodies moving to tapedeck music we can't hear through the soundproofing.

At least it's not night. At night, in areas like this which police cars avoid, they search us out and try to back us against walls with their fucking cars. They come up on the pavement after us. They're positively scary, weird shadows moving behind tinted windshields, tightassed monsters out to joyride. When we can, we steal their license plates, which is not often but each time gives them hell to pay down at the bureau. Ah, I know they always get new licenses. Once a safedry, always a safedry. But at least we twist their guts with red tape. The license plates, we bend them out of shape and bury them in the ground.

Street debris clings to my trousers. Dust flies into my eyes. I need something different. My whole life needs a kick in the balls. Work, when I can get it, is sleepwalking from desk to desk or being a zombie behind counters. Home is sneaking looks at my Dad sneaking drinks. Play is dodging the traps, play is bumping bodies to drumbeats you can't hear. Sex is just bumping bodies. I can't wait to get behind my own fucking steering wheel.

The cops may crack me for illegal driving.

But they got to catch me first.

2

EASY time slipping past the fuzz checkpoint—they are, after all, trained to supervise the passage of blackfolk in and out of the ghetto, a white complexion on the way in is same as invisible. Not so easy crawling across the natural barrier, the rubble of the blownup abandoned buildings. I walk through the sniper zone unscathed, though a distant shot keeps me alert. Lincoln Rockwell X told me to get to the corner before eleven and I'm just making it. He's a demon for appointments. Like he says, you're late and you've missed me.

He's at the corner, turning some business with some really disreputable looking types who have the words Don't Shit Me Dude printed on their white tee-shirts. I stay out of their way till the dealing is done. Then Lincoln Rockwell X notices me. His eyes get wide and I get a sharp pain in the pit of my stomach—he's going to do his darkie act with me, to entertain his associates.

Well, Master Lee, he says (at least he doesn't do the act in dialect, that's some comfort). I am so pleased to see you. How may I serve you, Master Lee?

The other blacks all put on these shiteating grins, picking up the routine with a bit more eagerness than I'd like, frankly.

It's time, I say. You said eleven.

Well, indeed I did. How considerate of you to be so punctual. I am properly humble of the honor, sir.

Can we go?

I am almost whispering as I submit this request. After all, I'm quite familiar with Lincoln Rockwell X's darkie act. We grew up together, him and me, both in the same ugly suburb—before the laws of the New Enlightenment forced him and his family out. We hung around a lot together, and he always got a terrific kick out of playing this darkie act. When we were kids the game was fun. See, I'd give him orders and he'd fulfill them, like bringing me imaginary mint juleps on a real tray or acting out rude passenger and shrewd porter on a train. He used to wear this old white labcoat we found on a junkpile. It was ripped at the pockets and smeared with what we hoped was blood.

We had no reason to believe that we wouldn't grow up together all the way, playing our comradely game into our adult lives. We just never figured on history interfering—first the Grand Rapids Massacre, then all that combat shit out west. Then the South delighted at the new historical turns muscling in on it all. I cried when Lincoln Rockwell X had to leave our suburb with his family. Shit, my family was out of the place within two years ourselves, after Mother took off and Dad started his affair with the bottle.

So now Lincoln Rockwell X had to have that damn special encoded card to function at all—and everybody with an ounce of intelligence complained about the regressive New Enlightenment laws and there were still skirmishes and here I am putting up with his darkie act on a streetcorner in his own turf and hating every fucking minute of it. He sees the pain in my eyes, calls the act off, takes me by the arm, bids farewell to the others, and we go off down the street.

Tone down, Lee, he says, it's only a couple blocks from here to the wheels.

The blackfolk citizens of the territory stare at me but leave me alone.

Only an idiot sneaks into their territory, he mutters, and they don't think it's Christian to maim idiots.

I walk along with my tongue sticking out the corner of my mouth.

He leads me to wheels. It's in the basement of an abandoned Afro-Methodist church. We have to maneuver around upended and broken pews. To get to the car we have to go down steps behind what's left of an altar. We pass office doors with broken windows, shards of glass unsteady stalactites and stalagmites. You can only see junk inside the offices.

He takes me to a recreation room. No electricity.

He says, I'll light candles and you get the Big Show, dig?

He makes an elaborate thing out of placing the candles on the stage. Lights each one with a swishy hand move. The front of the stage is littered with the pieces of broken light bulbs and torn-up hymnals. He sings a trumpet call through his nose as he opens a curtain that's got burn holes all over it.

And there you go, he says. Wheels.

Which is so, though it's not exactly like I imagined it. All the cars you see on the street are shined-up no matter how old they are. Harold does a spit-shine on his Pontiac every Saturday. I've seen him polish the car in the rain. Safedrys think a glossy car's better than a big prick. And they don't allow any bumps anywhere on the body of the car. I nudged a tree once with Harold's Pontiac and he had a heart seizure right there, further complicated by a stroke when he examined the tiny scratch on the fender. Scratches like that, bumps, they're the end of the world for safedrys. If anything happens they quick go to a black market garage before anybody official finds out and they get points against them. They'll pay anything to keep their record clean, to keep their license.

But this car! This car's got pain in every curve. It'd choked to death and gone to hell. It looks menacing. Like if you touched it, you'd get cancer.

Five hundred dollars, says Lincoln Rockwell X.

Five hundred dollars? I say. For *that*?

You got a better deal, you go make it. No small talk on my time, man.

I know better than to argue. I'm deep in his territory, more than five hundred bucks in my pocket. Lincoln Rockwell X's got blades for teeth and he's not one to let old friendship stand in the way of profits. Sight unseen I'd already bought this baby.

Still—I make like a reluctant buyer. I walk around the car. I kick a tire; it wraps rubber around my foot. I grab a door handle which almost comes off in my hand.

What do I know about cars?

Nothing.

But I pretend.

What year? I ask.

'67, he says.

'67 what?

'67 Mustang. Saved from a graveyard and reconditioned, my granddaddy did the job himself.

Shit. Shit, that's an old fucking car then, qualifies as antique.

Don't say that. Antique makes it all the more valuable, man! I might be tempted to add a c-note to the list price.

Okay, okay. Don't get your back up, old buddy.

Soon as I say it, I know that old buddy is a mistake. Lincoln Rockwell X glares at me, but says nothing. The glare is enough. Forget the old days is always his message. I make mistakes, but I do respond to communication like that.

I just, I don't know man, I just expected something more *recent*.

This is as recent as is on the market these days, friend.

The way he says friend does not sound anything like the way I say my old buddy. But he's right. None of the late models, the ones put out just before they stopped carmaking a decade or so ago, when Ford went down fighting, were ever available. Hell, you hardly even saw them on the streets. They were all protected, guarded, kept behind barriers. Their owners couldn't afford chancing them in open territory. That was the kind of attitude Harold had and, hell, he didn't even have a late model. His Pontiac was only a few years younger than this Mustang. He'd reconditioned it himself right after the New Enlightenment laws that drove the auto companies right out of existence.

Well shit, this Mustang's my car, going to be when the formalities are terminated. I brush away a layer of dirt. The car is dark green underneath. Dark green where it's not rust. I run a finger along the fold-line of a dent. Dark-green flecks come off onto my fingertip.

Jeez, I say, how'm I gonna drive this heap around? Look at all the dents. Cops'll crack me in a minute.

Your PR with the fuzz is your business, baby. You wanted wheels, these're the only bootleg wheels left in town. You got five hundred dollars, you got wheels. You can leave the small talk in your wallet.

Okay, okay, but how'm I gonna get this junkpile on the street? Drive it through the ceiling?

You got five hundred, I'll open sesame for free.

I open the door on the driver's side real easy and get in. Dashboard's in scarred leather. Seats are ripped bad, too. A part of the steering wheel's missing, making it look like a broken-off piece of pretzel. I try out the accelerator. Creaks on the down motion, cries on the up. I move the automatic floor shift, the only undamaged part of the car.

I tell Lincoln Rockwell X okay I'll take it, and hand him the five bills. Motioning me over to the passenger side, with an imperious hand-jerk, he takes over the driver's seat. He produces a key with another swishy flourish and puts it in the ignition. The car moans, gurgles, trembles, threatens suicide, but doesn't start.

Don't worry boy, Lincoln Rockwell X says. Just need to find the right touch. Cars're like this when they're not used everyday.

He invokes a tribal curse and re-presses the accelerator. The car curses back but gives in.

He gets the car out of the building through use of a freight elevator at the back of the stage.

Up a ramp and out in the light, I get my first good look at my wheels. I see all the bumps and dents I missed in candlelight. The thing looks like a crumpled piece of paper. Front and back windows both have cracks in them, short thin cracks yes but it looks like with a little nudge they'd spread wider. Headlights point in opposite directions. Fenders are separating at the seams. Bumper's rippled like sea waves. The mustang on the insignia's laid down and died. Another hole in the roof and it'll be a convertible.

I look over at Lincoln Rockwell X, try to screw my face into the kind of subtle anger he's so capable of (but fail, I know) and I tell him:

How you ever had this heap on the road I'll never know.

Around here cops see a car in this condition riding the asphalt, they lay off cause they know the driver's got blades for fingers.

But how'm I gonna get it across police lines?

You own the car now, friend, you make it run wherever you want to make it go. There's gas cans in the trunk. Filled. A bonus for prompt payment. A gift for old Master Lee—I don't forget anything, man. Call me when you need more. Lowest prices in town.

Drive it, sure. Where the fuck can I take it?

Take it anywhere but keep it moving. Only white allowed around here by dusk's gotta be blurred.

It was a long while till dusk but I didn't want to stay around anyway. Still, I didn't know what the hell to do.

You got a responsibility to me, I say to Lincoln Rockwell X.

Shove that, friend. I put you in the motherfucker seat and that's all is necessary.

He walks away, waving the five bills like a flag. I locate the horn, push it in to get his attention. It wheezes shyly but makes no other sound. I'll get out, run after him, snatch the five bills, run like hell. The door handle comes off in my hand.

I've had the course. What can I do? Stay in the ghetto, dodge between blades? Race cops around the city? Drive only on moonless nights?

My Mustang, motor running, has a coughing fit. I quick depress the accelerator, run it hard to keep the engine from dying out. The accelerator pedal vibrates. The whole car begins to shake.

I better get this car moving before it really gets angry. I shift to D, press the accelerator pedal. A delay before the car responds, then a growling jump forward. Spinning tires set gravel flying, striking the underside of the car with hollow clanging noises.

I pass Lincoln Rockwell X at the end of the block. In the rear-view mirror I see him bounce the five bills off his forehead, tipping them to me like a hat.

Ghetto streets make good practice runways. I see only two other cars, each dilapidated, though in better condition than the Mustang. The streets are filled with obstacles—potholes, chunks of broken pavement, jagged trash, traffic lights laying across intersecting roads, bricks from fallen buildings, the twisted remains of old newsstands. People jump into doorways when I drive along the sidewalk.

The Mustang is reluctant. When I try to gun the motor, it groans and waits a second before granting the speed increase. None of the dashboard gauges work right. The gas gauge doesn't work at all. Maybe I should just joyride, let the gas run out, abandon the car, leave it for some kids to have a lift to their day by burning it. Kiss the five bills goodbye.

Getting through the police line is easy. Both cops're busy beating up a rummy. They got him backed up against a piece of building and they're trading off who slams the club into his gut. The black man shouts out old militant slogans. A carful of white kids parked on the safe side of the line call out ratings for each blow. I speed by them and they hardly glance at me.

3

THE Mustang, which rattles a lot at slow speeds, quiets down with acceleration. I realize how inexperienced I really am at driving. Harold's Pontiac *handles*. Driving it's not driving at all. I try to remember all the times I rode with the social worker—that slouchy old man with a car almost as beat up as this one—and studied the way he drove, trying to learn driving by osmosis. Memory doesn't help. I have to just make the mistakes. Okay. I learn fast.

I can't go home now with no place to hide wheels. If I keep driving around the city, I'll have fuzz scrambling around the windshield in an hour or two. Or the nightroamers'll run me off the road once they see the car's illegal. Or I'll make some dumb wrong turn and wind up back in the ghetto just at dusk.

It took almost three workdays to get the five bills—the longest job I had this screwed-up month and I suffered for it—so I might as well get some value for my money. I'll take a chance, drive around till something happens. What can happen? I can get the shit beat out of me, that's what. I can get five to twenty for driving without a license, another rap for the illegal vehicle itself. I can get sliced up. I can die.

Still—what's a few risks if you got wheels?

• • •

Suddenly I'm in the country. Open fields, overhanging trees, telephone poles, soft shoulders, road signs—the works. I look in the rear-view mirror to make sure the city's still behind me, that it hasn't disappeared. The change is too fast, too abrupt. I'd expected a police line, or some barrier. A sign saying This Is The Countryside.

Instead, there's just country! All around me, nothing civilized to break up the pattern of country. Well, a couple signs ordering me to eat at a couple homey restaurants, but the signs are old and peeling with stuff growing all over them, I doubt these eateries still exist. Trees, all the trees I've seen in the past few years, at least in the days since Dad lost his safedry status, have been scrawny, growing out of little squares of earth in the cement, held up by rusty wires attached to sticks with spinal conditions. But these trees, these trees are frightening. Some arch backwards like they're avoiding contact with the road. Here and there others bend forward, crowding the road, ominous. I edge out to the middle of the road to avoid them. In between the crouchers and the leaners are some straight fir trees, the kind we used to have at Christmas before Dad's habits cancelled Christmas. I pass a whole field of dead trees, still standing but barren. Wonder what did them in.

I begin to notice signs at the side of the road that have nothing to do with eateries. Around a circle each says To The Expressway. Inside the circle is an arrow pointing the way. We got expressways in the city, great cracked-up roads with their entrances blocked off with walls. Kids play on them cause they're safe. I decide to check this expressway, *The* Expressway after all, out.

I give the Mustang its head. I slam down on the accelerator. Gradually the car picks up speed, I don't know how much because the speedometer needle jams at 50 mph. Well anyway, at least I've topped my best speed in Harold's Pontiac. At a certain speed the car begins to vibrate menacingly. I slow it down to the fastest safe speed.

The car has a tendency to veer to the right. I have to clutch the steering wheel to keep the car on the road. I'm learning that the Mustang does what it wants to do. I have no control over it, I just make suggestions and hang on.

I pass another car, wheels screaming. Scared, I look in the rear-view mirror. The other car kicks into action and begins to follow me. I know right away I've broken some code; maybe

I've challenged and now I got to play out the fight. I push the pedal to the floorboards. Vibrating like hell the Mustang goes faster, reaches its top speed. It is not enough. My wreck of a Mustang is no match for the sleek tuned-up model chasing us. I try evasive tactics, hogging the middle of the road so that our pursuer can't pass. Around a curve he glides to the outside, comes alongside, and convinces us to pull over.

You can read fuzz all over his face. He's skinny but he walks like a fat man. His little eyes look out between the only bulges in his face. Cram-course muscles hang from his thin shoulders like meat on hooks.

He pulls open my door. It makes a loud snap like it's going to break off. He grabs my collar with huge hands and drags me out of the car. My feet get tangled and I start to fall. He tosses me the rest of the way. I hit my head against a rear fender. The pain makes everything blur.

You pukes're getting braver all the time, he says.

I don't know what you're talking about.

I'm talking, you asshole, about how far you're willing to venture from the Cloverleaf. Which group of bums you belong to—the Roadrunners, the Mechs, the Hundredplussers?

I tell him I don't understand. I stand up. He gives a kind of nasal grunt and slaps me across the face backhand. He grabs my shoulders, twists me around, pushes me against the trunk. I double over, a sharp fender edge caving in my stomach. He frisks me, takes away my wallet. He looks inside, there's nothing in it but the left-over money from my great wheels transaction, a few bucks. He counts it, and it looks for a minute like he's going to pocket it, but he puts it back inside. I start to stand up again. He pushes me down again, harder this time. Pinpoints of colored light flash like TV interference and I black out.

4

As I wake up, I hear the cop saying:

Get your ass here pronto. I can't sit on the lid all day just for this jerk. Okay, sure, okay. Ten-four and other great numbers of the western world. Over and out. Goodbye. À demain.

I'm laid out on the ground, on my back. He must've put me there, arranged me carefully like an undertaker with a corpse he really likes.

You okay, old buddy? he asks.

I test all my breakable parts.

Yeah. Okay, seems.

Stupid, you shouldn't take such chances.

Chances?

When you got a gang, stay with them. You guys that think you can go it on your own—why that car of yours couldn't outrun a fat nurse pushing a baby buggy.

I don't get it.

What are you trying, getting off on a schmuck defense? Stupid's not an excuse. We're not going to baby you jerks any more. Any day now, we're going to tear up the roads and pour your skulls into the new cement.

His voice is strange. Like, he's telling me how his side is going to brutalize me and he sounds like he's giving me friendly advice.

18

I sit up. He leans against a car door, puffing on a joint.

You jerks, he says, wish I could nail you all. Then I'd get myself taken back onto the city force. They'd stop all their chickenshit excuses about how *valuable* I am to them out here, how I make so many outdoor collars, all that shit. Outdoor collar! Jesus! I hate cop talk.

I shake my head to clear it. But there's still a dizzy wavery layer that makes it hard to focus my eyes. The cop looks at me and his face edges an inch closer to kindness.

It'll go away. I'm well-trained, never killed anybody yet. Not with my fists anyway.

With a gun?

He doesn't like me asking, that's clear.

Old buddy, that's for me to know and you to shut up your face about.

He looks off toward the hills, takes another puff. Across from us is a field where thin stalks, most of them with spotty leaves, move about erratically as if there are at least five different breezes stirring them up.

Jerk, he says, exhaling.

He looks my way again.

Funny, you don't look like a jerk. You're not scruffy enough.

He hands me the joint. I try not to look surprised. I accept it and take a big drag. It makes the pains better.

You know who you look like, old buddy?

No idea.

No, wouldn't've. You look like a guy who used to be my partner on a city beat. We'd go off to a coop and rap about things. Rap was his word; he used it like it was still in style. He didn't know shit about being a good cop but he read a lot and was real good at talking about it. In a few words, a few words, he could tell me the gist of what he read. Always amazed me, that.

I pass back the joint. His fingers are so big he can hardly take it out of my hand. Little clumps of hair grow on the wide backs of a couple of his fingers, looks like you could hide contraband in them.

He'd been one of you jerks, or at least a jerk like you jerks. Maybe that's why you remind me of him. He could explain the radical line so it almost made sense. Shit, I think he figured on revolutionizing the force.

He takes another drag, holds it for a long time.

Nice kid. Got sliced from hairline to heel by some punk out looking for wheels to cop. Ain't run with a partner since.

I hold onto the fender of the Mustang and pull myself up. The fender almost breaks off under the strain of my weight. My gut feels like it's ripped to pieces.

You'll be okay, kid. Just be glad I didn't give you my patented Sergeant Allen special. They can't get up from that—they beg for amputations.

You Sergeant Allen?

Yeah. You heard of me?

No.

He seems disappointed.

You ain't been on the road long then, he says.

I look around. We seem to be in the middle of a curve, just off the road on the shoulder. Except for the nearby field and the hills beyond it, you can't see far in any other direction.

You got any information, I can get you off easy.

He seems embarrassed to be saying it.

No. I don't know shit. Really.

He gives me a strange smile, like he likes the answer.

Ah, you jerks, he says, and I think he means something good.

I wonder if he's jazzing me. He talks like no cop I ever heard. I mean, he makes me want to talk to him. I decide to.

You like being a cop?

He laughs. An explosion.

You really are a dumbass from the word go. Shit, I bet if we still had to read off the rights to you jerks, I'd have to spell out every word for you.

I don't understand, but I'm learning it's better to keep my mouth shut. He takes a last drag on the joint, then crushes it between his big fingers and throws it away.

Jerks're the foundation of my whole goddamned life, you know that? he says. No, you wouldn't. I gotta drive around twelve hours a day collaring jerks, I gotta listen to jerks tell me what to do, jerks jerking off, I gotta go home to—

He stops talking, stands up suddenly, his body tense. I hear the sound of an approaching car. I wonder how long I've been hearing it. Allen reaches into his glove compartment and pulls out a gun. I haven't seen a gun close up since I was fifteen. That was when mother first introduced me to her new friend Harold and he showed me all the firepower he kept in his cellar—better than Prudential for insurance, he called his guns. I haven't been in his cellar since. Allen's gun has a short barrel and a thick grip. He holds it like he wants to use it.

Squad car's coming from town, he says, ain't nobody else out here on patrol. So that must be buddies of yours. You got something arranged, jerk?

I can't tell him the only arrangement I ever made is buying this screwjob of a car.

The sound stops just around the curve. Car doors open and slam. Feet glide across gravel. Moving shadows through a clump of trees.

I hear you, you stupid bastards, Allen shouts. I don't know what you're up to but I got four rookies just testing out how to use their clubs joining me any minute.

As if to prove his declaration, a siren begins to sound in the distance. I see something on the other side of the Mustang, a dark blur in the bushes. I look to see if Allen noticed. No, he's watching the other side of the road. His body's crouched. The siren gets louder.

Rescuing this dummy's not worth your time, Allen shouts.

Something flies out of the bushes at me. It comes at me chest-level and I catch it. I look down. It's a monkey wrench. A flying monkey wrench. I look at Allen; he hasn't seen. The siren sounds very close. The dark blur jumps silently out of the bushes and crouches beyond the Mustang. I walk three steps to Allen. He hears only the last step and turns. I swing the wrench back-handed, hit the side of his head, scrape the wrench across his forehead, hit him a second time cheekbone level.

Get moving, calls a voice behind me. The siren sounds like it's next door. I run to the Mustang, climb in, too panicked to look at the dark blur, who now occupies the other front seat. I turn the ignition key. The motor wheezes.

Get moving, you dumb shit, says the dark blur, hitting the dashboard with both fists. I can tell by the voice it's a girl. The Mustang must be scared of her, cause it starts up right away.

I push the Mustang to its limit. Every time I think it's having its death rattle, instead it finds a new resource of power and keeps going. The other car, the one from around the curve, joins us and we ride side by side down the highway. Four guys are in the other car. They wave and make odd signs at me.

This car's out of sight *bad*, my companion says. What you got under the hood, a rusty sewing-machine motor?

I look over at her, try to examine what can be seen of her.

Which isn't much 'cause she's so small. She's black. Very dark, so I suspect she wears a darkening makeup, the kind they advertise as AfroBlack. Lincoln Rockwell X told me all the *real* sisters, whatever he meant by that, were using AfroBlack these days, except for the few who were dark enough not to need it. I don't know whether to credit him or not, since he was doing his darkie act while he told me.

Keep your motherfucking eyes on the road, she says. Up ahead it's all broken up and you got to ride the shoulder. It's only a mile to the Cloverleaf.

I continue to sneak looks at her.

Where'd you guys come from? I say. How'd you know Allen had me?

She has white-girl texture hair and she ties it back as if ashamed of it.

We keep tabs, she says. We got a good lookout post up in the hills with a high-power telescope. They saw Allen beating up on you, sent out the message. Guys over there received. Lucky bastards, they got a working CB.

What's your name? I say.

She has childlike shoulders and arms, a series of round pipes with ball-bearing joints.

Cora. Cora Natalie Townsend. What's yours?

She has practically no tits at all, just a hint of nipple beneath a tight sweater.

Lee Kestner.

She has thin but well-proportioned legs.

I want to see her eyes but she won't look at me.

We come to the Cloverleaf. The other car speeds ahead and leads me through its maze. We cross a bridge. Down below are eight lanes of highway, four on each side of a center mall. I see at least three abandoned cars at the sides of the road but not a moving vehicle from one horizon to the other.

This is the Expressway? I say.

Shit, you really *don't* know. Where you come from, a cave?

No, I just never been out of the city before.

The bigass cave. You mean to tell me you never rode the Expressway?

Yes.

Well, you're about to now. I should've known when I saw this rotten car that you were a dumb-shit newcomer. Because it's so slow. Newcomers' cars're lucky if they do 75 on a straightaway.

I just bought this car.

You *paid* for this wreck? Boy, you must be the Newcomer of All Time.

The other car stops by a Merge sign. Its driver rolls down his window. Cora tells me to stop.

The Savarin? the other driver shouts.

The Savarin, she shouts back.

As the other car pulls away, picking up speed fast, she says:

Chuck's impatient. Doesn't want to drag along at your speed. He doesn't believe in wet-nursing other vehicles, leaves them on their own. C'mon, let's see how fast this horsecart can go.

She looks at me and I see her eyes finally. They are dark, expressive. They say, you fool with me and I'll slice off whatever part of you I want.

5

WE go to the Savarin, Cora cursing the Mustang all the way. The
Savarin comes into view after a sign saying Service Area Ahead
1 mi. It is on top of a hill at the end of a long curved access road.
Parked around it are more cars than I've ever seen at one time.
Some of them are being worked on. Others have people sitting in
them, on them, leaning against them, eating off them.

A knock on the window by my head. It's Chuck from the other
car. I roll down the window.

Need anything? he says.

Since I can't even figure out categories for what I'd need, I
start to shake my head no. Cora says,

Everything's straight, Chuck. Check in with you later.

Sure, Cora. Happy trails.

Happy trails.

He walks off.

Chuck's kinda the dutch uncle around here, Cora says. He'll
keep an eye on you for a while, probably. What's the matter?
You look startled.

It's the cars, all of them.

What do you mean, all of them?

With so many cars *here*, how come you don't see any on the
road?

Cora gives me a dumb-shit look.

Two reasons. One, to conserve gas and materials, which are becoming harder to get and more expensive all the time. The legal service stations that deal on the side charge an arm and a leg just to negotiate. So we have to do a lotta down-time whatever we do. Two, it's safer to travel at night unless you're in the mood for real joyriding and we've had to be cautious lately. In the daytime we're more vulnerable to sneak attacks from the fuzz. Once we're on the highway they see us as legal game and they get all kinds of plaudits when they round up a few of us.

Why don't they just come here and get a bunch of you all at once?

Too many of us, not enough of them. It's volunteer duty out here: the smart cops stay in the city and they can only get a few freaks like Allen to take country duty .

That's not the way he tells it.

Oh?

He says he wants to get back to city duty, didn't sound like a volunteer to me.

Who knows with him? He tells you one story one day, switches it around the next. Maybe he's a volunteer, maybe they exiled him. Now you mention it, I might buy the exile jazz. Other cops hate him almost as much as he hates us. Might be. I don't know, he's got his points. Anyway, where was I?

Volunteer duty.

Oh? Anyway, the fuzz likes to keep us as far outside the city as they can, no room for us in the jails or those goddamned camps any more. So they don't bug us much. They hide at the access roads and exits, and look for strays. They only attack when the odds are in their favor. Except Allen. He wants our blood and he wants it flowing. C'mon, I'm going to introduce you to the one man you need desperately right now.

She takes me to a tall, heavy-set man in grease-stained coveralls.

This is The Mech, she says, some reverence in her voice. If anyone can resuscitate that corpse you drive, he can.

The Mech says he'll get to it later. Cora and I go to the squatty building they call the Savarin. On the way I ask her:

That's his name, The Mech?

Her eyes are both amused and angry.

Shit, of course it's not. It's a name, that's all. He hates his real one or he has to keep it a secret, people vote for both reasons around here. But he knows cars, everything that goes in between bumpers. Keep on his good side.

In the Savarin Cora introduces me to a lot of people and then sits me down at the remains of a counter to eat. Chuck, in a nearby booth, waves to me. The room is crowded. Some people sleep in cots lined along the wall. Children run in and out. One man works on a long poem which he is inscribing in Magic Marker around an enormous coffee percolator.

Cora, her eyes taking in everything, seems to look for an excuse to escape from me. I set traps to keep her with me.

I want to touch her—but so she'll know I touched her because I wanted to. Instead I brush against her arm reaching for a sugar shaker, graze knees while swaying the counterstool.

This Allen, he's mean, huh?

Mean? Yeah. Yeah, I guess. He's tough, I'll give him that. He can scramble your brains with one punch if he wants to. But you got to respect him.

I don't understand.

You wouldn't. See, he's a loner and they're hard to come by out here. Most of the time, they cram four-five pigs into one car, but he comes after us all by himself. He digs it, taking us on by himself. He's a spooky dude.

You ever had a run-in with him?

Once. Almost took a bunch of us in. He was pretty nice to me, told me some legal tricks I might use. When he got an emergency squeal and he had to go and leave us behind, he almost seemed happy he didn't have to take us in for booking after all. Strange cop, like I say.

Outside, a score of engines start up. Nervous laughter and fidgeting indicates the eagerness of the crowd to hit the road. The sun is low on the horizon—coming through the large front plateglass window it casts weird shadows over everything. A mock fight starts up between two of the guys. Children scamper around their legs. There is a steady flow of people coming into the Savarin to fill up thermoses with water.

A tap on my shoulder. Chuck, a pleasant smile on his face.

Call for you, he says.

Call?

Phone. Over there.

I look over at a scarred pay-phone, its receiver dangling down, swaying from side to side.

The phone works, I say. Out here? Out here the goddamned phone works?

Sure, Cora says. The ones the phone company can't maintain,

we keep up ourselves. We need them. We need to keep up a network of phones so we can assemble in an emergency or suchlike.

Who pays the bills? I mean, how can you—

Again Cora's eyes suggest the depth of my stupidity.

God pays the bills, she says. Go on, you're keeping somebody waiting.

Two things go through my head. First off, who the hell could be calling me *here*? Who'd know my whereabouts? Second, if I go to the phone, will Cora be here when I return? I am so afraid she won't that I'm almost tempted to have Chuck tell the caller I'll call back sometime. But Cora gestures me away. It's a gesture I know I better obey.

I almost don't know how to use a pay-phone any more. I mean we have a phone at home, but it's just an old black table model. Wall models threaten me. Pay-phones are demonic. Especially ones that work when they shouldn't. I speak into the receiver, feeling that it is absurd to think that the thing will talk back to me.

Yeah, who's this? I say.

Are you, let's see a moment, are you Lee Kestner?

Yeah, that's me.

A pleasure to hear your voice again, old buddy.

Who is this?

You know.

Okay, I know. Sergeant Allen, right?

You got it.

How'd you know where I was?

Not hard to figure. Where else'd they take you?

I don't know.

Got your name off your wallet. You want your wallet back? I can arrange to return it to you. A little meeting . . .

Keep the wallet.

That wouldn't be ethical.

Maybe not, but I'm not about to have a rendezvous about it. Why'd you call me?

Just to let you know I'm alive, case you were hoping otherwise.

I wasn't hoping other—

Maybe not, bastard! His voice has deepened, seems to come out of the phone hissing. Anyway, just wanted to say hello.

Look, I'm sorry for what I—

A click on the line. He's hung up.

6

Who was it? Cora asks when I return to the counter.

Wrong number.

Do you have to be—never mind, keep it to yourself. Your right, rule of the road. Privacy.

Chuck says, you need anything you let me know, and walks away from the counter.

Let's go check out your wreck, Cora says.

We go out to see if The Mech's revived the Mustang. He's taken it inside the garage half of the Savarin building. Crouched over the engine, he's taking pieces out and throwing them over his shoulder. Parts lie scattered all around him on the concrete floor. When he sees us, he says:

Not ready yet. Got a lot to do before I can make this baby even run a straight line without wobbling.

Is it salvageable? I say. Cora grunts. The Mech taps a screwdriver against the palm of his hand and says:

It's salvageable all right. But never expect it to chase rabbits. With new parts and a tune-up and a speed booster, it might hit 85 or 90 but you can give up any hopes of it being a hundred-plusser.

So long as it runs on more than wishful thinking I'll be satisfied.

I can do a salvage job on any make o' car, the Mech says. Make it run good. Up to a point.

Do your best, I say. But, man, you got to know I'm wiped out financially.

Did I request an appointment with your accountant?

Well, I just wanted you to know. Cop took my wallet, I got zilch.

The Mech nodded his head.

Well, you get ambitious, come and see me. I usually know where a reasonable profit can be turned. For now get out, okay? I don't like people looking down my coveralls while I work.

Cora pulls at my arm and we leave the garage. As we walk slowly back to the restaurant building, car motors all over the lot are being revved.

Allen took your wallet? Cora says.

Yeah.

Not like him. He's no ripoff artist.

Well, give him his due, he was unconscious when we left him and the wallet behind.

You shoulda taken the wallet from him.

Yeah. I should've. Oversight.

Oversight's your way of life, sounds like.

As night falls, cars leave the parking area, usually in groups of four or five.

Any more crowds their piece of road, Cora says.

Where do they go?

Anywhere.

I mean, why go out on the road at all?

The dumb-shit look again.

They got to, she says.

The Savarin restaurant empties, becomes barnlike in its emptiness. I decide to test out the phone, try to call my Dad. The connection is made, I hear the click of answering at the other end, but no voice. He's just taken it off the hook, is probably just staring at it blurrily. Or blearily. I hang up.

Cora and I sit in a booth. She wants to get out on the road, you can see that in her fumbling hands, her overeager smiles, her vacant look. Many people invite her to ride with them, but she says no.

I hate being just a rider, she says. I had my own car but I

totalled it, smashed it against an abutment. I'll get wheels again, soon's I find a deal.

Many accidents along this road?

Not many. Sometimes a spinoff or a car that dies completely. Not many fatalities. We take care of our own when anything happens. If only the cops'd leave us alone completely.

Pretty soon there's hardly anybody left inside the Savarin, just us, a few others who look like they're not so eager to go traveling, a tall skinny old man who starts cleaning things up. The old man smiles at Cora. It's a very toothy smile. He either has all his natural teeth, or a sensational job of bridgework.

Who's that? I say to Cora.

That? Oh, just Emil. He hangs around here. Cleans up, makes coffee sometimes. Stay away from his coffee. But he's a fixture, never goes out on the road. This's home, I guess.

She clearly doesn't want to talk about Emil, about anybody, about anything. We talk less and less. I watch the front of her sweater, trying to locate the shape of breasts behind the vaguely outlined nipples. She is so tiny. Standing up, she comes to chest level on me. She must weigh under a hundred pounds.

The Mech comes in.

All transplants've been made, he says, and the car still lives.

Good, I say. I was thinking . . .

Yeah?

Like I said, got no money, but there's gas cans in the trunk. Why'n't you take some?

He shrugs, says okay. Back at the garage I notice that he'd already taken half the gas cans.

Shall we try her out? I say to Cora, patting the Mustang on the hood.

We better wait. Till somebody can drive out with us.

I don't want to run in packs. Look, you heard what The Mech said, it can't even go as fast as the other cars. Who'd drive out with us? Who wants to wet-nurse slower vehicles?

I don't know. There's Allen and—well, it's risky.

Good, let's go.

She's hot for it, I can see that. She looks at the Mustang like it's a souped-up racer. I take her hand—a legal touch—and lead her to the car.

7

I SLAM down the accelerator. A roar shakes the whole car. I take it down the exit ramp and onto the main highway, giving it a little gas at a time, letting it speed up by degrees.

The Mech's done a good job. I can feel a thousand little differences. The steering's steadier, the engine smoother, the car's responses more immediate. It holds the road with sureness. Cora flicks a switch and the goddamned radio works. She finds a program of chant-rock. The heavy beat underscores the evenness of the Mustang's ride.

Finally I hit top speed, glancing sideways to see if Cora's impressed. She isn't. As The Mech says, the car's not going to set any speed records, but it does glide along. We enter a stretch of road with woods on each side; shadow trees fly by. We pass several abandoned cars, some with their hoods up, many with windows broken, most apparently stripped of valuable items.

The scenery flashing by, the car rumbling pleasantly around me, I think of making love with Cora. I glance over at her, trying to devise a way in which fantasy might meet reality. There's a tingle in the tips of my fingers as I think about caressing those small breasts. Cora smiles at me, a hopeful sign. I reach out my hand. She squeezes it, but does not hold it, a gesture more like affirmation of brotherhood than love.

Still—she's here in the car with me, and we're cutting a wide slice through the night. I'm better off than when I didn't have wheels.

As we leave the wooded area, a metallic glint of light flashes through the last trees. Cora doesn't see it and I don't say anything. I alternate looking at the side-view and rear-view mirrors. Another ray of light, but this time not in the forest. Out on the road this time. The third gleam and whatever it is, is closer to us. The Mustang is already going as fast as it will go. I try to nudge the gas pedal further into the floorboards. A sign informs me it is twenty-three miles to the next rest area. Cora senses my tension. She twists around, looks out the back window.

What's back there? she says.

I'm not sure.

Dumb-shit look.

It's another car, I guess.

You guess?! It's a pig car. It's Allen, it's got to be. He's the only one with nerve enough to buzz this stretch.

What'll we do?

I don't know, I can't think—keep going straight ahead till something happens. He's got the speed, but it'll still take him a few miles to catch up.

Maybe we should ditch the car, make a run for it.

Shit, I got to be in a spot like this with an idiot who don't know his ass from a crack in the road. It's open country here. We'd never get far. We'll have to chance what comes. Keep driving.

It catches up with us quicker than she'd guessed. It slows down behind us, staying on our tail but far enough back to remain a black ghost. A black ghost, its headlights off, stalking us.

It's Allen all right, Cora says. He likes fun and games. We got to make the first move. Hit the brake.

What?

Hit the brake, shithead!

We burn rubber in a long skid but hold our lane. The other car eases past us. He's in front of us before he realizes what happened. His brake lights flash on, but we're controlling speed now. He tries to slow but we stay right on his tail. With four lanes leeway he can't set up a block or run us off the road. He guns his motor and pulls away from us.

Okay, Cora says, we've got him taking a chance.

This's like a chess game to you.

Yeah. You got it.

Let's turn around, head back.

Can't, too risky. He'd catch up. No, forward's best. We have to wait him out.

She's tense. She hugs her legs to her chest.

Maybe we should slow down and get off the road, I say. Maybe he won't try to find us.

No, if he did get to us, we wouldn't have a chance. Shut off the headlights so at least he won't see us coming for miles.

I can barely see the road in the dim moonlight. Once I swerve around what I think is a tree across the road, but there's no tree there. The Mustang hums steadily, going along at about 40 mph. A couple of times it slides off the road onto the shoulder but most of the time finds its own way as if it had built-in radar.

Maybe you should pull over, Cora says, and let me drive.

I don't say anything, I just keep going. She mutters something that I'm glad I can't hear. I roll down a window, listen to the night noises. A shadowy blur turns out to be nothing more than a shadowy blur. I slow down further. To my left we seem to pass the sound of a quiet engine idling. The sound skips and I hear tires against gravel.

Open her up, Cora screams.

I increase speed. I have to turn the headlights on again so I can see where I'm going. He flashes his on, too. So he can take aim, as it turns out. The first shot, although it doesn't hit anything, is close enough to frighten the bowels out of me. I get a quick mental picture of Allen, leaning out the window and taking aim, a fat hand around the tiny gun, the other hand on the steering wheel. An anatomical absurdity, but if it's Allen, it's probably what he's doing.

I swerve but regain control. Next shot goes through the back window, leaving a circular area in white-lined little fragments. A third ricochets off the side of the car.

Switch lanes, Cora shouts, and keep switching.

I start zigzagging. He guns his motor and comes up even with me on the outside.

Get out of his way, damn it, Cora shouts.

He sideswipes me. A terrifying crunch of metal. I almost go into a spin, but the Mustang responds and I ease back into a lane. Through my side-view I see that he's had the worst of the swipe.

Body damage my Mustang can take in stride. He's skidded sideways and has to straighten out.

I feel a weird sense of satisfaction, but can only hold it for a second because he's catching up again.

I pass a sign. Exit, Food, Gas, Lodging, one mile. I keep dodging from lane to lane.

Exit, ½ mile.

We'll get off there, I say.

Cora looks terrified.

No, you dumb shit.

Why the hell not?

He'll cream you there. That's his territory, man.

What the fuck are we supposed to do? He'll cream us here.

I'll think of something.

I already have.

I let him almost catch up. At the last minute I swerve onto the exit ramp. He overshoots it. His tires scream as he turns around. Cora screams at me, but I can't make out what she's saying. I go around the long curve, over the bridge. Behind me I can see Allen's car at the far curve of the exit ramp. I turn right onto the access road and floor the gas pedal. The Mustang makes the long curve. On two wheels, feels like. I mutter long, involved promises to it. Under the bridge I execute a skidding U-turn and stop the car.

I grope for the monkey wrench which is behind Cora's seat.

What are you going to do with that? she says in a frightened voice.

What do you think?

She makes a grab for my arm as I get out of the car. No, she screams. Don't! She says it again as I run across the road, the monkey wrench a dead weight in my hand. I hear his tires screeching around the curve.

It's like my own death. Everything important flashes before my eyes. Not the events of my life—the events of the day. Maybe they are the events of my life. I see Dad wearing a doughnut. I see the car and Lincoln Rockwell X and Cora's hidden tits. I see all the blurs and bumps and rising dust of the road. I see myself running scared. All the things I always wanted to do. I see the road stretching to its perspective point, trisected by the flashes of oncoming headlights.

All this at once, as I watch the car round the last curve of the access road and come directly at me. I release the heavy wrench and my arm feels weightless. The wrench shatters the windshield glass, sails on across the side of Allen's head, floats out through the rear side window.

Inches from me the car swerves and heads across the four lanes. Cora screams, but it misses the Mustang, bounces off an abutment, hits another abutment broadside, and stops.

I don't want to look but I do.

His left arm is part of the mangled steering wheel. The rest of his body is relaxed, leaning slightly forward like someone exhausted from heat. His head rests against the splintered glass of the window. I avoid looking at what the wrench did to the side of his head.

I return to the Mustang. The wheels. Its motor throbs; the whole car shakes. I get in and turn off the ignition.

I touch Cora's arm and she slides away from me.

You dumb fucking shit, she says.

She begins to beat her fists on the scarred leather of the dashboard.

PART II

1

CORA sleeping: her head twisted, exposing her skinny little neck. Her mouth open, releasing the most grotesque noises. Her eyes squinched tight, looking in pain.

The blanket's slipped down to her waist. She sleeps naked. Her tits are still hard to see, a pair of gently curved shadows. I know them better by touch than I do by sight.

At least there's touch.

I lay back against a pillow, choke on the musty indoor odor clinging to its surface like an extra pillowcase. I don't know how Cora knew about this motel, nestled so far back in what looks like woods that haven't been pioneered yet. No wonder it went broke years ago. Even when cars were plentiful, how many'd find their way down that road? The road looks like it hasn't been resurfaced since the administration of Calvin Coolidge. A bunch of small cottages at the back of what used to be a gas station, this motel looks Early American. Wood peeling all over the outside, wallpaper peeling all over the inside.

Why am I awake so suddenly? I jumped up with a start, I remember. Probably that dream about Allen again. This time when I take the wallet out of his jacket pocket, his eyes open and he grabs at it and I hit him again with the wrench, which has floated out of nowhere back into my hand. It's always some variation on going back to his car and searching for my wallet.

Funny, that obsesses me and not the killing of Allen itself.

Cora stirs in her sleep, rolls over onto her stomach, nearly crowds me off my side of the bed. Her spinal line is just barely curved, a straight ramrod up her back. I remember running my hand along that line over and over just—how long ago? A couple of hours. Running my hand along the line, afraid of going any further either with my touching or making love to her. She always makes love to me as if her mind were somewhere else. When I asked if she had orgasm a few days ago, she said of course. Aren't you satisfied with our fucking? she asked. I said sure I was, I just wasn't sure about her, especially the way she always seemed to submit instead of join. It's my way, she said, don't feel centered out, it's the same with everybody, I am just reserved about fucking—but you can be sure I enjoy it.

A noise underneath the floorboards. Some animal skittering from one side of the cabin crawlspace to the other. Happens three or four times a night. That many animal runs when I'm awake, who knows how many of them work their way through when I'm asleep? Cora's left the porch light on and about forty different kinds of moths are flapping against the screens of the two small front windows. There are insects around us inside, too, but I don't like to think of them at night. In a corner, a spider mother has recently given birth, or at least that's what we think those tiny globules that look like a grey-blue galaxy are the result of. Another spider, a big black one, is hanging over my head right now. Him I especially don't like to think of when it's night and smelly creatures are foraging in the crawlspace.

What was that? Cora says suddenly. She is lying on her side now, here eyes wide open. Her head is lifted from her pillow just an inch or so, and she's straining to look at something past me. I look toward that wall, see nothing.

What was what? I say.

The noise.

I didn't hear any noise.

It was a sudden thump, the noise.

There was nothing, believe me, you were sleeping.

No way. I've been lying awake here for hours.

Wrong, Cora. I'm the one's been sitting awake here while you've been in dreamland where no doubt you heard that noise.

We got to get outta here.

Thought you were the one liked it here.

My taste for the pastoral has diminished. It always does after about four or five days. I still feel the muck from the pond all over my skin.

Well, if you'd take a shower—

I took a fucking shower, white boy. I still feel the muck. I like my swimming better at that Holiday Inn.

Where all the creeps are hanging off the patio balconies.

That was unfortunate, I admit. I can't help the creeps, they're interfering everywhere. Everything was so nice before—

I don't know about before. Wasn't here then.

No, you came 'bout the same time as the creeps.

Cora, please lay off. I can take just so much of—

Ah, sweetpea my darling, you're still so sensitive. I didn't say you were one of them. Only you just came at the same time. It's different.

What you say and what you mean aren't always the same.

Look, man, it's you that puts creep into your own head, don't lay it off on me. I thought we settled all that kind of shit already. Part of the truce.

She's right. It's my part of the truce not to fly off the handle at her remarks, just as her part's not to mention that first night and the killing of the cop. Okay, I'll back off.

Sorry, Cora. I'm getting edgy. Like you say, it's time to move on.

Fine. We'll clear the grounds tomorrow morning. Any heat we've collected should be off by now. When we get to a working phone, I'll call Emil or Chuck. They'll know what's safe. Between the two of 'em, they got a pipeline to everywhere.

She snuggles up to me, a peace gesture, and kisses me lightly on my right shoulder. The kiss sends waves of reaction through me. I haven't told her that she's the first woman I've slept with for more than two consecutive nights, that all the rest were one-night stands, forgettable and interchangeable. I have to be careful what I tell her. If I told her that I'm at least halfway in love with her, she'd probably hop the next mail train out. If they have mail trains any more.

How much money we got, hon? she says. She's now kissing my neck and it's all I can do to just let it happen, let her proceed her own way, which is the way she likes it most of the time.

Not much. My wallet was pretty much cleaned out even before Allen copped it.

He didn't cop it. The money was still there, wasn't it? He didn't intend to keep it.

Sure, he was just going to kill me, then give it back.

She laughs, one of her rare laughs without a mocking undertone.

How come you came outta the city with so little bread? she says.

I tell her about Lincoln Rockwell X and the buying of the wheels. It's the first time in our five days together I've had nerve enough to tell her about it. I mean, she mocked me out royally when she first heard I'd paid anything at all for the Mustang.

So he put the swindle on me.

Good for him. You were ripe for picking.

But we were old friends and it was five bills he took from me.

More power, baby. Anyway, you each got what you wanted. What are friends for?

I suppose. I could use those five bills now.

Well, we'll figure something.

What?

I don't know, we'll ask around. There's little jobs where we can pick up some loose change. Some doperunning, that sort of stuff.

I don't like to mess around with dope.

Only suggest you run it, not use it.

But that's exploitative.

Do what you want, I don't care. I gave up all judgement shit when the law and order folks all started sounding like Marxists.

Well, I hope we can get something better.

Ah, who the fuck cares? Right now I need you inside me.

Which is where I'm heading.

2

TURNS out The Mech's got deals up the ass. And some of them are doperunning deals. When the money comes in, I find I don't mind the dope. I tell Chuck that and he just laughs, says:

Course you don't mind it. It's high-class doperunning.

Why high-class?

Well, you notice what kind of vehicle waits at the pickup points.

Usually a pretty classy one.

And you notice that your packages get taken by functionaries, even uniformed chauffeurs?

Yes, have to admit I've noticed that. But I thought it was just some sort of middleman disguise.

Not at all, youngster. Not at all. They *are* the middlemen. That dope's going to mansions, summer hideaways, the boardrooms of corporations. That's what I mean, high-class. I got my standards, too. I don't deal dope to impoverished areas, that's my kind of code. Ghettoes, no; Shaker Heights, yes.

I think you show definite Robin Hood tendencies.

You got it. Dope to the rich, food to the poor. In time society'll stabilize.

Cora goes on the runs with me. Sometimes I let her drive, which makes her ecstatic. The one time some fuzz flushes us out, she's driving, and she couldn't be more delighted. She leads the cop car on a merry chase. Finally, she zips into one of the small rest areas, starts maneuvering around it, and maneuvers the cop car right into the wall of an abandoned information center. She laughs and returns to the expressway.

I don't get it, I say.

Don't get what?

How you can get so gleeful over making a carful of fuzz crash into a building wall, and yet you make me feel guilty about what I did to Allen.

I thought we weren't going to talk about that.

You're not supposed to. All right if I mention it.

You son of a bitch!

She drives on, silent for a long time.

Allen died, that's the difference.

Well, maybe some of the fuzz in that car back there have bought the farm.

I didn't see any of 'em die, did I?

That makes no—

You go by your rules, I'll go by mine.

Further driving on in silence.

Anyway, anybody dead back there is a legit kill.

How legit?

They were chasing us.

Allen was chasing us.

You don't see the difference, okay, then you win.

I can't get her to address the subject any more.

Every second or third run I take the car to The Mech for further servicing. He always tells me the job is beyond his capabilities.

I thought you could fix any car, I say to him.

Sure, I'm the best, he says, but I'm afraid I skipped the class about mouth-to-mouth resuscitation back at Mech School.

But he always takes the Mustang out of my hands and makes it run better. It even looks better. On the side, The Mech has been hammering out some of the dents and applying a dab of paint here and there. You can tell the parts he's painted. The green is plenty lighter in color and tends to look like rash marks on the Mustang's body.

When Cora's not around, I prefer to spend my time with the old man, Emil. The Mech and Chuck chat with me some, but I'm uncomfortable around them. They make me feel too inexperienced, too much like a kid they're indoctrinating. Anyway, there is just too much mech in The Mech and we don't have much to say to each other. As for Chuck—well, he's just too efficient, too roadwise, too knowing. He never really talks to me like a friend, and if I'd needed an uncle I would've had warm relationships with my own uncles. So Emil is the only person I can feel natural around. He treats me like just another of the old men, as if we're sitting around the town square beneath the statue of the forgotten hero and all that, except that we're in a cavernous abandoned restaurant sitting beside the remains of a coffee urn. Emil hangs around the Savarin, rarely goes out on the road—if he does, he's quickly back behind his post, the restaurant counter. He's your typically tall old man, bent and gaunt in all the right places. Maybe I like him because for a short time years ago he was in show business like my Dad. A psychologist would make something out of that, I guess, but the hell with it. Emil's just an old man and I've always liked old men so I enjoy his company. Old men, most old men, don't treat you like a kid. Mostly they treat other old men like kids.

Cora out on the road somewhere? Emil says.

She never tells me where she pops off to, I say. But she's probably riding a car somewhere, like you say. She can't get enough of riding. And, if you let her drive, well then the circus's come to town.

She's got the urge all right.

What? What urge?

What I call it. The urge. The urge to wander, the urge to be more than what you are, the urge to get somewhere even if somewhere's just next door or back in your own backyard. It's just Cora's not really focussed on any one thing. She tell you anything about her background?

Now that you mention it, no, not much.

Thought so. She's not talkative when it comes to that. Would you like some coffee?

Normally this could be a trap. We all try to avoid Emil's coffee. It is his special act of misanthropy to serve you his coffee. But today I'm lucky.

We're all out of coffee, remember?

Yes, you're right. That's what's been making me edgy. I don't feel right if I'm not making coffee. Shall I tell you about Cora?

I want to hear, but I say:

Well, maybe you should respect her privacy, her right to secrecy.

That's true, but do you want to hear about it?

Cora adores Emil. I'm sure she'd tell him more than she'd ever tell me, and I do need to know, so I nod yes. Emil looks awkward for a moment, as if he's looking for some coffee to pour, then leans forward, puts his knobby elbows on the eternally sticky counter top.

Cora's not had what you'd exactly call a pretty life, he says.

I figured as much.

She grew up in one of those suburban havens blacks fled to before all the whites fled out. By the time she'd reached her teens, there wasn't much left of the genteel middle-class respectability her folks had so strived for. Her mother was on the needle at least part-time, certainly popping pills most time. Her brothers and sisters, and Cora had a flock of 'em both younger and older, were all running free. Crime and dealing and agitating and everything. Cora ran counter to them and their life. She went to school, worked at a legit job after school so she could stay in school. She was the only one allowed into her father's study. He'd read to her, she told me. The way she said it I gathered those were pretty happy moments. Her mother also seemed to have an amount of affection left for her. Whatever time she could spare from the needle and pills. Certainly she showed no love for her other children. It was as if, Cora said, the shreds of their respectability were still being maintained—but only for her.

A car buzzes the Savarin. I hate the creeps who think the noise of their motor is some kind of proof that they breathe.

So one day Cora came home from her part-time job and, well, what she found was everybody in that shaggily terraced rotting-wood suburban home was dead. The whole family, all of them. Sprawled on the floors, it seemed, of every room. All her brothers and sisters lying bloody and dead from cellar to attic, some of them blown apart by gunshot after gunshot. In her parent's bedroom she found both her mother and father lying separately dead on their separate beds. There was a whole damn arsenal of guns piled between the beds. They looked serene, she said, and she doesn't know from that day to this whether it was her father who ran amuck and killed everybody, or maybe it was her mother. Nobody official ever had a yearning to discover who killed whom. The corpses were all the information they ever needed. Cora thinks maybe both of them ran amuck, though she'd rather believe all the killings were done by an intruder, though that's doubtful, even she admits that.

God, I say, I never realized. That's how she wound up here then, fleeing from *that*?

More or less. Nobody ever winds up here that simply. I think she tried to go back to school but it was no good for her any more. All I know is eventually she stole some wheels and showed up around here. She smashed up her wheels the first month, hasn't had any since. I'm not sure, of course, but I think she may've smashed up the car on purpose.

What?

Just an hypothesis, youngster. I think she might've gotten into one of her moods, and she can get deeper in a mood'n anybody I ever saw, and she run the car against the abutment. But I'm no shrink. It's just a guess. How could I know? Some coffee, Lee?

We're out.

Oh, right, you told me.

Cora comes in and she looks disturbed, as if she's overheard what Emil's been telling me. But it turns out she's pissed off because Chuck's told everybody not to let her drive for a while.

That bastard! she says. He thinks he's some kind of dictator, the rest-stop Mussolini.

He say why he did it? I ask.

Sure he did. He said I am too volatile. Volatile, that's his word, volatile.

Calm down, Cora, Emil says. Sit. Let your nerves unglue.

Emil, you know better. Nothing'll help.

Sit anyway, lady.

Cora sits. I put my hand on her wrist. She tightens her fist and moves her wrist around in my hand. I tighten my grip.

He could not trust me behind a wheel, that's what the shitprick said. Jesus, I can outdrive anybody. Anybody but Chuck, maybe. You know that, Emil. You know that, Lee—no you *don't* know that.

That's not fair. I let you drive some—

Oh, sure, *let*! When it's all right with the Gestapo commissars, then I can have a piece of steering wheel. Well, screw off, all you guys. All you guys who think—

Lay off me, Cora. Chuck's the one who—

I don't fucking care who told me. You all told me. All you bastards with your own wheels told me. I'm leaving here.

Her words frighten me. I don't mind her mouthing off, even at me, but she can't leave. I won't let her leave. But if I say that to her, she'll only hear the word *let* and leave anyway. Wait her out, that's all I can do.

Emil, she says, why don't you have a car?

I hate cars, you know that.

Get one anyway. Just let me drive it.

Sorry, Cora, can't. Merely owning a car, even if I never saw it, would drive me crazy.

She smiles at him. She has a way of smiling at Emil that's like none of her other smiles. It has real love in it. I want her to smile at me like that. But it's no good. Even if I try to shut my eyes and imagine her smiling at me like that, it doesn't look right when pointed in my direction.

Sure, Emil, I wouldn't put you through that for anything.

What can I get you? he says.

Poison.

Cora!

I think I'll go out to the garage and lie under a car with a bad radiator, drink the drippings.

Emil leans on the counter and starts whispering in Cora's ear, the ear turned away from me. I strain to hear what he's saying, but I can't make any of it out. Whatever it is, it works. Cora starts laughing. She kisses Emil on the cheek and hugs the arm closest to her.

Emil, she says, you're so far out of your tree you must be floating above redwoods.

I'm certified, he says. Was, anyway.

You get *officially* released?

Nope, just walked out one day. Told the guard I had a shrink meeting in town. Might not've gotten away with it but I was asylum gardener and I was in my gardening clothes, so the guards figured I must be a doctor and passed me right through without even examining my fake I.D.

You were, I say. You were, were—

Spit it out, Lee, Emil says. I'm not gonna answer you unless you say the word.

Forget it.

No, I especially can't forget it. Spit it out.

Crazy.

I am whispering when I finally say it.

Crazy, Emil shouts. I was a loony! he says even louder. By definition I am still a loony. His voice echoes around the room.

You don't seem crazy to me.

Emil laughs. Traces of madness in the laugh.

The almost universal reaction: you don't seem crazy to me. You know what you're saying? Do you, Lee?

No.

You're saying if you don't perceive craziness in me, that it must not exist. You're saying that if you had to recognize its existence in old Emil, you might have to recognize its existence in yourself.

Damn it, Emil, I'm not crazy.

I might judge that you're not, but you see I've learned not to trust my perceptions. So I allow for the idea that you might be crazy. And if you happen *not* to be crazy, it does not make me any the less insane. Just as you're not crazy for failing to perceive my madness.

I take it back, Emil. You are crazy. I believe you.

I can convince *anybody*.

He laughs again as he says this.

A voice behind me: Hey, Lee. I turn around and see Chuck standing in the doorway. Chuck filling the doorway. I sometimes forget how big Chuck is. He carries it so well that he seems normal height and weight to me. I can sense Cora's body tense at the sound of Chuck's voice. They've already had their fight and she is resisting the temptation to start it up again.

What's up, Chuck? I say.

We're scheduling a food run. You got to help.

Sure, what's it about?

We're going to town tonight. Arrangements're all made. We'll convoy to exit 12A, some of us'll veer off there—you'll be in that group. Others'll split at other exits. We'll rendezvous at the objective, do the raid, make tracks like hell outta there. You game then?

Sure.

I glance at Cora who's now crouching over the counter, looking for a way out.

Chuck turns in the doorway to leave, but I say:

One condition, Chuck.

You got it, Lee. What is it?

We'll use my wheels like you say, but Cora's gonna drive.

Chuck's normally affable eyes suddenly become quite fierce with anger.

C'mon Lee, he says. No power plays.

I want her to drive. I've never done a food run. Need somebody with experience behind the wheel.

All right, I'll get you somebody. Mike, LeRoy, And—

Nope. Cora. It's my deal, my condition.

Shit, Lee. It's not possible. I know what you're up to. You favor the old romantic gesture, right? But the run's what's important, goddamnit. I can't let you ruin it just to impress your woman.

I got off my counterstool, felt it still swinging against the back of my jeans.

Fuck off, Chuck.

Standing there, my spindly legs spread apart defiantly, I become very conscious of Chuck's height. Why in the bloody hell can't I stop myself from challenging him?

Forget it, Lee, Cora whispers. It's a stupid gesture like he says. I don't want you—

Never mind. You're making the run, and you're driving. I know the score, how much supplies are down. You need this run, Chuck, and you need every vehicle you can get, and we can do it on my terms or—

Or what?

Or my wheels'll find some blocks to sit on while you idiots make your goddamn run.

Chuck takes a couple steps into the room. I am about to escalate my offensive, call him a three-dollar-bill Hitler. But he looks at me, then at Cora, and his voice goes softer as he says:

Maybe you got a point, Lee. Maybe you shouldn't drive this one, after all. Not if it's your first food run. But Cora—damn it, Cora, you toe the line. This is a mission, a mission, and you treat it like one. Nothing fancy, just get the job done. Drive the limit when you're supposed to. Burn rubber only when the situation dictates. Any decisions relating to the mission, you let Lee make them.

She takes a deep breath. She's resisting obvious comments. The pause is so long I almost forget what we were talking about.

I'll, um, toe the line, Chuck, don't worry.

Chuck contributes a long pause of his own. The two of them stare at each other. Their eyes could start fires.

Well, Cora, Chuck finally says, guess I can trust you as much as I can the rest of the troops. Okay, we'll do it your way. Briefing meeting at six, we'll be on the road by seven, in the city by eight. Other words, just at dusk. Check in with The Mech before the briefing, okay? Okay. Well . . . happy trails.

We all happy trails Chuck, even Emil, and Chuck walks out, still looking doubtful.

I wait for Cora to thank me for getting her assigned to a driving gig, for letting her use my old Mustang. She remains crouched over counter, her fingers daintily ripping into shreds an old paper container of sugar. On the side of the package is a picture of some old Bird of America, probably extinct by now. All of the sugar packs in the Savarin are either Birds of America or Important Women in History.

Well, I finally say, guess you'll get in some driving time tonight.

Don't go into a lousy orgy of self-congratulation, Cora says. I recognize your generous impulses, but you're just as stupid as Chuck.

Cora, that's not fair.

Nope, it isn't. But I won't kiss your ass just so you can win points with me and yourself.

I wasn't trying any—

Like shit you weren't.

Cora, I—

She swings around on her stool, looks me right in the eye.

You want to display your generosity? Show me what a keen dude you really are?

What're you talking about?

Simple. I'll believe you're straight up if you do one thing. You want to hear?

Sure.

Give me your wheels.

What?

Give 'em to me. Let me drive 'em away so you never see either me or your Mustang again. How about that, Lee? Can you do that, Lee? Huh?

Emil looks like he'd like to help me, but even his active and crafty mind can't come up with a way of handling Cora in this kind of mood.

Cora, I say, you know I can't—

Yes, I know that. All I'm really asking is for you to stop begging me to get down on my knees and lick your prick just because you're such a fucking nice guy. That's all I'm asking.

I thought you'd like to drive tonight, that—

Stop it, Lee. You never stop trying. I can lay it out in clear numbered instructions and when you get to the last number you still can't understand what I said. Stop trying. I'll be happy behind the wheel tonight, ecstatic. But you get no points, comprehend?

Whatever you say, Cora.

She groans.

I give up. I really give up. He won't ever change. I want to kill myself. Right now. Mix me a cup of your coffee, Emil.

Can't, dear. Outta coffee. One of the reasons you're all making the food run, no doubt. I'll make you some when you get back.

Hell, I'll probably want to live by then. Nothing ever frigging works out for me. Let me take the car over to The Mech, Lee. I need to talk to that reactionary bastard.

I'm sure she sees the disappointment on my face. I really like to deal with The Mech myself. But I tell her yes, take it over any time she wants, and hand the keys to her.

You got a heart of gold, Lee, she says. Which somehow seems the appropriate material for your heart. See you, Emil. And be on time for the briefing, Lee. Chuck gets pissed if you ain't punctual.

She laughs. It's got the sarcasm in it, but it's such a beautiful musical laugh I don't care. Emil and I are silent for a long time after she goes out the door.

Would you like a Danish, Lee? Emil says.

What?

A Danish. Sweet roll. I've kept one stashed.

He takes out this Danish, in a cellophane package with blue marks all over it on the inside.

It's a few days old, Emil says, but we can pick away the moldy parts.

You're crazy, Emil.

I told you that.

Yeah, but now I believe it.

Because of a Danish?

Something like that.

Well, you're the type sees symbols everywhere, I reckon. Even where you don't want to look for them.

You sound crazier by the minute.

Be nice to Cora.

What?

You heard me.

He opens the Danish, starts tearing away the whitish blue moldy parts. My stomach starts climbing and I swing my stool away, watch Cora stand beside the Mustang which is parked just outside the front plate-glass window. She's goddamn dusting it with an old rag. Her movements are easy and gentle, loving.

3

WHAT does that asshole think he's doin'? Cora says. Even with a pillow under her, she seems to be peeking over the top of the dashboard. I keep finding myself looking down to make sure her feet really reach the pedals.

What asshole? I say. I am very sensitive about such words lately, always want to verify that she is referring to someone else.

That asshole. Chuck. What does he—he think he's honchoing a funeral or something? What kinda creepshow is this?

He's just being cautious, Cora. A lot of fuzz out lately.

Cautious, hell. He's a coward. He's got a retractable prick. Acts tough with us back there, but out on the road he becomes Miss Prissypants.

Take it easy.

But Jesus, Lee, Chuck used to be the fastest. The Roadrunner God, somebody called him. He's been spooked. I don't know, maybe it's the cares and woes of leadership. The old lousy loneliness at the top. It's been since he's started running things that he's started actin' like your average village schoolmarm.

Oh, can it, Cora. Chuck's looking out for us.

She leans back against the bucket seat, works her shoulders against it. Her head's tilted back, but she keeps track of the road.

Sorry, love, she says. I'm edgy. That's all, just edgy.

She leans in toward the steering wheel and, before I realize what she's up to, she's pulled out to the outside lane.

But I'm dying of this goddamned snail's pace, she says, and rams her foot down on the accelerator. The rush of the engine, heard from inside the car, is like a sudden blast of thunder. Somewhat neurotic thunder, but thunder.

Don't Cora! I say, but she just laughs. It takes her about half a minute to reach the head of the convoy. Twisting her body upward, Cora leans partway out the open window and yells:

Happy trails, Chuck!

She settles back behind the wheel. I twist around in my seat and watch the convoy diminish behind us. I sit back, put my shoulder against the door, watch her stare at the road ahead, the happiest possible grin on her beautiful gamin face, spots of reflected light gleaming off her newly applied AfroBlack, and I decide against saying the obvious things—which would, after all, only draw the obvious responses. She knows Chuck'll try to ream her out later and she'll try to ream him back. What good is it for me to do a sneak preview of it now?

Hey Cora, I say, what're ya draggin' tail for? Faster, c'mon, faster.

She shrieks with laughter, and lifts her tiny ass off the pillow by at least two inches. She laughs harder as she slams down the gas pedal and continues to bounce on her pillow.

Hey Lee, she says. I love you, you know that? I love you to pieces.

I resist saying that pieces is what we're going to wind up as. Then I realize the rest of what she just said and suddenly know what people mean when they say they feel a glow and I lean back in my seat trying to keep the glow going, as I listen to the Mustang rattle, registering its protest against a high speed which it nevertheless manages to maintain.

Cora parks in a side street about three blocks away from the rendezvous point. The Mustang gurgles a bit as she shuts off the ignition. High speeds aren't always kind to it, so I guess I'll let The Mech give it a lookover again tomorrow. The street is dark. Either the houses are abandoned or everybody in this part of town retires early.

Why here? I ask Cora.

I got my caution, too, she says. Even behind the supermarket we'll be vulnerable. Since we're early, wouldn't be a bad idea to look things over first. Case there're any traps set, we can flush 'em out before the rest get here. Chuck shoulda thought o' this in the first place, the stupid bastard. C'mon, let's get rolling.

We walk the three blocks to the rendezvous point. This street is quiet, too, but not so dark. I keep looking over my shoulder. It bothers me more that I don't see anything than it would if there was an occasional passing car, or maybe a drunk in a doorway. I begin to feel that the street and the side streets are all facade, all fake with no people living there. I'm glad to get to the rendezvous.

The supermarket's an old A&P, somewhat gone to seed. One of its overhanging signs says Double Coupons and, with the rest of the message broken off. Front windows have been broken, wide taped patches cover their many cracks. A couple of bullet holes have been corked with some kind of hard putty.

Around the back, Cora says.

What?

Rendezvous point's around the back. You know that. C'mon.

We keep to the side of the building, although the parking lot, carless, stretches about a hundred feet or so away from us. I can smell a garbage area ahead and I make Cora circle around it, even though she doesn't want to go out into the light. I convince her it's still dark enough so nobody can see us from the road, even if there were somebody in the road. The garbage is piled high, as if waiting out a sanitation-men strike. Boxes are soggy from ancient rainstorms. We round the corner of the building and proceed to the loading platform where, in a matter of minutes, we expect to be piling goods into convoy vehicles. Everything's quiet. I pull myself up to the platform edge and sit.

Any gentlemen around here? Cora says.

What?

Give me a lift, mamadiddler.

I pull her up and she sits beside me. She can't sit still. She bounces her leg off the pilings of the platform, pulls at splinters with her fingers.

I don't like this place, she says.

How come?

I don't know. The rhythms are wrong. Something.

There is a noise on the far border of the parking lot and we both tense. A person comes out of the bushes there, takes a cinemascopic look around, seems to think everything's okay and motions back toward the bushes. I expect to see a gang emerge from the foliage, but instead it is a much smaller form who scampers to the legs of the first figure, taking its proffered hand. The two of them approach the A&P. Cora is coiled, ready to leap off the platform and make a run for it.

Take it easy, I say. Nobody can book us for lounging around an A&P.

Maybe, maybe not. I don't like the look of this dude.

As the two figures approach, I can see that the taller one is a black man, dressed in dark shirt and levi's. The smaller is a child dressed similarly. I hold my breath, put my hands against the surface of the loading platform and am ready to move.

Lee my man, what's happening? says the black man. And I let my breath out in a loud sigh.

He know you? Cora says.

Friend of mine, I say. Name of Lincoln Rockwell X.

You're the last person I expected to find here, he says.

Same for me, I say. What're you up to?

Just the usual. Just dealing. You cats with Chuck?

Before I can answer, Cora says:

Don't call me cat.

Lincoln Rockwell X smiles, more engagingly even than his usual, and says:

That's straight with me, babe. But what's the A to the Q?

Yeah, I say, we're with Chuck.

That's where you wound up then, huh? he says. Better'n I might've thought. Chuck honchoes a good outfit. Wheels still operating?

Good as gold, I say. He seems surprised. Astonished might be the better word.

Well, what'd I tell ya? I make the deal, you know you got the goods.

You're the stingman sold him that dirty asshole of a Mustang? Cora says.

Lincoln Rockwell X drops the smile, superimposes the mean scowl.

Don't rile me, babe.

You got me wrong, Cora says. I don't mean to get your bile astir. I just want to shake your hand, man, you gotta be number one.

The intricate set of handshakes and slaps they go through makes me nervous. How come neither one of them ever gave me handshake lessons? The way Lincoln Rockwell X grins, I can see he likes Cora. A whole lot. Maybe too much. I'm getting edgier by the minute.

This your woman, Lee? he says.

Don't answer that, Cora says. I run my own life, man.

I don't like the way she says that. What happened to all that loving me to pieces she was talking about back in the car?

You want to stay in town a couple o' days, Lincoln Rockwell X says, I can show you the grids where the heat is, babe.

Not this time, Cora says and I feel better. Maybe later, man, she says and I feel worse.

The child who's holding on to the one loose spot behind the knee in Lincoln Rockwell X's tightfitting levi's watches us with wide eyes, and the side of a finger stuck in her mouth. She's a bit chubby and looks to be about five. Her hair is twisted in curls close to the scalp.

Who's this? I say to Lincoln Rockwell X. He lights up, gets back to the easy smile.

My daughter, Lee, he says. The fruit of my loins.

She's gorgeous, Cora says. What's her name?

Norma.

At the sound of her name, Norma puts her arm around her father's leg as a defensive measure.

I didn't know you had a kid, I say.

No surprise, he says. I never told you.

And five years old. Norma, how're you, Norma? Norma Rockwell X.

As I say the name, I realize its source.

Hey, I say. Norma Rockwell? You don't mean you named her after—

Sure shit, man, and I wouldn't make critical footnotes, I were you.

No, course not. Sounds good. Norma Rockwell X, sounds good.

Righto, old chap. Thing a beauty is a Norma forever, right? I got a right to my sense of Americana, too, dig?

Sure.

He is about to say more, but the first platoon of the convoy quietly edges into the parking lot and creeps over to the loading platform area. The other sections arrive soon after, Chuck among them. Chuck nods at me, says nothing to Cora, and we get to work.

• • •

One thing about Chuck, he's got the operation planned well. After Lincoln Rockwell X opens a bunch of locks from keys on an overcrowded chain, Chuck puts each group of us into action, motioning the motions he'd demonstrated at his briefing, directing the traffic in and out the doors leading to the loading platform with an alert, crisp, often graceful efficiency.

As Cora and I enter the store, Chuck stops us, putting a massive hand on my less than massive shoulder.

Where's your wheels? he says.

Um, I say, parked near here. Side street. About three blocks away.

He looks like he's about to ream us out, then sucks in a breath and nods.

You want me to go back for it?

No, the time's off. You fucked up, Lee. You two just go help others for now.

God, Chuck, I'm sorry, I—

Get moving, will you? Haven't got time for a formal debate right now? Hey you guys, yeah you, be more careful, you might break every damn glass in the damn box, damn it!

I think he's irritable, I mutter to Cora as we slink away from Chuck. My stomach linings feel singed by his words. I don't like him disappointed in me. Cora apparently isn't feeling sorry.

That shitface motherfucker, she says.

He's right. We're not supposed to go off on our—

That don't make him no less shitface nor no less motherfucker. I'm gonna stick his balls into an overheated radiator.

Best not to argue with her in this mood. So I say:

Who'll we help out?

Let 'em all do the fucking work. Let 'em all be drones. You and I, we'll trouble-shoot. Wander around, find something of more value than Sugar Pops and meatloaf mix.

But Chuck said—

Screw what Chuck said. C'mon.

I follow her down a dairy aisle, sneaking looks over my shoulder for Chuck, hoping he won't catch us goldbricking. We skirt around colleagues who are busy loading milk cartons and cheese packages into shopping carts which, when full, are rushed to the loading platform. I feel lousy. Somehow I am sure that Cora no longer loves me to pieces and I got to get back to that. Somebody tugs at my pants leg. I look down. It's Norma. She smiles up at me.

Well, *you* like me, I can see that, I say to Norma.

Cora glances back at us, smiles.

Hey, little lady, where's your daddy?

Norma shrugs and continues to walk alongside me, her chubby little hands keeping a firm grip on my pants leg.

I think we got an accomplice, I say.

I think *you* got a friend, Cora says. She grabs a package of Hershey Kisses off a shelf, opens it, carefully untwists the silver wrappings on one candy, and hands it to Norma. The child stares at the chocolate bit as if she's not sure what to do with it.

It's all right, Norma, you eat it, Cora says. Norma stuffs the candy into her mouth. She lets it melt down on her tongue. Cora tosses me a Hershey Kiss, starts nibbling on one herself.

We roam the aisles. Cora keeps muttering under her breath as she eyes the shelves trying to find that elusive something of value she wants. Norma stays by me. I offer to pick her up, carry her a stretch, but she shakes her head no. Apparently she's unwilling to give up the security of a clutched pants leg. I grab off a bag of marshmallows, which I intend as another treat for Norma. Before I can open it, I bump into Chuck, who's riding herd on a couple of dilatory workers. He sneers down at my bag of marshmallows.

That your contribution to supplies? he says.

No, I was just—

Ah, hell, just stay out of my way, okay? Hide Cora someplace. Jesus, why don't you two hook up with some other outfit?

Chuck, you got everything mixed—

Move on! C'mon, you guys, put a little spirit into it, some muscle, we only got a few minutes left to use.

Now I can't find Cora. She's disappeared into the darkness of an aisle. I remember how bright a store like this used to be with lights full on. I always hated that fluorescent glare, now I long for it. I offer Norma a marshmallow. She doesn't want it, makes a face. Taking it out of my hand, she throws it, scoring a neat two-pointer into a wicker basket of ChoreMaid dish scrubbers. I toss the whole bag into the basket.

C'mon, Norma, let's go hunting Cora and your daddy.

I can find Daddy. This is the first time she's said anything. She has a sweet husky voice.

You know where he is?

Nope. But I can find him. You want to find him?

Sure, let's do it.

We proceed down an aisle which turns out to feature pet food.

Since our outfit has little need for pet food, the aisle's unpopulated, a small blessing. Norma pulls me along determinedly. I'm sure we'll find her father any minute, perhaps peeking out from behind a sack of Cat Chow.

Suddenly there's a thunderous sound of gunned motors coming from the parking lot. Streaks of light dance along the top of the aisle, glance upward toward the ceiling. Somebody to our left hollers, Fuzz!, which is followed by the sound of general scrambling. I feel frozen to the spot. Norma blithely walks ahead of me a few steps, then looks back as if she wonders why I'm not following her like I'm supposed to. In the darkness I can just see her, just read the expression on her face.

There's a resounding crash of glass at the front of the store, then a lot of rustles and clumps—probably the sounds of thousands of cops diving through the A&P front windows. Ceiling lights begin to flicker on in erratic rhythm. I am still rooted to my spot. Down front, a cop races past our aisle. He doesn't even look down it, guess he doesn't expect to see anybody looting pet food.

Norma walks back to me in what is a pretty confident stride for a five-year-old.

What's that *noise*? she says. She's genuinely annoyed, I can tell.

They're called policemen, Norma, I say, and we are in trouble.

Oh, fuzz, she says. We got to *hide*. Scrunch down.

Immediately I scrunch down, although I feel a bit ridiculous for following the orders of a five-year-old so obediently. Yet there's a sense of knowing the turf in that child voice and I've always believed that when-in-Rome shit. Norma scrambles into a low shelf of pet food sacks. C'mon, she says. I manage to fit myself into the narrow space, lying flat next to her. Straining every muscle in my body I manipulate a couple of sacks to the front of us. The sacks might not be necessary, no cop seems at all interested in checking out the animal food section. The smell of cat chow and doggie treats is even mustier at this low level. It's making me sick. I turn my head, seeking clearer air, and am immediately assaulted by birdseed odors worse than the pet food. For a moment I'm sure I'm going to throw up.

Norma and I lie stiff for about five minutes. I can tell by a kind of low humming that's going on in the back of her throat that she is enjoying all this immensely. Like a little hide-and-seek from the coppers is part of her daily life, a favorite game. We hear a lot of running around and some growled orders and responding curses. In the next aisle there's some rough stuff, I'm sure. Sounds like cops pushing a couple of our guys against some bottles. Cracking glass and angry oaths, shoving, howls of pain.

Gradually, silence returns to the supermarket. Cars drive away outside, a couple of them with sirens sounding. A last voice or two drifts to us from nearby aisles, the final cops making the final checks. Then they leave, too, and Norma and I continue to hide out for a few moments longer.

Pushing away the sacks, I feel a crick in my back as I try to slide out onto the linoleum floor. The last cops turned out the lights when they left and now the store seems darker than ever. Norma scrambles out beside me, stands up right away, and starts walking toward the rear of the store. She stops, looks back at me, says:

Let's go, lardass.

And right then I know she's Lincoln Rockwell X's daughter all right.

4

NORMA leads me to the back door, the one her father had opened with keys from his packed key chain. I peek out. Three cars from the convoy are still out back, parked at odd angles to each other. Nobody's anywhere near them now. The cops apparently decided to leave no guards. I motion Norma forward and we cross the loading platform. As we go by the three cars, I check each one to see if there're any keys left in their ignitions. Not key one. Directing me with a gesture of her thin left arm, Norma leads me across the parking lot to the bushes, retracing the route she and her father had taken earlier. Being out in the open like this makes me nervous and I'm checking all directions. Norma doesn't even turn her head, just strides on in jaunty little-girl steps.

We reach the edge of the parking lot and work our way through a break in the shrubbery. On the other side of the bushes is a small cement-surfaced playground. Doesn't look like it's used very much. Only one or two functional swings, empty chains hanging down from the other places. The remaining see-saw is split in half, both sides touching the patched rubber foundation. The slide looks like if you try it you'll get metal ass-splinters.

Daddy, Norma whispers.

Lincoln Rockwell X answers:

Over here, honeybun.

Norma leads me to what turns out to be a sandbox. A fence surrounds a deep square hole in which there're only a few grains of sand. Lincoln Rockwell X is crouching there. So is Cora. I'm so glad to see Cora safe I break into a smile. Either she doesn't see it in the darkness or she chooses to ignore it.

Norma climbs over the fence and into her daddy's arms. He hugs her to him. She puts her arms around his neck and smears kisses all over his face.

See, babe, I told ya, he says to Cora.

Yeah, I see.

See what? I say.

I told your ladyfox that I told the kid where to go if there was trouble. Norma's got more brains than her daddy already and you make any sarcasm about the state of her daddy's brains and you'll find a blade in your throat, babe.

His angry reference to sarcasm tells me that he's had a chance to chat with Cora for a while.

So—a little child has fuckin' led you, he says to me.

She saved my ass, man, I say, feeling a glow of camaraderie for my old friend.

Well, he says, I can't speak well for her judgement there but at least she knows how to get the job done, right?

Some of the camaraderie feeling leaks away. I lean on the fence, say to Cora:

You all right?

Why wouldn't I be? she says. I just happened to fall into the arms of the man here just as the cops made their noisy entrance. The man knows all the escape routes.

That's right, babe.

He knows the escape routes so well that I'm thinking he might have figured escape into his original game plan.

What the fuck do you mean by that, bacteria-tits?

I mean like you mighta set us up, shine-face.

Lincoln Rockwell X looks like he might take a slice at Cora if he didn't have Norma squirming in his arms and loving the hell out of him.

I don't set anybody up, he says. The mean is in his voice at double its usual intensity.

Cora laughs. I wish she'd get some sense and stop pursuing this particular subject. She's always got to make her play against the leader, damn it. I mean, when we're alone with Lincoln Rockwell X in a deserted playground and there's nothing but cops and darkness all around us, it doesn't make no nevermind whether or not Lincoln Rockwell X set us up. It's all right if he sent out engraved announcements. But Cora goes on prodding him:

You don't set anybody up. That is fucking rich. What about our mutual old buddy Lee here? You tell me you didn't set him up when you dealt him that shitpile of a car? You deny that?

That's a different sort of dealing, and I don't want to stand here arguing the philosophy of legitimate business with a titless wonder like you.

You did set us up, didn't you?

Lincoln Rockwell X gently removes Norma's arms from around his neck, kisses her almost demurely on the forehead, and sets her down. She immediately grabs his pants leg.

Look, no-tits, I don't have to explain a fucking thing to you.

He towers over her. I can tell she's trying to stand as straight as possible. She doesn't realize she's doing it, but she always glances briefly down at her chest a moment or two after each of his references to her small breasts. He clears his throat, says:

The deal between Lee and me was up and up. He saw the wheels, he knew he was buying, he knew I was overcharging. That, titless, is business. The setup is part of the contract, dig? Tonight'd be something else. I don't set up my clients, not to the cops anyway. The only way I set up clients is in my fee, which is always more than I'm willing to accept if anybody's willing to argue. No matter how much I despise the motherfuckers, these're my clients and I don't set them up. Nobody sets anybody up. This crew tonight's so dumb they probably put out signs. Robbery In Progress, Next Junction. Rip-off, two miles ahead. Well, their dumb is none of my nevermind. Course I know the escape routes, 'cause I know dumb. If I trusted my clients to have smarts, I'd be right there in the slammer with 'em. Got it? Answer me, no-tits! Got it!

Cora leans sideways, against the fence. I reach out and touch her shoulder. She moves away from my hand.

Yeah, she says. Guess so. Sorry to step into your shit, man.

That's all right, ladyfox. You treat old Lee here well, okay? I wouldn't admit it to anybody else but there're moments when I come damn close, damn close, to liking him. Damn close.

I'd like to believe him. Can I? Probably not. He looks up at me and I can't tell what the hell he means, either from the look on his face or from his voice. He's been this way as long as I can remember and all the intelligence units in the world working together would be unable to crack his codebook.

Well, he says, it's past teatime for my kid and me. We gotta be splitting, goin' on down the road. I drop you two anywhere?

I explain our wheels are parked three blocks away.

Okay, I will deliver you there in style, he says. Norma and me, we got our own way out of the park. You lead, child.

Norma takes us through some more shrubbery on the other side of the playground and across a couple of backyards. Out an alley and we're on a dark street. Lincoln Rockwell X takes over the lead and points us up the block to where a car is serenely parked beneath a willow tree. Branches of the tree hang over and obscure the car from anybody except those who know where to look.

He is not kidding about the stylish part. His car is one of the late-models. One of the last ever made, he says. Ever. It is two-tone maroon and cream with large windows all around. Inside, the upholstery is genuine leather and the dashboard looks like it belongs inside an airplane. The sound system alone looks like it could receive signals from Aldebaran or Betelgeuse. Cora slides into the middle of the front seat, her eyes bulging with pleasure.

Man oh man, she says to Lincoln Rockwell X, you must really make a living!

He laughs heartily and takes the driver's seat.

Yeah, pretty-eyes, I can be said to make something of a living.

She smiles at him. I can see it's her best smile, the one I'm still waiting for from before.

Can I drive? she says.

The air inside the car changes, as if clouds have zipped in the window.

Nobody drives this buggy but me, Lincoln Rockwell X says. Nobody. Ever.

Fucking shitface motherfucker, Cora says.

Suddenly, without warning, he gives her a backhand slap on her near cheek. He hasn't got enough leverage to really hurt her, but the point is made. Cora stares silently ahead, her eyes moist but stubbornly without any falling tears. Lincoln Rockwell X starts the motor—I can just barely hear it's running—and the car edges smoothly away from the curb. The droopy ends of the willow tree caress the windshield and pass out of sight.

The only thing anybody says for at least three minutes is when Lincoln Rockwell X mutters:

Nobody. Ever.

5

CORA mutters tribal curses at Lincoln Rockwell X as he drives his monster-car away. His last words to me were, you got my number, you need anything call! Norma's waving out the back window as the car drives up the street and fades out of sight around a tree-lined curve.

You want to drive back? I say to Cora, interrupting an imprecation that probably would've continued to eternity.

She looks at me for a moment as if she doesn't understand the question, so I say:

If you'd like to drive again, it's okay.

Some further blankness on her part, then:

No. You.

As she slides in the passenger side, she says:

After being in that supercharged Cadilleac, I can't drive this piece of junk for a while.

She actually says that, Cadill-e-ac. I feel like I should apologize to the Mustang for her. Maybe Mustangs understand about Cadilleacs.

Hit it, Cora says.

After that fiasco back there, Chuck's not exactly going to be glad to see us. Maybe we should take off for someplace else.

I don't give a shit.

I just don't know where. Any suggestions?

Plenty, but none you'd take.

We just sit and carefully don't talk for a minute, then Cora says:

Hell, no, I don't want to go anywhere else. Screw Chuck. I want to see Emil again, talk to him.

Wouldn't mind a chat with the old man myself.

So let's turn the key and make it, huh, Lee?

I turn the key but that is all that happens. Almost all. The Mustang does manage a couple of chugging noises but refuses to start. I work the gas pedal up and down several times. Cora leans over, looks at the dashboard, then points to the E on the gas gauge.

It's empty! she says. How could you be so—

Don't Cora! Look, I did fill it. Wait a minute, what am I saying? Filling it was your job, you took care of the car before the briefing.

That stops her for a minute, as she thinks back.

Then something's the hell wrong, she says. I did fill it. I was careful to shake out every little drop. I remember. Clearly. What's wrong?

Gas leak in the line, maybe.

Let's get out and check.

Did you put gas cans in the trunk?

Sure, The Mech gave me an extra. We're straight, so long as the car works.

Outside, the evidence confronts us. A broken-off piece of tubing lies near the left rear wheel. The trunk's lock is broken, there are marks where it's been pried open. All the gas cans are gone.

Son of a bitch! Cora says. We been ripped off. Some son of a bitch siphoned off all the gas in the tank then stole the gas cans! What a fucking shitty thing to do. Couldn't they leave us one can? If they wanted the cans, why'd they bother with the siphoning? What kind of a son of a—

Take it easy, Cora. It's done.

Oh, sure, it's done. What're we gonna do? Walk back? Or you got some kind of miracle up your sleeve? Turn your piss into gasoline or something?

Stop! Let me think for a minute. Let's both of us think, okay?

Won't the noise wake up the neighborhood? No, don't answer. All right. Think.

The solution I'm trying to avoid keeps intruding on my thoughts.
I have to acknowledge it.

Got a quarter? I say.

You kidding?

No. I ain't got a cent either.

Why you want a quarter?

Phone call.

What, you want to phone the cops, report stolen gas?

No. Matter of fact, I was going to phone my mother.

That stops Cora.

Your mama! she says.

Well, she lives about two miles from here, but it's one of those
guarded communities. Only way we can get through is to call her
and have her tell the guards to let us in. But we need a quarter to
call.

What's the advantage?

No advantage. It's just a place to go.

Yeah, what we could use. Well, lead the way. Maybe we can
find a quarter in the gutter.

The quarter comes easier than we'd anticipated, if not by a
route I could favor. We mug a guy out walking his dog. You
don't see that many guys out walking anything these days, and an
opportunity's an opportunity. Cora distracts him and I jump him,
hold him down while she goes through his pockets.

We only want a quarter, she says to the guy. He struggles
harder in my grip. The dog, a chubby hairy monster, barks at us
but keeps a wise distance. She finds the quarter, hollers Voila!, I
let the guy go, and we run like hell away. Looking back over my
shoulder, I see the guy start to chase after us. Then his dog trips
up his feet and he falls. He hits the pavement with his hand as if
the dumb quarter was really important to him. I'll never understand how people can go bananas over small amounts of money.
As we realize it's safe to slow down, and do, I say to Cora:

Hell of a way to make a living.

She laughs.

Ah, the bastard deserves to be mugged. Walking his ugly
goddamned dog.

Why does walking a dog make him an eligible victim?

Ah, I don't know. Just that there's enough dogshit around, you
know? What good's a guy out in the dark of the night contribut-
ing dogshit to all the other shit that's out there?

You may have a point. Let's find a working phone.

That may be the miracle of the week around here.

We walk a few steps. Out of nowhere comes this car. A nightroamer. Some jerkoff inside looking out like it's not him that's trapped in the cage. He just creeps along beside us, doesn't even roll down his window and shout at us. Cora yells a couple of her choicest obscenities at him. He probably doesn't hear. He probably has fifty tracks of loud music enveloping him, shell within shell. I'm furious. This is what I bought beatup wheels to get away from. Finally I notice an empty garbage can on its side in an alleyway. Darting into the alley, I pick up the can and hurl it at the nightroamer's car. My aim is off and it just bounces harmlessly off the side door. But it makes the jerkoff take his face off the glass and zoom away. Cora gives him the finger, but I doubt he sees it.

We find a working phone. For a minute I'm not sure of the number, then I dial what seems like the thousand digits that compose it. As I hear the ringing inside the receiver, my heart starts to beat faster. The beat seems to be saying, let it not be Harold, let it not be Harold, let it not be—

But there's a click, a voice says Hello, and my heart seems to fold up. It is Harold.

Harold, this is Lee. I—

Ah-ha, a voice from the dead. And at midnight. Perfect timing. Goodbye Lee.

Wait a minute! Please! I'm in trouble, Harold.

So, what's new?

Harold has this keen sense of humor always, as if he's collected every old comedy routine and situation comedy gag in the history of banal humor.

I need to come over there.

Over there, over there, send the word, send the word—

Harold is actually singing a song in my ear! Songs are another part of his comedy repertoire. I wait it out.

Why do you want to come over here? he says finally. Did the welfare finally go out of business?

Please, Harold. We can do bits later. Tell the guards I'm coming there and bringing a friend.

Is your friend human?

Why do you say that?

There's a full moon tonight or perhaps you haven't noticed.

You bring anything that howls and I'll wooden-stake the both of you.

Will you tell the guards please?

Of course. I wouldn't endanger familial harmony. I'll wake your mother. She's always glad to be shaken out of a sound sleep to see you.

Thank you, Harold.

Don't mention it, Lee. Or do mention it. Again, or I'll reconsider.

Thanks, Harold.

Okay, I'll inform the guards. You know what to say to them when you get here.

Sure.

And no sarcasms this time.

Yeah.

They don't take kindly to sarcasms.

I understand.

I'm still hearing about you from the day shift.

I'll behave.

Okay. See ya later, alligator.

Goodbye.

Wait. See you later, alligator.

He is pronouncing each word precisely. He is demanding the ritual response. I try to mutter it so Cora won't hear.

After while, crocodile.

I hang up before he can tell me louder. Cora's heard everything, but she's either too tired out to mock me, or has had a sudden attack of consideration for my feelings.

6

TALK about alligators! Standing at the door of his modest-sized but over-decorated house, Harold looks something like an alligator who's just mastered the upright position. Except what this reptile wants to do is get back to the floor and start devouring us at ankle level.

Harold, this is Cora.

He gives a bit of a start as she ambles into the living room light. He had not expected my friend to be either female or black. I've scored a point, but points don't count for much with Harold. He takes her skinny little hand and puts it almost to his mouth.

Je t'adore-a, Cora, he says. She's a bit taken aback. I had decided not to prepare her for either Harold or my mother. She hadn't asked any questions anyway. After glancing my way, she flashes him a different brand of smile. The obvious staginess of it reminds me of Lincoln Rockwell X's darkie act.

Where's Mother? I say.

She's in the boudoir, arranging her face. The sculpture takes somewhat longer nowadays.

Harold's lips look wet. They always do. He used to have a walrus moustache that hid his mouth and that was better. He's wearing a blond wig these days, shaggy with a few locks falling over his forehead. He doesn't need a wig, he's not bald. He just doesn't like the natural color of his hair and hair dyes make him

73

break out in a rash. I feel like I always do when I enter Harold's happy home: I don't want to be here.

Harold's added a lot of junk to the living room. I am particularly taken by the plastic replica of a spinning wheel. Mother lets him do whatever he wants with the house. With anything, for that matter. How she can stand to live in a tacky junkyard, I'll never know. He's added some new pictures, framed reproductions of covers from *Popular Mechanics*. I almost like them.

Cora inspects the living room by walking a circle around it. She says:

Nice place you got here.

I nearly choke on that, and she notices.

There's no place like this place so this must be the place, Harold says and beams happily.

It's good to see you again, Lee, says my mother, who has managed to come into the room without anybody noticing her. No mean feat, if you look as good as my mother. She's wearing a pale blue bathrobe pulled tight about her to emphasize the fact that she still has the same figure she had when she was twenty. Her hair looks like she's just left the hairdresser behind in her bedroom; I expect him to rush out to pat the last few locks into place. Her most recent beauty treatment, the Swiss miracle Dad told me about, has moved the age of her face back a few years. Again. She will go to the grave looking no more than thirty-five, I'm sure. She will become the poster girl for Old Age Clubs of America Inc., if such an organization exists and it probably does. Every time I see her my eyes tear up, both from gladness and appreciation of art. At the same time I remember I hate her for turning myself and my father out to the wolves. Some day, some day when I'm good and drunk or doped or out of my mind or canonized as a saint, some day I will tell her what I think about her leaving us—some day when I'm sure she won't hate me for saying it.

Hello, Mother, I say. She puts out a cheek for me to kiss. It is not like kissing skin. Rubber or porcelain, but not skin. I introduce her to Cora.

You're black, Mother says.

Am I? Cora says. Really? Doggone!

That is Cora's usual rejoinder to whites who feel compelled to point out the obvious. Mother is a bit disconcerted.

Of course I did not mean any racial slur, she says, I just let a thought rise to the surface and vocalized it unintentionally.

Mother is well-read. What she just said probably relates to whatever self-help book is currently on her nightstand.

She takes Cora's hand (she and Harold are compulsive hand-grabbers) and says:

My dear, you're beautiful. I am quite willing to take you into my family as a daughter. Then, glancing at me: That is, if the intention of this visit is for us to welcome you as our new daughter.

I am always amazed by the alacrity with which Mother leaps to conclusions.

I'm not in the market for a family, Cora says, an edge of bitterness in her voice. I recall what Emil told me about her slaughtered family and I understand.

Cora and I just need a place to stay, I say, hoping to diminish the tension in the room. And some help later, if possible of course.

Always glad to chip in to help a chip off your mother's block, Harold says, and grins again, looking for a reaction. I've usually found it better to just ignore his jokes. In a way, they're better than chatting about knick-knacks, lawns, and TV.

What do you need from me? Mother says warmly as if she's always in there pitching whenever her son requires a helping hand.

We just had all our gas stolen from our car, I say and am about to explain in detail when Harold interrupts:

You have a car? A real gas-driven car, not a kiddie car?

Of course it's a real car. And some guys took—

Since when have you been a safedry? Harold says. I can see now what he's up to. Why didn't I just wait until I could talk to Mother alone? Because, dummy, Harold never leaves Mother and me alone. Smart Harold.

I'm not a safedry, Harold. It's bootleg wheels.

Ah-ha, an outlaw then?

If you want to call it that.

What else should I call it? It's against the law to own a car without the proper licensing, right?

Sure, Harold.

And those who drive without the proper licensing are outlaws, by legal definition, right? By legal definition.

He is clipping off his words again.

All right, Harold. Outlaw. I need your help. Just one can of gas, half a gas can, enough to get us back to—

No way, stepson of mine, no way.

But all I need is—

No way. N. O. W. E. I. G. H.

Mother takes a couple steps toward him. He backs up a step, away from her.

Harold, she says. Dear. It's only a little gas. Why can't we help him out?

He sighs, the patient commanding officer about to address his shortsighted subordinates.

You know I can't. I worked hard to get safedry status. Being a safe driver is an achievement, not a privilege.

Depends on what side of the thruway you come from, Cora mutters, but apparently neither Mother nor Harold hear her.

It's only a small thing, Harold, Mother says in her smoothest gentlest voice. I have to acknowledge a begrudging admiration for Harold, for being able to resist the pull of that voice. I never could.

A small thing! he says. All I have to do is give him a thimbleful of gas for his stupid joyriding. If they trace it back to me, there goes my safedry status, and all for nothing.

What are they gonna do, I say, follow the gas trail right back to your doorstep?

Don't get angry, Lee, Mother says, then turns back to Harold: It won't hurt, dear, to take a little risk once in a while. Make you tougher, more masculine, more—

Damn it, don't hang that masculine rap on me.

I don't mean to insult your masculinity. Of course you are masculine from my point of—

A eunuch'd be masculine from your point of—

Calm down, dear, we don't argue. Remember that, we don't argue.

Harold, amazingly enough, settles right down.

You see, Lee, he says, I just can't let you have the gas. Your mother means best but she knows, too. If we get into any kind of trouble, the council might get together and vote us out of the community. Think of that, dear. You know what happened to the Steeses and that was just for—

Yes Harold, I understand, Mother says. Of course I understand. I had just hoped for otherwise. I am sorry, Lee. But please stay the night. In the morning things always look better.

A little sun brightens the son, Harold says.

I nod wearily.

Mother leaves the room without looking back at any of us. Cora stares at a metallic portrait of a wide-eyed clown, purses her lips and nods as if she thinks it's fine art. I have a duty to make conversation. Only catch is I got to make it with Harold.

How's your Pontiac? I say.

Resting in peace. Requiescat in pizza.

Huh?

The Pontiac has gone to the happy hunting grounds. Get it? Pontiac? Hunting grounds? Pontiac was an Indian name and—

Okay, I get the joke but what happened to the car?

Traded it in. Somebody bought it off the lot the next day. Some imbecile who'd just gotten his safedry papers and promptly racked it up into the nearest wall. Totalled it. Made me unhappy, I'll tell you. I put so many years of care into that vehicle, should never have traded it in, in the first place. As the fellow says—

Why *did* you trade it in?

It was time. A time for reaping, a time for trading. Time to move up, as they say. I've been promoted and I'm at the Buick level now, so I managed to arrange for a nice reconditioned Buick. I'll show it to you in the morning. What's the matter? You look like you've seen a ghost or something.

No, just shock. I can't imagine you without that Pontiac. Somehow it's all wrong, you without the Pontiac.

Some are born with Buicks, some achieve Buicks, some have Buicks thrust upon them. From the look of you, you'd like to thrust a Buick right on my head. Sorry, Lee. Really.

Don't, Harold. I understand the safedry mind. Even from my *outlaw* point of view.

You're entitled to your views, but I say no views are good views.

He's used that line on me before. I feel if I stayed around Harold long enough, I'd experience a cycle of the same lines without any new ones to break it up.

Mother comes back in, carrying a tray of tea and cookies. She always ignores my hatred for tea. I don't much care for cookies, either. She's been giving me tea and cookies since I was a baby and she sees no reason to change the habit. I gave up long ago telling her I don't want them. I take the tea, which is in a pretty pink willow pattern teacup. Mother has always had such good taste in her own things, I don't see how she can stand to allow Harold's junk to dominate the look of the house. It's been one of the great mysteries of my life.

Cora devours her cookies.

You must be hungry, dear, Mother says to her.

In a way, Cora says, but really I'm a freak for cookies.

She's never said she was a freak for anything before. Sounds like slang from teenage rebel movies that show up at two a.m. on the TV. Freak? She says it so sweetly I begin to wonder if she is fitting in here or something. When she laughs politely at Harold's pair of word plays on the word freak, I really begin to worry.

Mother remarks that it is the wee hours of the morning and we all need our sleep.

I can't of course allow the two of you to sleep in the guest room, she says, so we'll put Cora there and you can have the couch here, Lee.

I had that couch back when I was a bachelor, Harold says, used to call it my debauch-couch.

Cora goes hysterical over that one. Harold clearly likes her. Even Mother seems to like her. What is Cora up to?

I should demand to sleep in the same room with Cora. I should say I fuck the woman, and it's right we should be housed together. But that's the kind of thing I can't say to Mother.

Cora stretches her pipestem arms and yawns.

I *am* tired, she says. Thank you for your hospitality.

Think nothing of it, dear, Mother says. We are happy to have you as our guest.

Gladda see ya, Harold says in a peculiar voice and blinks his eyes several times. Gladda see ya.

Whatever that means.

Mother leads Cora out of the room. Before leaving, Cora says goodnight politely to Harold and gives me a kind of dainty feminine wave that she would make fun of in others. Harold and I sit around in silence for a moment, then I say:

Say something about wooden nickels.

What? Oh, you mean don't take any. Hell, these days don't take *any* nickels. Even dimes are suspect. It's hard dimes, everywhere, kiddo.

Fortunately Mother comes back into the room with some linens for me to use on the couch.

We must let Lee get some rest, Harold, she says.

Harold looks bemused for a minute and then gets the message that he's supposed to leave the room.

Happy trails, I say to him. He looks back, startled. Then he decides he likes it, says gosh Roy happy trails too, and goes off.

Mother makes up the couch for me while telling me where everything I might require for any emergency, from hunger to sudden blindness, is located. As she retreats from the made-up couch, she says:

That should do you just fine. She touches me as she walks by, a light stroke on my arm, I can barely feel it. Then, leaving the room without turning back to look at me, she says:

I love you, Lee. I wish you'd come and see us more often.

She's out of the room and I'm feeling lousy. Lousy about me and her, and lousy about touching those clean sheets with my dirty clothes.

7

IN my dream I am suddenly in a monastery. It's got stone walls and religious icons in alcoves. But there's also metallic pictures of gardening tools on the walls. A monk passes by me, muttering. He says, Hearty Burgundy, Gallo Be Thy Name. He goes into a time step, but is chastened by a passing Mother Superior, who is of course Mother. The Monk, of course Harold, shuffles off to Buffalo. I become more and more aware of the tinkling of bells in the distance. The tinkle has been there throughout the dream, it seems, and it is getting louder.

I am suddenly awake, staring at the soft copper reflections of the clown picture which hangs above the couch. The tinkle continues, next to my left ear. I turn my head toward the sound. It originates from what appears to be three dark lines rattling directly in front of my eyes now. They are drawn back and I see that it is a set of keys on a chain and Cora is holding them. She whispers:

You're 'bout as hard to wake up as anybody I've seen.

I point to the keys.

What're those?

Whatta you think? Our exit visa.

Exit visa? Cora, what've you—

Keys. Car keys. Buick keys. Mr. Harold's Buick's keys.

Harold's. How'd you—

Keeps 'em under his pillow, the obvious place. No imagination, that man. I can see—

You stole 'em?

Crept tiptoe in his room. Didn't need the tiptoe, he snores like a freight train going uphill. My dainty little hand under the pillow and voila! Let's get outta here.

Put 'em back.

What? Lee, what're you saying?

Put them back. I'm not gonna steal from Harold. Not from Harold.

Cora leans back on her haunches, stares her squint-eyed stare at me.

Oh? she says. Not from Harold. Not from your mama, you mean.

Not from either of 'em.

Not from your mama.

Okay, you say so. But put the keys back, whatever you think.

Go to hell. I'm using these motherin' keys, and you can go on back to dreamland, wake up all innocent in the morning and commiserate with your mama about how this evil demon child you all trusted has put the double hex and double cross on you. Those hand puppets you call people in there'd probably love it, you commiserating with 'em. Sleepy-bye, Lee.

No, wait.

You give the alarm, you bastard, and I'll stuff your balls 'tween your teeth 'fore you can say sorry.

I give up. Okay, let's go. That's your blacker-than-thou voice and I can do naught but obey.

Naught, huh? You got high-quality shit for brains, know that?

I love you to pieces, Cora.

At first she doesn't get it, doesn't remember. Then she does and her eyes become fierce.

You bastard!

Oddly enough, I mean it.

That's not the point. Oddly enough. You been saving that line just to slice me once. And I don't like that. I don't like that ay-tall.

Let's get out of here.

Harold's Buick is a bright yellow. Canary, I think. As usual the garage looks like it's tended by a live-in maid. All the tools on the shelves are shiny, polished. Whatever stuff he uses to take the grease marks off the cement floor works. There's another damn clown portrait hanging above an empty garbage container with a neat ribbon of green plastic bag encircling its upper rim. The bag is clean inside.

You got the keys, I say to Cora. You unlock the trunk.

What do you mean, unlock the trunk?

Harold keeps gas cans in the trunk like everybody else. If we're gonna steal one, we've got to unlock the trunk.

She doesn't like the sarcasm in my voice. She puts her hands on her hips, says:

Look here, white boy, I ain't gonna grab no gas can, sneak by those ugly face guards, and trek back all those miles to your wheels. We're taking Mr. Harold's car.

All the blood drains out of my body. I glance down at the floor, fully expecting to see my blood staining its pristine whiteness.

Jesus Christ, Cora, no! Take Harold's car? That's insane, that's—

That's what we're gonna do. What I'm gonna do, anyway.

You don't know Harold. He may act like a real simp but you touch his car and suddenly he's—

Look, Lee, he's not *my* Mr. Harold. I don't give a shit he's got a hardon for this Buick. All I want is to get out of here, back to where I can breathe again, where the bedsheets don't stink of Clorox.

He'll have the fuzz on us before we get two blocks.

Look, Lee, the way that man cuts logs when he snores, he won't wake up for an explosion.

That's what you think. When it comes to messing with his car, he's psychic. He'll be on the phone and—and anyway what about the barriers, the guards, how the hell do you expect to get the car out of here? This community's—

Use your head for something besides jello. The guards, they're out there to keep people from crashing into this place, they're not ready for somebody crashing *out*.

But then—but then we've really had it. I mean, that canary yellow's not exactly the kind of unobtrusive color we need for an escape run. Too conspicuous.

She leans against the car door, fiddles with the side-view.

No matter, Lee. This's the way we're doin' it. I'm doin' it, anyway. You come, not come, your decision.

Her voice is firm, sure. You can't win with her when she's in this kind of mood. Lately, you can't win with her when she's in

any kind of mood. I look at the Buick, whose brilliant color is
hard on the eyes even in the dim light of the garage. I look back
toward the house, get a mental X-ray picture of Mother and
Harold sleeping away. No matter how this works out, I won't be
exactly welcome home again. But I don't do what she says, I
lose Cora. I'm damn sick of having to give up something to get
something. There's got to be some other way of running my life.
I look back at Cora. Her face is calm. She is being ostentatiously
patient, as if she reads my mind and is willing to wait for all the
rusty gears to click into place.

Okay, I say to Cora, give me the keys.

You son of a bitch! I want to drive this baby. It's my right.

Don't see how it's your right.

I come up with the plan, I stole the keys for it, I get to carry it
out. That's only right. Even you can—

No, Cora. If we're gonna steal from Harold, then it's me that's
got the rights. Harold's Buick's my responsibility, I'll drive.
Give me the keys.

You sonofabitchin' bastard, she says but gives me the keys.
She sulks all the way around the front of the car, shoots furious
looks at me across the hood. When we've settled—collapsed
into—the plush seats of the car, she mutters:

Okay, I agree, you got the right. But that don't make me like
you for it, you crapmouth bastard.

Cora I—

The key there goes in the ignition, the ignition is the doo-
hickey next to the—

Please shut up.

Yes, sir, master.

The car starting up sounds like just the sort of explosion that'll
bounce Harold right out of bed. I'm sure he hears it. Cora insists
on using the electric garage-door opener that's set into the dashboard, and we back out into the dark street. I think I can feel
eyes gaping at us from inside the house, as I swing the Buick
around and drive past.

8

HAROLD'S car is customized, just like usual. Cora loves it. She works the panel of buttons, makes all the windows go up and down several times. Then she inspects all the gadgets in the glove compartment. She discovers the tape deck, puts in a cassette, squeals with delight even though it's only one of those thousand-stringed orchestras playing songs that were dull even before they got their schlocky violins wrapped around them.

She turns out to be right about the guards. We zoom through the gate without even seeing them. I'm sure they see us, but we're in the clear before they can lift a phone receiver or press an alarm button.

Cora, bopping to the draggy melody, says:

Hey, what're we doing going back to your wheels? Might as well be in for the pie as the slice.

What do you mean?

I mean we've already stole Mr. Harold's Buick. The deed is done. Chances are, we get it back to the Expressway, nobody's going to send out search parties for it. This car's got some power. We won't have to blush when—

Forget it. I'm not gonna keep Harold's goddamn Buick.

Dumb shitface motherfucker. Now I seen your mother, I know you must be the motherfucker of all time.

Damn it. Be reasonable. This car's like putting out a flag.

We'd get to keep it about a week, and that's with luck, then either somebody'd rip us off or some cop is gonna make a special effort to take us and the car into custody, so he can let *us* go and keep *it*. You know that, Cora.

Yeah, know it. But, Jesus Christ, Lee, we'd at least have a good set of wheels for a week. That'd be better than a year in your—

I want my own car back.

Yeah, you and that stupidassed Mustang. Shit. That's your car awright, you deserve each other. Okay, you go back to your rotten wheels, leave me these.

I can't do that, you know that.

What difference does it make really? They catch me alone in old Harold's Buick, you're better off. You're off the hook, or at least only dangling from it by your lip. I know you, you can sweet-talk your mommy into thinking the whole thing's my fault.

Not that easy. She don't care if she never sees me again.

I remember how she told me she loved me without looking at me. The pain's still there.

You just don't know your mama, Lee.

I suppose you do, after ten minutes' acquaintance.

I can do anything in ten minutes that takes you your whole frigging life to figure out. Let me keep this car, Lee.

I'd let her drive any other car, but not Harold's Buick, it'd be like giving a doper a full key of anything, and I don't know any way I can tell her that. She goes on grumbling as we turn the corner onto the street where we left the Mustang. Up ahead first thing we see, next to the Mustang, under a bright streetlamp that hadn't been working before, is a flashing red light. Just what I need right now.

God damn it, I say. Cora says it too, just slightly after, an echo that almost overlaps.

Fuzz? Cora says.

Looks like it. Flashing red lights don't usually mean the Goodwill's come to call.

I slow down, pull easily over to the curb, switch off my lights as if I'm just a nightroamer arriving home after a pleasant evening of terrorizing street people downtown.

Looks more like a truck than a police car, Cora says.

It hits me what it is.

Shit, I mutter.

What?

It's a tow truck. A police tow truck. They're going to tow the Mustang away.

Cora laughs and mutters, hot damn.

What're you laughing about?

Tough titty, Lee. We got to keep the Buick now.

Maybe, maybe not.

What're you thinking of?

If I tell her, she's going to mock me out. Instead, I remove the keys from the ignition so she can't get her hands on them while I'm out of the car, then I get out and casually walk around to the back of the Buick and take two filled gas cans out of the trunk. Sliding back into the car, I hand the cans to Cora.

These ain't going to do us any good, she says. We can't gas up now. They've already got your wheels hooked up to the truck. They're just tightening it now, see?

Yeah, I see. You take the gas cans and—

Hey Lee, I don't know what kind of dumb play you got in mind, but drop it. The Mustang's lost. It's now your contribution to city charities, get it? It's on its way to that great junkyard in the sky, all compacted and absolved of its sins. No use wasting us trying to get it back. Let it go, Lee, let it—

Cora, you take the gas cans and when I honk—

I don't want any part of this.

You don't have to do much. Just splash some of the gas onto the trunk of one of those trees on the lawn to the rear of the Mustang. Don't say anything, just listen. When you hear me honk, you set a match to that gas and get out of the way quick. The fire should draw off at least one of the cops. I'll take care of the other. You just get yourself to the tow truck and climb in streetside. I'll join you.

Fuck you.

Cora, please.

I don't want any part of this chuckle-headed brainstorm, Lee. And I'm not going to be accomplice to another cop-killing.

I'm not going to kill 'em, just get 'em away from the truck.

With your fucking record, somebody's liable to get killed.

All right, all right. You walk back to the Expressway. I'll figure out some other way.

She stares at me for a long time. The tow truck cops seem satisfied that the Mustang's attached tightly to their chain. One of them pulls on the chain at least four times. The other climbs into the cab of the truck and works the lifting device. The chain raises the Mustang into the air. When the lifting abruptly stops, the car sways momentarily from side to side. For a moment it looks like it's about to slip off the chain, but it's just an optical illusion caused by the shifting shadows around it.

Awright, you sonofabitch, Cora finally says. Never copped a tow truck before. It's suicide. But I'll help you. Those fuzz-brains better leave the keys in the ignition or they'll be throwin' us into the compacter along with the wheels.

Cora . . .

But she's out of the car and lost in the darkness quickly. Too quickly. I'm scared. I take the legendary deep breath, then start the Buick again. Putting it into reverse, I back quietly to the corner of the street without turning on headlights. The cops don't take any notice. They're standing by the truck and chatting. One of them seems ready to climb into the cab and haulass away. I stop the Buick, shift it into drive, take another breath, and honk once. Almost immediately, a plume of flame rises from a tree behind the Mustang. Good, Cora, good. One of the cops whirls around and runs toward the flame. The other one takes a couple of steps, draws a gun. Well, I'm going to have to get his attention. I ram my foot onto the gas pedal. Cora's right, Harold's got himself a vehicle with real power this time. It picks up speed faster than I'd expected. I almost can't time things right. Steering the Buick first right at the tow truck, I suddenly switch on its lights. The cop with the gun looks toward me, shading his eyes with his free hand. Damn it, he's pointing the gun at me. Shifting the steering wheel slightly to the left, I point the car at him. I can almost hear Cora whispering no, and I swerve back again. The windshield becomes a spiderweb as the cop's shot hits it. He's turned now and he's running like hell away from the Buick. Twisting the steering wheel more to the left so it won't collide with the tow truck *or* the cop, I open the Buick's door and leap out. A hundred pains shoot through my body as I hit the ground and start to roll. The Buick just misses hitting the hood of the truck, seems to glance by its bumper, and careens on down the sidewalk. My arm throbs with pain as I complete my body roll and stand up. Holding it to my side, I make for the tow truck. As I open up the driver-side door, first I see Cora scrunched down against the opposite door and second I hear a basso profundo voice behind me yell:

Freeze, punk!

One foot in the cab, the other dangling free, most of my

weight supported by the door which I cling to with my throbbing arm, I freeze.

His large frame turned into a moving shadow by the firelight behind him, the cop who'd gone to inspect the burning tree moves cautiously toward me, his gun arm raised.

You got any weapons, you throw them down right this minute, he shouts.

I'm clean.

Who is it? shouts the other cop. Sounds like he's halfway down the street.

Don't move punk, my cop says.

I'm trying hard not to move, but it's hard to keep my dangling leg immobile and the pain in my arm makes it jerk unintentionally.

Where are you, Bill? my cop says.

Over here. The other side of that stupid yellow car. It's crashed against something. Can't tell what. Looks like a lawn ornament. A giant black jockey, I think.

Well, get the hell back here. I need help with this jerk.

I've got to find my gun!

Your gun?

I lost my fucking gun when I was running away from the fucking car. I got to find it. It must be here somewhere.

Get back here.

Screw you. They're fining a week's pay for the loss of a sidearm nowadays. I'm gonna fucking find it. You take care of the punk.

But he might have help, he—

You take care of it, Jerry.

Behind me, I hear soft rustling sounds. Cora sliding over on the seat. What the hell is she doing?

Get down out of there, the cop says to me.

Stall him, Cora whispers.

I'm comfortable, I say to the cop.

Get down or I'll pull you down, stupid!

Stall, Cora whispers.

I'se comin' boss, I say.

Comedian, says the cop.

Stall, Cora whispers.

My foot's caught, I say.

I'll chop it off for you if you don't—

Now! Cora yells.

She starts the truck and it lurches forward. I fall away from the cab, my one foot still wedged into something inside, my arm still clinging to the door. It swings outward and I hang on for dear life. Cora applies the brake heavily and I swing back. She reaches out her left arm and grabs my belt. She's got a good grip. I see a seatbelt hanging down and latch onto it, hold it as tightly as I can.

Hang on! she screams and slams down on the accelerator again. The truck has great pickup and we zoom off down the street. Cora's grip and the seatbelt keep me from falling to the pavement through the ravine between the truck door and the cab. I try to ignore the sound that seems like a shot. Cora stops the truck smoothly when we are about a hundred yards away from the cops.

Get in quick, she shouts, 'fore they start to chase after us.

She has slid a bit sideways, away from me, making a space on the seat for me. She still holds tightly to the steering wheel. I don't ask to take over. I pull the door close to me, there's not enough room to shut it.

As we lurch forward again, I sneak a glance back. Harold's Buick, on display beneath a streetlamp, looks quite battered by its misadventure. It doesn't seem likely, but the hood seems bent sideways. Looks like a club fighter's nose. Harold won't be pleased.

9

AFTER we're safely distanced from the cops, Cora tells me to drive the truck the rest of the way. She doesn't feel like driving, she says. When we're outside the city limits, I hold the truck at what seems the safest fast speed, one that won't damage my Mustang dangling so forlornly on its chain.

Cora grouses all the way back to the Savarin. All the way. She can't get it out of her head how we might've kept the Buick. I don't know what's got into her. She knows I wouldn't abandon the Mustang, especially not for Harold's Buick. You got to be practical, I tell her. The Mustang may be no prize, but it does the job. The Buick'd only be a toy. She says she wanted it for her toy and for me to shut up.

At the Savarin she practically runs into Emil's arms. I can tell she doesn't want me anywhere near, so I take the truck to The Mech's garage in order to have the Mustang disentangled from the chain. He's delighted to see the truck, says he's been wanting one but figured he'd never break lucky enough to ever get one. It's about as close to effusive as I'll ever see The Mech.

Some of the survivors of the supermarket caper gather around my prize and congratulate me for snagging it. I try to tell them that the credit for bounty should go to Cora, but they just nod, say of course sure yep. The don't want to believe me. Or they hold so many grudges against Cora they prefer to lay their praise on me. Well, I can take part credit. We wouldn't have obtained the truck if my plan hadn't botched up so effectively.

Not many of the troops were captured in the raid, they tell me. One odd note. Chuck's missing. He was definitely with them during the escape from the parking lot, but he's not turned up since. He's probably off brooding somewhere, or dreaming up a punishment for Cora and me.

Eventually Cora rejoins me, takes my hand. Apparently Emil's calmed her down, what he usually does for her. I'm glad Emil likes me. I might've lost Cora by now if he didn't calm her down at regular intervals, and send her back to me.

I lose Cora anyway. Not that day, not for several days. But I think that day's the reason, even though I can't really understand why. I do everything I can to keep her. Let her drive the Mustang more than I do. Her eyes light up when she drives, but that's about the only time. Every time we return from a dope run or an errand or some joyriding, she runs straight to Emil. I try to get her to go back to our abandoned motel for a few days, but she says she can do without any more spiders thank you. Chuck never does get back. Cora asks Emil about him every day. I thought you were mad at Chuck, I say to her. That's true, she says, but I want him back here so I can rage at him. She's got me so riled, I start screwing up the runs, make mistakes. Everybody starts insulting and joking at me. It's like Cora's scripting their lines for them. Finally she stops going out on any kind of run with me, manages not to be around when I get back. It's a while before I realize we are split. I have to ask Emil, and he has to tell me. When I confront Cora with it, she doesn't want to talk about it. Just shrugs, says it's so, walks away. I try to change her mind a few times, but after a while even I give up.

PART III

1

THERE I am, cruising along at 75–80, and this punk kid comes zooming up beside me and honks his horn twice, grins over at me, honks the old horn two more times. The sign for challenge. He wants to challenge me. The punk kid. He looks about twelve, probably is twelve. They let anybody take a run outside the city limits these days. Not like my day. I had to fight my way out of the city, sneaking across guard lines, coping with rogue cops like Allen. It was a lot harder to get launched onto the road in my day. My day! Shit, my day was only a few months ago. The kid guns his motor and slides on ahead of me. He's driving a souped-up Pinto. A Pinto! For God's sake, a Pinto! And he wants me to play in his yard. Goddamn roadrunner in soggy diapers. I'll take him. I pat the old Mustang on the dashboard, mutter to it in that way that Cora always found so stupid. I'm about to accept the challenge but, just as I press down on the accelerator, I hear a couple pops in the engine and I lift my foot straight off the pedal. I've been driving this car long enough to know it's disaster to ignore its complaints. The Mech taught me anything, he taught me that. Hell. I got to let the punk kid slip over the horizon, his dumb Pinto emitting a pair of explosive backfires that I have to interpret as derisive farts.

All right. Okay. That's it. That's all I can take. Punks are driving me off the roads, I can't even stand being in the same lane with them. And the fuzz, the fuzz're getting so straight, you got to make appointments with them to do two day's worth of slammer time. It's just a game with them. Run us down, lock us up, give us lectures, send us back on the road, run us down again. Penny arcade shit. Ping-ping-ping, we goose-step across a horizon of neon trees; pop, they hit the light in our bellies, we fall, then ping-ping-ping comes around again. The first time I got hooked by the cops, some paper-shuffler found my name on a list, and was ready to hit me with a felony charge for copping Harold's Buick. But asshole Harold refused to press charges. I called home. Mother answered, said Harold refused to come to the phone and talk to me. She said she still loved me but I better not come around to their house for a while. She said to take care, then hung up before finding out if I have any intention to.

Harold, Mother, my alcoholic dad who still breathes into the phone when I call him, the goddamned fuzz, Cora. Cora.

Cora's gone so far off my case, I can't even figure any more why she stayed with me so long in the first place. Once in a while I pass her on the road in her new car, sitting next to her new guy. Soon as she sees me, she looks straight forward, crouches a bit. Her new guy drives a beatup Plymouth Duster. A Duster, can you beat it? All I see on the road nowadays: Pintos, Dusters, I expect kiddie cars linked together in a line any day now.

The few good guys—the stubborn roadrunners and hundredplus-sers who're still hanging around—are avoiding me, calling me screwup. Worst is, I don't even care to go out onto the highway anymore. It's too much for me. My wheels are just not fast enough. Anyway, now Cora's given up on me, there doesn't seem to be any sense in staying around this tar-patch and performing my loner number anymore.

Well, let them shove it.

Let them all shove it.

I'm taking my wheels and going on down the road, heading west, across the great plains and through the mountains, where the fields are greener and so, I'm told, are the punk kids and cops.

The punk kid is in the parking lot of the rest stop, deliberately intruding on my home-base territory. He's just leaning against his Pinto, which is hardly dented and looks like he's just this moment shined it with a toothbrush. Shit, a prepubescent Harold. He's so short he must have to use raised pedals. He looks *less* than twelve standing up like this.

A Pinto, for God's sake!

I'm about to stop and explain to him why I didn't accept his challenge, but he just grins to show off his black and brown baby teeth, gives me the finger, climbs in his car, and zooms away.

I got to get out of here.

I go to The Mech, ask for a tune-up. He gives me the usual look. Ritual, damn it. His answer is ritual, too.

I don't think a symphony'll help the old Mustang much less a tune-up, he says, but I'll get to it, see what I can do.

He wipes sweat off his brow with the back of his hand, after wiping the back of his hand with a clean cloth first.

I really appreciate what you've done for the car, I say—my part of the ritual.

Sure, he says. How you fixed for money? Need any runs, anything?

What's on the docket?

Not much. Crap, really.

Well, I'm fixed okay, I guess.

Not even any doper jobs now. Things're tight.

I have a question I want to ask him, but he doesn't like personal questions, so I hesitate. But I really have to ask it, so I say:

Emil told me last week you been offered a job.

Yep. Supervisor in that shiteating new inspection program back in the city. You know, where they give the new *government-approved* vehicles the once-over, take their payoff, and stamp their seal of approval on the hood. Not even work, just checklisting big charts.

You're not going to take it, right?

He glances around the garage, which is getting so barren it's beginning to look neat.

I don't know. Might.

Ah, c'mon, you—

Look, man, I gotta check your wheels. Don't look over my shoulder. I'll come get you when old Musty's ready.

I hate it when he calls it old Musty, but I am getting good at responding to the voice of authority. I give him a kind of casual air-corps salute and go off. The Mech won't take that job. He'd die in a day.

2

I HAVE to hang around the rest stop, so I go up to the Savarin to see what's doing. Nothing's doing. Hardly anybody there.

Where's everybody? I say to Emil. Emil looks tireder than usual. The hollows in his cheek seem cosmetic, as if he's waiting for a traveling roadshow to offer him a character part. He looks like my dad looks at his worst.

Wedding bells are breaking up that old gang of mine, Emil says.

What the hell do you mean by that?

He shrugs and hands me a cup of coffee. I especially don't want any coffee today. But you got to take it, and you got to drink it in front of him, give yourself a caffeine tracheotomy. More ritual. It's the only thing makes him happy.

Guess I should say goodbye, Emil old buddy, I say.

You just got here. Drink your coffee.

No, I mean I'm taking my wheels and heading for the sunset.

The Sunset Drive-in? Man, you'll never hack it there. That's blade country.

I never know whether Emil is putting me on or not.

No, I mean when The Mech has given my Mustang the once-over, I am leaving the territory. You'll never see me again.

Emil acts angry. Cora used to say that when he got angry at you, you must be doing something right.

What are you, co-opting? You believe all that leaflet crap about Reorganization? Dumbie, they got more rules, that's how they *reorganized*! Look, you had trouble getting a safedry license, right?

Sure, that's how—

Well, now they're going to slip you one on a silver platter provided you return to the fold, and that's worse.

I see that license, think of my dad's driving record and how it cost me safedry status, and I'm almost tempted to go back.

I don't understand, I say to Emil, how could it be *worse*?

You don't know about the new monitors? They don't even need fuzz to make you toe the line. Even the roaming safedrys who used to terrorize pedestrians by goosing them with the points of their hood ornaments—even they've gotta obey the rules now. Everybody tells everybody else it's paradise, and everybody stays in their hovels getting wired in to every new device comes along. Gee-odd in Heaven, I don't know how people can—

The monitors, Emil, what about the monitors?

Ah, they're butterfly's assholes, they are. There's one installed in every approved car, transmitting every move a driver makes to a central agency. A monitor picks up every mistake, no matter how trivial. Two points against you for each mph over the limit, a point for failing to signal, ignoring a stop sign, that sort of thing. It's like taking a driver's test each time you go out on the road. It's like a permanent learner's permit. Pile up enough points and you can apply for a tricycle license.

Emil always gets fired up about social topics. His habit, he's an old-line political activist. Once I asked him which extremist groups he was connected with, he said republican. I don't know anything about republicans, except my alcoholic old dad was against them, so they must've been extreme all right.

Ah well, he says, no use ranting. Man, I was born when F.D.R. was elected president—fourth or fifth time, don't remember which—and here I've lasted several years into a new century. You probably don't know anything about F.D.R. Do you even know there's still a president holed out down there in Washington, forging new improved invisible chains to keep the citizenry in line, do you know that, buster?

Yes, well, I think so. I never voted, but I guess his name is—

Who cares what his name is? Their names haven't mattered since, since I don't know when. You go right back to where you came from, vote for him, or is it her, like everybody else. Become a nine-to-fiver like all the rest.

All the rest of what?

All the rest of you dumb bastards. Look around. Nobody's here because nobody's riding the roads anymore. Everybody's copped out, gone back to the absorbent middle-class, sold their wheels and bought kiddie cars. Yeah, I can see you in one of those lousy new machines, car polish on your teeth, chrome epaulettes on your shoulders. Gee-odd in Heaven, I knew you'd be one of them. I never knew what the hell you were doing around here in the first place.

I feel hurt, Emil's been on my back ever since Cora said so long. I feel hurt, but damned if I'll let Emil see it.

I'm not copping out, Emil, I'm—

Your voice is shrill, drink some more of that coffee. That'll drop it an octave.

I take a sip. My tongue dissolves, the trickle down my throat leaves scars. Emil looks like he hopes I'll choke. My new low voice may be permanent.

I am not returning to the goddamned city. I wouldn't go back there if they paid me, I—

They *will* pay you. Amply. It's the new thing. Ask the fuzz.

Nobody ever said anything to me about that.

No, maybe they might forget to tell *you*.

That's an insinuation.

That's what it is, all right. So, where in this land of opportunity and sudden ambush do you plan to go?

I don't know. Somewhere west of here.

Ah, west! Of course. Robert Penn Warren, *All the King's Men*, west is where you have to go, something like that. West is, when you go there, they have to take you in. No, that's not right. Forget quotes, misquotes. People used to pursue their dreams to California. They died there, which was all part of the dream according to some. I've heard it's not so pretty there any more.

So what? It's pretty here?

A rare smile from Emil.

You may have something there. Would you like another cup of coffee?

It is not a question, it's an order. I haven't drunk that much of my first cup. I hope The Mech gets to my car soon. Before I die would be good. A lot of the coffee spills when Emil pours it. I never noticed before how much his hand shakes. I touch my coffee cup cautiously, not wanting to get any of the spilled coffee on my skin. Emil stares off toward the bug-splattered glass window behind me.

That whole myth, the California dream, California trip, died when I was quite young, Emil says. It died first, then it traveled across the country and left grave-dirt on the paths it walked.

What do you mean by that?

I don't know. Drink your coffee.

He means something by all this chatter about deaths of myths, but it's nothing I really want to hear about. You get tired of people telling you that everything you wanted has decayed long ago.

Hi Lee, what's on?

I recognize the voice immediately. Just exactly who I don't want to see. But I swing around in my stool anyway. Smiling.

Hello Cora.

She's looking as compactly beautiful as ever. She's cut her hair, an attempt to look more African, but it doesn't work, still looks like a white woman's hair. Large-looped earrings hang from her newly pierced ears. She's wearing Afro dress, a dashiki or whatever they call it, and it isn't quite right either. Sad: no matter what she does, she'll never look black enough. At least she has stopped using that cosmetic that made her skin darker than normal. In spite of all the tinkering with herself, and all the fights we've had, I immediately want to fall to the floor and beg her to take me back. But she won't, wouldn't ever, and so it's no use bothering with the floor.

You look good Lee, weatherbeaten or something, Cora says.

All that sun. Guess it affects the skin.

Affects the brain, too.

I wince, and some tears come to Cora's eyes.

Sorry Lee. I don't want to hurt you with cheap talk. You know that, not anymore.

I don't like her being delicate. She should've let the insult stand.

Saw you riding with some, with a new guy. Who is he?

A guy. Nice guy, you don't know him.

Where is he?

Oh, the fuzz got him yesterday. I was with him, but he made me run away. He'll be back in the usual coupla days.

Sure. That really a Duster he drives?

A brief flash of anger in her eyes.

Don't start mockery, Lee. That Duster's in good condition, better than your—ah, fuck. Blue's a good vehicle, leave it at that.

Blue? You named it Blue?

Let's not start squaring off, all right?

She looks around the room, runs her skinny little finger along the edge of the counter, skipping it over an upraised metal sliver.

Fuzz'll have him back two days, exactly. Everything's very formal these days. Remember when this place was crowded?

Emil and I were just talking about that. He says we've lost a lot of people from the ranks. They've gone back to the city and civilization.

That's the new hustle all right. Rip it off, rip it up, rip away. They really screwed us when they repealed some of the old anti-car laws. Don't get me wrong, those laws were dumb all right. Well-intentioned, maybe, but dumb. But look at it this way, we all got out of our traps just because some dumbie legislators cooked up a lot of profitmaking ways to restrict the use of the old automobile. How'd they know their profits'd disappear when G.M. and Ford went down the tubes? Still, it was great—gave *us* all this space, all these roads.

Cora's eyes glow when she talks like this. I told her once it was like she clicked on her high beams, and she ridiculed me for days for saying it.

Well, she says, the good old days are departed. Now you can go back to the city, the megalopolis of megalopoli, and get a brand-new machine that's got so many special devices hidden in it, it can't even outrun a snail. So you can plod along, low-pollute the air with low-pollutants, and take a luxurious half-day job with all-day pay. For all-day suckers. Shit, why'd anybody want a half-day shift when they can have a no-day shift?

I don't know, Cora.

How's your wheels?

Okay. They always say they'll impound it the next time around. But they don't really want it.

I know what you mean. They don't really care. They're not going to do any impounding or anything. They're too out of it to even pull out any red tape nowadays. Gonna let all outlaw vehicles die natural deaths. They've got your number, Lee, that's all.

Not my number.

Oh come on Lee, what—

No, I mean it. I'm clearing out. Heading west.

What's west?

Without waiting for an answer, she walks away, stands by the plate-glass window. It's a grey day outdoors, and it puts her in a shadow, makes her for a moment as dark as she wants to be.

Emil taps me on the shoulder. Without speaking he puts a piece of paper in my hand.

What's this? I say.

Telephone number here. That wall-phone, that one over there.

I know where it is. Thought it broke forever.

Nah, it works. Chuck came back one night and threw together a few wires and fixed it.

Chuck? You've seen Chuck?

Day-amn, I wasn't supposed to say anything. Okay, yeah, I seen him. He pops in sometimes, the dead of night, when nobody's around. Just appears at the door out of nowhere, asks for a cup of coffee. His face is always white against the night, like a ghost. Maybe that's what he is. Anyway, he fixes phones. Coffee urns, too. And he's worked out a gasline system for the stove. Ghost or no, he's handy.

If Emil is really off his nut, like some people say, then Chuck may exist only in his demented mind. Nevertheless, I say:

Next time you see him, say hello from me.

Okay, but he doesn't like to hear about anybody. Always shuts me up when I bring up a name. Spooks me, I'll say that.

The phone really works?

Course it does. Hardly anybody ever uses it, that's all. I never tell anybody it works.

I look down at the piece of paper with the number on it.

Well, what should I do with this number?

Call it, schmuck.

He says this affectionately, then walks away without further explanation. I pocket the paper with the number on it, wondering why I'd ever want to call this miserable place.

Then the sun breaks out from behind a cloud (Cora steps backward), and The Mech comes in.

Your wheels're about as healed as can be expected, he says, but I really recommend a sanitorium for it. Matter of fact, I got an address right here—

Thanks, I'll run it a little longer. You take out the usual gas cans?

Not this time.

That's really decent of you. I mean, you—

Shut up, roadrunner. Look, these days I got no need for extra gas in extra cans. Just weigh me down.

What he says worries me but I decide not to pursue the subject. Instead, I mumble goodbyes to Emil and Cora and, without looking at either of them, follow The Mech out of the Savarin. Checking the trunk, I find that not only has The Mech not taken his payment, he's added a couple of filled cans to my supply. Looks like I can get out west on what I got. I crawl into the Mustang and, swinging around a broken and fallen gas pump, I am off. I forget to look back at the cafe window to see if Cora waves goodbye. I know she did, though, and I'm just as glad not to see it.

3

As usual, The Mech has put the magic touch on my vehicle. It never goes so good as when he's just worked on it. At its worst, just before I hand it over to him, nothing responds right away, everything seems to take a moment of contemplation before the Mustang will allow it to happen. But, after The Mech has left off his working of wonders, its responses come much quicker. So quick that it seems like the car's reflex actions damn near ignore stimuli.

I go smooth for many miles, almost half the afternoon. I don't want to attract the attention of any stray fuzz looking to fill last week's quota. But the roads are clear. Not only that, they're in good shape. We have our own road teams, who work at night, making repairs with what material they can find, making the road safe for roadrunners. I've heard the roads are worse farther on.

I only see a few other cars, mostly going in the other direction, on the other side of the median. It bothers me I don't see any familiar faces. Drivers I'd normally snub for their meanness, moral corruption, and coldhearted stupidity would seem like old-school-tie chums to me now. The people I do see are cretins, testing whether or not they are alive by riding the roads.

Finally I begin to feel free, and I floor the accelerator pedal. The Mustang springs forward without any argument, the way I like it. We pick up speed, the cool wind gusts in through my open vent-window, the rumble of the motor is mellower than it's ever been. If the speedometer worked, I'm sure it'd reveal Musty's highest speed. Everything flies by. I have not felt this good, so at-one (a favorite expression of roadrunners I have known) with my machine. It's all illusion, I know that, but I love it. I want to cry, I am so happy. Then I want to cry because I am so sad, knowing the happiness is phony. I'm not free, I've just managed to drive away a few miles. But I've got to keep up the illusion, it's important. Why the goddamned hell did Cora have to show up at the Savarin? It wasn't right, it cast a pall over the whole goddamned trip. Hell with that, I'm going to keep this goddamned car moving. It'll get me somewhere.

That night I stop the car, take a blanket out of the back seat, stretch it out, and sleep under the stars. No, that's part of the fantasy. I can't see any stars, but I know they're there, and I sleep.

In my dream Cora and I make love in front of a penny-arcade mirror. The images of our bodies in the mirror, hers especially, are elongated and wavery. She is tender with me, the way she was when she wasn't telling me off or throwing sarcastic remarks my way. Like in that abandoned motel, or when she was in the afterglow of driving the car. We both lose interest in lovemaking and become more fascinated with the mirror. She asks what right have I got using conventional mirror imagery in my dreams. I say I have no control over it and like conventional imagery anyway. She says I am a dumb shit, always was. She says I don't amount to diddly-squat on the wall. I say, forget the mirror and let's screw again. She laughs. I recognize the laugh as the same one she laughed the night she finally admitted she was splitting with me, when she simply said it was all off and walked out the door as if on a quick errand. I realize that laugh is stored in my brain and so it comes into my dream easily. She turns toward me and begins caressing my face with the back of her hand, the way she often did when she didn't think me such a dumb shit. Then her expression changes to a deep-furrowed frown. She pulls her hand abruptly from my face, stares at the back of her fingers. They are now smeared with blotches of white. I look toward the mirror, expecting to see myself in a clown getup. But my face is normal, except where Cora's been touching it, where there is now a dark patch. As I stare into the mirror she puts her hand on my face, rubs it around. With each of her strokes an area of my white skin comes away. I look back at her, at the white now all over her fingers. In a troubled gesture, she rubs the hand on her own face. The white comes off on her skin. She now has a light patch to balance my dark one. She begins working on my face in earnest, taking my whiteness away, smearing it on her face. Soon her face is white and we both look into the mirror again. Cora is now a white woman, and it looks right on her. She looks smashing. I am a black man. A rather odd-looking black man, but I kind of like it anyway. Cora screams. Both her hands go to her face and she tries furiously to remove the white. I know she wants to smear it back onto me. But she can't remove it. She starts tearing at her skin, as if she wants to pull all the layers off. As I wake up, it begins to look like she might be successful at it.

Next morning I wake sore as hell but feeling wonderful. I tramp around a little, working out the body cramps, exercising a few muscles. What strikes me best is I don't see much litter. One or two rusty cans, crushed. A pizza carton, grease-spotted. Some old wrappers, that sort of thing. But nothing big, no old tires or car seats or cars. No rusty or disintegrating monuments to the decline of the road in the last decades of the twentieth century. Perhaps I am in a new land. It starts to rain and I return to the Mustang.

The rain continues all morning. It is a misty rain, annoying because it makes me drive slow and carefully. I can only see a few feet in front of me and have to maneuver around all the cracks and potholes in the concrete. Once I have to stop altogether. There's a wide crack bisecting most of the road. I wonder what the drivers along this way must be like, to let a crack like this go unrepaired and unmarked. It really pisses me off. Back in my own territory we always put up signs warning others against road hazards. Chuck, when he was in charge, regularly inspected our stretch of Expressway. Cora and I made regular runs putting up signs based on the information he and his crew brought back. Sometimes the fuzz came and took them down, but we kept pretty good track. No sign before this monster of a gap, I'm sure. If I'd hit it with any speed, I might have totalled my wheels. Damn drivers—but what drivers? Come to think of it, I haven't seen any cars in some time. My temptation is to attribute this to the miserable day, although rain never discouraged any roadrunners I've known. Ah, well, no tragedy. I maneuver the Mustang onto the soft shoulder and it tiptoes by the obstruction. Back on the road, I drive even slower. I don't know what might be coming up next. I wouldn't be surprised to see a Minotaur blocking my way. Or superintending a rotting tollbooth.

For many miles the road is clear. The rain stops. I begin to relax, settle into driving. I lean back against the bucket seat, enjoy the kinetic sensation of the car moving along. God, this is the life. The road, the Mustang, me, the horizon ahead. Nobody in sight, haven't seen another car in over an hour. I get the feeling, at least for a moment, that all the highways are mine.

4

I APPROACH a rest area beside the road. I'm tempted to get out and stretch my legs for a minute but, hell, I'll never get out west if I take rest stops all over the place, so I decide to drive on. As I pass the area, I see quick movement there, near what used to be an information building. Somebody throwing something at somebody else. I can only get a quick look because trees then obstruct my view. I slow down a little, cruise along on the edge of the rest area, try to see what's happening through the trees. They're too thick, too clumped, can't see a thing. Soon I'm at the exit road. Going past it, I look over my shoulder. Somebody's running along a sidewalk, but I can't see much else because there's this huge shack of a comfort station in my way. The running person falls, there's a scream, and I hear the zooming sound of what is unmistakably somebody gunning a motorcycle engine. I slow down to a crawl. The exit road is a few feet behind me and I can only see the shabby roof of the comfort station above a new set of trees. At first I tell myself to drive on. Whatever it is, it does not need my investigating of it. Nevertheless, my quick glimpses have caught major details, and I can't ignore them. I stop the Mustang, put it in reverse, and slowly back it to the exit road. I can't see anything now, but I can hear what sounds like an argument, interrupted irregularly by derisive taunting laughter. Nothing I can do but take a look. First I ease the Mustang onto the exit road and slowly drive up its gravelly surface. My shoulders cringe each time a stone clangs against the car's underside. But the argument and laughter continue, so nobody up there must be hearing it. I come to a one-way sign bent over and across about half the road. There's something of a ditch on the other side of the road, so I have to pass by the sign with care. As I come near the comfort station, I can see movement on the other side. I stop the Mustang, not knowing what I can or should do. Best thing would be to approach on foot. Whoever they are, they might get distracted by a passing car. I want to be able to get back into the Mustang if I'm in a hurry, so I leave the keys in the ignition and the car doors open on both sides.

I edge along the side of the comfort station, compulsively reading several of the obscene slogans scrawled all over its splintered surface. Reaching the corner, I take a careful peek around it. What I see looks like a ritual. A bunch of guys in a semicircle around another figure. I wonder if it's some kind of occult ceremony, like I've seen in movies. Some motorcycles are parked along the driveway leading to the abandoned information center. Something tells me it's not smart to fool with cycle jockeys, and I consider slinking back to the Mustang and driving gently away. But, no. Motorcycle gangs are not exactly the high society of the road, never have been, and if this particularly repellent group of bikers is gathered around somebody, that somebody is in trouble. I got to help. I don't want to, but life has its prerequisites. One of mine is, if I don't do something, I worry a lot afterward. I can't allow bad things to happen. I am not heroic, but I must respond to the needs of my fellow man, even if it means going up against a half-dozen mean bikers. I am insane, is what I am.

I crawl around the comfort station corner, crouching low behind a foul-smelling leafless set of bushes. Anybody looking my way could easily see me there, but they are all intent on the ritual. Hell, it's no ritual, it is business. They are stalking. Their object is turned away from me, but she seems to be a slim-hipped and tall young lady, in a flower-patterned dress with a long skirt. Long blond hair and fairly broad shoulders. I am impressed with what I see of her from the back and wish she'd turn around.

I take a position behind the wooden panels that form a two-sided protection against anyone spying on the ladies room. Nobody notices my move there. They're intent on their prey, don't expect an intruder. An intruder! Great, just how am I going to intrude on six brawny tattooed ugly slobs, each with a weapon in his thick hand? One of the men is pointing a gun at the girl. Jesus. All I need is to get a bullet through the heart, just when I am on the verge of finding the west. On the other hand, the girl is in real trouble. It looks like they're going to do all the numbers bikers are famous for. Beating, clubbing, shooting, raping.

Backing away from them, the girl stumbles, falls. A biker helps her up with mock politeness and she springs away from him, staggers a few steps backward, toward my watching-post. I still don't get a good look at her face.

The bikers regroup around her helper, who is apparently their leader. They face the girl. The leader's about ready to say it's time. I don't know what to do. The girl falls again, crouches. She shouts to the leader of the pack. She tells him she'll rip his balls off. She sounds like she can do it. I wonder if she is going to need me. Her voice is hoarse, as if this isn't the first insult she's screamed at them. The leader shows no reaction, makes a gesture with his gun hand to one of the other men, who is wrapping a tire chain around his hand ostentatiously. The tire chain looks like a locket chain in his beefy hand. They're about to make their move. I have to do something. I can't think of anything to do.

Hey you guys! I say, stepping out from my shelter. Stop that!

Some great thing to say. I think I startle them with the girlishness of my voice. They look toward me, all six of them. Not a single one would weigh in under 180. That's at least 1080 pounds if they all decided to jump me at once. Shit.

A bit delayed in her reaction, the girl looks at me, too. Even though I'm scared, I am also stunned by her looks. It is the right kind of face to go with long blond hair and a tall slim body. Healthy, red-cheeked, long. She has a pointed chin, strong, makes her look like a tennis-player mannequin. She smiles.

Who the fuck are you? she says.

I am not ready for that question from her. Fortunately the bikers, dumbstruck, are not ready for me. They are obviously not afraid of me, just not ready.

I got three buddies in the car, fellas, I say (gesturing backward toward the Mustang which they probably can't see), and each one of us's got a piece. I suggest you stand right where you are.

I try to sound as anti-gun-control square as I can. I can see they are not quite ready to doubt me. A couple of them take steps backward. The leader stays where he is, but is no longer as poised for action as before.

Okay, young lady, I say, ma'am, uh, you—

Well, um, she says, you can call me Vicki.

Okay, Vicki.

Wait a minute, the leader of the pack says. Vicki stands up and begins walking toward me.

Okay, Vicki, I say.

The leader takes a step forward.

He ain't got no piece. He's a fuckin'—

Okay, Vicki, I say. Run!

And I rush back to the Mustang without looking around to see if anyone is following. I nearly trip on a bush as I turn the comfort station corner. Vicki keeps pace with me. I zip around the open door and somehow make it into the driver's seat. Vicki scrambles in the passenger side, does not think to shut the door behind her. Her head knocks against my shoulder as she tries to swivel around in her seat. As I press down on the accelerator pedal with all the force that my somewhat less than 180 pounds can muster, one of the bikers rounds the car on her side, his body crouched, apparently to take a jump at the car. The open door hits him right in the face.

Shut the goddamn door! I yell at Vicki.

Reacting quickly she pulls it shut. At the same moment there is a sickening thump on my side. I look that way over my shoulder and see a falling biker hurling curses at me. The leader of the pack is rushing toward his cycle as I speed past him. In the rear-view mirror I can see two of the bikers running after us, waving their clenched fists at the car. One of the casualties is sitting on the ground, holding onto his leg and rocking. I pat the Mustang dashboard, glad the car responded so quickly.

I have to make a wide turn out of the rest-area access road, in order to head west again. A biker, apparently taking a shortcut through the trees, emerges at the side of the highway, but too late. In the rear-view I see the leader of the pack, leaning over the handlebars of his cycle, taking the wide turn from the entranceway and starting his pursuit. His cohort, oblivious to the approach of his noble leader, runs onto the road, as if he thinks he can catch me on foot. The leader has to swerve to avoid him. His cycle skids and he and it slide down into a depression in the median. The other biker runs toward him. They are both soon out of sight.

Beside me, Vicki is twisted around on the seat watching. I look over at her. Her face is quite pretty, although the look of healthiness is due to artful makeup. Rather too much lipstick. I glance down at her chest. She is like Cora, in that I can't quite detect tits, although there is a suggestive roundedness.

I return my attention to the road ahead, letting my elation sweep through my body. Here I am heading west, freedom in my soul and a rescued maiden at my side.

Jesus Christ, Vicki says, can't you get this crate going any faster? They're souped up, the bikes, they can catch us.

I push the Mustang to its limit. We are now flying down the road, but Vicki is still nervous.

This may be fast enough, she says, maybe. Don't see any sign of them. Just keep it up, sweetheart. Keep your balls in gear and we'll get outta this yet.

I notice a small protesting sound from the Mustang's engine. I think we should slow up a bit, but I'm afraid of upsetting Vicki. I'll keep it up for a few miles, then gradually decelerate. Vicki turns in her seat and stares straight ahead. I am a bit annoyed at her—she has yet to say anything grateful to me. A small sweetly muttered thank you would be sufficient, but she just stares ahead and smooths out ruffles in her skirt. The hand I can see has short stubby fingers on it. Each finger has a jewelled ring.

They looked like a mean bunch, I say. The guys that were attacking you.

Mean, yeah. They abducted me. Hurtled into town on their filthy machines and fucking abducted me. They're monsters, is what they are.

What town?

What?

The town you live in, where they abducted you.

Jesus, I didn't live in that creepy place. I don't know what its name was. Truth is, way the town was, it was preferable to be abducted.

Well, Vicki, I guess it's good I came along when I did. Looked to me they meant business.

Business?

Well, at least they looked like they were gonna rape you any minute.

Vicki laughs.

Look, rape they coulda had for free. I woulda been glad to

take on any of them. No, it's murder that I couldn't cotton to, frankly.

Well, yes, Vicki but—

Look, it takes a minute to get my head together. I know you think you're Lochinvar and all that, sweetheart, but one thing I think you gotta know right off.

What's that, Vicki?

It's the Vicki business. Well, I do call myself Vicki from time to time, and it seemed natural to be Vicki when you showed up with your armor shining in the haze and all. But, Jesus Christ, I always feel ridiculous when I have to say this—but my name isn't really Vicki except for fantasy purposes.

Well, names . . .

I'm Victor. Victor Whelan.

Victor.

Look, man, I'm a transvestite. Let's not make anything out of it, okay? I like to dress up and wear makeup, and that's that. I can't help it. My psychiatrist couldn't help it. He liked evening gowns.

I look over at him, try to imagine him without the pretty clothes, the makeup, the blond wig. He still looks very beautiful.

Okay, Vicki—Victor. Vic. I mean, I'm tolerant. I been on the road a long time, know all kinds of folk. Some of your kind, too, and—

Don't be so fucking condescending. All right, you knew some gays. Good. But I'm not gay. Some gays like to dress up, yes, but a transvestite is not automatically gay, get it?

Oh, sure. I wasn't saying that you were at all when—

You were saying then that you run into transvestites regularly?

Well, no—

Then shut up till you know what you're talking about.

But—

Anyway, I hate fags.

The sun is shining now and the glare begins to hurt my eyes. I find myself edging away from Victor, leaning against the door. He doesn't notice. He just keeps smoothing out his skirt, adjusting his wig.

We drive fast for a long time. Finally I have to slow down, for the good of the car. Victor doesn't seem to care now. There are no signs of any bikers behind us. I haven't even seen a car in hours.

5

VICTOR'S getting to be a real pain in the ass. For two days I've been hinting that it would not cause in me great grief if he decided to stay in one of the dumb towns we've been passing through. He says he doesn't like the midwest.

He's got one habit he could've picked up from Cora. He keeps asking if he can drive. I make up a story about how the Mustang has an odd feel to it (part true) and I don't like to have other people drive it. He seems to understand but always asks again an hour or two later. I can't say I just don't want him behind the wheel.

There are more vehicles on the road now. Even some trucks clearly engaged in interstate commerce. The cities don't seem so ugly and even seem to be functioning reasonably well. When we go into them or pass through them (some stretches of the turnpikes are impassable), the citizens don't stare much, unless of course they realize that sweet Vicki ain't so sweet. Some of the cities that slip by our car windows look deserted. The ones that seem deserted aren't, Victor says, they got people in them, they just died, that's all—the cities, not the people. Midwestern fuzz don't want to bother with us. Some of them wave when we go by.

I am getting damn sick of Victor's patterned dress, both for looks and odor. He's got nothing else to wear, he's lost all his clothes and possessions to the bikers. I almost offer him some

115

clothes of mine, but I don't like the idea of him in them. Finally I tell him I'll rip off something in his size. He says he can do his own ripping off, thank you, and steals a couple tee-shirts and a pair of jeans at a smalltown store. I'm sorry about that. It's a nickels and dimes place and even the proprietors look tarnished. I wish I could leave them a few cents afterwards.

I keep wanting to stop the car and ask him to get out, but I can't. That would take the edge off having saved him.

It's almost evening. I have driven most of the two days, with only a couple stops to rest. I need to get west as soon as possible. Victor says I'll never get this car through the Rockies, not even the foothills. I tell him he doesn't nearly suspect the Mustang's capabilities. His laugh is like a sneer printed in block letters.

Special markings ahead, beside the road. Rest stop, one used by our kind. I've seen so few cars on the road that I don't expect to see people there, but I have got to stop for a while.

Think we'll lay over at this place, I tell Victor just before we reach the access road.

Whatever you say, sweetheart. Maybe there'll be a clothing exchange. I need some new duds. That dress has had it.

You'd buy a dress? Like that?

Like what?

Openly, I mean.

Sure, nobody cares.

I can't tell him that I care. I can't give him that kind of a lever. We drive up the road. It turns out that the place is more populated than I'd expected. Cars parked all over the lot, it's hard to find a spot to leave the Mustang.

This is not my kind of place. There may be a lot of vehicles, just like in the good old days back east, but it's not the same. These cars are not well kept up. They have the dust of the road on them, sure, but it looks like last year's dust. Drivers back east took pains to keep their vehicles shiny and relatively undented. These cars are lusterless, and their bodies look like they've substituted for practice drums. The few people in the parking lot remind me of the cars. They are lethargic, battered. They just lean against surfaces, not doing anything, not even talking to each other. The Mustang, with three days' driving debris scattered over its unglamorous surface, looks better than any other car in this whole goddamned lot. And that, Cora might tell me, is a switch.

I walk toward the building which had once been the rest stop restaurant. A Hot Shoppe, didn't think that chain had extended this far inland. One of its walls has partially collapsed and people are using it as an entrance. The gas pumps in the distance are working, that's something. Although we picked up two cans of gas in one of the towns we passed through yesterday, it is always exciting to come upon a place with working pumps. Although the cost or barter is always high, it's worth it to drive off with a newly filled tank, especially now that there are so few functioning gas stations left that will serve us.

I follow Victor. Rustling his still-stiff jeans, he walks with a cowpoke's lope. I've never seen him walk this way before. People leaving the restaurant have the same kind of walk. Victor, I have seen, is ever adaptable. What I really can't get over is that he's even beautiful in men's clothes.

Victor, hey man, over here! some freak says when we enter the Hot Shoppe through the hole-in-wall entrance. And I do not use the word freak lightly, even generically. This guy is a freak. His head isn't on straight, it looks like it's been pushed over onto his left shoulder. His face is arranged casually. I feel uncomfortable looking at him, I want to take the features of that face and put them where they belong. He is wearing half a beard, on the right side of his face. He is quite muscular, barrel-chested, but his legs would look better on a ballerina. He is so freaky-looking, I should feel an instant kinship with him, but I don't.

The freak is standing with a weary-looking group. We walk to him.

Link, Victor says. What're you doing here?

Just drifted here from the last place, like usual. Who's your friend?

Oh, right. Link, this's Lee.

Pleased to meet you, Lee.

Hello, Link. Link, short for Lincoln?

No, missing. But don't let it throw ya.

Link and Victor get to reminiscing. Turns out Link was in the town where Victor was kidnapped by the bikers. He had tried to intercede, but they had run him through a shop window. After picking shards out of his clothing, he had decided that the town, which was biker-controlled, was not for him, and he caught the next ride west. He must have been just ahead of us most of the time.

But our wheels died just south of here and we trekked to this place, been here a couple hours. Three of us. You guys got room in your car for us?

Sure, Victor says.

Victor, I say.

What's the matter, you can't be hospitable to a bunch of guys in trouble?

Link's two friends are bigger than he is. They all stare at me as if I am completely lacking in the milk of human kindness. I don't want to have anything to do with any one of them.

Okay, I say. Sure. The more the merrier. But one thing, I do the driving and right now I need rest.

Can fix you up immediately, Link says. Cots set up in the back.

He starts to lead me to a back room. Victor lopes along beside us.

Anybody dealing threads around here? he asks Link.

Let's see, yeah, I think you can be accommodated. Let's get our friend here some shuteye, and we can take care of that.

Sure.

The sleep room's not my idea of luxury accommodations, but there are several cots spread around the area in no logical pattern, and I am too tired to care. I select one that looks like it's relatively new, with only a few layers of dirt and grime. I sit on it. None of the other cots is occupied. The room is dark and I know I can drop off to sleep right away.

This do? Link says.

It do fine, I say.

Link smiles. The bland pleasantness of his smile becomes freaky on that peculiar face.

You're okay, Lee, he says. The kind of easygoing dude who's immediately likable, you know?

You say so.

Victor is irritated.

C'mon, Link, I want a look at those threads.

Okay. Sleep cool, you hear?

I don't believe his phrasing but I am beginning to like Link. He takes Victor's arm and leads him out of the room. Victor's walk is now perkier, more rhythmic. Like Link's.

I test the cot. Looks like it'll hold me. I take off my shirt, but keep my trousers on, because that's where I keep my car keys. There's no real safety in protecting your car keys in a place like this. Anybody wants them bad enough, they can get them. Still, I feel safer with them on me. I stretch out on the cot. It is hard on the back but more comfortable than grabbing a few winks in the bucket seat of the Mustang. I find myself thinking of the keys as I drift off to sleep.

6

I WAKE up suddenly, with a start. The room seems much darker. It is a minute before I realize that somebody is standing over me, another minute before I realize it's Victor. He has apparently been successful in his search for threads. He has discovered a lovely peasant blouse with full sleeves, white with some red at the fringes. And a multicolored skirt in bright hues—orange, yellow, and green—running downwards in a rainbow pattern from the waist. I find myself compulsively turning over in my cot to check out his footwear. Only a tip of what might be a high-heeled plain black shoe peeks out from underneath the hem of the floorlength skirt. I look up again. He still stares at me. He has done something to the blond wig, wound up some of it in braids by the ears, while letting most of the hair fall onto and past his shoulders.

I try to see if there are any sleepers on the other cots yet. There are not. We are alone in the room. Something about Victor's eyes frightens me.

Abruptly he sits down on a cot across from me. He lifts up a hand. There is a tube of lipstick in it. He holds it in front of his face, examines it. He has already applied some rouge and is beginning to look like Vicki again. He applies a little of the lipstick, then works his lips to spread it. He can apparently do this sort of thing without a mirror.

I sit up, decide I should make conversation.

What's doing, Vic?

My voice seems to echo around the room and come back to me, sounding more false than when it had started.

Victor doesn't answer. He merely works the lipstick. It is orange, the lipstick's color. It suits him.

Did I sleep long? I ask. I have absolutely no sense of time.

Long enough, Victor mumbles, between compressing his lips and running a finger along the edges of his mouth to remove excess. When he puckers, it is remarkable how evenly he has applied the lipstick. The orange goes beyond the border of one side of his upper lip, but the rest is put on as well as if he had a mirror.

I feel rested, I say. Where's Link, and the rest?

Out somewhere.

They'll be coming back, won't they?

Sure. They're just dealing for some food. Some cat up in the hills has a lot hoarded away, and he sells it at inflated prices.

Victor's voice stays in a monotone. He seems to be done with the lipstick, though he still holds it in his hand. Rings on his fingers again, reflecting more light than seems logical for the room. Maybe they store up light. His other hand is toying with a strand of hair while he stares at me. I feel I should say something more, try to break the mood or something, but I have forgotten my native language. Victor runs a tongue along his upper lip, as if tasting the lipstick.

Lean forward, he says abruptly. In a louder voice.

Why?

Don't get tensed up. I'm not trying to seduce you or anything. I just want to touch you.

But isn't that—

No, it is not the same, if that's what you're trying to say.

That's not what I was trying to say.

Well, fuck it anyway. Lean forward. C'mon. I'm dangerous, even you must've figured that out.

Dangerous.

I guess you haven't. Well, maybe dangerous isn't the right word. Maybe unpredictable. Lean forward.

I am out of responses. I lean forward. With the hand that had been twisting his golden locks, he touches my cheek. He doesn't stroke or press or do anything with the hand, he just puts some fingers against the skin. His hand is cold, as if it's abandoned circulation. We sit like this for quite a long time. It is hard for me to hold my head steady in this position, but somehow I do it. I am afraid to remove my cheek from his hand.

Sit still, he whispers finally. Like that. You're doing fine. Just for a moment. Still.

I am staring at his forehead and so at first I am not sure what he's doing. Then I sense his other hand coming at my face. It still holds the tube of lipstick in it. I start to spring back, but he moves fast and presses the stick against my upper lip. In another quick move, his other hand goes to the back of my neck and stops my retreat. His grip is surprisingly strong. As if reading my thoughts, he says:

I'm stronger than you are. I've taken some courses. Martial arts, shit like that. Just sit still.

He applies the lipstick to my lips with the same care he had used on his own. For a moment I let him, then I twist my head sideways. I feel the lipstick slide off the corner of my mouth onto the skin.

Shit, Victor says. I can't do this if you squirm.

I don't want you to do it.

I really don't care about that, sweetheart.

He tries again, manages hardly to touch my lip as I twist my head away again. I feel like a dental patient moving out of the way of a drill.

Goddamn it, sit still or I'll kill you.

Something strange in his voice makes me stop squirming. He releases my neck. Touches my hair.

You really should shampoo once in a while.

What's it to you?

Nothing to me. Absolutely nothing.

He smiles and presses his free hand against my cheek again. It is a curiously nonsexual gesture. On the other hand, it may not be a completely sane gesture.

With his thumb, he tries to fix where the lipstick has smudged. He curses under his breath.

Do with your tongue like this, he says. He runs his own tongue along part of his upper lip. Without protesting I duplicate the move, then look at him quizzically.

Like the taste? he asks.

Not especially.

I do.

We are a curious tableau for I don't know how long. When Victor speaks again, it is in a soft and friendly voice:

There's something I'd like to tell you.

Although I know I don't want to hear anything he has to tell me, the situation dictates that I say:

What?

He sits across from me again, seems to be thinking about something. His hands fidget deliberately, almost with a plan. The rings flash. Where the hell do they find all that light?

Well, he says once, but does not go on. There is something oddly appealing about the way he slumps, the contemplation in it. Suddenly he stands up, saying:

What was that?

What?

That.

What?

That, you asshole.

Then I realize what. It is a rumble slowly growing louder. The noise of an engine, but not an automobile engine. It is a sound Victor apparently recognizes right away. He springs away from me, goes to the door of the sleep room. I touch my lips, wonder if I can even dare go out the door right now, but Victor hollers:

Jesus Christ!

The tension in his voice makes me forget the way I look. I run out the door after him.

Even though the front window is crusted with dirt, you can see out just enough. Weaving in and around the parked vehicles is a gang of motorcyclists. Bikers. For the moment they seem to be treating the parking area as a big fun maze. The people who'd been lounging against cars are checking out in all directions, most of them making for the wooded area behind the rest stop.

Victor stands to the side of the window, watching, his eyes wide.

Is that them? I ask.

Of course it's them, he says. I don't cower in a corner for every bike gang that comes along. They must've been following us all the way. I knew it.

Well, they coulda caught us easy if that was true.

They're goddamn catching us, aren't they?

I mean before this.

Maybe, maybe not. We kept a pretty good pace, not stopping

and all. They're patient. They could've—what the fuck am I doing here analyzing? We got to find a way out of this.

We got to?

Victor glares at me. For a moment he looks more frightening than the biker gang.

Of course we, I say quickly. I didn't mean any—I mean, we can—if we can just make it to the Mustang.

And how the fuck are we going to do that? They're all, the entire gang between us and the goddamned car. What good is the car, anyway? They'd catch up in two miles.

I don't know. It's something. Better than here.

You may be right.

When he turns away from the window, his wide eyes dominate his face, and not just because of the eyeliner he used on them. He reminds me of the kind of frightened lady you see on the cover of some paperback novels. He rushes past me, to the middle of the room. Only a few people remain here, most of them pressed against a wall.

Those bastards out there, Victor shouts, are after me. They're going to kill me probably. Going to try. Anybody here willing to—ah, shit, forget it.

He turns back toward the window. His skirt takes a wide swirl, revealing his stockinged legs, his shiny black high-heeled shoes. Of course they're basic black, Victor has taste. People are edging their way to the door of the sleep room. Except for Victor and me, this room'll be empty in a minute.

If only Link'd get back, Victor says. And his friends. He'd know what to do.

He wasn't much help the time they abducted you, was he?

What difference docs that make?

No difference.

The bikers have finished their fun with the maze now. They are pulling up their bikes in front of the building. I recognize the leader now, he's already got his gun out. He'll remember me, I realize suddenly. This time I'm not the anonymous intruder, the innocent bystander. I made a fool out of him, he won't be pleased. Suddenly I want to retreat to the sleep room, too. Why do I want to help Victor? What's he ever done for me? No time to decide that issue. The bikers are spreading out into two flanks, one group on each side of the leader. Sort of an unbalanced line. The leader shouts something. I can't quite make out each word, but mainly he's hollering for Victor to come quietly. He says *Vicki* derisively. Even I get pissed off at that kind of smugness.

We need some kind of weapon, I say. I run to the lunch counter, hoping there'll be a sharp-edged knife there. I'm stopped for a moment when I catch my reflection in the mirror behind the counter. Victor has put more lipstick on and around my mouth than I'd suspected. A long thin orange line streaks out from the corner of my mouth. The shape of my mouth is indistinct. I rub the back of my hand across it but the orange is only smeared more.

It's no time to make yourself beautiful, Victor says.

I look behind the counter. It's been cleaned out, nothing we can use as a weapon.

Look, we better get out of here, I say to Victor. We can't do anything against those bastards.

No point running. Besides, I got a piece.

He pulls up his skirt and reaches inside his panty hose, down to where an athletic supporter would be if he wears an athletic supporter. He pulls out a gun, a small calibre revolver.

Where the hell did that come from? I ask.

You just saw.

I don't mean that. Where'd you get it in the first place?

Always had it. Just never told you about it. I had it in my crotch that day you rescued me. I was trying to figure a way to get at it when you stuck your nose in. Then I didn't need it any more.

Well, okay, so you got a piece. What good is it? There're six of them. If you get one you're lucky, and then it'd have to be at close range.

I'll just have to get close.

You'll never.

You have an alternative suggestion?

No.

So.

Victor—

C'mon, out the side.

I spot a two-pronged cooking fork next to an encrusted griddle. I pick it up, it's got scum all over it, and follow Victor toward the opening in the side wall.

The bike gang is heading toward the main entrance of the Hot Shoppe, so apparently they didn't notice, or didn't care to use, the wall opening. At least we have room to maneuver then. Victor starts through the opening, hesitates.

What's the matter? I ask.

My clothes, my other clothes. I left them back there.

This is no time to sort out your wardrobe.

You're right.

He takes another step, then mumbles:

I'm always leaving my duds behind somewhere.

We get outside. The day is terrible. Humid, murky, that unpleasantness that comes with dusk on awful days. Outside, we are worse off, since we can't see the bikers any more.

Maybe we *can* make a break for it, I say, they don't know where we are.

I want to kill that bastard.

How about some other time, maybe we—

One of the bikers strides around the corner of the building. What teeth are left in his mouth seem white and shining, adding a conditional brightness to his smile. He wears a tee-shirt (little underarm rips) with the words *I'd rather eat shit than ride Jap bikes* printed on it in threadbare block letters.

Hey look at this, he shouts over his shoulder. Victor's arm moves backward, he hides the gun in the fold of his flowing skirt. The biker turns back. He is particularly ugly, some criss-crossed scars on his cheek, the shape of his face doughy.

Remember later, Vicki baby, he says. I found you first. Remember I got rights.

You got about as much rights as you got balls. Zero on both counts.

Dough-face feints a blow. Victor steps back. The others appear around the corner of the building. The leader pushes Dough-face aside. He is a lot prettier than his gang, but you'd rather spend a casual evening with any one of them. There is malice in his eyes above and beyond any provocation.

Well, Vicki, he says, it's been a thrilling chase, honey, now we've got matters to—

Victor shoots through his skirt. The leader, stunned, grabs at the side of the building, at the border of the wall-opening. I glance quickly toward Victor. He seems about to collapse. Dough-face is first to react. He lunges at Victor, past me. As he goes past, I bring the scummy fork upwards. Amazingly, I get both prongs into his beefy neck, just below the jaw line. Some blood starts running down the prongs as Dough-face falls sideways.

Victor is still retreating, ignoring what I've done, staring past me at the man he's shot. He's scared shitless, I can tell. Suddenly there is movement all around me. One of the bikers jumps at me, I hear some shots off to my left. The biker hits me twice in the stomach, once against the side of the head. Last thing I see is somebody else's fist coming at my face.

7

LINK is looking down at me as I come to. At first I see his face in fuzzy outline, an improvement on its normal state, then I see him more clearly. He is smiling.

What's so amusing?

That you're alive. Considering, it's worth momentary amusement.

Okay, guess you're right. What happened?

You all right?

If I move any more I'll discover my whole body's in pain. Other than that, I'm okay. What happened?

You had a run-in with some bikers.

I remember. I mean, after I got knocked out.

Well, not much after that. I saw you two and the bikers as we came out of the woods. I saw the shot and what came after, dropped the box of food I was carrying. You were falling as we ran into the parking lot. A couple of bikers came after us, and we had a good old brawl. Course we outnumbered them three to two and we managed to win out. I carried you in here about ten minutes ago and, oh, about forty-five seconds ago you woke up.

You're leaving out something.

Yes, well, I am assigning priorities to certain pieces of information.

It is all too confusing to me. I shake my head to clear it, but that only makes it hurt more. I wonder if I have a skull fracture. A concussion, at least.

What happened to the bikers? I ask.

You mean, besides the dead one?

Which was the dead one, mine or Victor's?

Yours.

I was afraid of that. What about Victor's?

I don't know. He isn't around anywhere. None of them are. His bike's gone, too.

Suddenly I discern a missing piece of information.

Where's Victor?

Gone, too.

Where? How?

He took off in your car.

In my *car*?

Zoomed it outta here on two wheels down the road.

Oh, Jesus.

I lie back and think about it for a minute. Then something occurs to me and I reach in my pocket. My keys are gone.

That son of a bitch! I shout.

Which son of a bitch?

Victor!

Oh, should've known.

The son of a bitch stole my keys. He must've, *had* to do it before those bastards even showed up. He picked my pocket back there when I was asleep, he had to. He *intended* to steal the car all along.

That'd figure. For Victor, I mean.

I am about to ask Link to explain that remark, then I realize he doesn't have to. I understand it completely.

Rest a while, he says.

I try to rest, but I can think only of that rotten son of a bitch and how he must've picked my pocket. I can see his hand sliding in, him watching me breathe deeply, perhaps stopping for a moment if I snored or stirred. That son of a bitch. I put my hand in my pocket, scrounge around to see if maybe I have missed the keys and they're still there, hoping that maybe Victor ran off in somebody else's Mustang. Nothing. At the very bottom I come upon a crumpled-up piece of paper. I pull it out, open it up partially with the fingers of my one hand. Just some numbers. It's a minute before I recognize them. This is the paper Emil gave me before I left. The telephone number there. I stare at it for a long time, then I start to get up. Link is beside me immediately.

What's the matter? he says.

That wall-phone. It works?

I think—yes, it does. Somebody used it the other—

I'm gonna make a call.

Later.

No, now.

Your move, I guess.

Link sees I'm determined, I can tell that. He helps me to the other side of the room, where the telephone hangs unsurely on a decaying wall. Every step is agony, pain shooting up and down my arm.

This one work like back-east phones? I ask Link.

They all work alike, don't they?

I mean, do I need coins?

Oh, that. Course not. It's all doctored, I'm sure. We can beat Ma Bell every time.

I dial the number and wait through several rings before a recorded voice answers and tells me the number I have dialed is not a working number. Hell it ain't, I shout at the voice. She tells me all over again that the number I have dialed is not a working number. I redial it, get the recorded lady again. She sounds like she's ready to die as soon as she finishes with me. I try to slam the receiver down on the hook, but it slips off and out of my hands, dangles like a forgotten string. Link gently replaces it but I continue to stare at the phone. I want to tell Emil I am almost out west, hear him cackle so what. I want to go and chase the ghost-Chuck across phantom highways. I want to talk to Cora, ask her to consider meeting me out here somewhere. But how the hell could I meet her or go back there, with no wheels and no luck?

Link comes up and says some new dude is offering the bunch of us a ride and would I like to come. I say yes and hobble out of the restaurant.

8

WE drive in bleak darkness. I keep dozing off and, after one of the dozes, suddenly awaken to bleak sunlight. The guy who's given us the ride, a short professorial type, seems to be antiventilation. He won't let us open any windows. The inside of the car is unbearably hot. I can't breathe. I press my head against the side window, as if I could somehow draw air through the glass. We drive for a few miles, then I spot an overturned motorcycle off the side of the road.

Stop! I yell at the driver.

I ain't got time, gotta barrelhouse to—

Stop, you can leave me here, it's okay.

I'll go with him, Link says, stop the car.

Jesus, the driver says and pulls to a stop. I am out of the car before it comes to a halt and running down the road on my aching legs. I hear Link's ambling footsteps behind me. Even when I get to the motorcycle I have no way of knowing if it belonged to any of the gang. I look past it and see a flash of green, the shade of the Mustang's paintjob, behind some trees in front of me. Link catches up with me and says:

What do you think?

Over there, I say, and we both head toward the trees. It is the Mustang all right. Overturned, the windshield glass shattered, part of the top crushed. I am looking at the passenger side. I slowly walk around the car and see what I expect to see. Victor, the upper half of his body sticking out the driver's-side window, pieces of broken glass and other debris around him. I find it odd that his new blouse has only a couple of stains on it. I lean down to him. Beside his face there is an upper denture plate, split in half. He must have spit it out. How it broke I can't figure out.

How is he? Link says.

He's still breathing. But I don't know.

We should do something.

What can we do?

I don't know. Something.

What can we do?

Maybe we should—but no, I don't know where we could go, or how to get anywhere.

Then what should we do? The roads are—

You could start by pulling me out of this goddamned wreck of a fucking car, Victor says.

Link looks at me and I look at him and, without commenting, we begin pulling Victor out of the Mustang. As we work on him, I notice more and more that is destroyed on my car. More things twisted out of shape, more things that cannot possibly function again, more places where it is smashed in completely. It looks worse than it did when I first bought it.

Victor complains about the way we are delicately removing him from the mangled vehicle. I kick him in the ribs and tell him to shut up. Link laughs. Victor continues to grouse anyway.

We finally get him out. As he stands up, he tests his body. Apparently he is in no more pain than I am. His mouth when he talks looks funny. Because he's half-toothless, of course. The condition does not seem to alter his complaining abilities, but it sure looks weird.

What happened to the biker? I ask.

Beats me, Victor says, shrugging.

Link taps me on the shoulder.

Over there, he says. Noticed it while we were extracting our friend here.

I look where he points, and see the biker. Or the body of the biker. I guess such distinctions should be made. Upside down, feet aimed at the sky, the body rests, reclines almost, against the trunk of an old leafless tree.

We should check him out, I say, see if he's still alive.

No way he's alive, Link says.

He looks into my eyes, seems to see something there. Misery maybe.

Well, okay, he says, I'll check it out. You two stay here.

He goes to the tree. He walks like a gorilla in traction, he looks weird even from behind. I follow him a few steps. Victor stays behind, leaning against the car, looking toward the body as if it's a normal piece of the landscape. His eyes are cold. Indifferent is the word, I suppose. How many gods can dance on the end of a pin?

As Link leans over the body, I see its face for the first time. The biker looks much better dead. His face looks angelic in a kind of strangely colored way. Like in one of those very old no-perspective paintings you sometimes see on religious calendars. I remember the cop I killed, Sergeant Allen, and the calm on his face in death. It had been a coplike calm that looked like it could be reanimated by a staticky call to duty. Then of course there's my own second kill, the other biker back at the crumbling Hot Shoppe, lucky I never got to see his dead face. Shit, now I've chalked up two corpses, I could notch a gun grip, does that make me a success? How many corpses can lie peacefully on the head of a—shit, I've got to stop thinking like this.

Link walks back to me.

He's dead all right. Dead as a piston rod. C'mon.

We return to Victor, give him the news.

I'm heartbroken, Victor says.

What did those guys have against you anyway? Link says. Victor just shrugs.

Usually they don't chase a guy down for nothing, Link mutters.

I lean against the Mustang.

Do you think it'll run again? I ask Link.

Who the fuck cares? Victor says.

I don't know, Link says. It's possible. I heard of a dude, at a place not far down the road. If the challenge is impossible enough, he'll work on anything. He's good, I hear. Let's go see.

Okay.

I remember The Mech, who has given me great faith in mechanical miracle workers.

Jesus Christ, don't you two guys have a car? Victor says.

We did, I say.

But we don't any more, Link says.

Jesus Christ, you mean we got to walk?

Take off your goddamned heels and c'mon, I say. Victor is about to reply, but thinks better of it.

We all stand still for a minute, nobody ready to take the first step out. I look away from Link and Victor, examine the underside of the Mustang. It's spotted with rust, just like the overside. Hell, I should just leave it behind, get another set of wheels. But, shit, what would I do with a different set of wheels? Make the same mistakes twice, Cora would probably say. I turn around. Victor is smirking at me as if he realizes how stupidly sentimental I'm getting. Well, why shouldn't I? Here I've maybe lost my wheels forever and I'm stuck with Victor for who knows how long. Not too long, I hope. I know I can ditch him. How seems to be the problem.

Let's go, Link says.

Okay, I say.

Finally, Victor says.

As he passes the Mustang, Link gives one of the front wheels a good spin. He and Victor go on. I watch the wheel's spin diminish, then give it another good spin before starting after them.

PART IV

1

I CAN'T believe there's any hope for the Mustang when I get a good look at it dangling at the end of the tow-truck chain like a fish that was already dead when it bit the hook. I also can't believe the polyester leisure-suited clean-skinned mechanic (well, there's dirt embedded in the grooves of his fingers but they go to the grave with that) who says sure he can fix it, there ain't a car was made by any worldeating conglomerate that he can't resurrect if somebody's really praying for it. The third thing I can't believe is that he wants more than just the usual couple of gas cans as payment.

Look, I tell him, I haven't got a penny to piss on right now.

That's not precisely true, but I really don't have the price he's asking for, and I'm not willing to settle for handing over what little money I got left.

Well, he says, I got plenty storage space and I can wait until you get the funds together.

And if I can't get funds?

Don't worry about it. We'll think of something, my lad.

He wears horn-rimmed glasses, this mechanic, and his sunken cheeks make him look more like an undertaker. No muscles on his body, but an intrusive and oddly uncharacteristic pot belly. The skin of his face is scrubbed so clean, it has the appearance of a tile surface—a touch of gloss on the unreal paleness.

Staring at his benign and bizarre visage, I'm beginning to
realize that I'm no longer back east and that this ain't The Mech,
and I wish I could figure a way to cry.

While I stand there in silent frustration, a battered Caddy
drives up to the open garage door. A bearded driver leans out his
window, hollers:

I needa get laid, Anton.

Okay, the leisure-suited mechanic hollers back, you know
what to do.

I even know how to do it.

So see Maria, tell her I okayed you. And, if I don't see she's
got the money from you upfront, I'll personally invade your
room and screw off your prick with a pipe wrench.

I got the money, Anton. I got the money. Made a pile at the
casino. Blew away a couple rubes in a game of bac. So don't
sweat it, Anton.

Not sweating.

See you later, Anton.

Bye, sport.

The Caddy drives off. *Anton*! This guy's name is *Anton*? And
he's a mechanic? Something's not right. If The Mech had a name
like Anton, he'd have changed it. If The Mech had a name. I
think of the confident pleasant feelings I always had around The
Mech and I resent being put on the defensive by this asshole who
looks like a faulty and inefficient copy of good mechs everywhere. Like one of those new translations of the Bible that come
out every few years, Anton seems to have the words okay but not
the poetry.

Well, what's it to be? he says blandly. Fix it, junk it, or sell it?
Tell the truth, I recommend junking, but I might be persuaded to
buy it off you.

I don't know.

You got to decide soon. But take your time.

I don't like this Anton. What he's saying is I might as well
resign myself to dying today but it's all right to wait an hour or
two for the actual event.

That guy in the Caddy, Link says to Anton. Link has been
standing to the side, watching us and scratching his tilted head
actively as if its itch is perpetual.

You know the guy in the Caddy? Anton says.

No. Just wondered what the deal was all about. Don't have to
know if you don't want to tell me.

Don't mind telling you, sport. It's business, after all. You might be a prospective client. I have converted what used to be the Ramada Inn here into the biggest brothel in the west today. You must have noticed the building as you drove in. Ramada sign's still up. I prefer to have it that way, although—would you believe it?—there're still people, older people, who stop by the lobby and ask for a room for the night. That really overwhelms me. You don't see many older people willing to venture out of their comfortable enclaves in the cities. You wouldn't think they'd take the risks of traveling our highways and expressways. I hope they survive, I really do, but I expect not. I'm not that old, but I always go out with protection. Ah, I don't have to go out much anyway. So—if you want to use the facilities, the prices are reasonable and the girls are clean.

Well, says Link, not my style but I'll keep it in mind case some windfalls drop my way.

You do that. (To me:) What about the Mustang then?

I'll have to see, get some money.

I can save you the trouble. I can use some of its parts at least before junking it. Say, a hundred dollars for it.

Hundred? I paid five bills for it in the first place.

You were cheated. Hundred's as high as I can go.

No, I want to fix it, get back on the road again.

Well, how about a trade for a car in good condition. I got a reconditioned Pinto that—

Shove it! No Pintos. I wouldn't take a Pinto if you—

Link touches my arm to calm me down. I glance down at his hand. Its skin has a purplish cast to it. Never noticed that before. I'm probably conscious of it because of Anton's unnaturally glossy skin. Link's got a take-it-easy look in his eyes. His eyes look purple too, maybe it's the fluorescent lighting of this damn garage, turning Link into more of a freak than he already is.

The garage is so neat, everything on a shelf or a hook or a goddamned bright nail. I can't really believe a mechanic actually works here. There are a few grease spots on the floor but they look like they could be wiped up with one piece of a paper towel.

I wouldn't *trade*, period, I say, as calmly as possible.

Perhaps, Anton says. But you have to do something if you want your car back in any kind of drivable shape. I might have some ideas.

I remember The Mech and the special jobs he used to arrange

for Cora and me, the doperuns and all. Okay, if a few runs'll get me back my car, I'll even do them for Anton.

Okay, what? I say.

That young lady over there, he says.

What young lady over where?

He is momentarily taken aback by my confusion, but then whispers to me:

The young lady leaning against the Coke machine of course.

I come close to laughing in his face. I stopped seeing Victor as a woman some time ago, even when he was, like now, wearing his Vicki outfit. On the way here, he said the first thing he'd do after we got the car deal straightened out was deal himself some new threads—though without money I wasn't quite sure how he could buy so much as a handkerchief.

I decide not to let Anton in on Victor's secret. If he's going to persist in being a transvestite, it's up to him to tell all. I'd feel too foolish to spill those particular beans, so I say to Anton:

Oh? You mean Vicki?

Pretty name. I had an aunt named Victoria. Used to make all sorts of jokes about the Victorian age, etcetera. Your Vicki is very attractive. Even in her, well, somewhat battered condition.

Battered's the word for it all right. Without his upper plate, Victor's upper lip sinks in toward the gum unattractively. He's got a ninety-year-old mouth on a twenty-five-year-old face. The encrusted dirt on his face and clothes doesn't add to his overall appeal either. Still, there are the eyes and the finely sculptured face and what Anton undoubtedly imagines is a slim teasingly curvaceous body beneath the torn clothing. If the dress had been ripped in a couple of different places in the accident, Anton would know right away it isn't *Vicki* he's ogling. I don't know whether to establish a complicated and dangerous con or to try to escape from the problem by changing the subject. I hate Anton so much already I'd really like to play him along for a short time. However, he seems to be the chief honcho around here and I don't want any chief honchos infuriated at me.

One thing we should clear up, I say to Anton and Link looks ready to explode. You said *your* Vicki. She's not my Vicki. She's just a—well, just a friend.

There, that ought to get me out of any reprisals that might come from Victor's identity becoming suddenly revealed. Link seems relieved by my answer.

Just friends, eh? Anton says. His voice sounds lascivious but the hell with it. I take a step back, pretend to examine a tire rack, as a way of trying to disengage myself from the subject.

Well, Anton says, I can suggest to you how you might obtain money for the car. A different kind of in-trade situation, as you might call it.

Victor is walking forward, toward us. He's been listening closely to the conversation. Anton had meant to include him in on it from the first. Oh, God, he's going to do his I'm a transvestite not a fag number. I gird myself for the worst.

Link takes a step toward Victor, makes a hand-wave that looks like W.C. Fields frustrated, but does seem to mean something to Victor.

Vicki, he says, I'd like you to meet Anton. He's going to fix Lee's wheels if we can come up with some cash.

Victor nods, rubs a hand across his forehead as if he can apply further beauty by some kind of magic in his fingertips.

We're just flush out of money, Anton, Victor says, a guarded sweetness in his voice.

Yes, I heard, young lady, Anton says, brightening up at Victor's interest. But there's something might be done about it.

Yes?

I have never seen Victor look more provocative. Jesus God in Pittsburgh, the worst, the truest and deepest worst, I can feel it coming.

I run a little, um, establishment over at the Ramada, Anton says. A little business for the relaxation of, as you might call them, the knights of the road.

You needn't be coy with me, Anton, says Victor. I'm quite familiar with the concept of whorehouse. Brothel. Bordello. Catshack.

Then you have some experience in them? I can pay more for—

Experience? I tell you, Anton, I was born to the breed. I know any trick that you can imagine.

She's right there, Link chimes in. She got top prices back east.

My stomach runs through a shredding machine. This is even more dangerous than the con I was thinking of and rejected. What's gotten into their heads? Link nods knowingly at Victor's every word and innuendo. Victor's voice has slowly descended the scale to sweet and husky. I've hooked up with a pair of lunatics. One of us's gonna wind up dead, maybe all of us, but me for sure. There must be a way out. I can run. I can do that, I can run. I look at the car, hanging helplessly from its hook. It doesn't appear to be fixable, but I want it fixed.

I don't know if I can offer top prices, Anton says to Link. For a moment my mind is in a complete muddle. Is Anton talking about Vicki or the car? At least, Anton continues, not until we've let a couple of our boys have a run or two at her, but your Vicki's as good as you say, young fellow, and you might have this car repaired and paid for in less than a week. Who knows what I can get you if you stick around a while?

I think we can negotiate, Link says.

We can *negotiate*? I say.

Can it, Lee, Link says, then turns to Anton: Lee don't exactly approve. A bit of a prude, you see, but he's straight. Just give him a job that's not tied in with the main business of your institution.

Hmmm, yeah, Anton says, I do need somebody to clean up the kitchen.

Good, Link says, he'll take it.

I'll take it? Damn it, Link—

Won't hurt you for a week, Link says, and then makes a peculiar wink at me. I don't know how to interpret a wink from that face—a body language expert would be baffled by messages from that complicated physiognomy—but I keep quiet anyway.

Anton strokes Victor's arm. Not lasciviously—more like an inspector of prime meat, which is what he is, I suppose. Or maybe he's exactly what he appears to be, a mechanic looking for the vehicle's body flaws. Angling his body away from Anton's touches, Victor is carefully keeping the man from letting his busy fingers suddenly discover any of the more revelatory areas.

All right then, Anton says, after satisfying himself that Vicki passes the initial inspection. A deal? he says.

Deal, Victor says.

Deal, Link says.

Deal? I say.

But first, Link says, you got to assure us you'll get right to work on the car.

Done, Anton says. My boys'll be starting it soon as you boys get out of the way. I'll dip in and attend to the hard parts—you know, where skill is absolutely required. Looking at the state of that car, I'd say maybe more than skill will be needed. I'll get out one of my old missals. You all go over the Ramada and ask for Maria. She'll assign you, give you instructions, feed you. Show you the ropes.

Sure thing, Link says. We'll go over there now.

Wait! Victor says.

Link looks at me worriedly and I can tell the same thought is going through both our heads: What's Victor going to do to screw us up now?

What is it, young lady? Anton says. I can see by his growing familiarity with Victor, Anton'll be looking out for a staff freebie any day now. What the hell am I thinking of? *Any day now?* How can Victor and Link hope to carry on this masquerade more than a day, a night, an hour, a few minutes? What *is* going on in their twisted minds?

I wanted to say, Victor says, I got pride in my profession and I don't like to do things second rate.

Good, exactly the policy of my organization. Good business with the people, good business with God, that's my motto.

The God reference stops Victor a moment, then he says:

I can see you're a real pro all right, sir, and so am I. That's why I can't, um, turn any tricks until I look the part better. I'm certainly not useful to you looking like this.

Anton laughs.

I'm always amazed, he says, that—whatever social change alters her status—one thing never seems to depart from woman: vanity. Ecclesiastes had it right on target so long ago. You'll look beautiful, young lady, believe me.

I'm grateful, but clothes aren't my greatest worry. Clothes make the woman and the woman makes the man and all that, I agree, but in this profession good looks are a mite more vital for good business. I can't do the job well with damaged looks.

Well, we can provide you cosmetics or—

Not just that, sir. Victor stares, quite primly, at the shiny garage floor. You see, this is embarrassing to talk about but my dear friends know anyway. You see, when we had the dreadful accident that damaged yon car—

Did Victor really say *yon car*? *Dreadful* accident? *Dear* friends? Things are really getting too messy. I better take off before I find a limp grey mop in my hand as defense against ten layers of dirt on that kitchen floor.

—that accident damaged, well, my teeth. My, well, upper plate fell out and it's broken and I can't imagine how I can face a man looking like *this* and I'm afraid I can't take the job if, oh, I don't know what to say.

Suddenly Victor goes into this convincing crying act. So convincing that I scrounge around in my pocket to see if I can find a Kleenex. Anton puts his arm around Victor's shoulder and begins patting his back, saying dumb there, there things. Victor moves a step sideways to keep out of any possible detecting maneuvers Anton might try.

Don't worry, young lady, Anton says. I don't keep a dentist on staff but I'll send for one. Be out here tomorrow, next day at the latest. It'll take him no time to fix your plate or make you a new one.

It's so embarrassing, Victor says. He manages a shy but tight-lipped smile. He looks for a minute like an old woman who hates being on the dole.

Jesus, don't worry, Anton says. I understand. I've had a full set of choppers all my adult life.

They look so real.

Here. Look.

And damned if Anton doesn't take out his false teeth and display them for us. They are as clean and shiny as the man, his garage, and his tools. Seeing them disattached from his mouth makes me feel queasy. Even faint. Really. With no self-consciousness, he pops them back into his mouth and gestures us away. We start off up the many-colored stone path to the Ramada.

What's this all about? I whisper to Link.

His face twists into something approximating amusement.

It's all like an old sex farce, kind of play like *Getting Gertie's Garter* or *Up in Mabel's Room*, which no doubt you've never heard of.

Oddly enough, I have. My dad's an actor.

(I wonder why I speak of his profession in the present tense?)

Victor and I've pulled this before, Link says. And it's like one of those plays, where the good guys' real dilemma is keeping the other guys from discovering the awful truth. We just have to put all these dudes off as long as we can, then figure something else.

Oh, great! What something else?

We'll face that when the time comes. We've got more time than I'd hope for, thanks to Victor and his teeth ploy.

Damn it Link, I *want* those teeth, Victor says, some menace in his voice. I won't *leave* until after the dentist does the job.

Time's in our favor, Link says.

But is fate? I say.

2

I AM paralyzed. It came over me, swept through my entire body, as soon as I sprawled out on this motel bed. I don't think I could move if God came down and said, Lee, well, you done some good deeds in your time, not sensational but B-plus good, and I'm gonna let you off from this shithouse mess, but next time keep your bum clean, hear? I'd have to beg Him to just let me fall beneath a shower of martyr's stones, I want blankness so much just now.

The room is painted all white. What with the sun glaring in the wall-to-wall window, I get shooting pains behind my eyes every time I raise a lid. As far as decor goes, there's none of the usual motel room landscapes and scenes of pastoral simplicity adorning the white surfaces. Instead, we have delicate erotica. The dominant print in this room is of a rather fleshy naked lady lying on a purple velvet divan backed by red curtains. Her skin is painted with a suggestion of bright red that carries through the color scheme of the curtains. I don't know what I'd do if I actually met a woman with skin color like that.

Ever since we got in the room, Link has been lying on the other bed, but he's hardly paralyzed. It's one of those beds where you put a quarter in and the mattress vibrates for a half-minute. The management has thoughtfully supplied a pile of quarters on the bedstand, and Link keeps feeding coins into the slot and vibrating away. If he's getting any sensual pleasure from the experience, he's keeping it to himself.

Victor is watching TV. Anton's got his own closed-circuit setup and, apparently, videocassettes in a wide variety. Victor's intent on some episode of an ancient series called *It's a Man's World*. He keeps repeating the title to me so I'll appreciate the irony. I have to admit he maintains the womanly disguise with efficiency. His curled-up pose in a red and white striped chair seems quite feminine. (Link told us on the way over that we better behave as if Anton's got concealed cameras in every room, which, considering his fascination with electronics, he probably has. It's frustrating. I desperately need to discuss our situation with Link and Victor but am not allowed to say a word about it.)

Maria keeps coming by to check we are okay. She's a pretty thing, Maria. Short, a bit too fat to be a client's first choice, but large-breasted and small-waisted, the appropriate whore for the nineteenth century pictures. Whatever, she certainly has a vast repertoire of sexy moves and gestures. Only thing that distorts her appearance is her blind left eye, which she keeps half-shut with only the white staring out under the lid. She has what may be a Spanish accent, although her skin seems a shade too light for that background, and she has light-brown hair whose color looks natural. I kind of like her, or would if I were not so paralyzed with fear to feel much other emotion.

Knock on the door. Three taps, light. Maria again, she uses the same knock each time. Link shouts come in. The vibrator device of his bed runs down just as she steps daintily through the doorway. She's wearing a tighter costume this time, a dark-blue turtleneck sweater that emphasizes the roundness of her tits, and levi's that don't let in much ventilation. I think the high-heeled red shoes with a line of red sequins around each rim are incongruous, but I've never had much fashion expertise.

I can see by your outfit that you are a woman, Link says agreeably.

Maria smiles. The only accurate word to describe that smile is enchanting.

'Stime for assembly, she says.

Assembly, Link says. Are we back in high school or something?

No. Mr. Anton likes to bring all of us together at four o'clock each afternoon for announcements, orders, little talks, on Friday distribution of bonus commissions, and silent prayer.

Silent prayer? I say, finally stirring from my paralysis.

Mr. Anton is a very religious man, Maria says.

There it was, a suggestion of accent. She almost said wery, the sound of the first consonant wavered slightly between V and W.

Well, let's go, Link says, springing off his bed as if one of its special features is to launch its inhabitant.

Not yet, Victor says, irritated. I want to see the end of the program. It's almost over.

Mr. Anton don't like anybody be late, Maria says. Her words sound more like a command than advice.

I won't be late. It's almost to the end. You three go, I'll be right behind you in the other elevator.

Maria considers this for a moment.

Okay, she says. (It comes so close to sounding like hokay that I wonder if there is such a linguistic event as a half-aspirated H.) Mr. Anton is sometimes forgiving on first days, but I strongly suggest getting your ass down there on time. That's as much as I can do for you skinnybitch.

She says skinnybitch as one word. The sound of authority leaves her voice as quickly as it had entered. The enchanting smile returns.

She walks over to my bed, stands by it.

We would appreciate your presence, too, she says.

Oh. Sure. Yeah. Sorry.

I stand up, try to do a few clandestine muscle stretches to revive my inert skin and bones.

You're a nice-looking fellow, she says to me. Link almost lets out a whoop of laughter, he is so amused by her attention to me. I resent that. I mean, I'm no Victor, masquerading my sex. Of course I can appeal to Maria. My God, she can put more suggestion of passion into her one-eyed sexy look than most women can with full operative power.

She takes my arm to lead me out of the room. She pats Victor on the top of his wig, says:

See you damn quick, skinnybitch.

Link, with mock courtesy, clears way for the two of us to pass. Well, shit on him then. Maria manages to bounce her hip off mine with almost every step. I enjoy the sensation. Hell, if we're all going to get wiped out when Anton finds out about Victor, I might as well have some fun in the interim.

3

ANTON'S come over to the meeting directly from work apparently. He wears coveralls that look freshly pressed. Not a sign of grease or dirt anywhere on them. Large buttons so polished-up they look like an even row of enormous sequins.

The room is fiercely air-conditioned. I'll probably wind up with at least a cold. My throat already feels scratchy. This is a really bizarre place, this Ramada cathouse. Doesn't look or feel like any bordello I ever imagined. There should be garish colors all over the rooms, maybe cloth on the walls, sequins and gewgaws. There should be a heavy, even overpowering, odor of perfume mixed with the musky drifting emanations of warm and sensuous bodies. There should be jazzy music from a skinny piano player, a whorehouse professor. There shouldn't be all this pristine cleanliness, this whiteness, these mundane chattering ladies in tasteful, even expensive, but dull and plainly patterned garments. There shouldn't be the oily cold smell of the too-efficient air conditioning.

Maria starts the assembly with what I suppose is her version of a pep talk:

Okay. Quiet down there. Alice, save your mouth for better duties. Okay. Short comments today, then some introductions. Okay. Moves. Listen up, Alice. You move like an elephant on the way to the graveyard. Moves're important in this business.

Walks, for instance. Walk with style, sexiness. Remember for most of these guys you're the only things near to beauty they can see when they come off the road nights, heaven help them. Get the right look, so you're light in the middle of their darkness. Extra dividends that way. Get the moves right and the looks right. Too much hip swinging in your approach across the encounter-room to a client, too much sordid eyeplay caused by too much of that silly makeup you ladies continue using like it was an endangered commodity, and you lose the effect and therefore the dough. Grace, that's the word, ladies. The right look in the eyes, the right flow to the hair, the right thoughts in your head. Think of that, ladies, thoughts. Think clean, that's what they like. At least down here. Upstairs it's another story and I leave that part to your own individual instincts and styles. But down here we like sweetness, the pretense of purity, got it? It's all in the head, most of this business is in the head, ladies.

What could only be described as a titter of amusement goes through the ranks of casually dressed unmade-up unhappy-looking ladies. I'm not sure which possibility for *double entendre* is causing it.

Okay, you laugh, okay. You think most of the business is in the body. I tell you no! It's in what your head projects, ladies, what your head projects. The rosiness in your cheeks, *that* comes from healthy happy thoughts. The smoothness of the brow, from not bitching in your head about the amount of money you're clearing. The softness of your appearance, the serenity of your moves, the eloquence of your entire presentation, that's what the fellas come here for. Remember smiles, be conscious of color in yourself and what you select to wear. Like, that purple velvet with the blue pumps last night was tacky, Alice, tack-ee. The thing is, ladies, illusion. You must look as if all of your days have been filled with good thoughts, good acts, a good sense of how to treat a client. Keep your mind in line and it'll link up with what's below. No, I don't mean below *there*, ladies. I mean your heart, dear ones, your heart. If you have the proper attitude toward yourself and your business and your clients, then innocence and love will emerge from your heart. And don't you forget it!

The stare that Maria now spreads around the room draws absolute quiet. There's so much dignity and even beauty in the way she looks now that, if there's ever a committee to collect money for half-blindness, Maria should be its poster girl.

Her part of the assembly done, she turns the podium over to
Anton, who immediately launches into a talk about profits and
how there are never enough. Maria walks down a side aisle
slowly. Watching. Inspecting. Checking out discrepancies in dress,
making sure there's no more horsing around from Alice. Anton's
voice is so monotonous I stop listening to it. I look around the
room, which obviously used to be the Inn's lobby. I notice the
remnants of what used to be a pseudo-nautical decor. Anchors
and ropes, miniature jibs and mainsails, and stuff like that. At
each of three entranceways to the room, a brawny man stands.
Every time I notice one of these guys my heart drops to my inner
soles. Link thinks we can get out of this with our heads on
straight? Exactly the kind of thinking one would expect from a
man whose own head is on so crooked.

At a curt nod from Maria, the woman sitting next to me
abruptly stands and leaves her seat. Maria replaces her, nudges
up beside me, places a stubby-fingered hand on my thigh. I'm
sitting on her blind side, so I don't have to react. Good, I
wouldn't know how to react if I had to, not just at this moment.
In some ways I don't mind her attention. I've been so celibate
since Cora (and I was so close to ascetic before her that I'm not
sure if celibacy isn't my norm) that the strain of denial is
beginning to tell on me. And Maria is certainly tempting. She is
the living example of the kind of demeanor and behavior she was
suggesting to her charges during her pep talk. The body beneath
her turtleneck and levi's combines the kind of curvy fleshiness
that makes you wonder where you should first grab her, with a
girlish demureness that implies she should first give permission
where you can grab. Her round cheerful face framed by waves of
curly light-brown hair fascinates me, in spite of her blind eye. Or
perhaps because of it. The eye adds a kind of sinister contrast
that, for some reason, appeals more than repels. Oh, yes, she is
surely tempting. Still, I doubt she's the best one to fool with in
this organization. I have a feeling that, if I crossed her, I might
as well lie right down and pull a tombstone over my body for a
blanket. That dangerous tone's always there in her voice, whether
she's giving an order, making a lecture, or telling me how nice I
look. I stare down at her hand on my thigh. I watch her chubby
fingertips stroking me like she's petting an animal, and I am
suddenly afraid. I want out of this place.

Anton's voice rises sharply in volume. There's perhaps a touch
of anger in it. Not having been listening to him, I look up,

half-expecting to find out he's just been accusing me of some awesome sin. But no, his eyes are glued to the back of the room, where almost everyone else in the audience except me and Maria are now looking, too. I turn around. Of course. Should have known. For a pleasant moment or two I had forgotten him. For a pleasant moment or two he had vanished into limbo. Victor now stands arrogantly in the rear doorway, looking as if he doesn't give a damn whether or not he enters any further. I sure hope he enjoyed his TV program.

Come in, young lady, Anton says. I was just getting to the point, young lady, where I'd introduce you and your friends. I'm sorry you missed the earlier part of the assembly. Come in and sit among us.

Anton's voice is calm, forgiving. I wonder what he has just said to cause the entire audience to turn around and gape at Victor. Victor shrugs indifferently. Anton again tells him to enter, this time with more authority in his voice. Victor enters all right, but he might as well have exited. He's showing everybody he doesn't give a damn. Damn it, Vicki, neither do they. He takes a vacant seat in the last row, a further hint of antagonism in the way he settles. Anton makes the introductions with some formality, asks the three of us to stand up. Link, I notice, is trying to look pleasant, bland, at least as pleasant as he can with that face and the simian curvings of his body. I try out a just-folks smile that doesn't seem to offend. Victor looks around like this outfit's too bourgeois for one of his/her accomplishments. I can see a lot of the young ladies are not exactly taking to their new business associate.

Anton clears his throat dramatically and says it's time for prayer. Everybody's head looks down at their laps in neck-jerk unison. I follow suit. I'm not exactly comfortable looking at my lap, where Maria's investigative fingers are now surveying a wider area.

We never know enough of God, Anton says suddenly. No, no. God beckons to us with His flirtatious fingers, and we draw back, knowing how befouled we have made our souls with our reckless actions. But God, He doesn't give up easily. When He sees our reluctance at the old pearly gates, He comes closer, asking us, darling, what do you require? What can I do for *you*? That's His way, ladies. And gentlemen. We may say we should not be allowed His great mercy. But you know what God says?

I could sense a congregation of bowed heads shaking no.

Well, people, He says of course darling you are welcome in My house. Your sins were your human destiny and they are forgiven with a mere snap of My heavenly fingers. What do I care about *human* sins? I can imagine greater than that, darling. You're just a raindrop on the pond, an atom on the slide. And what do you say then, young ladies? You say, are you talking about me, Lord? Me, the sinner? Me, the whore? Me, the broad who ain't done an honest day's work for the church since I begun turning tricks? Me, who couldn't think of anything during Mr. Anton's period of silent prayer? Lord, I can't be a part of any heaven of yours. I'd bring down the values of the neighborhood. Then, you know what?

Around us, everyone said, no, what?

God, He'll throw back his massive head and laugh so hard you'll suddenly know where thunder's been coming from all these years. And what He'll say then, what He'll say—*is* look, darling, Who do you think made the mess you got yourself in? Who do you think made the world that brought you down from day to day? Who do you think gets His biggest kicks outta forgiving sin? And you'll say, because you'll be just as stupid in heaven as you been down here, you'll say, you'll say, you'll say—Who? And He'll say, he'll say, why, Me, o' course. Old Lord o' Hosts and all that Stuff. Every little inch of you is My creation and you got to commit some pretty big sins, some smasheroos, to get yourself assigned elsewhere than inside the old pearly gates. And you'll spring backward, young ladies, 'cause you know you're undeserving of such wondrous mercy. And you'll say, no, Lord, I may be Your creation but I'm the reject model. I can't come in there. No, no, Lord.

The congregation: No, no, *Lord*!

And the Lord'll say, darling, you've been missing the point consistently. The fault is Mine for toying with My models so. I mean, darling, why do you think I sent My beloved son your way if not to test your powers of sinning? The ball is in My alley and you can stop fretting about your worthiness. Come on in. And, young ladies, you pause at the doorway, and look around, and sigh, and with your tendencies toward easy emotions probably you'll cry a little, and then you'll know. You can serve the Lord, and you will. You can serve him just the way you serve old Mr. Anton. Duty is duty wherever you find it. And the Lord, whose hospitality is my hope to copy, He'll say come to My arms and I'll give you the kind of loving embrace you so missed on earth, no matter how many times you sought it, no matter how many rushed embraces you experienced. And you'll go to Him and Love will finally be yours. This Ramada Inn is a step along the way to your salvation, honeys, a roadside waystation smack on the expressway to heaven, and you can believe in Him, honeys, in just the way you believe your checks'll be in your mail slots every Thursday. Amen. Now, this time put some real effort in your own silent prayers.

Dear God, I pray, if You do exist in that strangely perverse way Anton describes, get me the hell out of this, make Victor behave, and get my wheels fixed.

I look up cautiously. The way the muscles in those necks I can see are strained, I gather that a lot of the ladies are putting some effort into their silent prayers. Even Maria's hand lies still for a change. Anton's head is bowed but I can sense he's glancing around from under the edge of his brow. I look down again and wait for the end of the silent prayer period. Anton clears his throat, everybody looks up, Anton gives final announcements for the day, walks up the aisle, and the meeting is over. As I stand up, Maria says:

Look, I got some business to attend to, but check with you later. Hang loose, honey, and I do mean hang.

She smiles prettily, even demurely (an aftereffect of the sermon, perhaps), and strides quickly up the aisle. As she walks, she's giving orders to her charges, who listen attentively. None of the ladies go near Victor. He's now lounging against a wall. I don't think he realizes that one of Anton's goons is eyeing him steadily, for who knows what purpose. Sex or violence, those are the sure choices. A tap on my shoulder. Link, smiling, his head as unbalanced-looking as ever.

Maria likes you, right? he says.

I'm afraid so.

Don't be afraid. May work to our advantage.

Nothing'll work to our advantage unless Victor starts acting like a normal human being.

Which normal?

What?

Which normal? Ours? Theirs? Anybody's? Let him be. You make him think he's got to act a certain way, you can be sure he won't. Look, I'm going to check a few things out. You learn what you can from Maria. I'll tell Victor to maintain a cool profile if he can. Sometimes he listens to me. Sometimes.

With an awkward twist of his left hand, a wave perhaps, Link walks off. I wish I could have his confidence, but I guess I might as well follow his instructions. Learn what I can from Maria, before I pack it in forever.

I wonder how one goes about maintaining a cool profile.

4

IT's been a long time since I've encountered such an agreeable blend of know-how and awkwardness, Maria says as she sits up in bed and works a cigarette out of the pack she'd so meticulously placed on the bedside table before climbing into bed with me. She lights the cigarette and takes a deep drag. Looking sideways at me out of her good eye, she says:

A long while.

I'm not sure what you mean.

Maybe you shouldn't hear.

Okay. Whatever.

What makes you so cooperative?

I lose out a lot.

She furls her brow, absentmindedly runs a finger along the line of the scar on her breast. I wish she had not refused to tell where the scar came from. Probably from an operation, though. The line of it is too straight and too neat to be the aftermath of an attack, unless the slasher was particularly methodical.

What I meant, she says, is that you're, let's say, a bit deficient in technique. And that's no crime. Everybody and his brother knows all about technique, it seems, these days. Like they've been practicing nothing else since the cradle, reading all the manuals, like that. I don't take on many clients any more because— well, that's another story. I like your fumbling techniques. They're

155

preferable to the kind of coldhearted efficiency most of you road-guys usually take pride in.

But you said something about know-how, too.

Maria smiles. I really like that smile.

Know-how, yes. Affection. Warmth. I can tell you've been in love. Right?

Well . . .

You don't have to tell me. I envy the lady, envy you. You—

Don't bother envying us. We split long ago.

Well, you had *something*, right?

Sure, I guess.

Don't guess so much. You had something. Something good. Don't regret it. I think I wouldn't mind being the lady you loved. She must've been something.

She was, I suppose.

I guess, I suppose. You have to be more definite, Lee.

All this talk about love, Maria—sure I loved Cora but—

Cora, that's her name. I had an aunt named Cora.

But Cora didn't love me, I'm sure. I think she never loved me. And that was that. She wanted the split, nothing I could do.

Nothing?

Nothing.

If there was nothing you could do, might mean you didn't love her as much as you thought.

But—

Or else you just don't know what to do with the love you got in you. I'm getting maudlin, curse of the seasoned whore. Not good for business.

I don't get it.

Business and emotion. Don't mix. Old adage. Works, too. One of my girls gets emotional over one of the johns, that's it. She might as well be put out to pasture if you can't cure her. But, well, we can't control our emotions, right? I can cope with it, it's my job. I teach emotion, really, is what I do. The girls learn about emotion, they can control them, it becomes less of a problem. Good job, what the hell. And I got to get back to it. Hostess-time for me, I'll have to get into my trick-suit.

Trick-suit.

My joke.

Oh.

Never was much good at humor.

As she gets dressed, and I get my last glimpse of the mysterious scar, she hums to herself. She puts on her clothes as if she is no longer aware that I'm there. I feel like a voyeur. After she's dressed, she sits on the edge of the bed, puts a hand on my thigh, almost in the exact same place she'd put it back at the meeting, except it's a different thigh.

Look, she says, you need anything, just ask. What I *can* do, I will. Promise.

Sure.

Just stay out of trouble. For real trouble, I can't help, *won't* help. Right?

Well, okay. What kind of trouble do you mean?

Nothing special. Just trouble.

She stands up, makes a phantom gesture of straightening her levi's, stuffs more of her sweater into the beltline. Wouldn't have thought anything more'd fit there.

Trouble, she says. Like the kind your friend Vicki can get you all into, if you guys don't rein her in. That was a bum show she put on down there. God, Anton don't usually show such bad judgement. Means he's got the hots for your Vicki. Usually he keeps his hands off the girls. When he don't, it means trouble. Rein her in, right? Keep her out of sight, is the best thing.

I'll do what I can, but Vicki isn't exactly the easiest—

Yeah. I know, I know. She might as well have a neon sign saying danger mounted on her forehead. Hey, keep smiling, right?

If I could smile as nice as you, I would do just that.

She gives me the smile I'm looking for, something Cora never did.

You're sweet, too sweet. I better keep away from you. I probably won't, but I should. See you later.

She walks across the room with a little extra bounce, a little extra briskness. I like her. Problem is, I don't like her liking me.

5

CHECKED out the garage, Link says when I return to our room. Victor is sulking in front of the TV, watching a Daffy Duck cartoon with the sound turned off.

What you find out? I say.

Your car's not in as bad shape's we thought. Engine survived the abuse admirably, just a bunch of little things need doing. Most of the work's hammering out the hood, back into something like its normal shape. We might blast outta here sooner'n we think.

I get my teeth fixed first, Victor says without looking away from the cartoon. Without his teeth, he sounds a bit like Daffy Duck.

You and your damn teeth, Link says amiably. Don't sweat it. Dentist'll be here tomorrow, car won't be near fixed by then. Mechanics've already quit for the day.

Find out anything else? I say.

In a way, Link says. I know where the arsenal is. It's locked pretty good but, we need it, we can probably find a way into it. How about you? Maria tell you anything?

Yeah. She said to keep Vicki out of sight. Anton's lusting after our little beauty, she said.

'Twas beauty killed the beast, Victor says.

That's right, says Link, but which one are you?

Screw off.

Link laughs. Which one am I? he says. Laughing, his mouth twists in a different slope from the angle of his head.

I mope around the room a while. Victor's program changes from cartoon to sitcom. Hard to tell the difference. I guess I make Link nervous. He says:

Phone out in the hall.

I saw it, I say.

It works good. Better than any illegal tie-in I've seen yet. Anton's work. Dial one-one-one then any number you want. Why don't you go play with it a while?

I don't know, Link, I—

Get outta here, all right?

I get out. The phone's an old Princess model. Pink. I stare at it for a long time, then fish out the number Emil gave me. If I get the recorded lady this time, I'll—well, I better not get her this time. I dial the one-one-one, then Emil's number, and listen to a lot of purposeful but indecipherable static. Then there's a loud click, a buzz, and the ringing at the other end starts. It rings several times, and I keep hearing the recorded lady's voice in my head. But when the ringing clicks off and someone answers, I know it's got to be Emil or else the recorded lady's caught a bad cold.

It's your nickel, Emil says.

For a moment I'm too confused to talk. What's a nickel got to do with anything?

Anybody there? Emil says.

Yeah, I say. Yeah. Emil, it's me.

You? Who's you?

Me, Lee. Lee Kest—

I know which Lee. Ain't but one guy named Lee ever blighted my life. How are you, Lee?

Good. Fine. Well, maybe not so—

You out west?

Sure. It's wonderful out here. Beautiful.

Like the colors in the mountains?

Well, I haven't exactly gotten that far yet. Only a little farther and—

You ain't west yet then. If you're in the flatlands, you ain't west.

No, I guess not. Encountered some obstacles, you might say.

You mean you screwed up as usual?

Not *exactly* that.

But almost. I don't want to hear about it. You're not hurt or anything, are you?

No, I'm okay.

Well, that's something. With you, I always worry you're going to split your head open or something. Glad you're okay.

You okay, Emil?

I hang on, you know that. You didn't call to check out my health.

Not exactly.

Exactly why?

Is Cora around? I'd like to talk to—

No, she hasn't been around here since her accident.

My heart does stag leaps across my chest, and my stomach folds up. I'm afraid to ask Emil what he means.

Accident? I say.

Don't fret, Lee. She's all right. Guy she was riding with got back from jail and told her he was splitting with her and she stole his Duster. Ran it at top speed for miles, then slowed it down—or at least the report I got says she slowed it down first—and she aimed it at an abutment. Ran into the abutment once, the car was still running. She put it into reverse, ran into it again. Still running, she did it again, finally wrecked it. She's got some determination, that girl.

Why'd she wreck it? Why didn't she just keep it?

Ah, they wouldn'ta let her keep it. Somebody woulda tracked her down, returned the guy his car. Rules of the road and all that, you know. Anyway, you know as well as I do she's got a penchant for wrecking whatever car she gets her hand on.

She didn't wreck mine.

She never had to steal it from you. I detect a lonelyhearts sound in your voice. You miss her, am I right?

Well, um, yeah, right.

Come back here then. You don't need to—

No, I can't do that.

Suit yourself. Gee-odd in heaven, I'll never understand young people.

Maybe that's cause you were never young, Emil.

No, no, I was young all right. I remember it perfectly. Look, I don't understand myself then. But at least I didn't total cars on purpose or wander off on a fruitless odyssey westward.

I ask Emil how things are going generally, and he says lousy and goes into his familiar speech about people abandoning the road and returning to the cities and all that crap. Finally we have a long silence and then he says:

Glad to hear from you, Lee.

I tried to call before, got this recorded lady all the time.

Yes, know about that. Something went wrong with the machine. Chuck was by early today. He fixed it.

How is Chuck?

He kept looking transparent to me. I'm sure he's a ghost. He says he's heading west, too. Any day now. It's the new fad. I've asked around about Chuck. Other people see him once in a while. Usually he gets people out of jams. When their cars are stuck or run down or when there's fuzz around. You see him waving by the roadside and you know there's danger ahead, that's what they say.

Maybe it's what they used to call an alternative life-style, Emil.

Maybe so. Death is certainly an alternative life-style all right.

I'll call you again, now I know your phone's working.

Sure, do that.

He says this like he doesn't expect me to call. I say goodbye but he just hangs up.

I let time pass. It passes, and I dial one-one-one, then my father's number.

Noise. Click. Buzz. Rings. Another click. His voice:

Hello.

Hi Dad. It's Lee. How you been?

A long silence. But I can hear him breathing. He always did hold the mouthpiece awfully close to his mouth.

Have you abandoned me, Lee? he finally says.

What are you talking about, Dad? I'm just out west and I wanted to say hello and let you know—

Son o' mine. We thought you'd disappeared, faded into the gloom of—

We? Somebody there with you now?

A long pause. Heavier breathing.

Dad? You there?

No, I died. I died when you went out the front door. Right now I have decayed considerably and someone out in the hallway will soon detect the odor and call the—

Stop it please! I'm sorry I took off, I really am. I just had to get out, get away. There wasn't any—

Test your wings. Leave the nest. We thought you were testing your wings, that's what I told her.

Who are you talking about?

Another long pause, breathing.

Your mommy, of course, he finally says. She called me couple, three weeks ago, told me you'd gone outta your head, were now playing pirate or—

Are you all right?

Except for being dead, fine. How are you?

Oh good, real good. It's nice out here in the west, Dad. Nice. There're mountains and pretty colors and—

You're lying.

No, Dad, I—

Let me give you piece of advice.

I know all about doughnuts, Dad.

What? What you mean?

Nothing. Go on, pop.

That's another of the roles I play with him. Charlie Chan's number-one son.

I want to tell you about. About something. I forgot my lines, never used, forget my lines. Hundreds of plays, never dropped a line, missed an entrance. More'n I can say for some others. Remember one time I was doing repertory out in, I don't know where, the boondocks somewhere. Buffalo, Stockbridge, Cincinnati, somewhere. Shakespearian troupe, real toney, except all the productions were stinkers. Nobody had an ounce of invention. An ounce of invention's worth a pound of manure.

That's good advice, pop. Say, I've really got to get going, got a real line on a clue to—

I am not through, son. Your interruptions are. Are distracting. And, far as your Keye Luke imitation goes, you've lost the rhythm. Catch one of the movies again. It's the way he inflects the verbs, you used to have it, now you don't.

Gosh, sorry, pop.

Now, about the. About. About, yes, the Shakespearian troupe. We were doing, I don't know, some of the plays. *Hamlet*, yes, and. And. And *Twelfth Night*. There was this fellow. Fellow thespian. Always hated that word. He always used it, this actor I'm going to tell. You about. I always use thespian when I'm referring to those who cannot act. Like this actor I'm.

Silence, breathing.

Pop, you there?

Just my corpse. I have left.

You were telling me about—

I *know* what I was telling you about. Just lost the picture for a minute. When you get old, memory's like an old TV with tuner problems.

Sure, pop.

Condescending little bastard.

I've really got to be—

This actor. Let's call him John Barrymore, for that apparently is who he thought he was. Whom he thought he was. Who, whom. Anyway, he thought he was John Barrymore. He used to enunciate with revolting nasality in I guess the way Barrymore used to sound to him. Offstage he drank and made epigrammatic little jokes that he pretended made sense. He got the best roles, the bugger, best roles. Everybody kissed his ass. Each bad review he got, and he got many bad reviews, everybody had to hold his hand and come up with tears to match his. Everybody except me. I kept my distance, except on stage. I was a professional.

For a minute I'm afraid he's going to go into his you-don't-know-what-it-means-to-be-a-professional speech, but fortunately he doesn't.

This Barrymore used to upstage me, step on my lines, forget his own and make it look like I was the one at fault, invent his own variations on the lines. Vary Shakespeare's words, mind you. He was. Was a stupid sonofabitch, he was. Well, about this time we were doing, as I said, *Hamlet* and *Twelfth Night*. You can always tell when a Shakespearian troupe's in trouble. That's when they resort to the surefire items. *Hamlet* and *Twelfth Night*. Three-quarters of your audience can't tell the difference if they're done badly or well. So—*Hamlet* was fine, okay. Barrymore was, naturally, essaying the title role, doing To Be or Not To Be as if it were a grade school question on logical positivism. I was doubling Polonius and Osric, which was all right with me—not so many encounters with our star attraction. He always managed to mess up the method in his madness scene, but I always managed, with a touch of hamminess to counter his, make it look to the audience like the man was really mad. And Osric, always liked Osric—doesn't matter what the Hamlet does, Osric is a nice turn, a lark to play. But *Twelfth Night*, that was another. Story.

Pause. I get scared because I can't hear the breathing this time. *Twelfth Night*, pop.

His voice comes back. He must've looked away from the phone for a moment.

—*fth Night*. I played the clown. Feste. Sang my own compositions. Good songs, too. Should have. Kept them. Lost now. Barrymore was playing, naturally, Sir Toby Belch. A mistake. Didn't look the part one whit. Thin, had to be padded with so much stuffing he always had to keep his hands somewhere on his costume, plugging up leaks. And his face. An Aguecheek face maybe, just the slightest maybe. But not Belch. Too villainous for Belch by a mile. Tiny beady eyes that looked at you from eye sockets that seemed to be circled in skin-folds. He always brushed his hair straight back, guess to make his forehead look higher, more intelligent. Just served to make him look like some hick who liked his hair brushed straight back. Later, when he went into the movies, they styled his hair, made it wavy. I knew the production was going to be shoddy, and resolved, as any actor worth his salt must, to make the best of my own opportunities. Well, came the official first night, official because we'd given some wretched previews in which everything had gone wrong. First night of *Twelfth Night*. First. Night. Of.

Pause. A sound like small explosions coming through the static. Dad is chuckling to himself.

Well, he resumes, the kind of arousal that can come to even a weak company when there are critics in the audience seemed to stir up our troupe that night. I was even enjoying my scenes with Barrymore-Belch. Oh, Maria missed one of her entrances by a few seconds, the actress playing Maria.

He pronounces the name Ma-rye-a, not Ma-ree-a, as in our lovely one-eyed madam. Nevertheless, suddenly my Maria is onstage with my Dad in the odd scene that's playing in my head.

Maria, Dad says. Charming woman. Left me alone onstage and I salvaged that moment by improvising a song on the spot. *Completely* in character. I went off from that scene feeling genuinely triumphant. Our brilliant Sir Toby, waiting in the wings, said something like nice little bit but take care you don't screw us up. His remark had exactly the effect he wanted from it—it made me edgy. Had trouble playing the next scene with him. Didn't matter to him, he was getting the big laughs. I'd put the proper emphasis on a line, do a perfect Feste-gesture and quick little move on my feet, lifting a step or two from Aguecheek's galliard, and there'd be no response from the audience, zero. But they loved Sir Toby, every little overplayed inch of him. Well, no matter, I thought. We're getting a sense of ensemble in the production tonight, and that's what's important.

Well, we came to the Sir Topas scene. I was beginning to get that anticipation I always got near the end of a performance, especially an opening night. There was just this one difficult scene to play, then a couple of easy turns in the last act, and that'd be it for the night. There's a turning point in every performance when, unless all hell is breaking loose, you lose your fright, that fear which pushes you around the stage, and can relax into a characterization that you've been, after all, building for so long. I had reached that point just before the Sir Topas scene. It was perhaps the trickiest scene for me to play, since the master's left little indication of the shift in Feste's character at that point. Why does he turn so darn mean, with Malvolio at his lowest ebb? Not like him. A puzzle, but I'd found some business I could use to create a relationship with the Malvolio actor and in rehearsals we had worked well together, so the scene did not stir any great apprehension in me, and Barrymore-Belch could not make much use of his few lines during the sequence, so all was well. I thought. But all that's well does not always end well.

I'm getting shooting pains all over my arms from holding the pink receiver up for so long. I don't know what he's talking about. Sir Topas? Who's Sir Topas? Was he just mixed up and drunk and calling this Sir Toby Sir Topas? I don't know the damn play. Shakespeare, shit. I only like *Richard III*. I'll be turned to stone by the time this call is over.

In rehearsal and previews, Dad goes on, the actress playing Maria and I and Malvolio positioned ourselves stage-left while a scene that involved Barrymore-Belch was proceeding. He would make his usual overplayed angry exit stage-right, then work himself and his padding through the narrow backstage area to us, where he would wait to make his entrance just after ours. Usually he reached the stage-left point just as Maria and I made our entrance. Sometimes he was a second or so late and, eyeing the wings, I'd play my cue speech in a bit slower rhythm until I saw that he was in place. This time, as we waited, somewhere in the back of my mind I noted that, after the angry exit, I didn't hear the usual rustling and bumping noises from the backstage area. I figured that he'd finally learned to manipulate himself and his padding through the narrow passageway. I was always an optimist, remember.

Yes, I say, you always keep your eye upon the doughnut and not upon the—

Nonsense. Please to stay shut up, number-one son.

He does the last remark in his Charlie Chan accent. Pretty good, too. He still has some of the old pizzazz, I guess.

Well then, Maria and I made a smooth entrance and I could sense a solid base of audience approval from which to work the business of the scene. Still, after Maria had made her little speech and exited, I looked after her. Barrymore-Belch was not waiting in his usual place. Thinking quickly, I decided to buy a little time by extending my bit of playing with the Sir Topas disguise. Looked over it, around it, under it, with as long a silence as I could dare before the audience would get restive. I managed another glance stage-left, where I saw Maria waving her hands and looking puzzled. Off stage-right I could hear some scurrying noises, a stage manager off on a mad dash to locate the missing Sir Toby. I felt some panic. Where was the sonofabitch? I started my speech, measuring out the words as slowly as I could. Since I had the Sir Topas costume to put on, I improvised some stage business with it that the audience took to be part of the performance. As I reached the line cueing the entrance of Toby and Maria, I could hear some more stage-right noises and some heavy footsteps coming up the stairs that led to our downstairs dressing rooms. Barrymore-Belch had been found, but it would take him time to get to his entrance point. I reached the end of my speech. Had to ad-lib for the *second* time in that opening night performance. I made a rather good pun as I donned the Sir Topas beard about the other Elizabethan meaning of the word beard. Of course nobody in that audience was up to Elizabethan puns and I sensed it was becoming clear to them that something was wrong onstage. As I listened to the frantic rustling sounds of Sir Toby making his way across the backstage passageway, I improvised a proper little caper, very difficult in the Sir Topas robe, believe me. As soon as Barrymore arrived stage-left, I spoke the cue line and made my habitual graceful gesture. Maria came promptly out, but Sir Toby held back, then he did an overtheatrical drunken stumble onto the stage. Completely inappropriate for that particular sequence, but the audience got a charge out of it. He'd never used the drunken side of Toby in this scene before, and I was furious at him. He continued to deliver his lines as if in a drunken stupor and, for one of the rare times in my life, I was thrown right off. Even though most of the scene was between Malvolio and myself, its rhythm was severely affected. I know I appeared to be more cruel than ever to the audience, who tittered at Sir Toby's drunken moves behind me. My voice went flat on the song I sang at the end of the scene. My later scenes did not draw their accustomed laughs. At curtain call I didn't get that sudden burst of applause that I received in other performances. Barrymore-Belch striding onstage of course got a thunderous ovation. The critics' reviews barely mentioned my performance—at least they were wise enough to suggest that Barrymore over-Belched his part. I confronted Barrymore in the dressing room. He made a fake apology for missing his entrance, said he'd simply forgotten about it and gone off to the dressing room. For a bit of a tipple, no doubt, the sot. I knew if I claimed that he planned it, nobody'd believe me, and the tension'd be no good for the company, so I made light of it and backed off. God, I was happy to leave that fleabitten troupe when the run was over.

Sounds to me like you were better off away from it.

Perhaps, son, perhaps. Never did much good for me, that company. Didn't hurt old Barrymore, though. He went into the movies. Used a different name there, forget it too. He was in, oh, that space station thing that was a remake of *On The Water-front*. Do you recall his name?

Never saw that film, pop.

No, you don't often go to movies. Unless they're certified trash, anyway. Uh, can't recall. Name. He starred in a couple more flop flicks, then killed himself some way I don't remember either. All I could think of was how beneficial his death was for the theater. Hated myself for thinking that. So cruel. Don't know why I just can't forgive and forget. There's a lesson for you here somewhere.

Pause. His breathing's beginning to sound like sleep.

I'm afraid I don't understand, pop.

No, I do not know you; nor I am not sent to you by my lady, to bid you come speak with her; nor your name is not Master Cesario; nor this is not my nose neither. Nothing that is so is so.

That's way above me, pop. Could we—

Yes, of course it is. Course.

He is getting sleepy, I can really tell now. He's about to drift off.

And thus the whirlagig of time brings in his revenges. Keep your eye upon the—

Silence. The heavy breathing of sleep. I hang up gently so as not to wake him.

6

I TRY to call Mother, but Harold answers. I hang up without talking. I fish Lincoln Rockwell X's number out of my wallet, dial it, get a busy signal. Figures. I feel sleepy. This chair's so uncomfortable they might as well electrify it. I shut my eyes anyway.

When I open them again, I wonder if I dozed off without being aware of it. Link is now standing over me, his disarranged face almost forced back to normal by a scowl of concern.

What's up? I say.

We're in trouble, he says, and crouches down next to my chair. I've never looked at Link up this close before. The harsh fluorescent light emphasizes tiny pockmarks on his skin. And strange reddish streaks, almost like a rash, on each cheek.

What happened and what's Victor got to do with it? I say.

Didn't you see Anton go into our room?

No, I was on the phone. Or sleeping, maybe.

He must've crept past you, the bastard. Anyway, he came in the room without even knocking first. Used a passkey. Victor didn't even look up from the TV. Anton ordered me out of the room. When I asked why, he just said shut up and get out. I knew if I didn't he'd call in a couple of his goons, so I got out.

Oh, Christ! I say.

Don't give up yet. Victor's buying us some time.

How?

He's refusing to pay any attention to Anton until the program he's watching's over. Would you believe it, Anton took it like a lamb, just sat down on my bed and started watching the program himself. So I snuck out here to you. I'm going to the arsenal. It's locked but not so I can't get into it. You stay here, stand guard.

Stand guard? What am I supposed to do, something happens?

Look, I can only get my mind working as far as the arsenal. You improvise here.

I'm no good at ad-libbing. That's my Dad's—never mind. Get going. Anything does happen, you can step over my corpse and take care of it.

Okay.

He stands up and has disappeared around the corner toward the staircase and elevators before I'm ready for him to leave. For a minute I can't think of a thing to do. Going to sleep still sounds good. But no. I stand up, walk over to the door of our room, listen. TV's still going, all's well for now. No keyhole beneath the doorknob to look through. Shit. I go back to the chair by the phone. The paper with Lincoln Rockwell X's number is still lying on the phone table. I'll try it again. This time no busy signal. After three rings he answers. He almost doesn't believe it's me when I identify myself. He's happy to hear from me, he says. But he can tell by my voice something's wrong and he asks what. I tell him. He laughs at some of it.

So I'm stuck out here, I say, trying to figure out what to do. What do you think?

Easy. Punt.

What?

Get the hell out of there. Sounds like your Victor and Link can take care of themselves, man. Get your motherin' hide outta there and cut your fucking losses.

I can't. I have to help them. It's my—

No way you got responsibility for trouble people digs up for themselves. You save your ass. Be what *you* want to be. What you are not is no fuckin' knight in armor off to save the honor of a maiden with a prick as long as yours. Get it?

I get it. I just can't use it. I can't go off now, not—

Then don't. I can get along without knowing what happens to you and how you earned your six feet of boot hill.

You don't understand. I'm no goddamned knight in armor,

you know that well enough. But I can't turn my back on—and when it comes to—and there's the car, I can't leave it here, not to these—

Okay, okay. I can follow your parade, man, just don't leave so much horseshit on the street.

Guess I'll just see what happens. Improvise. Ad-lib.

You do that. Best way to act if you're gonna be a fool rushin' in. Listen, only advice I can give you: You was in one of *my* whorehouses in the same situation, my advice is, shoot anything that moves. Course that's futile in one of my places 'cause the anything that moves is liable to be me and you're gonna be fucked over anyway.

You really own whorehouses?

A couple. Part of my corporate holdings, got some partners. But, yeah, own a couple.

Never knew that.

I am an entrepreneur. My finger's swirling around the fillings of a lot of pies, man. You get out o' your jam, you come back here, I'll give you a job.

Thanks, but I want to get out west. That's where I'm heading.

Best o' luck, hombre.

Sure. How's your daughter? How's Norma?

She's just fine. Reading grownup books, she'll be into porn 'fore I know it. Maybe take over my part of that operation. I think she asks about you, time to time.

Asks about me?

That's my suspicion. Keeps talking 'bout somebody name of lardass, think she means you.

She's a good kid, pretty kid.

Come back here, let you babysit.

No. I'll work it—

Asshole.

He hangs up abruptly. His way—he gets tired talking to you, he cuts off the conversation. It's like his whole life is this Swedish art-film festival, where you can put up The End during any scene and the audience'll love it anyway.

Christ, where's Link? I go over to the door, listen. No TV. Victor's voice. I can't tell what he's saying, but it's got that mean sound in it.

Looking down the hallway, I see no Link yet. If I wait, who knows what old Anton'll do? For that matter, who knows what

Victor'll do? I wonder if he's still got that little pistol hidden in his crotch? Christ, I'd forgotten that gun. What if he gets it in his head to use it?

My choices are limited.

I turn the knob of the door.

Not only is it locked, for the first time I notice the Do Not Disturb sign hanging from its doorknob. Who the hell put that there? Must've been Anton, that sonofabitch!

I knock on the door.

Get the fuck away whoever you are!

Anton's voice.

It's me, Lee, I say. I gotta get in there right away.

One of my brighter lines, what'll I say if he asks why? Maybe say I'm a diabetic and my insulin's in there or that there's a werewolf in the hallway and they have to let me in or maybe—

What kind of a stupid—

Anton's voice halts abruptly. There is a thud, then footsteps, then the unlocking of the door. Victor lets me in. Anton is spreadeagled on Link's bed, his eyes closed.

What'd you do? I say to Victor.

I hit him with a Gideon Bible.

A Bible? With just a Bible you—

I told you I had some martial arts lessons. I know where to aim a blow. Or a Bible.

Martial arts. God no, is he—

No, he's still alive. I'll save killing him for some other time.

Don't try—

Don't get your socks all sweated up. I was just joking. I'm no killer.

Yeah? What about the bikers? You didn't exactly—

I didn't kill any of them. You remember right, it was *you* struck the fatal blow.

What about the other one?

He ran his bike into a tree.

I don't believe you. The bike was too far away from the body.

All right then. They parted company long before he flew through the air with the greatest of ease. How do you expect me to remember details? I was somewhat busy getting racked up myself, if you'll take the trouble to recall it. Anyway, this is no time for spilt milk and shit like that. We have a problem.

He points to the unconscious Anton.

Why'd you hit him, for God's sake? I say.

The second before you knocked he was starting to grab for me. A second later and one of his grubby little paws'd've been wondering what's wrong with my anatomy. You distracted him, I had no choice but to cream him.

He doesn't know you're—you're—

Not yet. I was about to tell him. Save him the trouble of pawing me. But the little creep moves fast, I'll say that for him.

What'll we do?

I don't know. What time is it?

What time is it? What the hell difference that make?

Program I wanta watch at nine. Is it nine yet?

Hey, we can't sit here watching TV while Anton—

Forget it, just another joke.

Your fucking sense of humor's too fucking subtle for me, Vicki.

He sucks in his breath a little.

Yeah, he says, I've noticed.

The question is still before the chair, I say, what're we going to do?

I think we should get out of here. Take your wheels and start goin' on down that road.

Haven't you been listening to *anything?* The damn car's not fixed yet.

Well, forget the car. Not worth a shit anyway. We can make better time walking. I know, you wait here.

Where you going?

Anton's close to my size. He must have a closetful of clothes, good ones, tailored. If I'm not gonna get any teeth out of all this, I'll at least cop some duds.

Before I can protest, he's got Anton's keyring out of his pocket. Victor's certainly an expert at going for a guy's keys. His fumbling about in the leisure-suit pocket dislodges a well-worn paperback. An anthology of Seventeenth Century Metaphysical Poets. What in hell'd Anton be doing with a book on the metaphysicals? Victor's going for the door, jangling Anton's keys at me.

Wait Victor, I say.

We haven't got time to jaw, he says at the door. Be right back.

I *can't* leave my car here, I just—

But he's out the door before I can finish the sentence. He

doesn't shut the door tight. Anton stirs. The door slowly swings open. I start to move to him, look for something to hit him with. Anton groans.

What the hell happened? Maria says.

I look up. She's standing in the doorway.

7

ANTON makes a small groaning noise in his throat but doesn't wake up. Maria takes a couple steps into the room.

Why'd you hit him? she says.

I didn't hit him. Who said anybody hit him?

Mr. Anton's not generally accustomed to take naps in guest's rooms.

He's changing his habits maybe.

Don't shit me, Lee. What's this all about? Why'd you hit him?

I didn't, I tell you. He was kayoed by—

I almost say Victor, but think better of it. I don't fill in the blank with any name.

She did it then, Maria says. Saw her scampering down the hall. I don't know what he saw in her in the first place. She's got all the grace of a baboon. She runs like a third-string halfback, the skinnybitch, and that old lady's mouth on her—she did it, I should have guessed right away. Heads're gonna roll tonight, soon as Mr. Anton wakes up.

I start to speak, can't, clear my throat, try again.

Heads, I say. Who—whose heads?

I'd start fitting your neck for a platter, I were you, she says, smiling. Or the end of a pole. Or—

You've gotta help, Maria.

Help?

Get us out of here.

Her smile vanishes. Logical perhaps, it's been a ghost-smile.

Not a chance, honey.

But we, you and me, we—

I know what we done, but that's just ice in the Amazon, far as I'm concerned. Melted away, cooled an alligator's tongue. Nothing you and me did has any part of this. I work for Mr. Anton, he pays me well, he *trusts* me. Guy like you have any deep feelings for the idea of trust?

Sure, well, but—

But nothing. I am trusted, I follow the rules that govern that trust, get it? You're a nice kid, Lee, but the only way out for you is, own up and take your punishment.

I didn't do anything!

You're here. She did it and she's not here. You didn't stop her. You did something. Anyway, you're in good shape, can take a bit of punishment. Afterwards, I'll take you to my room, care for you. You let your two scumbag companions go their way, they'll only get you into more trouble. I can take care of you. Nurse your wounds, as they say.

My wounds?! What're they gonna do, for God's sake?

Nothing that'll surprise you. They're tough. But they're not killers. Not usually.

Not usually! Oh, Jesus. Please help me, Maria, please—

Inadvertently I've pronounced her name Dad's way. Ma-rye-ah. Her eye widens in surprise.

Ma-rye-ah. Where'd you get that pronunciation?

Doesn't make any difference. I need your help, Maria.

This time I pronounce it right.

Ma-rye-ah, says Ma-ree-ah. It's years since anybody said it that way. My mother used to call me that. It's so pretty that way, don't you think? Well, don't you?

I sit down on the other bed, beaten.

How'm I supposed to have an opinion on that subject? I say. I'm about to be tortured. I'll call you Ma-rye-ah all night if you'll get me out of that.

Sighing, she walks over to me, sits beside me, puts her hand on her favorite section of my thigh, and whispers:

Take it easy. Don't be sad. I'll nurse you. I *will*.

I grab her hand and push it off my thigh. She reaches for my wrist but, with a quick backhand, I shove her hand away. As a second thought, I push against her shoulders. Not expecting that from me, she loses balance and falls backward onto the bed.

I'm getting the hell out of here, I say and move toward the door.

No, you're not, she says.

There's so much authority in her voice, so much of the madam running the house, that I have to look back at her. She has a gun in her hand now. Although it is a small weapon, one like Victor's, I wonder where in that tight outfit she could possibly have concealed a gun.

Maybe I'll stay then, I say.

No, we're gonna be going, says Link, who's now standing in the doorway pointing a short-barrelled rifle into the room. He holds it casually, his standard manner for everything, but his finger's on the trigger and ready.

I would reconsider, I were you, Maria says. She is leaning to her right a little, trying to see around me. Jesus Christ, I realize, I'm smack in the middle. The weapons of Link and Maria are both actually aimed at me. They want to have a showdown, they'll have to send their bullets through me in order to wound each other. I move a little sideways, to the left.

Stand still, Lee, Maria says.

I stand still.

Now I'd drop that rifle, friend, I were you, Maria says.

You're gutsy, say that for you, Link says and moves a short way into the room. He's dragging a bulky sack with his other hand. He, too, is leaning sideways in an effort to see around me to Maria. Reaching down, he pulls a pistol out of his sack, tosses it my way. I very nearly don't catch it.

What'm I supposed to do with this? I say.

Improvise.

You made your entrance on time, I'll just stay close to the script, thank you.

What the hell are you talking about?

Never mind.

Okay.

He sidles further sideways.

All right, lady, we each got a gun. Two weapons to one. What do you say?

Two weapons, huh? says Maria. She squints her eye at me. Well, she says, I'd say more a weapon and a half, as far as effective firepower goes, but it's still an edge. Okay.

She tosses her gun onto the floor. It skids a bit into a small throw rug, then rests there in the bunches it creates. Quickly I make it my business to move out of all possible lines of fire, including the one from the rug.

Where the hell's Victor? Link says.

He's gone on a scavenger hunt for clothes.

Victor? says Maria. Victor? Wait a minute. You mean she— you mean Mr. Anton's been courting a—

That's about, you'll excuse the expression, the size of it, Link says.

Maria starts to laugh. She leans back against a pillow and nearly has hysterics, actually. Anton groans a couple of times as if he's just getting the joke, too.

Clothes, eh? Link says. I shoulda known. Where'd he go, you know?

Anton's room. He stole his keys.

This information sets Maria, who has been quieting down, to laughing hard again.

Okay, Link says. We'll just wait.

You sure that's a good idea?

I don't know about good, but it's the only one I got.

Wait for what?

For Victor to get back and our mechanic friend here to wake up.

Okay, I can see waiting for Victor, but let's not mess with Anton any—

Nope, Lee, Mr. Anton's our ticket outta here.

8

I FEEL out of place, Anton's garage is so clean and neat. It's such a showplace I expect lights to come up and an orchestra beginning to play an overture. Link tells us all to stay back while he checks out the area. He trundles around the room, looking at shelves and in cabinets for I don't know what.

Maria stands next to me. Occasionally she brushes her fingers across the back of my hand. On one pass I take her hand, hold it for a moment. Anton, who has been steadily eyeing Victor since he's returned to consciousness, breaks his puzzled concentration briefly to glance disapprovingly our way. Maria immediately removes her hand from mine. I don't know why she's affectionate at all, not after what she said to me back at the room. She was going to let them torture me, after all. Now that that's cancelled, or postponed if Link's plan, whatever it is, doesn't work out, why is she being affectionate? Is she planning to nurse me back to health even if they skip the torture? I look at her. She's moved a couple of steps toward Anton, who's still staring at Victor. Victor's changed to sneakers, dungarees, and an androgynously provocative shirt. Nobody's told Anton about Victor, not even Maria. We just ordered him to go with us to the garage. I can tell from the way he's eyeing Victor that Anton hasn't quite figured it all out yet, even though Victor has removed his wig and makeup, even though Victor is now nervously clenching and unclenching his fists in a particularly masculine manner. I can understand Anton's confusion. There are still Victor's eyes, there are still the eyes.

Link checks even the inside of the Mustang to make sure nobody's crouched in it. Victor is getting very agitated.

Come on, Link, he says. Let's get to it, all right?

I *am* getting to it.

You're just walking around!

Yeah, I'm making the first checks on the maintenance chart, okay, so take it easy.

What do you guys imagine you're up to? Anton says to Link.

We're gonna nicely cruise out of here in our vehicle, Link says.

Anton laughs.

Hah! That wreck's not ready for the road. Half the insides are still on the shelves and around the car. The guys weren't going to finish the job off till tomorrow.

Well, we'll just do a little overnight work, won't we?

What, you expect me to go rouse the guys and—

You don't have to rouse anybody.

Well, if I—oh, I see. You expect *me* to do it for you alone. Cheap ripoff artists.

Correct.

Anton laughs, but this laugh is weaker, a little apprehensive.

I don't do the dirty work any more. That's what I hired a crew for. Built up a reputation over the years, built this place out of nothing, with hard work and God's help. Now I got employees. I only do the inspections, the diagnosis, a few adjustments here and there, a—

See? Link says softly. That's where you've gone off the track. You don't work with your hands any more. It corrupts you, to piece yourself out as a corporation, to hand out your abilities to subordinates. Each one of them is a lesser you, you see? You didn't check them out regularly, the quality of work in this shop'd be shit.

You can count on that. But it doesn't mean—

Oh, yes, it does. You need us, Anton. You really do. You need to get some grease on your coveralls. To crawl under a car and rediscover yourself. To weave your magic hands through that engine. It's a kind of salvation, understand?

Stop! Don't blaspheme.

Sorry. All I'm saying is, you're gonna do the job. And I know just enough to help. *And* make sure you don't booby-trap the vehicle. Okay, Victor, you stand guard while *Mr.* Anton and I get Lee's wheels in shape.

You're out of your head, Link, Victor says. Why don't we just—

We wouldn't get two miles down the road before Anton's goons'd be bearing down on us in a reconverted Mercedes. This is the way, Victor.

Victor, Anton mutters each time Link says the name—the light finally dawning. Do you mean that, that—

Shove it up your ass! Victor says. Do what Link says.

But—

Look, you stupid creep, I've played out this scene so many times I can do both parts. I'm not in the mood for it right now.

Victor, walking over to Link, takes the rifle from him, points it at Anton.

Get to it! he shouts. Now!

Anton moves in a dreamlike fashion, as if he's not willing to believe this tough guy waving a rifle at him is the tough broad he lusted for. I hate to think it, but I'm really enjoying his confusion.

With Link and Anton busy crawling into coveralls, Maria evidently feels it's safe enough to talk to me. She rubs the edge of her little finger against the outside of my thigh, while whispering:

I shouldn't probably warn you, but you should consider that eventually Anton and I'll be missed.

Maria, I think we're taking that chance. If you have any alternate suggestions you'd like to place before the board—

Don't get sarcastic with me. Please.

Sorry.

She brushes the back of her hand against the corner of her good eye. She's not crying but, I suppose, is about as close to tears as she ever gets.

Maria, I say.

What?

Why don't you come with us?

Affectionate mockery in her laughter.

You kidding? Aside from the fact in all likelihood you're not going anywhere, I wouldn't go with you anyway. I'd like to be a romantic, I really would like to go off and joyride, but—

Then do it.

Nope. For love maybe I could. But you're too hung up on your lady back east. You wouldn't stay with me.

Sure I would.

No, Lee, now don't get me wrong. I'd like to, just can't. It'd be a lark to take ninety days off, see some country, have some fun, do—

Why ninety days?

Guys like you burn out in about ninety days, at least with women like me.

Anton is now approaching my car. A bit tentatively, circling the front, putting off actually touching it for as long as he can. Finally he does make contact. He draws his hand back immediately. He's touched disease and, as a skilled diagnostician, knows it. Link hands him a spanner. He leans over the engine and begins tinkering with something. Still tentatively, but with a bit more effort.

God, this's gonna take forever, Victor says.

Your friend is impatient, Maria says, smiling. Victor whirls on her, furious.

Keep your trap shut, blind-eye.

Maria shouts at him:

You goddamn freak, where do you get off say—

Or should I call you white-eye, fatbitch.

Victor says fatbitch the way Maria used to say skinnybitch to him.

Stop that, I say to Victor. You've got no reason to—

Swallow your tongue whole, you creep, he says, turning his attention to me. If you think she's going to award you any points for playing her protector, then you got—

Shut up, all of you, Anton hollers. He waves his wrench threateningly. We got work to do here, we don't need to listen to any petty hassles, hear?

Yes, Anton, Maria whispers quietly. Obediently. Victor and I say nothing. Maria walks behind me, gets to my other side— obviously to put me between her and Victor. Another line-of-fire ploy, I guess. I'm uncomfortable with her on that side. It's her blind side and I can see too much of her blind, white eye. She's always placed herself on the good-eye side of me and I've usually positioned myself that way, too. Victor notes her retreat, then goes to a work table, holding the short-barrel rifle Link gave him at his side, pointing down. With one more angry look our way, and a slight scornful sound in his throat, he looks out the window toward the road. His body has assumed the threatening stiffness of a gangster, a B-movie hoodlum standing guard. I think of what generally happens to B-movie hoods who stand guard, and for a moment am deeply afraid.

9

ANTON works furiously now. He lets dirt fly without caring where it lands. His coveralls are speckled with black grease-dots and long ragged smudge lines where he's wiped his hands. He's doing all the work now, using Link only as surgical assistant to hand him the tools. I'm beginning to believe Anton'll revive the Mustang again, just like The Mech did each time I brought the car to him. Of course this time it's going to look more than ever like a cripple. Anton's men have hammered out the top well enough, but the overall surface is so rippled with dents a phrenologist would go crazy trying to give it a reading.

Off in the distance, toward the Ramada, there are sounds of laughter, some music. I can see Maria hears them and isn't too pleased. I can figure why. If they're in there laughing, they're not out searching for us.

What's all that noise? I say.

My girls, the bitches. They're having a goddamn party. I go away from them a couple hours, all discipline breaks down, things get raucous. They start playing their idiotic music and wiggle around like old-time whores for the clients. I got to get back there, I can't allow—

What's wrong with them partying? Doesn't that go with the job?

Not the way we run things. You heard what we said at the

184

meeting. We're turning them into good girls. That's the point of the place. Salvation.

Salvation?

Girls that leave us, always leave us for permanent relationships, marriage as often as not. The ones that return to whoring usually weren't here very long.

And that's the purpose of the organization?

Mr. Anton is a man of principle. He really wants to help them. Us.

How's he helping you?

It's a good job. I pretty much run that part of the operation by myself. He only interferes for the good of the girls and the business.

Why haven't you been saved then?

I don't get you.

Why haven't you grabbed off a husband, the good life, the—

I've had husbands, three of them. Mr. Anton's the third. Still is, legally.

I look from her to Anton and back to her again.

Anton? You don't treat him like a husband.

He hasn't treated me like a wife. Not for a long time anyway. It's a business partnership now.

You're so formal together, I just—

She smiles.

We were *always* formal together. That's his way. Became mine. He has his points, Mr. Anton does. And his spark plugs, for that matter.

Anton steps back from the hood of the Mustang, eyes the car as if checking the stitches, then drops a tool from each hand. The tools bounce and clang in unison.

Done, Anton says. A good job, I say so myself.

He looks down at his hands, sees more grease than skin.

Feels good, he says. Should do this more often.

Told you, Link says, smiling.

Let's get rolling, Victor says.

I'm going to have to ask you and Maria here to accompany us down the road a piece, Link says to Anton. A mile or so. Sorry for the inconvenience.

Sorry for the inconvenience, Anton says. You're so polite, young man.

Just a road sign I keep seeing.

Why bother taking them along with us? Victor says.

Hostages.

Well, don't expect me to sit in back with that bastard.

Anton laughs. Maria and I smile at each other.

Don't worry, Vicki, Anton says. I couldn't allow myself to be seen next to you. Not in that tacky shirt and with—

Victor, moving abruptly, hits Anton in the face with the stock of his rifle. Anton sees the blow coming, rolls with it, then swings around and charges at Victor. Victor, not ready for such a swift counterattack, can't bring the gun around in time to use it again. Anton punches Victor in the nose with a short but powerful jab. I think I hear a small crack. Victor reels back, a hand to his nose, blood appearing in trickles through his fingers. Anton makes a lunge for the gun, but Link runs up quickly and pushes Anton to the floor. Maria leaves my side and kneels by Anton. Victor takes his hand away from his nose, letting the blood run onto his lips, down his chin. He raises his rifle, points it toward the fallen man.

No, Link shouts and rams into Victor with his shoulder. Victor skids sideways on a grease mark. I stand there, wondering momentarily what is a grease mark doing on Anton's spotless floor. Maybe it's a bloodstain. Suddenly I realize that just maybe standing still is not my best strategy, and I move toward Victor, intending to deflect any further aim he might be considering taking on Anton or Maria. I am right about the aim but late with my move. He points the gun again at Anton, who is now crouching, ready to spring. Link makes another lunge, but this time Victor sidesteps him. I can see he's about to pull the trigger. At the same time I see Maria deliberately putting herself between Anton and the gun.

Get out of the way! Victor screams at her.

She just stands there. I make a move to grab Victor's gun arm, but he briefly aims the rifle my way and says quietly, don't try, Lee. I stop. He swings the gun back toward Anton and Maria.

Out of the way or I'll just shoot him through your body, bitch! Victor shouts.

Do that, Maria says.

All right, I—

Link's third jump at Victor is even less successful than the other two. He misses him completely, stumbles past him clumsily. Victor edges back against the wall, a maneuver to ward off further attacks. Everything is eerily still for a moment. Anton remains crouched behind Maria. Link, back on his feet, looks relaxed, his head and shoulders leaning again in Victor's direction, in a kind of simian stance. María stares at Victor defiantly.

Suddenly I realize that the Ramada's party noises have stopped. Outside, there are some suspicious cracklings that sound to me like twigs being crushed underfoot.

Okay Vic, that's enough, Link says, his voice steady.

Shove it, Link, Victor says. You're not gonna talk me outta this one.

But Vic—

Somewhere near the garage door somebody bangs into an oil can. Victor glances toward the sound. I use the opportunity to rush him. He sees me coming, gets his gun back aimed at me just in time to bring me to a quick unsteady halt.

Back up, Lee.

Vic, Link says, there're people out there. Anton's people. We gotta get moving outta here.

Better yet, give up, Anton says. You haven't a chance.

We won't have, Link says, if you don't cut this shit and get into the goddamn car. C'mon.

Victor seems about to relent when Anton says:

Go ahead, bitch. Do it, bitch. Get in the car, bitch.

Victor, with deliberation, takes aim on Maria and Anton. I realize he's too alert for me to try to deflect the gun. Instead, I remember every Kung Fu movie I've ever seen and take a leap, feet first, at his legs, to try to trip him up. I mistime my leap slightly, and fall down in front of him. As my back hits the floor hard, my right foot gets him right in the crotch. The foot hits something hard, sends shooting pains back up my leg. Christ, he's still got that stupid derringer hidden in his jockstrap! I don't have much time to consider this, as I hear the rifle go off above me and to my right. Maria's scream is almost drowned out by Victor's howls of pain. I twist around on the floor, see her ending a fall, her hand clutching her side. Squirming along the cement floor, I crawl to her. She sees me coming, whispers:

I'm all right. Been shot worse than this. Twice before.

I look down at her hand. There's only a couple spots of blood on it, but there's a stain slowly spreading on her blouse.

You sure you're okay? I say. She surprises me by laughing.

Of course I'm okay, she says. I almost died once. Felt nothing like this.

Get to the car, Lee, Link says.

I'm suddenly aware of inchoate vocal sounds outside the garage, the sounds of panic being countered by commands.

Do what he says, Maria says.

From the other side of her, Anton is nodding in agreement. He puts his arm around her shoulder.

I'll stay with you, I say to her.

C'mon, Link says.

Victor is limping toward the Mustang. Link stands between him and me, keeping guard but with his body showing a definite lean toward the car.

Don't be stupid, Maria says. You stay here, you're just going to get your ass torn apart.

The outside noises—less confused now, more organized—provide convincing support to her argument. I stand up, saying to her:

I'll call you, all right? Make sure you're okay.

You don't know the number.

I'll figure it out.

It's unlisted.

Don't worry about it. I'll call.

Get the fuck out of here, please! Anton?

Yes? Anton says, just as formally as usual.

Help me over to the wall so they can drive out.

Naturally, darling.

I hear the sound of that *naturally, darling* all the way to the car. Link nearly shoves me into the driver's seat, runs to the garage door. He's got a mean-looking automatic rifle in his hands now, a surprise from his grab-bag arsenal. He beckons to me to drive to the garage door. Which I do. Then he throws open the door, stands to the side and fires a barrage into outside darkness. I think I see people jumping for cover. Link races to the passenger-side door, which I've leaned over and pushed open, gets in, and shouts:

Floor it! Fucking floor it!

I slam down on the accelerator, and we speed through the gas station lot toward the exit road. Rows of lights all along the road come on suddenly. Up ahead, there's a regiment of goons lined across the road, a firing squad all with weapons held to their shoulders and aimed at us. I take a quick swerve around a gas pump, and head instead for the access road. Gunfire behind us, which I concentrate on ignoring. Anton better hire a new bunch of goons, none of these can shoot straight. I hear a couple of thumps along the side of the car, but that's about as close as they get. From my rear-view I briefly try to see back into the garage, but I can only glimpse one of the immaculate corners, no sign of Maria. The blasts from the artillery echo behind us as we reach the access road. In the mirror I see many of the goons heading down the hill toward the main road. By the time I reach the end of this access road and swing around to head in that direction, they'll all be lined up across the highway. They could easily get off a lucky shot. I can't go that way, no choice about it. When I hit the highway, I go the wrong way, head back east, watch the lights of the Ramada Inn become increasingly smaller in my rear-view. I'm so intense on looking back that I nearly rack us up into an oncoming car that swerves into the median ditch. Our route to the next exit is several miles and I rather enjoy dodging around the few cars we meet up with.

As we head down the exit road, looking at all the signs that say Wrong Way Go Back, Victor—who's been silent the whole ride out—suddenly speaks up:

Shit, now my fucking nose is broken. My fucking *nose*.

Sorry about that, Vic, Link says, but you—

I don't want to hear it, Victor says. Shit. What am I gonna do now? My fucking nose broken, won't stop bleeding. The god-damned fucking dentist never showed up. My balls ache because junior here had to play hero for his ugly lady—maybe I got a hernia, damn it! With this nose and no teeth, I'm gonna look like a fucking freak. I'm gonna look like you, Link. And—shit, goddamn it, fuck—I left my fucking bag of clothes, all those beautiful threads I stole, back there on Anton's fucking work table. Shit, goddamn, fuck, shit—

Victor's voice subsides to its habitual grating mutter and is then drowned out by Link and me laughing.

Part V

1

Now I don't even remember becoming an outlaw. I don't remember ever sitting down and thinking hey, this is what I want to do, my life's work, my goal discovered, hey, I want to be an outlaw. I probably never did that. Link's the one who really wants this life. He's forcing me into his fantasy, is what he's doing. I'm sick of being forced into things. I don't remember making any choices of my own since I made the choice to buy the fucking car.

Wish I could rest a while, think. Try to find my way to somewhere. Go to the end of the yellow brick road, take a swig from the Holy Grail, sing in the rain, keep my sunnyside up. I wonder if anybody remembers Janet Gaynor singing "If I Had a Talking Picture of You" in the movie *Sunnyside Up*. My dad took me to a museum and made me sit through that movie twice.

We've had about a hundred days and nights of playing outlaw, mostly robbing small towns. Give Link an arsenal and he thinks he's Clyde Barrow, Cole Younger, Jesse James, Teddy Roosevelt. He resents my refusal to carry one of his wondrous guns, says I'm a coward.

I am a coward.

I also hate guns.

Anyway, I've killed twice without needing a gun to do it. I'm an assassin with monkey wrench and cooking fork—what'd happen if you gave me a gun?

I don't much like playing getaway-car driver either. Waiting in the car, thinking every hick in work shirt and overalls has spotted you. You, in a rundown car in their rundown town.

The people we rob look mostly like ordinary types eking out small livings, small-timers whose lives are probably ruined by our brief appearance in them. A couple of nights ago we robbed a ramshackle health food store in an almost empty town. The proprietors, man and wife, both of them in their sixties if not older, cowered behind a dusty, unevenly arranged stack of whole grain cereals. Didn't even look like they'd had a customer in months. The woman had long straight white hair and wore a faded flannel gown. The man's hair, also long and white, had streaks of brown in it and the hairs of his thin long beard looked like they'd been soldered together years ago.

Link, normally the gentlest of robbers, got angry when he found only a few bucks in the cash drawer. He held his gun straight out, pointed it at the man's beard.

Where's the real dough? he hollered.

Real dough, Link? I whispered. You really say that?

The old man said Link held all the cash they had in his fist, and the woman added that we were welcome to take any of the stock, insisting that, for nomads like us, on the run from the law, from life, food was more valuable than money anyway. Then she started describing our obvious vitamin deficiencies. Link cursed and strode out. Before he got into the car, he sent a couple of wild shots into the air.

I took one look back. The man and woman stood at the door, pointed to the sack in my arms that contained the food and vitamins I'd hastily collected on my way out, and nodded knowingly. They waved at me quite cheerfully as we drove away.

Earlier today I felt really fed up. I told Link I was sick of ruining the lives of all the people we rob. He laughed.

These people got money up the ass, he said, cash under the floorboards, treasures in the attic. They got things worked out with bankers, accountants. They can't lose. Bankruptcy's sometimes the best thing happens to them all their lives. Ride with the music, Lee.

I remembered the old man and woman in the health food store. I doubted they had any annuities packed away anywhere, unless it was monthly deliveries of Vitamin B supplements.

Victor likes being an outlaw. He loves it. He steals clothes whenever he can. Driving away from a job, he throws the duds he doesn't like out the window. The best dresses he wears to the robberies, says it makes him look less suspicious. Not long ago we encountered a black market dentist and, with some of our loot, bought him a new set of teeth. He is almost pleasant looking, as pleasant looking as he gets anyway. He has also turned our getaways into a kind of bizarre art form. He leaps into the car in moves I suspect he choreographs the night before.

Each time it's my turn as driver and we speed away from a robbery, my heart nearly conks out. Throbbing pains all across my chest until we're miles away. Nobody ever pursues us out of these small towns. No pursuit, no roadblocks. Whatever happened to roadblocks? Seems law and order's broken down all over the nation. Still, I never feel safe until we reach an expressway. Things always seem better on an expressway.

We've been keeping the Rocky Mountains on our right for some time now. Link says we better not try to cross them, the car might not survive the trip. I am desperate to get to the coast. I want to see oceans, movie-blue water slipping and sliding over movie-grey rocks. I keep thinking, in a different kind of setting maybe I can work out a different kind of life. Link'd like to get to California, too, and figures we might be able to get there by a southwestern route. Although, he said sarcastically, the desert is probably just as likely to kill the car.

The mountains look misty today, drained of color. I want the color back, I want mountain contours that look less like a two-dimensional backdrop. There's been an almost continual cloud cover for days. The sun seemed dimmed even when it did break through.

We pass small towns and Link doesn't even glance at them. I guess he's moody today, doesn't want to rush in and rob a few unsuspecting slobs. All right with me.

He handles the Mustang well. Too bad he hates the car so much. Too bad he's always bitching about needing some real wheels. I'd let him have this car, if only he'd really like it.

Victor's nasal whine startles me awake. I hadn't realized I was dozing off.

Take the next rest stop, he says, I got to pee. Sign says two miles to it.

Victor's insistence on using proper lavatories instead of the side of the road once made Link angry. Now he just shrugs. The rest stop comes up and Link turns the car smoothly onto the access road.

At first sight the colony at this rest stop seems little different from any of a hundred others I've seen. There are fewer cars in the parking area, but that's been the general trend since I started west. Not so many people and vehicles. A bit of the wide open spaces. What I've been looking for, right? Wrong. I used to think so, but wrong. For all their well-pressed clothes and cars in better condition, most of these people aren't appreciably different from the types I used to work with in my infrequent office jobs. They're trapped behind the wheels of their cars just like the city people are sealed behind rotting desks. They wander aimlessly over roads they've seen so much they've memorized them. It's just another way of shuffling paper. You ask them about all this, they just say sure, fella, but at least we get to see trees and mountains instead of just a roomful of other desks. Maybe so, is my usual inspired reply. It's a good point, maybe, but I wish their eyes had more life in them.

Link parks the car a few feet away from any clump of parked vehicles, so there's lots of space around the Mustang. It's his way. Myself, I usually pull up closer to other cars.

Victor is out of the car like a shot. We follow at a more leisurely pace. The entrance to the restaurant building (once part of some chain called Harmony House) is casually ringed by a group of relaxed and happy-looking people who are distinctively dressed in bright colored work shirts and clean stiff jeans. Each of them has a leather pouch draped quite fashionably over his or her shoulders. Edges of paper stick out from the pouches.

What kind of gang is this? I ask Link, who shrugs.

You got me. Nice looking bunch, though.

He's right. They look like somebody's collected all the Most Likely to Succeeds and Best Personalities from all the local high schools and brought them together for a positive thinking conference.

Victor is stopped by one of the pretty girls, who beams a smile at him that would melt the heart of anybody with a heart, but of course it does nothing for Victor. It certainly would melt my heart if some of the right questions went with it.

Look, he says, I'd just love to talk with you about that, but I got to get in there and use the facilities. First things first, okay?

Well, sure, hon, the pretty lady says. God'd never care to have one of his workers interferin' with another's natural flow. You get on in there, hear?

Well yeah, thank you, ma'am.

She is getting to Victor. I never saw him so polite before.

But you check back with me, hear?

Victor nods. The girl steps to the side allowing Victor through the ring of smiling people. Two handsome young men stand on either side of the girl and watch her dealings closely. They approve with sunny smiles that reveal teeth whose shine would draw the Lost Dutchman into daylight. Not missing a beat as Victor slips past her, she turns to Link and me. She smiles. My heart starts beating rapidly. I think of how embarrassed I'm going to be to fall dead at her feet.

Hello hon, and you too hon, she says to us. My name's Theresa, you can call me Terry, and I'd like to talk to you about driving the natural unpaved road to God.

The what? I manage to say in spite of her mind-numbing smile. She ignores the question. Apparently she doesn't want to miss a beat of her prepared speech.

God is sure enough tired of sitting behind the billboard of heaven, watching degraded man drive by in his evil combustion machines, ignoring heaven as if it's just another pit stop on the race to oblivion. God'd like to zoom out from behind the billboard like the eternal and watchful traffic cop He is, but He can't, you see. He can't go pulling each and every one of us off to the side of the road and write a warning or a ticket that we don't intend to pay off on anyhow. God's got better things to do, hear? He can't be traffic cop and judge and warden and chaplain all at the same time.

I thought he could, Link says. I thought that was easily within his powers.

She probably can't detect the quiet menace in his voice the way I can, but his comments stop her spiel anyway. Her smile disappears for a fraction—oh, only the smallest fraction—of a second.

That's a good one, hon. First time anybody's thrown that one at me. Course I'm something of a novice, but I tell you, we don't often get a sharpie out this way. You're from the east. I'm right, right?

Yeah, sure. Look, I'd like to go inside, too, wash up.

Let's talk this out first.

Link begins to pull nervously at his half-beard. His other hand has formed into a fist.

Look, he says, I don't need this. Especially from a young punk like you, lady.

Terry's two handsome guardians stiffen up and lean toward her. She waves them off.

Lady? she says demurely. Punk? 'Zat polite? I thought you easterners invented women's lib. You don't have to treat me like a—

Link sighs.

I'm sorry if I insulted you. I'm tired out, on a short fuse. Look, I'm over forty and I don't need to listen to any young *person* tell me how to run my life.

You're over forty, Link? I say. Forty? You don't look like, I mean, you never said—

Course I never said. Think I want you to know I'm this old geezer traveling around playing games with kids? I've always passed younger. It's this ugly face, could be any age, so fuck off, Lee, all right? I'm tired of you putting your dime in everywhere. Just leave me alone.

Terry is smiling delightedly at us, happy to have caused so much trouble so quickly. She looks like everybody's favorite yearbook picture. God should create an eternal high school just for types like her. The minute you see her, you want to take her to the prom. You want a white tux jacket and an orchid in a silver box. You want to rub up against her, press yourself through the tulle or organdy layers of her multi-petticoated gown. You want to take her to the beach, mess with her under a blanket. Not that she'd mess with you under a blanket, you just want her to. It would not take long to convince me that she was real and the rest of us were just props in her world. I have to look away from her. It doesn't help. All the rest of this group is too good-looking. Terry's not even unique. There's a petite redhead down the way who may be even more beautiful.

Let's get down to basics, Terry says. I believe in basics. 'V' you accepted Jesus as your savior?

May I pass, miss? Link says. I got to—

You passin' already, cowboy. You passin' as a Christian, as a human being.

There're some who've even denied me that status, Link says. Now get the fuck out of my way. Ah, excuse me, *please* get the fuck out of my way.

The whole group begins to close ranks.

Cool down, cowboy, Terry says. You're on our land.

Your land? This rest stop?

Yep. Not only the rest stop, the whole area around, all of it belongs to God.

Link laughs.

It's God's rest stop? he says.

Yep. We own the land and you're a trespasser. Legally.

Somebody sold you a rest stop?

Yep.

They throw in the Brooklyn Bridge?

Terry laughs without really laughing.

Good one, cowboy. Nope, it's ours. This is the legal property of Wheelers for the Lord. We own a lot of the stops 'round here, not to mention some ranches, a few towns, our own railroad line, and a fast-food franchise chain we call Spokes.

I don't get it, Link says. How can you own a rest stop?

Easy. You freewheelin' dudes who run the roads may not realize but our federal gummint—gov-er-ment, always screw up that word—anyway, our government is practically bankrupt. As well it should be, with its godless ways and its refusal to recognize and support the spiritual needs of the people. They're sellin' federal and state lands just like they did back in homestead days. A bit more expensive than those days, but a bargain anyway if you buy in quantity and hire good lawyers. Wheelers got the money, we buy up what we can. After we've all talked for a while, I'd like to invite you guys to our main settlement hereabouts—just a mile or two down the road there. Beautiful place where our people can—

Sorry, we're not headed that way, Link says.

That's what you think, friend.

Without a noticeable sign from Terry, the ring of pretty people finishes closing rank in front of us, goes shoulder to shoulder. From out behind parked cars, more pretty people in stiff jeans and checker shirts emerge. They are all smiling. They all have bright teeth. For one of its brief moments, the sun comes out from behind the clouds and my eyes ache from the rays their teeth give off.

You guys are rough around the edges, Terry says, just the sort we favor as recruits.

I look over my shoulder. Some Wheelers have appeared from nowhere and casually surround the Mustang. I look back at Terry and her group. Their smiles are so appealing, their eyes so affectionate, that I am confused for a moment and don't know which one to ask to the prom. I feel dizzy.

Look, Link says, you want a fight you got one, but I don't get this at all.

We don't fight, Terry says and all her beautiful companions nod. Recruiters don't fight, we don't have to. We have some fighters over at the settlement, try them, but you want to throw a few blows here, we'll get out of your way. So—throw your few punches at the air, get the demons out, *then* we'll get down to business about Wheelers for the Lord. Go ahead.

C'mon, Lee, Link says. Let's get the hell away from this place.

What about Victor?

As if in answer to my question, there's a scream from inside the restaurant.

That's Victor, I say.

Let him catch up, Link says.

But Link, we can't—

We have to, get moving!

We walk, almost casually, back to the car. Sure enough, the Wheelers there make way for us, with smiles paralyzed in place. They remain smiling as we climb into the car. Victor comes running out of the restaurant, looking panicked.

Give me the keys, Lee, Link whispers as Victor rushes toward us.

You had the keys, I say.

Shit, Link says and begins hitting the steering wheel with the flat of his left hand.

What's the matter, Link?

I think I left the keys in the ignition. Shit. I don't do that. Shit.

The keys are gone from the ignition. Victor reaches the car and begins pounding on the window on my side, screaming for me to open the door. A Wheeler leaning on our hood sends a bright grin through the bug-spattered windshield, and holds up a clean well-manicured little finger, from which dangles, on a shining brand new chain, our keys.

2

I AM still disoriented by the Wheeler settlement, having never before seen a complex which integrates the best features of a utopian colony and a concentration camp. The place is more than Terry's mile or two down the road. Seems as if we pass into another country. Maybe that's because of all the checkpoints along the way, checkpoints staffed by more wide-smiling great-looking kids in checker shirts and jeans. They always step politely into the road waving clipboards at us to slow us down. Once our drivers are recognized and they make a friendly inspection of the unsavory trio squeezed into the Mustang's uncomfortable back seat, we're waved farther down the unusually smooth road, to the next checkpoint. Occasionally we pass other checker-shirted blue-jeaned young people working on the road, making the surface as smooth and well-scrubbed as your average Wheeler.

Our pair of Wheeler drivers keep up a run of incessantly cheerful chatter. It starts to rain. The Mustang's windshield wipers perform with their usual reluctance. Checkpointers and road workers wear grey raincoats with hoods. Victor hums to himself, using the wipers' off-the-beat phrasings as rhythm. Link curses nonstop. I feel caught in the middle of either an avant-garde symphony or a behavioral modification test.

We start down a long hill. The rain has subtly changed to mist. Everything seems eerie, as if we're being driven into the middle of a horror movie where we're merely going to be some vampire's conventional victims, the dodos he gets before the hero and heroine finally show up. We pass a bent sign that instructs us to watch out for falling rocks. Next few minutes I keep a lookout. No rocks fall. Disappointing. Once Link shouts at the cheerfully chattering drivers to shut up or he'll use their faces to line latrines. They laugh politely and keep right on chattering.

We reach the crest of a high rise and suddenly the Wheeler settlement is on view. A large meadowful of mobile homes, all shiny and gathered together in bunches. Well, not bunches exactly. It's all quite organized. Eight or ten of the mobile homes are arranged in a circle around a sort of mall which clearly is a meticulously planned setting of many-colored benches and vivid flower displays. The effect is both awesome and festive. Circular roads surround each grouping of mobile homes. Other, smaller and straighter roads link the larger roads to each other. It's a minute before I get the image. The homes are *spokes* around a central decorated hub with a rim of roadway around them. Spokes, hub, rim. Wheels for the Wheelers. This is a *deliberate* arrangement and there are many of these simulated wheels spread across the expansive meadow. I ask one of our drivers if this is the main Wheeler camp. He chuckles proudly and says no, this is only a district headquarters. It is only one of the many Wheeler communities. Some of the others are larger and have responsibility for wider geographical areas.

Wheeler communities are growing by leaps and bounds, he says enthusiastically. It's fantastic, isn't it?

It's stupid, Link says.

It's shit, Victor says.

It's, well, okay, I say.

A tall full-figured brunette named Lena delivers our indoctrination lecture. Although taller and bigger-boned, she still reminds me a lot of Terry. Her smile as she tells us we'll like it here seems electronically controlled, set alight by a whole board of microchips. She has a habit of raising her arms and her voice simultaneously, giving her speech the feel of a pep talk or football rally. Considering her size, raising her arms within the narrow confines of the inside of a mobile home is an almost choreographic accomplishment.

As she speaks I try to escape the sexy gaze of her luminous dark brown eyes by concentrating on the coffee table in front of the couch where Link, Victor, and I sprawl in various stages of ill-postured hostility. The coffee table is like a miniature plastic veldt, with tiny transparent statues of various animals arranged upon its glossy surface. I pick up a plastic antelope and study it. It is finely detailed, with many realistic lines and bumps on its head and body. I'm sure it'd be sold in a better store than your local five and dime. For a while Lena fiddles absentmindedly with a jaguar miniature while she talks. She strokes its body with her long thin fingers. In the course of her talk she mentions that the Wheelers manufacture these tiny animals down in Taos and then sell them in specialty shops all over the country.

Whatever else, you must believe in God, she says.

Not giving God much thought these days, I say.

Didja ever?

I shrug.

I understand, she says, life's hassle enough when you got to get out on the streets or the road and grab what you can.

You been reading my mail.

She laughs, a shade too loudly.

Wheelers know the malaises, she says, that guys like you face. The rootlessness of your lives, purposelessness of your existence. Wheelers aren't ivory tower gospel preachers with out-of-date teachings, and we aren't mindwashed cult members either. Wheelers become Wheelers by choice. Eventually, at any rate. We've traveled the roads, hung out in the cities, shoveled shit in the country. We have no formal set of ideas, just the need to bring God to everyone. We just care about people, simple?

Sounds quite open, I say.

It is, she says.

No restrictions, I say.

Lena has expected the comment.

Course there're restrictions, pal. Nothing's worth anything you don't give up something, that's one of our mottoes.

What do you give up?

We give up unnecessary diversions. Drugs, liquor, sex.

Sex?

Yes. I suppose that upsets you, pal.

Well, it does sort of reduce my interest. I was just beginning to take a shine to you, Lena.

She glares at me for that. She's mad. I feel a surge of energy, cheered by her anger.

Don't even make a joke about it, pal, she says.

She continues with her lecture. It's obviously prepared stuff. At times she reminds me of every preacher I've ever known. What am I saying, known? The only preachers I ever seen are on independent TV stations. Well, she does remind me of them at least.

She says the Wheelers offer everything anyone could ever want—food, clothing, shelter. Even luxuries.

We have our own cable TV system, stations from all over brought in by a vast array of our own microwave antennas. Most movies and TV programs ever made in the world are available on our library of videocassettes. We even got a porno channel.

But you don't allow sex, I say.

That's right.

What's the good of a porno channel?

Don't know, pal, I never watch it. Forget porno, we got to talk about God.

Does He have a show on the porno channel?

She looks like she wants to hit me. Link is amused, he keeps nudging me. But I'm not really baiting Lena, I am genuinely confused.

All we ask, Lena says, is that you believe in God—in your own way, in whatever system, in whatever bizarre set of practices. Whatever God you want. The God of the Christians or the Hebrews. The God of the Mohammedans, or Allah, or whatever those guys call him. Even some god from ancient Greece or Rome. We have one group that specializes in Jupiter and Hera.

That's really mixing it up, Link says.

What? she says.

One Roman, one Greek, he says.

If you say so, pal.

She takes a deep breath.

Look, she says, apparently getting down to basics. We don't give a fuck what God you believe in.

I blink a lot. Is this a new approach, speaking to the potential convert in his own language? I am shocked.

We just want you to take God to your heart, she goes on. Actually, we aren't so much for God as we are against godlessness. It's godlessness that's pressed us toward sin, decadence, the sheer confusion of life today. Godlessness has taken the vitality out of humans. That's what godlessness is, in a way, lack of vitality. God equals vitality, you see? So all we ask of you guys is that you believe in God, simple?

Why don't you just start up a string of health clubs? I say and Link starts laughing uproariously.

All right, idiots, Lena says. Clowns. Forget that shit. Look, we're gonna keep trying till you capitulate. The wheels are always turning here. Nobody gets out of a Wheeler camp without God to let you through the checkpoint. You'll all come around. Everybody does.

You're gonna keep us here till we believe, I say.

Right. You don't have to believe right off. Just live with us, let us convince you.

Let me ask you one thing.

Shoot.

What if I said I believe in God even if deep down I don't?

She laughs.

You're working your way toward the advanced courses, pal. That question doesn't usually come up right off like that. Okay. You *say* whatever you want. We don't worry about what goes on inside your head. But, see, it ain't as easy as you think. I look at it this way. You're no longer *saying* you don't believe, see, and that's better than damning God with your disbelief. At least the words are there, see? You say you believe in God even if you don't. You make a public declaration. You become another convert whether you mean it or not. You're listed on God's traffic log as a believer and whatever you really believe, you've helped anyway. The larger our numbers are, the more new people we can convert. So, even with your lie, you've helped us anyway. So, see, it doesn't matter what you think, long as you say it.

Okay, so I'll say it.

Uneasily, Link moves his body away from mine.

Okay, so we'll give you the fast shuffle in courses and you'll have your assignment in a week.

Assignment?

Yes, you have to act on your belief.

I thought you said we could go.

True, but first you got to do something for the Wheelers.

You've abducted us. This is a shanghai!

That's right, pal. We don't mince words.

Oh, shit.

Well, you guys think about it. We don't push. We like having you around. Enjoy yourself.

She starts toward the door.

Wait! I call after her. What kind of assignments?

Oh, we have lots of work. In the fields, taking care of the settlements, soul-recruiting at rest stops, computer programming. All kinds of work. Something right up your guys' alley might be our train gang.

What? We get to rail-split for the Lord?

It's not that kind of train gang at all. You'd be surprised. Later.

We stew in silence for a while after she leaves us. Link mutters, this is worse than Anton and his homilies, we should've stayed at the Ramada. Victor says it doesn't sound so bad. Link says, what's good about it?

Looks like a nice shuck. I might like to take them for all I can get. At least a few good meals and some duds.

That tears it, Link says. That's just like you. Selling your soul for some new clothes.

It's only practical. You could use a new shirt yourself, Link. That one smells like last year's garbage.

Victor squirms out of Link's reach, although Link doesn't even make a grab for him. I play with the toy animals. There's a particularly fierce-looking transparent gorilla. Resembles Link a bit. I don't want to be here. I don't want to flack for God. I don't want new duds. But one trap's as good as another and I say:

I'm going along with them. I'll say it.

Say it now, Link says. Say it to me.

I believe in God, I say. He's wonderful. He leadeth my soul and all that crap. I'll put on a prom suit with a clerical collar and, whatever their rules, make a play for Lena. Or that lady back at the rest stop, Terry. Now there's a goal worth—

You're out of your mind.

All we got to do is say it.

I can't.

Why not?

You heard her. It's not just saying it. If you say it, they use it. If you say it, they use you. What do you think your assignment's going to be, handing out pamphlets at a rest stop, short-order cooking at their fast-food outlet? I don't want to be used. I don't want to say it. I been more than forty years putting up with shit, I don't want any for supper just now.

We go on arguing for a long time. Link is stubborn. Victor looks on blankly. He's already phrasing his testimony, more than likely. I don't want to say I believe unless Link says he believes.

I don't want to leave him here. I would be uncomfortable abandoning him after all this time. I tell him that.

Buddies, huh? he says. Male-bonding. Shit. Go, Lee, take the low road, don't even think of me.

I am about to list all my arguments for going along with the Wheelers, when I'm interrupted by a gentle voice from the doorway. Someone's come in and we didn't even hear him.

Lena tells me, he says, that you guys might need some help in coming to a decision. I thought I'd see what I could do.

I recognize the voice before I look. Even under the thick scraggly beard I'd've known that face.

It's Chuck.

He's here.

He's a Wheeler.

Shit.

Chuck is wearing a white and brown checker shirt, with a suede vest over it. He has spangles all along the pocket linings of his jeans. He's wearing brown high-heeled western boots with spangles in the shape of wheels on the side.

Hi, Link, he says, long time no see.

I realize suddenly that Link is staring at him with as much startled recognition as I am. Link knows Chuck!

I recognize you, too, Chuck says to me. Can't say as I recall the name or the circumstances.

I give him the name, but not the circumstances.

But we've never met, he says to Victor.

I like your duds, Victor says.

You're close enough to my size, Chuck says. Skinnier, but big enough. I'll have them cleaned and altered and sent over to you in the morning.

Victor's mouth drops open. For a moment I'm afraid his new set of teeth are going to drop out. Then he breaks into a compelling smile. If Victor had any doubts about converting before, he's a Wheeler now.

So am I, I realize.

3

I BELIEVE in God! I shout and the assembled Wheelers cheer.

Victor smiles smugly at me as I step down from the platform. He yelled his declaration even louder than I and obviously feels superior about it. He is wearing the outfit Chuck gave him. It suits him.

Lena, presiding over the ceremony, asks Link to come forward. He looks away from her steady austere gaze. He moves his left foot spastically but can't seem to take a step. There is a strong aura of tension developing around him. All the Wheelers who've dealt with him know there's a chance Link won't perform the ritual testimony at all, since he has never quite committed to it, not in any of the classes or work periods. He sat through the classes with the rest of us, but in a relative stupor. Although he passed all the written tests, he refused to participate in discussions or exercises. Chuck came to his quarters nightly and talked to him quietly.

Now Chuck walks to Link and takes him by the elbow to lead him to the platform. He helps him step up onto it. The crowd hushes. Even the sounds of the surrounding woods seem diminished in volume.

I believe in God, Link whispers.

Louder, Lena cries. We can't hear you, Link.

Link's second attempt is only a shade louder.

Still not enough, Link. We got to hear you, pal.

Two more tries do not satisfy Lena. The crowd is getting restless. With an easy loping step, Chuck gets onto the platform.

I'll say it with you, Link, he says.

That's an old ploy, Chuck, Link mutters.

It sure is, but it works. Come on now, fill your lungs with it, then let it out.

Link nods at Chuck and takes a deep breath.

I believe in God! the two shout out together and Link receives a tumultuous Wheeler cheer. As it subsides, Lena climbs to the platform and hugs Link tightly. I resent that. She didn't hug me when I shouted out my testimony and I did it in one shot. These goddamned religious folk always have a soft spot in their hearts for the reluctant convert.

A few days ago, when I asked Link how he came to know Chuck so well, he just shrugged off the question, said they'd been buddies for a time a while back. But it's more than buddies, I can tell. You don't shift your belief a hundred-eighty degrees for a mere buddy, not when you're as stubborn as Link. Ah, well, no matter. At least Chuck got Link to come around, and that's what counts. We're already assigned to Chuck's team.

Victor, however, is another matter. As usual. He scored so high on the soul-recruitment matrix of final exam questions that the Wheelers insist he go out on rest-stop duty. I suppose his new clean-cut appearance, whose construction was supervised by Wheeler personnel, influenced the manpower people in their decision. Looks to me like they're grooming him to be their poster-boy.

Come with *us*, I said to Victor, without really caring if he did or not. I just had the odd notion that our team shouldn't be split up. When I considered what we'd gone through together, I didn't really know why I felt that way.

I don't like trains, he said, and I'm damn sick of cars. I like what I'm going to do. It may even be my vocation.

You're turned into one of them, I said. You buy their shit.

I guess so. They said I can dress any way I want off-duty. They understand me.

Which is more than we ever did.

Any more than you ever did anyway.

I allowed his remark to stand. I could not protest too much. I was too relieved. A little regretful, too, oddly enough, but I could hack it.

• • •

After a few joyless celebration speeches, the meeting breaks up. Some Wheelers go to a central pavilion area to dance (no close-dancing permitted). Others go to the nightly meditation session or to fulfill duty-roster jobs. Link and Chuck drift off to resume their nightly chess game. I can't decide what to do. Giving my testimony has made me feel fraudulent. I wonder how God feels about it. Lena sees me standing alone and walks languidly toward me, smiling rather enchantingly.

You look restless, she says.

Suppose I am, I say.

Nervous about your assignment?

In a way. I can't figure it.

Oh? Why not?

Well, it's—I mean, I just can't fit Chuck and his gang of, well, outlaws into your whole operation. You seem to disapprove of violence.

We do.

Yet you allow him to conduct these raids.

It's what he wanted to do for us. We didn't argue. Anything that will eliminate cars from the road is, after all, a blow for the Lord, one of many jobs we do.

See, you even talk of it violently.

I don't know what you mean.

You said it was a blow.

Everybody serves in his own way.

But why get rid of cars?

You find them useful?

I like them, yeah.

You should talk to Chuck about it.

He doesn't talk to anybody about much of anything.

That's his way. I'm afraid I can't explain him, or what he does. The council approves of it, so I go along. At least Chuck gets wrecks off the road. You should get some rest. You've a long day ahead.

I suppose you're right.

Good night.

Night.

And don't worry, pal. Whatever you do, it's for the Wheelers now. You don't have to justify it to yourself.

I resist telling her that that is not a comforting thought. She walks away slowly. I can't help noting, as I always do when she's walking away from me, the appealingly rhythmic swing of her ass. I want her, and I wish she could forget her vows to the Wheelers for just one night.

So I'm a shade surprised when she comes to my bed that evening. With Link playing chess, I'm alone in the mobile home we share, feeling just on the verge of sleep. She slips into my quarters without my hearing her. All Wheeler doors are open to all Wheelers. I look up to see her standing over me beside the bed. Instead of her usual Wheeler uniform, the checker shirt and jeans, she's wearing a dark blue slip under a checkered flannel robe. From this angle she is an even more formidable figure than ever, looking taller, bustier, fuller-hipped. For a moment I'm sure this is one of my recurring dreams.

Lee, she says, move over.

Why?

I need to get in there beside you.

Whatever you say.

I shift to the opposite side of the narrow bed, pressing my bare back against the frigid Formica wall. She slips off the robe and lies beside me, quickly pulling a blanket over her body.

Lena, I thought—

Shut up. See, I can't sleep. Happens to me sometimes. I get this, this lump inside my chest, and it begins to hurt, and I can't breathe right. I need to get sleep. You can help.

What do you—

I need to be massaged. It calms me down, lets me sleep. But I can't do it myself. Guy who used to do it, disappeared last month. I couldn't think of anybody to come to, then I thought of you after we talked. You have, you have a bizarrely gentle side to you. Please.

Okay, but—

Give me your hand.

When I offer my left hand, she grabs my wrist with a vengeance.

Right here, she says.

She guides my hand to her chest, places it palm-down just below her neck.

Stroke slowly, in a line, she says. Like this.

She guides my hand down her breastbone, in between her two formidable tits. Her skin is a bit oily with sweat. There are beads of perspiration in the hollows of her shoulders.

Then down here, she says, guiding my hand in a perpendicular line across the area just beneath her left breast. The stroke ends with my hand lightly cupping the underside of the breast.

Keep doing it like that, she says. In a pattern. Your hands are soft. For a road type, soft, anyway.

My hand slowly retraces the path she's shown me, in the pattern she demands. Her sighing tells me I'm doing it satisfactorily. She loosens her grip on my wrist, lets one hand clutch the upper level of the blanket, which she pushes away from her upper torso.

Feels better already, she says as my hand comes to a brief rest at its starting point below her neck.

More. Again.

When I finish the route this time, I let my hand rest more firmly on her breast. My thumb flicks briefly upward, makes contact with an erect nipple. She doesn't say anything about this liberty.

I massage her for a long time. She starts out breathing heavily, but does calm down. Sometimes when I touch her breast she gasps faintly, but never comments on it.

I lean the lower part of my body against her thigh, sure that she'll feel the firmness of my erection there. She does. She almost jumps out of bed.

No! she says.

But it's clear you need—

You don't know my needs. You don't know shit about my needs. I need to sleep is what I need. Massage me but don't touch me anywhere else, pal.

But—

Please. I need to sleep. Please.

I continue the massage, a little less enthusiastically than before. I don't even let my hand rest on her breast any more. Gradually her breathing becomes even. Sleepily, she takes my hand away from her chest and leans in toward me, her head on my shoulder. Her breathing becomes heavy. She is asleep. My body is twisted out of shape and I have to slowly ease it into a more comfortable position. I am almost asleep myself when she puts her right leg over my thighs. Lena is a big woman and the first thing I think of is that she's going to cut off the circulation in my legs, my feet are going to go to sleep, become numb and require amputation. I try to move my legs out from under her leg. Her response to my movement is to slowly, gradually, achingly start working her leg upward, leaning her body into mine. I whisper her name to see if she's aware of what she's doing. Clearly she's still asleep. I feel trapped in a vise. When her leg crosses my crotch, she stops, begins pressing me there gently with her thigh. My erection begins to return but, trapped by the pressure of her leg and helped by my own intense concentration on it, it becomes more painful than pleasurable and, for my own survival as a sexual being, it quickly goes limp. Good fellow. She presses against me for a long time, while the erection keeps threatening to come back. I try to keep my mind on atrocities. Eventually her leg movement is joined by a rhythmic pressing of her crotch against the side of my right leg. Oh God, I can't stand it. God, I'll validate my testimony, I'll believe in you for real, I really will, just save me from this. Her body begins to tremble spasmodically. I think she is coming.

Suddenly she's awake. Drawing her leg away and lying on her back, she cries:

Where am I?

I won't tell you, Lena.

For a moment I thought I was—what am I doing here? Wait, wait, I remember.

Lena, I'll take you to the prom if that's what you want.

What? What are you talking about?

Never mind. Just a thought.

You're really peculiar, Lee. I feel better now, though. Thanks for the massage.

Any time.

Are you sure you don't want to stay in the settlement instead of going out with Chuck and his bunch?

Could we go steady?

Well, sort of. I mean, I get this pain often and I can't get rid of it easily. It's not a real illness, I know, some sort of anxiety maybe—

I'll tell you just what kind of anxiety, Lena.

She stares at me angrily. Her eyes have the same kind of zeal in them that they have when she talks about God.

I know what's on your mind, pal. Just forget it. All I'm asking—and normally I ask nobody for nothin'—is that you stay behind, help me in my work, help me when I got the pain. Nothing else. Never anything else.

I think I'll go.

You atheistic bastard!

Why, Lena, I took the oath, said I believed in God, did what you told me. How could you ever—

Shut up, pal. I got your number and you know it. Anyway, thanks for the massage. And for the tenderness. You really are tender. Tenderness is in short supply, even among the Wheelers.

Whyn't *you* come with *me*?

The anger leaves her. She smiles.

I'd like to, pal. I'd really like to. But I found my vocation. I like it here. And I'm good at teaching, at recruiting. Believe it or not, for every questionable type like you we get, we get two or three genuine converts. The Wheelers are going places soon, I want to be there for it. In the heart of it. I like it here. Maybe I'll see you again, pal, if you don't fall off the train during the trip.

She's out of bed and out of the mobile home before I even know for sure she's going. I only hear the gentle padding of her feet, and that doesn't last for long.

4

VICTOR comes to see us off in a form-fitting checker shirt, red and black, and crisp new blue jeans. He's had a fresh haircut and his face is so spotlessly clean it looks like he's scrubbed it down with sandstone. He's handsomer than ever and looks quite happy. I realize that in all the time we've traveled together he never looked really happy before. His laughter has always been sneering, his exuberance unexhilarating. Maybe there's something in all this Wheeler crap after all. I mean, I'll never believe it but, hell, these people are happy in their ridiculous shells. Their illusions. Dad used to talk about protective illusions. This may be what he meant. Ah, what did he know? He probably read about protective illusions off the back label of a bottle of cheap wine.

Share the word, Victor says to Link. Share the word, he says to me. And that's about all he says. No nostalgia, no sentimental parting, no good to've traveled with you guys. Just, share the word. I'm already hating the Wheeler slogans, and I haven't really been a Wheeler yet.

Lena comes around, too, just as we're forming the caravan of cars going to the train. She stops by the Mustang and peers in at me, without emotion. I think she's already forgotten last night. No matter. I leave her to heaven, as the saying goes. Let her cheerlead her way to the education of recruits, let her tremble without love through long nights. I don't care. Why should I care? Why *do* I care?

I wave at her. She nods, then walks away with her usual languid stride.

That lady is programmed, Link mutters.

No, I say, she isn't.

How would you know, can I ask?

She's very disturbed, Link.

I never noticed. She seems very much in control.

Well, she isn't.

You been reading some old psychology magazine or something?

Nope. I just feel some of her pain, that's all.

What a crock of bullshit.

Yeah, I guess so. When's this show gonna get on the road?

Be patient.

We finally get started. The Mustang's been positioned in the middle of the caravan, probably so we can't sneak off, and I feel confined. The car ahead gradually opens the distance between us, the car behind seems intent on crawling into our exhaust pipe. Although it's a sunny day, the air is still. All the gas fumes from the immense number of vehicles in the slow-moving caravan make me cough, and I have to roll up the window. Link rolls up his, too. The inside of the Mustang gets too hot. Link rolls his window down a crack. I roll mine down a crack. We get whiffs of the fumes, but we get used to them.

Chuck's not too fond of this car, Link says abruptly. He says it's gonna fall apart at the first bump. He wanted for us to take a different car. I told him I didn't think you'd go for that.

You're right.

I told him I didn't go for it either.

Thought you hated this car.

I do. But, hell, we gave up our fuckin' freedom for these bastards, we gave up our self-respect, we lied in front of a fuckin' god who I don't believe in but if he's there he knows it and I'm gonna hate being on his turf when it's my time—so, anyway, I didn't see any sense in giving up the fuckin' car.

Link is staring straight ahead. His eyes are shut.

I appreciate that, Link.

Keep it in your head. I don't want to hear it.

The Mustang makes one of its odd choking engine sounds. No matter how many mechs work on it, the car seems to retain its various little noises. Maybe it has to keep up a running commentary. In a way, its noises are comforting.

One thing, Lee, Link says. You're gonna have to be ready to lose this car. The kind of drill Chuck's gonna run, a car's gotta be in good shape, and the best shape this car can maintain doesn't amount to a hill of carbon. If you don't find a way to cut out, you're gonna have to be driving new wheels in a month.

I don't want to hear *that*.

I know you don't.

I can almost hear Cora saying, see, Lee, I always told you you'd fuck up, you'd lose. Every time I hear Cora in my mind, every time I think of her at all, I'm angry that we couldn't stay together. I wish she'd turn up now, drive up now, say she's been looking for me all over the west, and wants to clear up all our differences so the two of us can settle down in a little shack and work on our own version of the good life. She'd never show up. She'd never look for me. But it's a pleasant fantasy.

To get my mind off the subject, I ask Link:

What kind of drill's Chuck gonna run anyway?

You'll see. Mainly we're gonna destroy cars any way we can. Burn 'em mainly, push 'em off cliffs when we can't burn 'em, smash 'em with mallets and axes when we can't do anything else. All sorts of good clean fun, Lee.

How about creating sculptures? That sounds less destructive, more useful.

You want to make sculptures, you talk to the man about it. The way Chuck runs things, he's probably got a set of welding tools stashed away somewhere.

Yeah, probably. Chuck's like that.

Where'd you know him from?

Back east. He was always around, getting things done.

Yeah, same here. Except I knew him down south somewhere. But he was getting things done there. Last spring he—

Last spring? You knew him last spring?

Among other times, yeah.

But he was with us last spring.

Couldn't've been. He was turning an abandoned state police station into a home for kids whose folks liked joyriding better than parenting. Took up a lot of his time.

But he was—never mind. Chuck seems good at getting around.

Seems so, don't it?

•   •   •

Two thickly foliaged trees bending toward each other form a natural archway to the Wheelers' train station. Or, rather, an eyestraining blast of bright colors that gradually assemble themselves into the station. Looks like the Wheelers, bright young folks that they are, have painted everything in sight. Particularly the damn stationhouse. Bright orange, windows in green. Maybe what they really want to do is transform the world into one vast fast-food franchise. The fence around the adjacent parking lot is painted in a single color located somewhere between yellow and green on the spectrum. Each track along the railroad bed is a different garish color. It all looks so happy I want to slit my throat. Just like these people, paint and bright colors. Saying you believe, pretending you're not sexual, arranging mobile homes as spokes, painting the railroad tracks. Surfaces.

Following the instructions of our briefing, we drivers line our cars up along the side of the tracks. Waiting for the train. With all the colors surrounding us, it's something like waiting for the showboat. The Mustang winds up between a Camaro and a Mazda. The drivers and passengers in each flanking car smile over at us pleasantly, the dazzle of their Wheeler smiles competing with the outlandish spread of color. For once, the smiles lose out.

Link hums to himself. Some song from the dark ages, early rock and roll. I try to make conversation, but he's in a mood, tied up in himself, doesn't want to talk. Both of us keep glancing nervously at the tracks, watching for the train.

The sun comes out and makes it impossible to concentrate on the tracks. All the bright colors send rays of pain across my eyes. I shut my eyes for a while. When I open them again, after the sun goes behind a cloud, the colors dim. I can see streaks of dirt now along the station walls, piles of dogshit along the painted tracks.

Finally the train comes. Around a curve in historical train fashion. I'm glad to see it's not painted any bright colors. Black engine, dark and dirty. Comforting.

The engine passes us. Link stops humming, leans forward, squints for a good look. Behind the engine are a couple of passenger cars and a dining car, then what looks like an endless string of freight cars. The train stops. We are right in front of a brown wooden car's sliding door. The engineer toots his horn one blast, the signal for drivers to start their motors. All along the line we comply, engines growl to life. I look to my left and right. The lineup of cars is impressive. It looks like the longest thinnest used car lot in history, Guinness record-book stuff. The engineer blows two short blasts. All along the train the sliding doors open and ramps slide out. We're assigned the number one spot for our four-car squad, so I barrel up the ramp at the next signal, the three other cars in our group following close behind.

The inside of the freight car is dark and damp, smelling faintly of the country. Barnsmells, old hay and older cows. After I back the Mustang into its assigned space, come to a stop, shut off the motor, and watch the other cars ease into their spaces, I become quite nauseated as the exhaust fume odor mixes with the barnsmells. The engineer gives a few more toots, I've lost count now, and after a long pause the train lurches suddenly forward and we're off on what Chuck so fondly calls The Outlaw Trail.

There's a rare smile on Link's face. He likes all this. I ask him why.

Thrills and chills, real-life adventure, I guess, he says.

Then why do I feel like throwing up?

A few minutes later somebody brings around food. Prepared in the dining car, it's laid out on trays. Looks something like airplane food. Tastes worse. Tastes like the way this freight car smells. I think I'll try to go to sleep.

Sitting in the passenger car, trying to ignore Link's and Chuck's eager chatter, I try to discern details of the night landscape that we're trudging through so slowly. We're going gradually uphill, across mountains. I can't make out much behind the bright reflections of the interior of the brightly lit passenger car. Some of it's trees, some of it's rocks, sometimes I see lighted windows in isolated buildings, houses, shacks. A few minutes ago we went through a dark village, apparently abandoned. I saw it in the light of tramps' fires. I shut my tired eyes, imagine our train climbing the mountainside, a little toy train with magically lighted tiny square windows traveling along fragile plastic tracks, the kind you have to force together by inserting the thin metal prongs of one into the slots of the next with the use of brute force and profanity.

A tap on my shoulder. I open my eyes, see a plastic cup of beer being offered by Chuck. I take it, even though beer is the last thing I want at this moment. I raise it to my lips, lick off a dab of foam. Chuck smiles approvingly, returns his attention to Link. I set the cup down on a table, intending not to drink any more. The cup slides along the table, almost tips over. I retrieve it before it slips over the edge. I'll either have to hold it or drink it. My stomach says hold, but I start sipping anyway. Oddly enough, it begins to make me feel better. Helps me to tune in on the conversation.

That school we built in Carolina, Link is saying, is that still going on?

Last I heard, Chuck replies. I'm told, can't say for sure, but I'm told they got so many kids now they built on another wing and're thinkin' about petitioning the state for accreditation.

Accreditation. I don't go for that. I don't go for that at all. Thought we built the school in the first place to provide an alternative.

That's so, but times change, Link. People who run the school, they figure they've made their point, now it's time to carry their ideas and methods further.

What do you say about it?

I got out, that's what I said.

Don't it gall you just a bit?

A bit. But there's lots to do. I don't have time for reflection. Why'd you get out?

Heat.

The law?

You got it.

Well, I don't ask questions, you know that.

I appreciate it.

I ask questions, I say.

I know you do, Lee, Link says. Now's not the time.

Even though he speaks calmly, I recognize the menace in his voice, so I shrug and take another sip of beer. It tastes good, but the calm in my stomach is offset by the onset of cramps in my intestines. Hell. I'm gonna have diarrhea, I know it. The god-damned food. I try to concentrate, will the cramps away.

I miss that school, Chuck, Link says.

I know you do.

I'd like to get back into a classroom, get a few kids under my wing. I liked teaching there. It was the one time in my life I felt I was really accomplishing something.

You were very popular. They miss you.

I imagine they miss you too.

Could be. But I had to get out.

I want to ask Chuck about his wandering ways, about how he

could manage to be leading supermarket raids with us while he was apparently down in Carolina working with schools and half-way houses. How Emil could have seen him a few days ago back east when it's clear he's been with the Wheelers for a while. How he can stand to be with the Wheelers at all. But I can't ask questions right now. The cramps have taken over. Excusing myself as coolly as possible, I stumble my way toward the claustrophobic bathrooms at the rear of the car. They all have their occupied signs slid into place. Damn. I feel myself turning green as I stand in the narrow corridor between the bathrooms. I try to think of butterflies but can't stop thinking of cramps. Finally one of the signs switches from occupied to vacant and one of my fellow outlaws emerges from the bathroom, looking as green as I feel. I grab the door handle just as he releases it. We exchange knowing looks, fellow victims of the food plague, and then I enter the welcome darkness of the closetlike bathroom.

5

THREE days on the Outlaw Trail and all mountains look alike to
me. We chug through pass after pass, slip through pitch-dark
tunnels, listen to the raspy grating sounds of tree branches brushing against the side of our freight car. Stones from the roadbed
pelt our underside. I try to listen rhythmically, create tunes out of
the many noises, but I can't. They are too uneven, discordant.
Too nerve-wracking. I am about to go crazy. Maybe I went crazy
yesterday and *this* is crazy.

Link's edgy too. He's eager to get at it, do it. I used to think
he was unemotional. But, seems the closer he gets to crime, to
participating in it, the more animated and excited he becomes.

He's been talkative lately. I think I'll try to draw him out.

Link?

Yeah?

The other day, when you were talking with Chuck—

Well, what?

You mentioned being in trouble with the law.

I been in trouble with the law all over the lot. What particular
grief you talking about?

I was *thinking* of you and Chuck in Carolina, but any particular crime that comes into your mind is all right with—

You're a leech, you know that?

That fair?

Fair enough. You want to draw shit out of me, needle the crap right out of my veins, take pieces of my life, right?

No, not at all. I'm just—

You're just nosy. That's worse. Well, ain't everybody nosy when you come right down to it? You're no better'n anybody else, Lee, that's what gets you down, right? You're no better than anybody else. But remember this: you're no worse than anybody else either.

Link has said this to me many times but I don't feel bad about it. It's about as close to a compliment as he ever gets. He goes silent on me now. I'm afraid to introduce the topic again. I get very cautious when his drawbridge is up.

You're entitled, he says suddenly.

What?

I'll tell you about Carolina. I wish I had a good unconventional story for you, but my criminal life is so conventional they couldn't make a B-movie out of it. Goes something like this: Three counts of armed robbery, coulda been more if they'd been any good at investigating. Actually, one of the counts I had nothing to do with.

Why robbery?

Why not robbery? There's always a good reason for robbery. You're greedy. You need money. You're hungry. You're angry at a society that elevates the worship of money to monumental levels, angry at corporations whose sense of public service is to pay for British programs on TV.

Which were you? Greedy, money-grubbing, revolutionary?

Practical. The school needed money, the school that Chuck and I ran. Well, hunger, too. The kids we hid out were starving. But to get back to the crime record: I think four counts of aggravated assault, one of attempted murder or manslaughter, the DA hadn't decided which.

Wait. What about the murder?

Or manslaughter.

Okay, or manslaughter.

Well, we coulda plea-bargained out of that one, I guess. But it came about because I went at the arresting officer with a knife. Wounded him good. A couple inches more and it woulda been goodbye fuzzballs. Murder one.

Or manslaughter.

Not likely. Do it to a cop and it's always murder.

Really?

I think of myself and Sergeant Allen. What if they ever found out? Murder one. They'd never believe I didn't mean it, that it was an accident. I wouldn't even believe it. I don't like thinking like this.

Well, I say, there are usually mitigating circumstances . . .

Are there? Maybe. Maybe in your life. But I think that's dangerous thinking. Hey, it was only self-defense. He was coming to shoot me, your honor. We're just poor Robin Hoods, stealing from the rich to give to the poor, and the poor is us.

Well, Link, there *is* something to that.

Yeah, something. A shitload of something. They're out to get us, so we're justified in getting them first. Wonderful paranoia, so comfortable and comforting. They did this to us, it's their fault, it's all because of them. Pronouns to hide our own failures, maybe. I don't know.

Link's voice has become gentler, lost some of its customary gruffness. He sounds almost professorial, genuinely like a man who had once headed a school.

Don't get me wrong. *They* do exist, I think. But not as a paranoiac conspiracy. They are just sets of values, clay pots of attitudes, disorganized but potent beliefs—all just bars of a prison we design for ourselves. *We* fail, *they* just make it easy for us. Easier for us, anyway.

As he talks, I see myself in a way I'd rather not. I rationalize my killings, I know that, think of them as accident and self-defense. They didn't deserve to die, Allen and that ugly biker. By seeing both of them as types, as characters who happened to play cameos in my life, I had taken away their humanity, seen them as lifeless hulks when they were around me, not much different than they were when I got through with them. An authority figure and a creep. Yet they weren't such easy stereotypes, I'm sure. It just protects me to think of them that way. Well, should I think like Link? Be realistic, rip away the illusions? I wonder for a moment what it'd be like to be like him, get inside his skin and feel what he feels. I doubt I'd like it. But I might understand what kicks he gets out of outlaw—no, criminal—acts. Jesus, I got to stop thinking about things like this. Next minute I'll be pondering the nature of evil.

It's the next minute and I'm pondering the nature of evil. The nature of my evil. And our evil, Link's and mine. If Link is right, we're criminals, the type (see, I even think of *myself* as a type) who'd be the bad guys in a children's game. I've seen those old westerns. All the bad guys have either thick moustaches, gaunt mean looks, or are stocky lugs about to go to fat. None of us looks like a bad guy. Not Link or me, not Chuck, not his band, not even Victor. We're frightening in the way we don't look like bad guys. Maybe Link is right when he says there is no real system out to get us. Whatever, we could've scrabbled around in the cities like anybody else, found a rathole to live in or maybe even done better, maybe even wound up with a car owned legally. But we went outside all that, kidded ourselves into thinking we were escaping all that. Just like outlaws. Just like criminals. No, not just like outlaws and criminals, we are outlaws, we are criminals, we are killers or potential killers, we are evil. We're not Hitler, but we're using his ballpark. Any time what you do touches another person, as we intrude on the lives of others, you have to be responsible for what you do. We don't make lampshades out of human skin, but we do affect lives. We are evil. No big deal, I just never thought of us that way before. Or myself that way.

Hey, Link says, we got off the subject of my criminal record.

It's okay, I can get along without any more.

But—

I've had enough, Link, all right? Just can it.

Link laughs.

You know, he says, you're getting a real tough edge, Lee. A real tough edge.

Tell me about it.

Maybe you're right, man, Link mutters. I pretty much told you everything anyway. You just missed the accounts of my two attempted jailbreaks, not to mention the later one that did work.

But I'd like to know about—

The train lurches to a sudden stop.

What's going on? I say.

Link smiles broadly.

I think we're going on the attack, Lee, he says.

I stare blankly at him.

It's a raid, Lee, a raid.

He says it like he expects me to respond by leading our army in a battle cry.

6

CHUCK sends Link and me on ahead for reconnaissance. He says it's not because of our inherent scouting talents but because the Mustang's the only car in the whole bunch that won't draw any suspicion. Our target's a group of nomads who're camping in a clearing a few miles away from any normal good roads.

It's suppertime and the people in the nomad camp are gathered around fires and Coleman stoves and cute little hibachis, cooking and baking and frying and barbecuing. Each of the appealingly domestic gatherings seems to have a number of children in it. The men are usually dressed in denim outfits, some with jackets, some with patched-up shirts. The women are in sturdy dresses, thick cloth and plain patterns. You wouldn't write home about most of these women, but they appear to be reliable, the kind who might, in better times, run health food stores or free libraries. In their often-repaired, sometimes frayed clothing, they look better dressed than the Wheelers. Several people are smoking and, judging from the odors drifting up to our hillside hideaway, some of it's good stuff. Chuck's gang goes for harsher junk, and I long for a hit of the mildness of the smokes these people are using. I think I'd trade my berth in Chuck's gang for a couple nights with these folk.

Link whispers into the walkie-talkie that Chuck assigned to us.

Everything's ripe, he says. Ready for picking.

Harvest is the general code metaphor for this kind of operation. Chuck's not particularly original when it comes to the practical use of language. Link signs off, after receiving a soft crackling response so muddled I can't make out a word.

They'll be here any moment, Link says, we're not to make a move until the rest start the attack.

Why don't we just stay up here and watch the whole operation? I suggest.

Link doesn't answer. He needs this raid so bad he can taste it. He doesn't like riding shotgun in the Mustang, so he wants to come out of this raid with one of the nomad tribe's cars. Chuck wants Link to be a driver, too. He told Link if he doesn't come back with a liberated automobile to use he'll be reassigned to a rest stop to hand out leaflets. Link doesn't want that. I mean, dispensing paper is no job for a true outlaw. I wouldn't mind an armful of Find God Now Or Else Damn It pamphlets. I'd give them out to the people below. Who obviously don't need them. But of course that's what religion is all about.

I sense the rest of the gang assembling even though I can't see them. If I got out of our own idling car and put my ear to the ground, maybe I could hear their engines idling all around us.

The raid starts suddenly, before I'm ready for it. Trees seem to part and cars emerge from between them like animals leaping into the small valley.

Step on it, Link shouts nervously. I slam down on the accelerator mightily and the Mustang plunges forward, down a more or less safe and unobstructed path that I've already chosen. We maneuver downwards in a zigzag pattern, narrowly avoiding large rocks and threatening tree trunks, looking like a pinball in search of a flipper lever.

We arrive at the raid a little late. The raiding party cars are already in the flat of the valley. Our victims are running all about. Their first concern, it seems, is protecting their families, making sure the children are hurried into the forest, although a few people, brandishing knives and axes, are attempting futile stands against our onslaught.

Link has this shiny well-maintained Toyota Corolla in his sights.

That one, he says, I want that one.

But that's foreign. You don't—

Shut up!

I rush at two men who are retreating more slowly than the rest, hoping and praying they'll get out of my way. Link waves his rifle threateningly at them. Chuck had wanted me to ride shotgun, but I refused outright. I told him I wouldn't touch a gun and he almost liked me for saying it. The two men jump aside. One seems to be reaching into his shirt for something. It's a gun, I know it, they've got guns and they're going to be shooting any second now. And damn it I'm right. Almost as soon as I think it, there are shots on the other side of the clearing. I swerve out of their way fast.

We come alongside the Toyota Corolla. Link leaps out of the Mustang and climbs in the Toyota with one smooth motion. He drops out of sight for a moment. We've all been given the course in hotwiring and Link proved to be one of the most adept at it. He remarked to Chuck that he'd had a bit of practice in his shady past. The Toyota Corolla's engine roars to life.

In spite of the gunfire, everything seems to be going smoothly. Nobody seems hit, none of our cars are down. I'll shepherd the Toyota Corolla out of the valley and our part of the raid'll be over. I feel strong, on top of things, ready to win again and again and again. Every time I feel like that something seems to go wrong. I should learn.

Link leans halfway out the Toyota's window and waves his arm at me in a circular motion, the signal that we better hit the road. I signal back and the Toyota Corolla lunges forward. And stalls. Glancing at me, Link smiles a half-smile through his half-beard. He leans down for a second and gets the car running again. My foot starts putting pressure on my accelerator. I'm anxious to get away from here. When Link rises again, he signals a second time.

I see the man coming around the Toyota before Link does. He's a short, squat, ugly man. Though beardless, he could pass as a relation of Link's—a younger brother, a close cousin. Before I can warn Link, the man grabs his signalling arm and starts to pull hard on it. The surprise of the ambush plus the attacker's strength makes Link's body straighten and his foot comes down on the Toyota's accelerator. It jerks forward, stalls again. The attacker skips along beside the car, keeping his footing with the same kind of determination he's using to maintain his hold on Link's arm. There's intense pain on Link's face. His arm may have been wrenched back unnaturally. Maybe it's broken.

Around me I can sense the meadow clearing of cars. Chuck

said the entire raid should last less than a minute. The short squat man reaches a hand in the Toyota and grabs Link by the collar. In spite of Link's holding onto the steering wheel with his free hand, the man gets Link partway out of the window. In a minute all our guys'll be gone and the nomad tribe'll come out of the woods ready for blood. I got to do something. Chuck said we should protect our partners but not be afraid to clear out if something goes wrong. I can leave Link behind. It's all right. Nobody'll blame me. Maybe. So I can go. No, I can't. I can't leave Link. Damn it. I got to help.

The man's attack is stalled. Link's grip has slipped off the steering wheel, but his thick body is lodged halfway through the window. The man keeps pulling fiercely. He releases his hand from Link's collar and jabs him about the head. Link, his eyes dazed, looks like he's going to pass out any minute.

Scrambling out of the Mustang and almost flying across the short distance to the Toyota, I leap at the man, grab his hair and pull at it hard. His head jerks back. My move loosens his hold on Link's arm just enough for Link to revive, pull out of the man's grasp, and twist his body back inside the Toyota. In the meantime, I've figured there's no way I can take the ambusher in a fair fight, so I manage a quick hard kick to his crotch and retreat without looking back.

I climb into the Mustang, fully expecting somebody's going to grab me from behind. Nobody does. Link has already got his Toyota in motion, this time with no stalling, and I follow him out of the valley and up the hill.

7

AFTER we've put a few miles between us and the clearing I begin to relax. The sting goes out of my shoulders, the pain out of my upper thighs. I feel all right. Now I'm a confirmed outlaw. The big time. Part of an outlaw gang. Loyal to my partner. Fighting when trouble appears. Fighting dirty. The real thing.

I feel all right, yes sir, all right.

But only for a moment.

This has got to be the sleaziest car I seen in my entire life, says a voice that's like a nasal jackhammer. A voice directly behind me.

I look in the rear-view. Sitting in the middle of the back seat, like a pint-sized tycoon, is a kid with the largest set of ears I've ever seen.

My *entire* life, the kid says.

I am too stunned to reply. I stop the car and turn around in my seat.

He's a skinny kid, the kind whose ribs show through several layers of clothing. He's got just enough hair so you can't call him bald. His eyes seem to look at me and somewhere else at the same time. He's got just enough nose so you can't call him a genetic mistake. His mouth is a genetic mistake, all disapproval and no shape.

Sometimes you see a kid and you get all tender. Not this one.

This one I want immediately to throw out of my car fingers first without opening any windows. I'm no good at guessing age, but I'd say this particular mutation checked in at around eleven or twelve.

Where'd *you* come from? I ask.

Up ahead Link's Toyota has stopped, and he gives me a horn-blast. Not knowing just how to communicate with a car horn, I just give him a single blast back. That seems to satisfy him.

We snuck in while you were busting Cap'n Chickenwings, the kid says.

Did you say *we*? I ask, panicking.

Yeah. Me and Scotty there, we climbed in this jalopy while you were out.

Scotty?

Yeah. There.

He points to the floor between the seats. I lean over the back of the front seat and see Scotty lying there, looking up at me.

Scotty isn't just another kid, he's a *little* kid. He's very blond and cute, a cereal commercial kind of kid. Except he's got marks all over his face. And his hands. And his clothes. In one hand he holds a black magic marker. In a shirt pocket (with large leak spots underneath) is a red magic marker. As I look down at him, he smiles tentatively. He's got an upper front tooth missing. After his brief smile he rubs his nose. With the hand holding the black magic marker. He leaves a new spot, a line of black war paint, across the bridge of his nose.

What're you kids doing here? I say, trying not to scream at them.

Handles, the kid on the seat says.

Handles? I say.

That's my name, he says. What they call me anyway. You think it's a good name, right, with these big ears on me and all.

Well, no, I wasn't exactly thinking that, I was just surprised at—

I have to tell everybody right away. So they know it's all right. I *like* the name. I *like* being called Handles. It's good for me.

Oh. Really?

My real name's Hamlet. After the prince. The melancholy one. My parents thought it was cute. To be or not to be. Shit. Rather be Handles than Hamlet any day. Wouldn't you? Well, wouldn't you?

I don't know. I'm glad I don't have the problem, I'll say that.

Another horn-tap from Link. I realize I'm sitting here chatting with this prepubescent mutation instead of getting on with our job.

Are you guys going to get out or what? I say.

Nope, Handles says.

Hey wait! I say. I've got to get hopping here. My—my partners are waiting for me. I can't ferry you guys around.

We're not asking for chauffeur service, Handles says. This is serious. We want out of that camp, so we're glad you came along. I wouldn't go back there if you paid me. What about you, Scotty?

What? Scotty says.

I said we don't want to go back to the camp. Right, Scotty?

Right.

He doesn't always listen, Handles says to me. He's always saying what, making everybody repeat all the time. So—drive on, we'll go wherever you go. Anything's better'n back there.

Hey, I can't take you guys with me.

Why not?

It's kidnapping. Abduction of minors. I don't know, some law covers it, I'm sure.

You ain't abducting anybody. We want to go. We're stow-aways. We're cooperating. We're joining up with you. See? You're not abducting us.

I can't take you back with me. You'll just get me into trouble.

Trouble, Handles says sarcastically. Jeez, I thought you'd be tougher than that. Some big outlaw! Afraid for his ass. Scotty, maybe we *should* get out of here.

What? Scotty says.

Never mind.

But what?

I said forget it.

I want to know. What?

You're a pain, you know, Scotty? I was just thinking of crashing out of this car.

Okay.

Scotty springs up, ready to get going. I look around. It's really dark along this stretch. All around us are trees and shadows and mysterious nightmarish patches.

You think you guys'll make it back all right? I mean, you can just follow the road.

We're not going back there, Handles says. We're not. Right, Scotty?

What?

I said we're not going back to camp.

I guess so. Do we have to?

Do we have to what?

We have to stay out here? I'm hungry.

You said you'd go out of camp with me.

I know that. I changed my mind.

Well, I'm not going back. You can find your own way back.

Let's go back, Handles.

No.

Scotty starts to cry. Handles sighs and reaches for the door handle. Link blasts on his horn.

Wait, wait, I say to the kids. Okay, you can come with me. Tonight. But tomorrow, you got to work out something else. If he wants, I'll take Scotty back to your camp on my own and you can do whatever in hell you want to.

Handles looks a little frightened. Maybe he's been bluffing all along. But he nods in agreement. He tells Scotty they're staying with me, Scotty says what, and he tells him again.

I signal with my horn to Link and we start up again.

Hey mister, Handles says.

Yeah? I say.

What's your name?

Lee.

Hey, Lee.

Yeah?

You really mean what you said?

About what?

About taking Scotty back to our camp.

Yeah, I meant it.

He laughs. Meanly.

Boy, I'd like to be there for that. I would. I sure as shitshootin' would.

Why?

I'd like to see your face after Cap'n Chickenwings decides to walk all over it.

Cap'n Chickenwings?

He's tough, man. Just you wait.

We hit the open road and start to speed up. In the distance I can see the gang's motorcade. Silently, I point them out for

Handles and Scotty. Scotty leans over the front seat to see better. He has been wiping his teary eyes with his magic marker hand. His eyes are circled with smudges of black ink. There now seems to be more spots on his face than skin showing. Even this dirty, he's pretty cute.

8

OUR rendezvous is at an abandoned recreation center. Link and I are the last ones to arrive, naturally. The gang is assembling in an open playing field adjoining endless rows of tennis courts. Soon as I stop the Mustang, Handles mutters I'll check with you guys later, stay close to Lee, Scotty. Before I can protest, Handles is out of the car and running. He has a curious way of running. Unsure but determined, none of his limbs working quite efficiently but with a kind of grace. He rushes up to Link and starts talking with him. Link shrugs, then Handles runs off. He runs first this way, then that, stopping only to talk briefly with members of the gang, all of whom seem bewildered by the kid's sudden appearance in their midst.

Let's go, Scotty, I say. I got to find out what kind of drill Chuck's running.

Outside the car, Scotty reaches up and takes my hand. The move seems automatic with him.

You still hungry? I say to him.

What? he says.

Come on, I'm going to get us some food, kid.

He nods. Obviously no big deal. He *expects* to be fed.

As we approach Link, he points a stubby finger at Scotty.

Another one? he says.

I explain about Handles and Scotty. Link seems amused, not at all troubled.

What'll Chuck say? I ask Link.

He won't mind. He loves kids. But we have to return them, Lee.

I know. I'm willing to drive Scotty back, but Handles refuses to go. I think he wants to join up with the gang.

Don't worry. Chuck won't allow it. He'll figure out what to do with him, wait and see.

Handles reappears, climbing onto the hood of one of the stolen cars, a Honda. Using what looks like four arms, he scrabbles over the windshield onto the car roof. Without a single cautious move, he stands up and raises his arms (there *are* only two) in the air. Some of the gang see him, point, laugh, then start a foolish mock dance around the Honda. Handles loves it.

One of Chuck's aides-de-camp informs us that we're to join an assembly on foot at the football field near the tennis courts. I take Scotty's right hand, and Link takes his left. I look down and, just my luck, I've gotten the hand with the magic marker. A thick black line divides my thumb from the rest of my hand.

At the assembly Chuck orders the drivers of the stolen vehicles to drive them to the outdoor swimming pool on the other side of the main building. The rest of us are to walk there. While Chuck speaks, Handles climbs around the bleachers. Sometimes he runs along the seats, sometimes he ducks under them and presumably plays Tarzan, swinging among the supports, sometimes he climbs onto the bleacher's iron railings and slides down a few feet. Every once in a while he stops and does a few hops, skips, jumps—again graceful in his awkward way. I think of Gene Kelly in the rain and umbrella dance in *Singin' in the Rain*, another of the many antique movies old Dad forced me to sit through more than once, and I can easily see Handles moving and dancing like that if he ever gets his muscles to respond in logically human fashion.

After the meeting Link and I take Scotty up to Chuck, and Link tells him about our stowaways. Chuck smiles down at Scotty while he listens to Link.

Okay, he says when Link's finished. I don't think with us is the best place for them, even though who knows what kind of life they're running away from. Lee, up to you. Somebody's gotta take 'em back, like you say, might as well be you. Okay?

Sure.

He stares at me, then says, I trust you to come back, right?

Right.

Time for the burning now. It's the part of all this I most look forward to. Let's go. Ah, Link . . .

Yeah, Chuck?

About that Toyota. It's no go on the Toyota.

Link looks downcast.

I know. It drove like shit all the way back.

But I might have something else for you. Check with me after the ceremony. So, for now, you know what to do with the Toyota.

Yeah.

Link gently disengages Scotty's hand and says to the kid that he's got to take care of something but don't worry he'll be back soon. Scotty seems regretful to see him go but walks patiently with me toward the swimming pool. On the way we stop by a campfire where a bunch of the guys are roasting hot dogs. I grab two for Scotty and me and deal for a couple bootleg Cokes. Before taking the food, Scotty makes an elaborate ritual out of capping the black magic marker and putting it in his shirt pocket beside the red one. Dots of mustard join the spots of ink on Scotty's face as he, with great seriousness, consumes his hot dog. We are passed by many of the stolen cars on their way to the swimming pool. I feel like we're at the center of some kind of sloppy, dirty, rusty parade. As soon as he finishes his Coke and hot dog, Scotty grabs my free hand again.

The swimming pool area is in the kind of organized chaos that seems to be Chuck's specialty. The pool itself looks like a chasm. It's empty of water and there are cracks running along the surface of its bottom and sides. You can hardly read the depth numbers. Chuck stands on the high diving board, his concentration intent on the array of cars coming to a stop on three sides of the pool. The autoless side is a set of bleachers where those not involved in the ceremony are expected to sit. Picking Scotty up (he seems quite heavy for his size, maybe he's an adult that's gone through a compactor), I make my way up to the top row. It's already almost filled, but a couple of the guys, smiling at Scotty, push and shove sideways to make room for us. I hold Scotty on my lap, hoping the ceremony is over before his mysteriously concentrated weight puts my legs to eternal sleep.

The last of the stolen cars is driven up. The driver shuts off its motor, swtiches off its headlights. I think it may be Link in the Toyota Corolla but it's too dark for me to be sure. At the moment the only light comes from a pair of spotlights which are directed toward Chuck on the high board. He looks ghostlike, I think spectral is the word, even his clothes seem washed of color. He raises a hand toward the bleachers and receives almost instant quiet. He glances around at the cars massed below him, to his left, and in front of him at the other side of the pool. For a moment I'm afraid he's going to bless them. I've never been able to fit him into the whole Wheeler shithouse anyway. Instead, he makes a circular gesture with his left arm. All around the pool, car headlights switch on simultaneously, blindingly. Most of the crowd in the bleachers instinctively raise their hands to their faces, shield their eyes. In a moment, though, I can see better, my vision only slightly distracted by a Dodge Omni's skewered headlight that seems pointed right at me.

Another signal from Chuck and some of the gang gather around an old Pontiac at the right end of the line directly across from the bleachers. One of them opens the driver side door, reaches in, and releases the handbrake. With a choruslike grunt, the group starts pushing the car toward the pool. They work slowly and the car eases forward. The front wheels clear the edge of the pool and, for the pushers, the job becomes momentarily difficult. The Pontiac seems to hang on the rim of the pool, stuck. An extra effort from the group forces it forward with a half-squeaking, half-scraping noise. It teeters for a moment, then slowly slides into the pool, striking the cracked bottom with a diffident gentleness and tipping over onto its roof. It rocks for a moment, then comes still. I can't tell if it has caused any new cracks on the bottom surface of the pool. The cracks that are there seem to correspond to the state of the wreck.

Down the line the group goes, pushing then tipping each car in the first row of plundered vehicles into the deep Olympic-length pool. The crowd cheers and applauds as each car hits bottom. After the first row has been pushed in, cars lie around the bottom and sides of the pool. Some are on their sides, some on their roofs, some flat on their wheels, some nose first like crashed warplanes. Wheels spin, bits of glass break off. The noise of the cracking metal sounds something like traveling electricity.

Another line of cars is arranged by poolside and the gang starts to work on them. These vehicles crash onto the tops of the cars that dived in first, landing with a series of crashing, crunching, shattering sounds that delight the audience who cheer, yelp wildly, applaud, and call out funny and obscene slogans. Some of the crowd spirit gets to me. I am awestruck. A small fire starts in a blue Chevy but is quickly put out by a standby fire brigade. Nobody wants the fire to start accidentally. Chuck was insistent on that at the briefing.

As the pile in the pool grows, Chuck stands tall on the high board. Once in a while, the excitement affects him and the board vibrates, but only slightly. Scotty is gradually heavier in my lap. Once in a while his head droops, but he pulls himself awake with a start. He is fiercely trying not to fall asleep before the ceremony is over.

A figure gets off the ladder onto the low diving board. At first his face is in shadow, then he steps into the light. It's Handles. Of course. He's working his way out the low board, the little bastard. First he takes tentative steps, testing. Then, more sure of himself, he starts lunging forward, his legs looking like they're resisting the upward tension of the board. Some of the crowd have seen him, and they begin to call out warnings. Chuck looks down, peering over the edge of the high board. He shouts something at Handles. Handles pretends he doesn't hear. Listening does not fit in with his current strategy. Grinning like the town fool or the underqualified court jester, he takes a short run as if he wants to dive off the board but stops way before the edge. However, the board vibrates up and down, and he loses his footing. He falls forward, just in time for the board to give him a good whack in the face. Stunned, he starts to roll sideways. A few people in the crowd gasp. Handles teeters at the edge of the board, just as the dumped cars had on the rim of the pool. Beneath him is the jagged open top of a VW. Swinging a leg backward, he pulls back from the edge. A gang member, who has climbed the ladder, works his way onto the board, grabs Handles' arm, and yanks him to his feet and toward the ladder. The rescue draws applause, which Handles thinks is for him. He manages a small bow, even while the rescuer is forcing him onto the ladder. As he descends out of sight, I realize I've been holding my breath, and I exhale with what sounds to me like an asthmatic attack.

The last cars are driven up to poolside. I see the Toyota Corolla. Link wearily gets out of it. When they push the Toyota over the side, he just stands there, still. Staring at the Toyota settling onto the pile, at the pushers, at the wreckage which has pretty much filled the entire pool. He seems puzzled.

Now Chuck raises both his arms, and a murmur goes through the audience. It's time for the burning. In a very orderly way, row by row, we file out of the bleachers. We have to get a safe distance away from the pool. Scotty is a dead weight in my arms. His head is draped over my left arm, his eyes shut, his mouth wide open. With each breath he makes a faint gurgling noise at the back of his throat. I wonder if that's normal sleep static for him, or is he coming down with something? God, that'd be just what I need now, a sick kid to attend to. I don't know what to do with sick kids. Well, no point worrying. All the smartass people around here, I can at least get help.

The crowd assembles behind an already roped-off point. I sense bloodlust in some of the people around me. Maybe not bloodlust, maybe flamelust. Or maybe it is bloodlust. Chuck has left the diving board and he takes up a position atop a high judge seat that a group of the guys have grabbed off one of the tennis courts. Gesturing imperiously, he orders the flame bearers to light their torches. Gathering around a campfire, each one ignites his torch, then they all line up in a straight row on either side of Chuck. With another kingly handmove, he orders them forward. They run at a steady even clip toward the pool, torchbearers for a destructive Olympics. Each one stops at the rim of the pool. At Chuck's next sign, they lift their torches high and, in unison, throw them into the pool. As soon as the torches are in the air, they start retreating from the pool. At first flames lick at some of the protruding metal. Suddenly, near the diving boards, there is an explosion as some of the fire finds its way to some gasoline. Then gas tanks all over the pool are exploding and fire is enveloping, consuming the piled-up vehicles. In seconds the separate fires seem to blend into one high-reaching thick flame. Explosions continue. Brightness grows. The low board, its flame retarded surface long since gone to pot, catches fire and a few flying licks of flame land in the bleachers. There is a long silence in the crowd while all this happens, then an explosion of yelling that matches in pitch and melody the sound of the exploding cars.

I'm tired of looking at it. I work my way to the back of the crowd. Clearing the last row of spectators is like stepping outside a stuffy building into fresh air. Scotty stirs but doesn't wake up. My spine is about to bend into itself. I've got to put the kid down somewhere. I choose the nearest vehicle, a dirt-streaked but shiny Buick. It's of more recent vintage than most of the cars in the outfit. Certain members of Chuck's gang pride themselves on the relative youth of their cars. They usually keep them pretty well slicked up. A lot of potential safedrys in this outlaw outfit. Even this Buick, despite the blotches of dirt, reflects the half-moon in the sky and sections of the fire to what looks like an almost limitless depth. I can see myself dimly though a clump of thick dirt lies crosswise across my elongated distorted face. Even as an impressionistic version of myself I look tired. Wiped out. Aging fast. I clear the dirt away to try to get a better look. The fire rages up a bit and my image becomes clearer, though still not particularly vivid. I don't look good, I surely don't. I've noticed that other times in brief secret glances at mirrors. No doubt about it, I've lost the lovable look. I look older, and not necessarily wiser. Well, that's the game, isn't it? Older and who gives a fuck about the wiser? You just get a lot of marks on the face and begin looking like Link and, if you live so long, like Emil. I don't need to look lovable. With Cora gone, I don't need it at all.

Carefully I lie Scotty down across the hood of the Buick. It's not a firm perch so I have to keep hold of him, but at least my back feels better. He lies sideways, his side crossing a stylistic depression in the hood. His body looks twisted in some unnatural way. I don't know, I guess kids can sleep in any position. Good old Mom used to say I looked like a pretzel when I was asleep in my bed.

I hear footsteps behind me, running up to me. I turn, ready for anything. It's just Handles. His eyes are brighter than the flames, his smile broader than the Olympic-sized pool.

This is wild, man, he shouts, really wild. What're you guys doing over here? I looked for you in the crowd. Don't you love the explosions? Did you see me on the board?

You almost killed yourself.

Not a goddamn chance. I knew I was all right. I got perfect balance.

That's hard to believe.

Perfect balance. I got perfect pitch, too. Listen.

He starts to sing. It's the most godawful singing I've heard since the last time I warbled into a tape recorder and played it back. He hasn't got perfect pitch any more than he's got perfect balance. Compared to him, ragged nails on a sandpapered wash-board have perfect pitch.

The fire has gone down. No flames appear above the heads of the crowd.

Are you gonna watch the big finale? Handles asks.

I think I'll skip it, I say.

Aw, come on.

What about Scotty?

Leave him. He sleeps anywhere.

What if he wakes up?

So he wakes up. He won't worry. He knows we'll come back.

I arrange Scotty better on the Buick's hood. Whatever you do to him, even if you jab your finger into his body, he stays relaxed, goes on sleeping.

Handles makes his way like an overbearing snake through the crowd, and I'm able to follow without any trouble. When we get to the first rank, I see that the fire's almost out. Handles rushes forward, beyond the safety line. No matter. It's safe now anyway. Up ahead, Chuck looks back, waves his hand in still another regal signal. I hear a great rushing sound. It's a moment before I realize it's water coming into the pool. Somebody somewhere has turned the pool's water back on. As it hits the smoldering vehicles, the water sizzles and flies upward in curling waves. The crowd surges forward to see better. Essentially we are all joining Handles who has reached poolside ahead of us. I hang back, resisting the push of the crowd. But, when I get to the pool, I take my turn at looking.

Looking makes chills run up and down my back. The pool is now filled with water. Some of it sloshes over the side onto the cement walkway around the pool. A few more torches have been lit and their light is reflected in the surface of the water. Beneath that is a frightening interweaving of broken and destroyed cars, metal joined and hooked into and melted with and, moved by the churning water, rubbing against other metal. Some pieces are floating on the water, their surfaces dully reflecting the light. A singed car seat floats by me. I look for a long time, seeing strange and gruesome shapes in the dark metal beneath the water's surface. I think I see living shapes, tiny monsters swimming in and out of the jagged cracks and openings in the wreckage. A justborn civilization of watery beings come to life and defining their existence by the twisted, burned, sliding terrain of their world. They should be able to thrive on such an existence. We can.

·   ·   ·

Afterwards, the pool filled and the fun over, Chuck orders us back to our cars. We have to clear this area in case anybody with law enforcement pretensions has been attracted here by the blaze. I retrieve the still-sleeping Scotty from the Buick hood without destroying anything inside my body. Is it possible for a kid to gain weight during his sleep? I see Handles doing his version of the scarecrow dance from *The Wizard of Oz* (another cutesy movie that brought tears to old Dad's eyes). It's not as if it's choreographed or anything, it's just that he achieves a kind of effortless clumsiness with it. He's heading right for me. My luck. Nobody's adopted him yet. I don't know why.

He falls in silently beside me. For once he's not talking. His motor's also running down. He's just able to put one foot in front of the other. I guess it's always a surprise when kids like Handles get tired, how it comes with such suddenness.

Link runs up, looking something like an awkward clumsy child himself.

I got wheels of my own, he says excitedly. Chuck's saved an old Merc for me. From the raid.

God, Link, I say. That's . . . good. That's all right.

Link squints at me.

What's the matter, Lee? You don't sound happy for me.

I'm happy for you. Really. Really I am.

No, you're not. But what the hell. I'm happy for me. I've needed to get my hands on a real set of—sorry, Lee. Didn't mean anything by it. Your Mustang's just fine. Musty's just fine. For you. It just isn't for me. I'm a driver, not a shotgun.

That's okay, Link.

He doesn't realize it's not the damn car I'm thinking of. All his great wisdom and he can't see that what pisses me is the split. I liked riding the roads with Link. I think he liked it with me. Now that he's got his own vehicle, that's just so much bent and rusted metal and chrome between us. It won't be the same. It's not the same now, even with him smiling at me so cheerfully, his worn-out face more at odds than usual with a happy look. Shifting Scotty around in my arms, I'm able to hold out a hand to Link. He takes it and shakes it eagerly.

We'll really be a team now, he says. The Merc and the Mustang.

Yeah, sure, Link.

Right, well, I'll see you at the train.

He runs off. I'd like to believe that we'll still be a team, that this will be a new phase. But it feels more like a break than a new phase, it really does. Ah, well, at least I'm not left alone. I got Scotty and Handles for tonight at least. I look down at Handles. He's asleep on his feet, his eyes closed, his legs working by rote.

When I settle down behind the wheel of the Mustang, I realize how tired I am. It's been a long day. My drive back to the train is accomplished as much by rote as Handles' weary steps had been.

9

I ALMOST feel sorry for Handles now. Subdued as he is, sitting alone in the back seat, sullen and fidgety, I almost long for the more active restless boy, the runner and leaper, the arguer and all-around pain in the ass. Maybe we're wrong in taking him back, maybe we should have kept him with us. Sure, kept him with us, trained him to be an outlaw, sharpened the cynical edge that's already so irksome. In a short time, four or five years, he could grow up to be someone. Someone like me. Now there's a goal for any soon-to-be adolescent. No, Chuck was right. He couldn't allow children into the operation, too dangerous, he said when we spoke this morning. He even managed to convince Handles to go back. Once he'd coaxed the kid out of his tantrum. Handles screamed, rolled on the ground, rubbed dirt into his face, punched Link's legs so hard it raised a couple of ugly welts. Even Link's patience was strained. It was lucky Chuck stepped in when he did. He took Handles back to his office in the caboose of the train and talked to him in private for an hour or so. When Handles came out, I hardly recognized him, he was so silent and his body was so calm. He didn't even start to fidget until he got into the car.

Well, he may hate going back, but that's better than what some of the gang had in mind. A few of our zealots wanted to ship him back to the Wheeler camp, make a proper disciple out of him. Chuck scotched that idea, said we're outlaws not recruiters and he wouldn't recruit Jesus when the Second Coming came. I was happy with Chuck's stand. I didn't much like Handles, but I'd hate to see the life squeezed out of him at the hands of Lena and her crew. Even more than that, I think I'd have fought to the death to keep Scotty out of their hands.

I've become very fond of Scotty in the short time we've been buddies. Sometimes I think he's got the goods on the whole world. Give him a couple magic markers, some sheets of paper, a calculator, and he's happy. I find I like making him happy.

Right now he's sitting on the seat beside me, papers all around him—on the seat, on the floor, in his lap. And he's working the magic marker energetically, writing figures all over the paper, checking them against the totals on the calculator that Chuck gave him (part of our odds and ends booty taken from stolen cars).

He's beginning to get ink all over his face again. Not much yet, a dot here, a small island there. I scrubbed him up good this morning but by the time I get him returned to his people no one'll ever be able to tell. He was even good about the cleaning up. He didn't squirm, pull away, yell, even flinch. I suspect he's used to being cleaned up a bit more than the average child is. He's probably seen a lot of ink-riveted water go down a lot of rusty drains in his time.

The sky's clouding up. That's the last thing I need, a storm. I have to rendezvous with the gang at a small town to the south, and I'm not sure they'll wait for me if I'm late. I suppose I could skip out. But I promised Chuck. And I can't leave Link hanging. I try to coax a bit more speed from the Mustang, but it resists. Seems like its top speed is getting less day by day. It needs a good session with the Mech to bring it back to good working order. But the Mech's back east and I'm here and none of the guys in the gang have the magic touch when it comes to breathing life back into a tired vehicle. Why should they? Anything goes wrong with one of their vehicles, they get their choice of the plunder from the next raid. Who needs to keep a car in good working order?

I'll clear out the first chance I get, Handles says suddenly. I won't stay. First chance, my feet will be a-running.

Okay, I say.

Okay?

Sure, why not? You do what you want to, once I got you off my hands. I'll be gone, I'll never know.

I'm not your goddamned responsibility, turdhead, so don't go making like I am.

I don't care whose responsibility you are, all I—

Nobody's, I'm nobody's responsibility.

Okay.

He lapses again into his sullen silence, but only for a minute.

You guys really disappointed me, you know that?

How so?

The way you all came streaming into our camp yesterday, I thought you gotta be hot shit. I mean, revving all those motors and sweeping in like the goddamned cavalry, I thought that was really something. Boy, what a crock.

Well, I suppose nothing's ever exactly what we want it to be, so—

What? What a jerkoff idea. Jerry Jerkoff, that's you all right. You think I wanted much? Hell, I didn't want much. Just something better.

His words hit me like the proverbial sucker punch. I don't want much either, I want to tell him, just something better. Just a way of life, just an idea that I can hold to my chest for more than ten minutes before it slips out of my hands, just Cora. God, no wonder I can't stand Handles. He's too much like me. I was just like that at his age. Christ, I'm just like that now. I've got to get him out of this car and out of my life.

That fire now, he says, that was something. Almost gave me hope. But you guys aren't hot shit. You couldn't get near hot shit even if you were inside a burning john.

I slam my foot down on the gas pedal, anything to get where I'm going faster. The Mustang shudders, shakes, rattles, and growls like a sonofabitch, but does manage a little extra speed. With a sigh of relief I see the exit road leading to the camp area. Only a few more miles now. Great.

Not so great. The camp area is deserted. Thoughts race through my mind like marathon runners who've misplaced their destination. We should have anticipated this. Why did we expect a group of nomads to be where they were yesterday, especially after we've made off with their vehicles? But, if they didn't have vehicles, where would they go? How far could they get? In which direction? If I can't find them, what do I do with Handles

and Scotty? Keep them? No way. Dump them? Where? Go to a
social agency, find foster homes? Why is Handles laughing his
head off? Why is he jumping up and down in his seat? Why not,
he doesn't want his people to be here anyway. What do I do
now? What do I do day after now? Why does the Mustang sound
like it's choking on a piece of food? What branch of heaven
arranges my life and who do I see for a reevaluation?

Back to the train, Handles shouts. Scotty, we're going back to
the train.

What? Scotty says.

Wait a minute, I say.

For what? Handles says.

What? Scotty says.

I'm going to drive down there.

Why? Handles says. You going to look for clues? Track them
down like a bounty hunter? Look for footprints, hoofprints, for—

Shut up, I say and start the car down the makeshift road
leading to the clearing.

For a moment I wonder if this is the right place. Maybe the
raid was somewhere else, two valleys down the road or something. But, no, this is the place. I recognize it. There's still
debris from the camp around, cans and wrappers and stamped-out
cigarettes, little joints still on their roach pins. There's the place
where Link copped the Toyota.

I get out of the car, walk around, doing exactly what Handles
said I would. Looking for clues, for footprints leading in a
direction I can follow. Handles leaves the car and starts doing a
victory dance, scampering here and there, laughing in a nasal
nerve-splitting way, a laugh that'd kill off any remaining buffalo
roaming the land. Scotty climbs slowly out of the car, a magic
marker in each hand, looking like he's ready to use them at the
first sign of trouble.

The morning's gradually growing darker as storm clouds fill
the sky. The air is getting heavy, damp.

Stop in your tracks, shouts a gravelly voice from somewhere in
the surrounding trees. At first I think it's Handles playing a trick,
but the voice is too deep, too adult. I whirl around, can't see
anything. I don't know whether to be frightened or happy. Happy
that I may get rid of Handles after all, scared I'll wind up dead
doing it.

That's the captain, Handles says. Boy, are you gonna get your
face rearranged.

I am somewhat uncomfortable with Handles' obvious approval of my imminent plastic surgery.

The captain? I say, the words catching in my throat.

The famous Cap'n Chickenwings. You remember from when he almost destroyed your buddy except you stopped it by fighting dirty.

I remember. As I picture the man in memory, the real thing emerges from between two moldy trees. He strides slowly, with determination, his muscular arms swinging in rhythm, his body threatening to split his clothes, his ugly face comfortable with its meanness. He is performing a ritual dance for me, exhibiting the potential of his power before actually using it on me.

He would show up now, Handles mutters. Now we don't get back to the train. I want to go back to the train.

Forget the train, I say. What can I do with this guy?

Do?

To talk him out of mangling me. I mean, isn't he glad to see you kids back?

Who knows with the cap'n? I never saw him glad about anything. Probably he's glad but he's just too ugly to show it. He's my pop.

What? Your father? He's—

Now you know why I didn't want to come back.

Cap'n Chickenwings has stopped a few paces from me. He's just looking. Looking me over. Sizing me up. What's taking him so long? He can see that he can wipe me out in a flash. So what's keeping him? He's probably the sadistic type, wants to savor the torture mentally before actually inflicting it.

Hey cap'n, I say as jovially as I can under the circumstances. What's doin'?

You're one of those Wheeler bastards, aren't you?

Well, not exactly, I mean I—

Not exactly. You're not exactly a human being either.

But, look, I'm here to—

You don't have to play cutesy games with me. You bastard, you took these kids away and I'm going to—

But, but, I didn't kidnap them or anything. They hid away in my car. I didn't even know they were there, really. And, look, I've brought them back.

And you were part of the gang that wrecked our camp, stole our vehicles.

Well yes, but—

But what? You know what those cars meant to us, for us. And you're gonna claim you did it for the Lord?

Hey I don't think I even believe in God, I—

Don't start that sort of crap with me. I know about Wheelers. I know you'll say anything to get what you want. And you want to stay healthy. Well, forget it. Start planning what size TV you want for your hospital room.

But I brought the kids back.

I'll give you that. It's why I won't kill you.

Cap'n, Handles says, this guy's all right. He's real nice to Scotty. Leave him alone.

An unanticipated endorsement. Handles seems on the verge of tears. Maybe he's only eighty or ninety percent monster.

Yeah, cap'n, Scotty says.

Scotty looks puzzled. I think he doesn't know what he's saying. He's just backing Handles up. Still, an ally is an ally, no matter what size, age, or magic marker spots.

Don't worry, Handles, the captain says. I won't do any permanent injury.

Cap'n, Handles says. Don't. I don't like it when you—you don't need to—I'll run away again, I will.

Of course you will, I know it. It's a habit with you by now. Just stay out of this, Handles.

Handles looks like he can't wait to grow up so he can take a swipe at his father.

The captain starts walking toward me, an oddly placid look in his eyes. Organs inside my body contract with fear. My skin crawls with fear. My vision changes all colors around me to fear. I can't hear anything but fear. I taste fear. I tremble. I really tremble.

The captain gives me a backhand slap across the face. My skull rattles around inside my skin. Before I'm accustomed to the pain, he punches me in the gut and suddenly I'm struggling to breathe in a vacuum. Doubled over, I watch his shoes move backward a couple of steps. I look up from my bent position. The captain is watching me, assessing when and where his next blow should come.

Handles is crying. So is Scotty.

Captain, don't you ever learn? says a soft almost whispering voice to my left. I can't look up to check out who it is. I may never look up again. My knees dissolve, they're gone forever, and abruptly I'm kneeling on the ground.

I know what I'm doing, Kay, the captain says. Punks like this—

I know, I know. Beat up a punk often enough and hard enough, and eventually he becomes a beat-up punk. Terrific.

But, Kay, he's a Wheeler.

Something like a whine has seeped into the captain's gravelly voice.

Captain, I despise the whole Wheeler thing as much as you do. But I don't think they should be beaten up in third-rate brawls.

Kay, that's where we usually part company, isn't it? Damn it, his gang attacked us, stole our cars—

We can get more cars.

It's not that easy any more.

So we'll get bicycles. Wagons. Covered wagons. What difference does it make? You want to beat up something significant, beat up his car.

Looks like somebody's already done that. And quite effectively.

Yes, it does, doesn't it?

Somewhere in there, while I was collapsing with pain, the captain's voice shifted from anger to amusement.

Are you all right, son? Kay says to me. She is just behind me, but I can barely hear her. Her voice is not only soft. It's weak and a little strained.

I'm getting better, I say in a voice not much stronger than hers.

Handles, come here, the captain says.

Not on your life, Handles says.

I'm not going to be patient with you this time, son. You know how worried you had me when I saw you were gone.

Not much, I'll bet.

Kid, I swear, I'll—

The captain takes a deep breath. He's clearly trying to keep calm. Against the odds.

And, damn it, if you had to go, why'd you have to drag Scotty along with you? Did you think of Kay, how she'd feel? Did you?

Captain, Kay says, it's over, all right? Don't torture him. Scotty's back, he's back, that's all that matters.

Kay, you'd forgive the God that's killing you.

I do, captain, I do.

My breathing is more regular now and that part of the pain that wasn't planning to stay around for a while has left me. I get up on one knee and look around. And see Kay.

Scotty is clinging to her skirt. It's a long skirt, heavy brown cloth with a black border at the hem. I look up past the skirt, past a white full-sleeved blouse with a lacy collar, past the string of green African beads, to Kay's face. It is an astonishing face. I see her eyes first. Anybody would. Behind colorless glasses, they seem brighter than the rest of her features. No, not brighter exactly. More vivid, more alive. She's beautiful but extremely pale, the whiteness accentuated by the delicacy of her features on a slightly too-round face, and the light blondness, almost albino-whiteness of her hair. The dark brown, almost richly brown hue of her eyes is about the only color in her face. The eyes, and the brown skirt, and the green beads against the whiteness make her look unearthly. I keep looking at her eyes. Besides being vivid, they also seem kinder than anybody's eyes I've ever seen. Beautiful. I want her for my sister, mother, wife, and mistress all at once. She smiles (her lips, the lightest pink) as if she has just read my thoughts. She probably has.

She reaches down and absentmindedly begins stroking Scotty's hair. Looking at her and looking at him, I realize now where Scotty got his blond hair. Even so, there's a difference. While his hair shines and sometimes turns bright yellow, hers is without sheen, almost as pale in color as her complexion.

Good to see you again, she says to Scotty, her eyes full of love.

Hi Mom.

I'm glad you decided to come back. I missed you.

I was gonna come back. So was Handles.

I was *not*, Handles shouts.

See, Kay, the captain says. I told you. He wants to run away for good.

That's right, Handles says.

No, he doesn't, Kay says. This is his third time running away, after all, isn't it?

I'm worried someday he'll get the hang of it, the captain says.

I will, too, Handles says sullenly.

The captain raises a hand as if to cuff Handles, and the boy recoils, a bit over-dramatically. Suddenly the captain makes a strange sad guttural sound, grabs Handles' arm, and pulls him close to hug him. Handles tries to squirm out of the strong man's grasp.

Can I go now? I say, standing up.

Kay turns to look at me. I have to stare into those wonderful radiant eyes.

Not yet I think, she says. You may not be aware of it, but there's a gash on your cheek. I'll tend to it. Then you can have something to eat. Then you can go.

I have to be somewhere by—

You'll be there. Don't worry. They'll wait for you.

They? How do you know I'm meeting a—a group?

She smiles.

You're wondering if I'm psychic, she says. People do, often. I'm afraid not, though I'd like to be. No, that was just a reasonably good guess.

Mom, Scotty says, I'm hungry too.

I know. You draw me a picture, and I'll take it in trade for some hot soup and toasted sandwiches. Deal?

Sure.

Scotty collects his magic markers, grabs some paper from his cache in the car, and, in confident and bold strokes, begins drawing.

While Kay applies salve and bandages to my cut, I try not to look at her. But, of course, her eyes draw me. As a lure, they could land anything. All the sneak looks I take do not clarify for me what shade of brown her eyes are. Up close, they seem darker. Just as radiant but darker. I notice that her eyeballs are quite bloodshot, tiny red bloodlines crookedly raying out from each corner, so thin they're almost invisible, as if they don't want to mar the overall pale cast of her face.

When she's done with my cut, she says she'll prepare some lunch.

Lucky your gang missed my truck during your raid, she says. It was probably too broken down to bother with. Without it, we'd have to revert to origins and build a fire. C'mon, Handles, help me.

Apparently her truck's parked in the woods somewhere. She returns carrying a Coleman stove and a tank of compressed gas. Handles has an armload of food.

Using a charred old frying pan and a battered misshapen pot, Kay makes each of us a toasted cheese sandwich—the cheese has an appealing nutty flavor—and a delicious vegetable soup. Then she apologizes that her stores don't allow for very imaginative cookery. I tell her not to be sorry, I haven't eaten this well since back east somewhere.

Scotty, who proffered three drawings, hastily executed but pleasing abstractions, sits beside us and wolfs down food. Handles and the captain sit behind Kay, who is not eating at all.

Not hungry? I ask her.

She smiles sadly.

Can't hold down food these days. Would you like some more soup?

Yes, thanks.

She spoons out more, careful to catch a good load of vegetables with each swipe at the pot.

You're sick? I say to her.

Apparently, she says.

You been to doctors?

Yes.

What'd they say?

That they're overworked and nobody pays their bills anymore.

I mean about—

About what I really don't feel like talking about. All right?

Okay.

She doesn't sound annoyed. She is matter of fact. Kay does not discuss what she does not want to discuss.

Scotty's your son? I say, to show her I'm willing to go by her rules.

Yes. No surprise there, right?

But Handles isn't.

Handles is the captain's son.

Scotty's father?

Gone.

Dead?

Gone.

You and the captain, are you together?

She hesitates before answering, clearly unsure whether to answer me at all.

If you want to think so, she says.

I don't want to think so. I want to know. Well, are you? Together?

Not really. He takes care of—let's pass on this subject too, ay?

I'd like to be with you. With you and Scotty.

She looks away. When I can't see her eyes, she seems to fade out a bit.

No, she says.

Why?

There's a reason.

But you're not going to tell me.

That's right.

She puts a lilt into her voice as she says this, a little musical enunciation that manages to be simultaneously kind and firm.

You and the captain, I say. Seems like an odd combination to me.

You don't hesitate to offer opinions, I see.

I don't mean anything by it. Just commenting.

The captain's a brilliant man.

That's hard to see. He doesn't act it.

He doesn't choose to. The captain walked out on his life some years ago. He doesn't look back at it.

And you? Did you walk out on your life?

In a way. In a very real way.

How so?

That's another thing I won't tell you. I'm sorry.

Look, let me stay. I don't want to go back to the gang. Wait. Listen. This is a different offer. I won't get in your way, just give me a job with your people. I can be a cook, a bottlewasher. I can be Scotty's nanny. I'd like that. And you could use the car. You really could.

She looks off toward the Mustang. She seems tempted.

No, I don't think so, she says finally. You have somewhere else to go.

I don't know where.

You're not a Wheeler, really, I can tell that.

Kay, I'm not even a hubcap. I don't even know what I want out of life. I've been wandering since, well, since I bought that damn car. Even before that, really. Before, I was wandering without moving my feet.

She smiles, a curious almost maternal kind of smile. The kind of maternal smile I never saw on good old Ma.

That's all right, Lee, she says. There's really no law that says you have to get anywhere. We all think there is. We think we have to have a plan, we have to succeed, we have to make something out of our lives. I don't think so. I've thought a lot about life, about my life lately. A lot. At first I didn't think it amounted to much. There was Scotty, of course, but giving birth to a child, even a wonderful one like Scotty, is pretty much standard, isn't it? But there wasn't much else. A marriage that didn't even fail, just came apart thread by thread. A failure at politics—oh yes, I was a city councilwoman, the token women's rights leader for rights they were willing to give. Other political type women achieved more. I dropped out of a postgraduate program, never held a job for more than a couple of years. Didn't add up to much.

More than mine, certainly.

Maybe, maybe not. But, see, when I thought it all out, suddenly it didn't seem so bad, my life. I didn't feel at all bothered by my failure to leave a mark on the world, leave behind a legacy.

I don't like some of her phrases. Leaving a mark, leaving a legacy behind. There's something final, or at least ominous, in those phrases.

All you've done is inhabit a body, I told myself, used up generations of living cells. But that was enough, see. The body may be wearing out faster than I'd like, my mark on the world might be less and less as time goes by, but I inhabited this body as best I could. Sort of like an artist. Here are the materials, the only ones you'll get, use them however you can. Make a gigantic mural, stitch tiny flowers in needlepoint, paint flattering pictures of sad passing tourists. I really think I went beyond the limits of my materials, did a little better than I should have. Sure, by some standards, I didn't succeed, didn't follow a plan. I don't have a collection of pretty things to show off, a work of art that anyone really wants to look at. But I did make something out of myself, did use the materials as well as I could. I made this out of myself—

In an eloquent gesture, she turns both hands toward herself.

I made this out of myself, whatever it is, whatever I am. I inhabited the body, used it up. If what some people believe is true, that perhaps wasn't enough. You know, put a different emphasis on the words, and they begin to seem like a justification of apathy, complacence, violence even. Maybe if I'd been apathetic or violent, I'd agree. Anyway, sometimes I think all we *ever* do is inhabit a body, intrude ourselves on a small section of time. The point is, we almost always miss the point.

Seems kind of negative to me, Kay.

Maybe. But it really isn't. See, I'm happy I tried. I may not have done much, but I did something and I tried. Whatever I believe, whatever the captain believes, whatever you believe, I made the effort. That's all the meaning I need, and it's not so negative.

I don't know, I—

Look, Lee, I'm not saying there isn't some sort of universal order, some God in the clouds, some reason to follow an ideal or a belief, I'm just saying I ain't doin' it. That's it. You want me to do such-and-such with my life, but I ain't doin' it. You want me to adhere to a plan, I ain't doin' it. I just ain't doin' it. In my way I tried, I made the effort, and that's it.

Her voice gets weaker as she tries to talk faster. All this talk isn't doing her one bit of good right now.

The sky is getting much darker. The storm that's been threatening for the last few hours seems about ready to pay off on its threats. I look up at the sky and say:

I better get on. I wish I could stay. No, don't get me wrong, I'm not making that offer again. I'd just like to stick around a little bit longer, but as it is I'm going to have to hotpedal it back.

She nods and we get up. Scotty takes her hand and they walk me to the Mustang. The captain glances our way, does something odd in his voice-box and strides off into the woods. Handles just sits and watches us.

Bye Handles, I say, but he doesn't answer, just looks sullen, as usual. I don't want to push it, so I just wave to him and keep going toward my car. As I reach the door, a few sprinkles of rain fall, disturbing the upper layer of dust on the Mustang. I turn toward Kay.

I hope we meet again, I say to her.

She shrugs.

Never can tell.

As the rain starts to come down harder, I look for it to do something to the paleness of her face. I don't know what exactly, reveal that the whiteness is cosmetic by stirring up some powder or at least bringing a flush to her face. She remains pale. I'm sure I'll never see her again, and I'm goddamned mad about it.

I touch Scotty on his head.

Bye Scotty.

Bye Lee.

I'll miss you.

Me too, I guess.

There's nothing more to say. I get in and start the engine. The rain is really coming down now and, with an apologetic smile,

Kay turns herself and Scotty around. They run toward the woods. Handles stays where he is, standing in the rain and watching me.

I start the car moving, drive by Handles to say a properly sentimental goodbye, but he begins shouting at me.

Goddamn shitpisser. Turdhead. I'm gonna get out of this, you bastard, away from here. I'll find you again and make teabags out of your balls. Fucker. Dirty rotten—

I accelerate, get out of range of his unpleasant voice. I look in the rear-view. He's still there, his body tense, shouting at the back end of the Mustang.

The way up the hill is treacherous, even with the short time it's been raining. The Mustang slips and slides, almost slaloms back to the valley. But I finally reach the top and the good road. I look back. Handles is still in the middle of the clearing, the rain pouring off his matted hair and soaked clothes. He's still shouting at me. I roll down my window and shout back even though I know he can't possibly hear me.

Give 'em hell, Handles!

It's almost like talking to myself.

10

I DRIVE out of the storm a few miles from my destination, a small junction town that Chuck's taking the train to before scouting up another raid. In the distance dark clouds hover over the hills, another storm ahead. I try to enjoy the splendid sunlit California countryside for as long as it's to be available, even if it is somewhat distorted by the pockets and streaks of mud that the heavy rain has left on my windshield.

The road along this stretch's in bad shape. The Mustang absorbs some pretty tough jolts and nearly takes up residence in one of the splendid sunlit California potholes. There are a lot of noises in the car's engine that I don't recall hearing before. I'm a little scared for the Mustang, out here a whole continent away from the Mech. I should have tried to learn something about maintenance and repair, become apprentice to the Mech or something. Who am I kidding? I could spend four years at a mechanics university and come out without a notion of what dark forces propel an automobile.

I can't get Kay out of my mind. I wonder what's wrong with her, what makes her so pale. I find I don't want to speculate on that. Too many possibilities are too frightening. Still, I'd like to have stayed with her and her group, even Handles and Cap'n Chickenwings. In the back of my mind, where she hangs around on streetcorners, Cora is laughing at me. Idiot, she is saying, you don't really want to be with them for any good reasons. You just want someone to tell you what to do, take care of you, give you hot soup, homilies, and road directions. Just look close at what you say you want. A woman older than you, and her son. Home cooking and a family. Everything but a suburban home. Why don't you just take your ass back to mama? She and whatsisname'll take you in. For about five minutes. Give up, Lee. Nobody wants to take you in. And don't ask, what about you, Cora, 'cause I'm not about to punish you any more, I promised myself remember?

I get glimpses of railroad track from time to time, laid across flatland in a depression beside the road. It's probably the same track Chuck's train has already used to get to the rendezvous point. God, I hope he waited for me. All I need now is to be stranded here in a godbenighted section of the west, my car rattling like a dying snake, and myself pained and bruised forever from the two blows Cap'n Chickenwings landed on me. I've forgotten how to scrounge. I'm not sure I could survive.

The track curves away and proceeds downhill as I head up a rather steep grade. Cresting the top of the hill, I see quite a bit of smoke up ahead, beside the road. I better check this out, in case anybody needs help.

It's lucky I pull off the road slowly, since I drive onto an overhang whose guard rails have mysteriously disappeared. The post holes are there, but there's no sign of the guard rails themselves. There's just a rusty anti-littering sign between me and the steep cliffside.

Somewhere down below, where the smoke is coming from, there's also one hell of a lot of noise drifting upward. I walk to the edge of the overhang to take a look. My first impression is that this would be a fine spot for one of those marked scenic overlooks along a road. Across the way trees seem crocheted into the side of rolling hills. In the distance, shape-changing in heat waves, is a small section of the ocean. It looks ethereal, as if it's hanging in the sky.

The smoke is off to my right, several thin wisps rising slowly from the band of railroad tracks, which now run directly below where I'm standing. At first the smoke obscures the scene below. I hear sounds of people shouting, sharp cracks that might be gunfire. Some of the smoke clears and I see a train, our train, stopped behind a pile of logs and garbage and other shit which have been thrown on the tracks with the obvious intention of ambush. I see figures moving about beside the tracks, but at this distance and with all the cliffside foliage obscuring my view, I can't see what exactly is happening. The smoke seems to be coming from a fire in one of the freight cars where we store supplies. Somebody's fighting with somebody on top of one of the other cars. There's a lot of activity all around the train and bursts of smoke in the bushes beside the tracks that probably come from rifles. Fire is being returned from the train.

From up here I can't get a clue to who's attacking the train, but it's definitely an ambush. And here am I, a spectator, hundreds of feet above the attack, with no way down. Not a path, a trail, a parachute drop. I'm tempted to just jump and see where I land.

There's a dirt road running along the other side of the tracks. Maybe I can find my way to it with the Mustang.

God, it's like running a maze in a dream. I can hear the blasts of gunfire and people shouting and sometimes it all seems very close. First off to my left, then later to my right, then front, then rear. I can't get a good fix on it. Maybe some natural phenomenon in this goddamned forest is misdirecting the sound. Whatever turn in the roads I take, whatever new road I take the car down, I just come to another road. They've got roads down here that don't go anywhere, roads that have no purpose, roads that have no community planning logic to them. I've driven across overpasses twice and actually seen the goddamned track without finding a goddamned way down to it. I've edged the Mustang along roads so narrow they might be footpaths, probably are footpaths. I've lost all sense of direction. I'm lost. The gunfire sounds fainter. I might be driving away from the train now. I probably am.

I stop the car. No sense in wasting gas just wandering around this area. Also, it's getting dark fast. I don't want to be stranded all night among a bunch of evil-looking trees that look like they plan to come alive and walk at sunset. I get out of the Mustang to see if, by being outside the car, I can get a better idea of where the sounds are coming from.

I still hear the gunfire. Now it doesn't sound so far away. I also hear something else. A voice, almost a voice. A phantom. I'm already being haunted and it's not even sunset. No, wait. It's a human voice. Groaning. Somebody's hurt.

The groaning stops and then comes a strong clear voice that seems to surround me:

Damn it, that's it. I've had it. I'm going to buy a tacky suburban home, keep all my guns in the cellar, and I'll have a workshop. Yeah, good, a workshop. I'll make uncomfortable furniture for all my friends, tables that need matchbooks underneath one leg, yeah, that's—ouch, damn it to hell.

It's a deep voice, resonant. Its pronunciation is precise, every syllable pronounced like in a diction lesson. I almost ask the voice if it's talking to me, but it begins again and I can tell it's not talking to me.

Jesus, this is the last time I play vigilante with the guys. What do I care, a bunch of punk kids out stealing automobiles. Let them, I say. Why not? I say. Please take my Volkswagen, I say. Junk it like all those cars they junk. Just let me run my lathe, is that the right word, a lathe? Just let me run my lathe. Maybe I can make a candlestick out of driftwood. Can you do that? Driftwood candlestick, sounds great to—goddamn the pain. This is the last time. The last time I get shot.

He starts to laugh.

Yeah, he says, I don't want to get shot any more. The fun has gone out of getting shot. I am retiring. No doubt about—damn it, damn it, damn damn damn damn.

The voice slips back into groaning. It's coming from behind a tree just off to my left. I can see a grey-suited shoulder almost merging with the greying bark of the tree.

The groaning stops for a moment. I watch the shoulder for a sign of movement. Then the man coughs.

Oh God, blood. I'm coughing blood now. Oh great. Oh wonderful, terrific. I'm not even going to get the tacky suburban home now, am I? Damn. This is the last time I play vigilante, last time I play mercenary. God, it hurts. Oh, damn damn.

Taking my steps carefully, I walk toward the tree. I can almost reach out and touch his shoulder now. The man groans. I step backward and my foot comes down on something hard and slippery. I can't get my legs to work. I fall.

What? the voice says. What was that?

I look down at my feet, and see what I've tripped over. A gun. One of those automatic rifles with the clotheshanger stock.

Is there somebody out there? the voice says.

Yes, I say, just me.

Just you, who the hell are—oh god damn it! Jesus, I can't stand it.

He coughs again. A small abrupt cough that sounds more like

clearing his throat. Then his shoulder slumps and he gradually slips sideways, toward me. His head hits the ground hard, just next to the rifle. He's dead, I know that right away. There's blood all over him. The blood and the darkness keep me from seeing his face well. His hair is almost all grey, so he's probably on in years. *Was* on in years. I don't want to know what he looks like. I just want to get away.

I pick up the rifle, it's lighter than I expected. I was going to take it with me but, now that I've touched it, I realize I can't. I don't want to feel its oily cold surface, don't want to feel its weight. I hurl it away, listen to it break through leaves, hit a branch, and fall, not all that far away.

I return to the Mustang. At first it won't start. Nothing seems to respond to the turning of the ignition key. Then suddenly the motor kicks in and I almost stand on the gas pedal to get it going. It does not respond well. It moves but there's not much speed or power. There's enough to get me away from the corpse, but the car crawls like a snail down the road. I start breathing again.

The battle's just about over by the time I finally find the train. I come around a curve in the dirt road and am suddenly, miraculously it seems, alongside the tracks. I can see smoke up ahead, and hear a couple of gunshots. They are almost reluctant. Afterthoughts.

The car now barely moving, I creep along the road. In a couple of minutes I see the train. Some members of the gang are putting out fires in two freight cars. Others mill about, stare at the hillside looking for signs of ambushers returning. I see Link, climbing on the engine, doing some task I can't figure out from this distance.

As I pull alongside the barrier of garbage and other debris, I feel the Mustang gradually losing the remainder of its power. Just as it rolls to a stop, I hear the sound of gunshots from the other side of the barrier. I duck. At the same time I feel the right side front of the car begin to sink. A shot has hit the tire. Great, wonderful, terrific, damn, I think, fully aware I am echoing the words of the dead vigilante. What the hell, he did have a few points in what he said.

I just want to go to sleep.

Are you all right? says Link. He is leaning in the driver's side window. You're not hit?

I start to laugh.

No, I'm not hit, I say. I'm not hit at all.

Then what's the blood on your forehead?

I reach up and touch the blood on my forehead.

God, I am hit, I say.

I stare at the blood on my fingers for a short time, then the fingers start to fade out. Everything fades out.

I wake up suddenly but don't open my eyes. Someone's talking near me. It's Link. Link and who?

Well, frankly, Link I don't think there's any real hope.

It's Chuck. What is he saying? I feel all right. I don't feel shot.

Is there anything we can do? Link says.

He doesn't sound very sad. C'mon, Link, I want to shout. I thought I was your buddy. Get a little emotional, will you?

I'm afraid not, Chuck says. We're simply not equipped for that kind of salvation work. Needs a specialist.

Specialist? I think. Salvation work, what does that mean? What kind of salvation do they mean?

What do you suggest? Link asks.

The scrap heap, I'm afraid.

I see myself thrown onto a pyre with a bunch of stolen automobiles. I see Chuck lighting the pyre and the flames enveloping my body. I see my face melting.

Is there anything we can do? I don't think Lee's going to care for the idea of the scrap heap one iota.

You're goddamn right about that, I say and open my eyes. You're not throwing me on any goddamned scrap heap.

Chuck and Link exchange puzzled glances and then begin to laugh hysterically. I'm confused but at least it's clear I've jumped to a wrong conclusion. I'm all right, they've been talking about something else.

Everybody needs a little Abbott and Costello in their lives, Chuck says.

Whatever that means.

How are you, Lee? Link says.

Okay I guess, for somebody's been shot.

Link laughs again, unfeeling bastard.

You weren't shot, he says. I don't know where that blood came from, but it apparently wasn't yours.

I remember the corpse by the tree. When he fell, some of his blood must have sprayed onto me. I never felt it.

Link sits beside me, a suggestion of compassion on his distorted face.

We wiped the blood off your forehead, he says. Funny, there wasn't any on your clothes or anywhere else.

Funny, I say.

But you're okay. You missed a whale of a fight.

I saw some of it, from up above there. What was it all about?

We don't know. These guys in suits stopped the train with their barrier, and opened fire without discussion. I guess we've made a lot of enemies. People want to protect their possessions. Chuck is thinking of giving up the operation.

What were you guys talking about just now?

Link nods, glances at Chuck.

It's your set of wheels. I think it's had it.

No.

I'm sorry, Lee. Couple the guys been working on it. They can get it to run, they say. I mean, it'd be all right for grocery shopping, herding sheep, stuff like that. But it's got no power, no speed, and they can't do anything about that. It's certainly of no more use to the gang.

The Mech'd fix it.

From what you've told me about him, I'm sure he could. Nevertheless, he's on one coast, you're on another. Chuck says you're gonna have to scrap the wheels.

Chuck can go to hell. I look over at Chuck. Go to hell, Chuck.

I'm sorry, Lee, I don't—

Shut up, Chuck. I don't want to hear from you. I don't trust you anyway. Who can trust a guy who pops up everywhere I go? You're haunting me, Chuck. You're a spook, Chuck. Go away.

Chuck looks very sad. His handsome face seems to collapse just a bit, his body deflates just a little.

Sorry Lee, he says. I really am. But that's my decision. I'll see you later.

He walks off before I can answer back. He's smart. He knows my mouth.

You're gonna have to, Lee, Link says. There's no way that car can—

Have to? Have to? Who the fuck says I have to? What are you guys, God? A fucking two-headed God? I'll take my wheels and—and—

And sulk in your tent, Link says quietly. I wonder what the

hell he means by that. I won't ask him. Let him be smug, what do I care? I care.

Link, let's bow out. Let's get away from these guys. You and me, like before.

Assholin' down the road, you mean?

Yeah, that's exactly what I mean. We don't need these guys.

I like it here, Lee.

Like it? Fuck, they had to force you onto that platform, force the words about believing God out of your throat, force you to study the—

I know. And I don't intend to go back there. But I like it here. I'm staying.

But why?

I like it here, that's all. I got a sense of, I don't know, purpose. We do some good, we—

Some good? Burning up wrecks?

As I say it, I get a flash of the Mustang on fire, its melting metal twisting into and blending with the frames of other wrecks.

It's not such an awful job, Link says.

Job? Job, Link? Man, Lena's got you right in her clutches. From hundreds of miles away, you're just one more fucking puppet. You're a Wheeler, Link.

He shrugs.

Maybe, he says.

Maybe? Fucking maybe? This is the criminal life, hell, you told me that, it's not a job.

Whatever you say.

He looks away. We get silent. In the distance I can see the Mustang, looking all crooked because of its flat tire. Hell, it looks crooked without a flat tire. It's got more dents, bumps, bruises, rust holes, and all that shit, than I'd remembered. New little scars it's received over the last few months. A couple of guys are crouching over the motor, lazily working on it. I look back at Link. He's almost as much the worse for wear as the car. How many bumps, dents, and bruises are there on his body? Hell, I can see why he wants to stay. Here he can be Errol Flynn and Gary Cooper, and nobody looking at his ugly face will think about it much. He'll stay. And I don't want to leave without him.

Okay, I say finally.

Okay what?

We'll scrap the Mustang. But not Chuck's way, definitely not

Chuck's way. I'm not going to just dump it in a swimming pool, then burn it and drown it. No sir, not that way.

What way then?

I'll think of something. I will.

— I'm sure you will.

Link smiles and pats me on the shoulder. I try to smile back.

Okay, I decide finally, we're in California, near the good old rugged ragged coast, I know what to do with the Mustang. I give Link the rundown. He likes the idea. We go to Chuck, who at first doesn't understand, asks me to go over it again.

It's simple, I say. I just want to send it off one of these splendid sunlit California cliffs. Like in the movies, you know?

Chuck smiles. Why is it so hard to stay angry with him?

I like it, he says. As they say in the movies, Lee, it's you.

I wonder what he means by that.

Well, whatever, I say. I just don't want it to wind up as part of a mangled pile of metal. I want to watch it roll and bounce down to the sea and sink beneath the water.

Chuck suddenly can't stop laughing. When he can talk, he says:

Whatever you say, Lee.

Why is everybody always saying that to me? Can't I do any goddamned thing without being the object of ridicule? I mean, Link and Chuck are on my side, for God's sake.

Link, you take your Merc and follow him. Drive him back when the deed's done, okay?

Sure.

I want this to be right, I say to Link as we walk to the car. It's ceremony, right, ritual? If you want to laugh at me any more, choke on it, okay?

Okay.

We should probably wait until morning to leave, but I can't stand the idea of waiting. I want to go now. Get to the coastal cliffs, say something appropriate as a eulogy, then send the Mustang over the edge. I want it to be quick. I want to watch it go, then turn my back on it and walk away. No wonder I'm afraid of Link's laughter. If I were split into two people right now, one of me'd probably laugh at the other.

11

I THOUGHT the coast would be easier to find than this. California's got more roads than they got jerks. Well, I hate to do it, but I have to admit it. I'm lost. I don't want to admit it to Link.

This road looks likely, and that rushing noise sure sounds like the ocean. I'll try it. I look into the rearview. Link's Merc is still there. Maybe he doesn't know we're lost. I took the directions from Chuck, after all. Ahead, the road seems to be getting worse. It's pitted and not well defined. Sand has drifted in elongated triangles onto the road. Well, sand's a good sign, I guess. Where there's sand, good chance there's an ocean nearby.

Only the headlights from our two cars illuminate the road. My brights aren't working, so I can see ahead only a small stretch in the pitch darkness. At this slow speed, the car's not running too badly, although it did have an attack of emphysema when I tried to speed it up earlier.

The farther we go, the more sand there seems to be. Sometimes the road disappears altogether and the car skids along the sand for a half-mile or so. I'm getting scared. I'm scared I'll lose all sight of road and wind up stuck for good on a rocky beach. I'm scared I'll skid on sand and slide off into a gully.

The land around me seems to be flattening out. The few lights in the distance—windows of homes, working roadlights and streetlamps, faded neons—are fewer. They seem to flash out on me like dying stars. The ocean smell is getting stronger. I'm scared I'll just drive nonstop into the sea. No cliffs, no romantic tumbles, just me and the Mustang following this old road right into the ocean. I begin to believe this could happen. I slow down more.

There's a high fence beside the road now. Well, it was formerly a high fence. Now it's bent over with age. In some places its barbed wire top nearly touches the ground or sand. There's a sign up ahead. I stop the car.

As I get out Link runs up behind me, his simian gait made more awkward by his slipping and sliding over the drifts of sand.

What the hell's going on? he says.

I'm gonna read this sign.

Look, Lee, why don't you follow me out of here? We get back to the main road, I'm sure I can get you to a better place than this.

I want to read the sign, Link.

Okay, read the sign. God.

It's a big sign. Its wood was once painted white but the air and sand and time have flecked away some of the paint, have greyed the rest of it. There are several lines of print on it. This must be some major sign. In the dark I can't quite make out what it says. I go back to the Mustang. Link watches silently. I drive the car up closer to the sign. The letters, those that can still be read, are clearer now that they're illuminated by the Mustang's headlights.

I get out of the car. Link, crouching and leaning close to the sign, reads its bottom line:

This says something about an air force base. V-A—I can't read a few letters, it ends in a burg.

Vandenburg, I say. Used to be an air force base out this way by that name.

How do you know?

My Dad took me to a lot of military-preparedness movies. And Vandenburg'd probably be around here somewhere. I want to read the sign, maybe we can figure out where we are or where to go or something.

In capital letters at the top of the sign, it says WARNING, then in regular block print it implores: Please take heed.

It goes on:

Land East of High Tide Line between Osa Flaka Lake and Point (the word is obscured, looks like Sal, wonder who he was) Except Parking Lot and Road—Private Property.

That's interesting, I mutter to Link. I think we've trespassed.

Under the general warning are some numbered specific ones. In each warning the word danger is colored red. It was probably bright red once. Now it looks like old lipstick.

1. DANGER! Rip Tides and Strong Undertow. Swimming and Surfing at your own risk.

2. DANGER! Dangerous Rocks and Air Currents. No Hang Gliding.

3. DANGER! Mouth of Santa Maria River Not Passible (It's really spelled that way) When Flowing. Dangerous Quicksand and Heavy Currents.

4. DANGER! Missile Fall our Area from 1 Mile South Through Vandenburg Air Force Base.

5. DANGER! Obstructed Vision in Dunes: Shifting Dangerous Surface. Watch for Pedestrians and Others.

I don't know what to do. Watch for the Pedestrians or the Others. I'm afraid to move. One step and I could get pulled away by a rip tide or fall into the quicksand or onto the dangerous rocks. I could impair my vision hopping around sand dunes or just simply stand here until the next missile falls on me. Good thing I left my surfboard at home, anyway.

What is it? Link asks.

I don't know, I say. This may be the checkpoint for the end of the world.

Oh. Well, I'm checking out that dune over there myself.

The dune he means is higher than any other rise in the vicinity. It seems populated with ragged-looking clumps of mysterious dark matter. It looks ominous. It looks like the kind of place where you'd find irritable mutated animals and corpses of dead pilots from the world wars.

That dune? No.

Why not?

You could, you could get lost.

Me? Bullshit. Don't worry.

He strides off, holding his low shoulder lower than usual. I retreat to the Mustang, almost get in it, ready to crawl underneath the steering wheel, stick my thumb in my mouth and wait. I read the sign several times. I look out at the sand dune. I think I see Link moving around out there in the darkness, dodging the mutants, stepping over the aviators' helmets of the corpses.

Are you all right? I holler.

Fine. There's not much out here but prehistoric beer cans, that kind of shit.

I'm fidgeting. I'm slapping both hands against my jeans in an erratic rhythm. To stop this, I reach in the car window and switch off my headlights. No sense in having the battery run down, not now. I resume slapping my jeans.

In the distance a car motor starts up. My heart leaps to my throat, where it's wanted to be anyway for the last ten minutes. It hadn't occurred to me that somebody else might be out here. On the horizon in front of me, I see a gradually expanding glow of light, the headlights of another vehicle. It clears a dune beside the road and starts coming toward me. It is two or three miles away right now, toward where the ocean should be. I hadn't suspected that the beach could stretch out that far. I'm scared. What if we've come all this way across the country and into the western paradise, only to be robbed and slaughtered by some cruising carload of beach bums? We're too alone here, isolated. What should I do? I try to holler to Link, but the words catch in my throat. I clear my throat and manage one good shout:

LINK!

He doesn't answer. Oh Jesus, maybe he has gone off and got lost. That car is closer now. It's not moving fast, just coming on steadily. I glance into the Mustang, looking for some kind of weapon, but my luck fails me now, no monkey wrench, no cooking fork. The car comes around a curve, and it seems to be slowing down. I close my eyes for a moment, see a gang of pirates emerging from the vehicle, brandishing already blooded swords, cocking for the first shot from ancient two-barreled pistols. I open my eyes. The car is now only a few feet down the road. I'm sure it's stopping. It's going to stop. Isn't that squeak the sound of a brake being applied?

But it doesn't stop. It barrels on past me, traveling much faster than it had appeared to me. In the streaked darkness following the glare of their headlights I can't even see into the car, can't tell what kind of people were in it or how many. I'm not even sure there was anybody there, it might be a ghost car, driven along these godforsaken sands forever. DANGER! Ghost vehicles. Beware of tire tracks after sand storms.

I holler for Link again. He hollers back this time, says to keep my shirt on, he'll be there in a minute.

I stroll around the Mustang, trying to bring my nervousness under control. On the other side of the road is a gentle downgrade. A few feet down it, I see something. It's probably a land mine. Still, I want to know what it is. Slipping and sliding, I run to it.

Just poking out of the sand, like a burrowing animal just checking out the outside world, is the front of a car. An old Ford, looks like. It's eerily dark down here and I can't see any of the lights I was using for reference points earlier, the roadlamps and lighted windows. There's only a faint aura, the headlights of Link's Merc. Much of the metal on the old Ford has rusted or eroded away. It's replete with holes that have rust-bordered rims. It occurs to me, wherever I leave it, the Mustang'll look something like this some day. Hell, it's at least halfway there already.

I scrape away some sand and discover the Ford's windshield which, amazingly, has remained intact under the assault of the elements. There are scrape lines all over the glass. I trace a couple lightly, safely, with my fingertips, try to look inside. It's dark. I fumble around in my jeans pocket, come up with a bent and almost crumpled matchbook. Like most of the matchbooks I carry, this one has a single match in it. One match, bent and almost ripped through. Carefully, I disengage it and gently strike it. At first it doesn't light, then it suddenly flares up. Quickly I hold it close to the windshield. I can't see much. There are still seats inside the car, they seem to be ripped, jagged metal peeps through the upholstery. There is a book wedged between the front passenger seat and the gear box. I can't make out what book it is. It looks like the pages would fall apart, turn into sand, blend with the natural sand of the beach, the minute they were touched. The match is almost burned down to my fingers. I try to focus on the rear seat. Just before I have to shake the flame out, I see something. Something large, something vaguely human or shaped like a big ambulatory animal, something moving.

I jump backwards, lose my footing, start to fall further down the hill, do a couple of backward somersaults, the kind that had always eluded me in gym classes. My back rams against something solid. Another car probably, but I don't look back. I scramble to my feet, start running up the hill. My left foot slides out from under me and I fall sideways. Onto what looks to be the remains of the cab of a diesel truck. It gives way when my shoulder hits it, makes a small moanlike sound, slips downhill a bit. I don't want to inspect it at close range, but it felt strangely light to the touch of my shoulder. I want to scream hysterically and be rescued. Instead, I manage to get my feet working again and, running and crawling, slipping and sliding, chewing on mouthfuls of sand, I get back up the hill to the road.

I am a few feet behind Link's Merc. I run toward it.

LINK! I yell.

I'm right here, he whispers. His whisper almost sends me right fucking out of my skin. For a moment the weirdest possibilities occur to me. Maybe something bad happened to Link out there by the sand dune. Maybe he's become one of them. One of whom? What's out there besides a lot of sand and a few old car shells?

Let's get out of here, I say to Link.

Why don't you leave the Mustang here? he says. Just run it off the road down that hill.

No!

Lee, it really doesn't matter where you—

No.

All right, you follow me. I'll find the coast for you.

No, not that either.

Then what are you going to do?

I look back down the hill, I can just see the old Ford poking its nose out of the sand, can just make out the outlines of what must be a couple dozen other abandoned vehicles. A breeze has come up from nowhere and, with it, the salt smell of the sea. I can almost feel the salt on my skin. I can hear the waves beating against the shore much clearer now, I don't know why I didn't hear them before. My throat is dry, and probably sandfilled. My tongue feels swollen.

I think my brain is swollen, sandfilled, dry. Maybe I should abandon my brain here, let it sit forever in the driver's seat of one of these derelict vehicles. I see the Mustang rotting and rusting away in sand until it breaks up into pieces, artifacts for beachcombing; I see it becoming pearl-smooth in sea water and discovered by future scientists out to see what went wrong with Earth's oceans; I see it on its roof at the bottom of a cliff, come upon by sleazy vagabonds who use it as a place to sack out and roast pig's tails; I see it floating to the South Seas and becoming a scrap metal god. I see it turning on me and going off on its own, leaving me only a roadbed oil slick to remember it by.

So what am I to do? Drive a new car for Chuck's gang, make raids on lonely aimless nomads, run the car to its inevitable ruin, get a different car, make raids, ruin another car, another. I laugh suddenly. By his benign expression, I can see that Link accepts the laugh as pure logic. I remember Kay and what she said to me, how pale she looked, her love for Scotty. I picture Cora standing by the Mustang and, like a doctor who's pulling the plug, shaking her head as if it's no use. I see myself as a toothless old man, hunching by the roadside, begging rides, telling tall tales of my life as an adventurer, as an outlaw, as a piece of shit that once traveled the roads. I can't do that. I can't be that.

I'm not going back, Link, I say. At least not to the train and Chuck and that gang. I'm not going to play out your little outlaw fantasies either. I'm not going to even stay in California, I'm heading back east, I'm going where Cora is. And I'm not going to send the Mustang over any fucking cliff or any fucking hill of sand or into any Sargasso swimming pool. I just ain't doin' it. That's all. I just ain't doin' it.

Link stares at me a long time. In the light from the old Merc, his face catches a lot of bizarre shadows. Then he smiles.

All right, he says. Okay. Okay with me. I like it.

He stands in front of me for what seems a long time, staring into my eyes. I realize that his face—his grotesque distorted face—now looks normal to me. It has not seemed strange to me for some time. I have not felt sorry for Link for some time. For some reason that's good, I know, but I don't know why the hell why. He reaches out the back of his hand and touches me lightly on the point of my chin.

Okay, he says again, then, abruptly, without looking back at me, he gets into the Merc, starts it almost before he's settled into the driver seat, backs up, turns around, and drives off.

Hey, Link, I say, just before the Merc disappears into the darkness.

So here I am, leaning against the rear of the Mustang, no desire to move, glancing at the sand wrecks to the right of me, the decaying warning sign to the left of me. I'm no longer scared. I'm in no hurry to leave here.

Well, that's not true. I am a little scared. I'm afraid I'll get into the Mustang, ready and eager to start my trek back east, and it won't start. That is too much the way my life goes. I even begin to believe that it won't start and I stay beside the car, enjoying the growing breeze and the smell and taste of salt in the air. Yeah, it probably won't start.

It starts.

12

AN afternoon in the care of the Mech and the Mustang looks, feels, sounds, complains like new. Well, maybe not looks, but definitely feels, sounds, and complains.

Even Emil, who lets me take him for a spin around the Savarin parking area, admits that a miracle has been wrought. For the Mech, the usual miracle.

Just don't hunt rabbits with it, was the Mech's parting shot when he returned the car to me, and I was pleased, hearing all the echoes of all the other times the Mech has said those words, or words very much like them, to me.

Want to go out on the Expressway with me? I ask Emil. His face goes ivory white.

No, this is a fine ride here. Fine. All the ride I need. Let's go back to the coffee shop. I feel better there.

I smile, to let him know I was just joking anyway, and let the Mustang glide to a stop in front of the coffee shop door.

Emil sits still for a while, then says:

You've been good for this car, Lee. I suppose, not to get too silly about it, it's been good for you.

I laugh.

Who knows, Emil, who knows?

Come in and have some coffee.

I think of his coffee and wonder if I could substitute a cup of percolated machine oil while he's not looking. But, no, I have to drink it. I have to.

It's very comfortable sitting again at the counter in Emil's coffee shop. I've spent the better part of the last two days here, sitting here and giving Emil a rundown of my escapades out west. I have a tendency to exaggerate details. That's all right, Emil doesn't believe me anyway. Before our ride I told him of my trip back east. All the times the car almost gave out on me, all the little repairs done by all the lesser Mechs in repair shops across the country. I told Emil of trying to locate Kay and Scotty and Handles and the captain, and failing to find even a trace of them. I told Emil of my sneaking into the Wheeler camp and spying on Victor presenting an indoctrination lecture. In shiny well-pressed new clothes, Victor looked great. His manner had become milder, really professional, and he delivered the standard lecture with a chilling sincerity. He convinced me the Wheelers are really on their way to somewhere, and I don't like thinking of that. I told Emil about my encounter with Lena, but I didn't tell him *all* about my meeting with Lena. Sometimes the curtain has to be drawn. I told Emil how I set fire to two campersful of Wheeler literature. (He said it was an empty, somewhat Pyrrhic gesture. I didn't care what he said. I liked burning pamphlets better than burning cars, I told him.) I told Emil how I parked the Mustang near the Ramada and stood outside the inn's windows and watched Maria laughing with a group of her charges. It seemed like a long time since I'd called Maria and been told by her that her wound was healing well. She said then that she liked me, but please I should not try to see or talk to her again. She said Anton had gone through a transformation and was treating her like a wife again. Spying on her, I wished I could talk to her, at least say hello, but instead I let the glow around her smile tell me that she needed no help from the likes of me. Maria was all right.

Emil enjoyed hearing about my experiences out west. He said they reminded him of yarns told around campfires.

I'm not lying, I said.

Not even about Chuck? he said.

What about Chuck?

Well, all the time you were with the gang, Chuck was showing up here regularly, *here* at the Savarin, usually at twelve o'clock at night, usually just looking in and not saying much.

C'mon, Emil, who's spinning yarns now?

One of us maybe. Maybe neither one. I'll ask Chuck about it, next time I see him.

You do that. You just do that.

It's been good times for me, talking with Emil. Whether he believes me or not. Anyway, he doesn't believe anybody. Not even himself sometimes.

Just as he's about to serve me a cup of his coffee and stare at me until he sees me take a sip, I am saved by the bell. The Savarin phone rings. Emil answers it, then hands it to me, saying:

For you.

It's old Dad.

Your mother called me, he says, gave me this number.

I had called her yesterday and tried to tell her about my western tour. She said come by for tea some afternoon when Harold would be there. He would just love to hear about it, she said. I said I love you Ma, and hung up quickly.

How've things been? Dad says.

Not bad. How's it with you?

Can't complain. You gonna come by? I'll split a pint of anything with you, son.

I'll get there, Dad. I don't know when, I'll ring you first.

No, just come. I often don't answer the phone.

Sure then. You feeling all right? I mean, your health, that sort of thing?

I'm tiptop, son.

You don't sound tiptop.

I figure I can breathe, that's tiptop. I look forward to seeing you, son. Lee.

My eyes suddenly tear up when I hear him say my name. He never says my name. Emil sees the tears and smiles. Here I am, dealing with two men simultaneously, you could paste them together, they might make one pretty good father.

I try to say goodbye to Dad, but he's already hung up.

I sit at the counter for a while, and stare at the surface of the coffee. There are no answers there, only big oil spills, so I ask Emil:

Where's Cora? You seen her lately?

I've been two days trying to ask those questions, and this is the first time I've been able to.

Not lately. But she's around, I hear. Looks good, too.

Why do you say that? She always looks good.

You didn't see her after that last time she racked up a car. Told you about the accident, just didn't want to tell you she'd been marked. I thought her face might have permanent scars. But they went away pretty fast.

I want to see her.

I know you do.

You going to do anything about it?

I guess so.

When?

Now, I guess.

He goes to the phone, picks up the receiver, with his back to me dials a number. When the call has gone through, he says hold on for a second, okay? Stretching the cord, he backs away from me, takes the receiver to the kitchen doorway, just manages to make it into the kitchen. He talks softly into the receiver and I can't hear a word of it. He comes back and says:

She already knew you were back.

I nod, not surprised.

Is she coming here? I ask.

No, she wouldn't do that. She says to meet her by the old Exxon billboard. Somebody'll drop her off there. The Exxon board is, oh, about ten miles down—

I know where it is.

I get up and head toward the door, realizing that I've managed for once to get away without drinking a single sip of the coffee. Something must be wrong with Emil.

I'll check with you later, I say to Emil.

If I'm here.

Won't you be here?

I heard your buddies, the Wheelers, have bought this property, don't know when they'll show up.

They're not my friends.

He shrugs.

Maybe not, he says and pours out my coffee at the sink. I can't tell whether the rising fumes are from heat or corrosion.

13

CORA leans against a tree next to the decrepit Exxon sign. She looks slimmer. Her face seems older and, for that matter, prettier. I take the keys out of the ignition, get out of the Mustang, and walk around it toward her. She has her thin arms crossed, and she stares at me noncommittally. I stare back, almost too afraid to talk.

You look, I don't know, earthier, she says. Your face is leathery.

The outdoor life, I guess.

About all the outdoor life you'd know would be what blows in a car window.

That's not true, Cora, that's—

Yeah, you're right. What do I know? I'll take it easy on you. I meant to. That just slipped out.

It's all right.

The day is almost unbearably humid and hot. It feels like the west. Well, it feels like California anyway.

I'm not going anywhere with you, Lee. Nothing has changed that way. And don't ask for a chance even.

I know all that.

Then what are we doing here right now? I don't even want to discuss—

We don't have to. Here.

I hand her the keys to the Mustang.

It's yours, I say.

She looks at me strangely, disbelievingly.

The wheels, I say. The Mustang. It's yours.

She stares at the keys, jangles them a bit. She looks over at the car.

It's more of a wreck than I remembered.

It's more of a wreck than it was then. But the Mech's got it running real good again.

She tightens her grip on the keys.

No strings, she says. I don't even want you riding with me.

That's okay, Cora. No strings. The wheels are yours.

She takes a few steps toward it, looks back at me.

I'll probably rack it up in a coupla days. I racked up every car I ever had.

Yeah, I know. I knew that anyway. Maybe you won't. I have a feeling you won't.

She stops by the driver's side door.

I'm taking it, she says.

Good, I say.

Want a lift back to Emil's?

I thought you didn't want me to ride with you.

I'll make an exception to back there.

I'm tempted, but I'm afraid to sit beside Cora, even for a short time.

No, I'll walk, I say.

Walk? It's ten fucking miles.

I know. Good to see you again, Cora.

Yeah, me too, guess.

She starts to get into the Mustang, then stands up again.

No, Lee, it *is* good to see you. You look good. Sound good, too. I really wish we could get together. I wish—but we can't.

Yeah.

Maybe we'll run across each other.

Right.

She starts to get in again, then emerges again.

Thank you, Lee.

Sure, Cora.

This time she stays inside the car. She holds onto the steering wheel for a long time, just holds it. Then she slowly puts the key into the ignition, puts the gear shift to P, and starts the car. The motor growls. Out here, it sounds louder than it ever did from inside. She starts to glance over at me, but doesn't quite make it. Then she leans forward, shifts to D, and the car accelerates, almost lurches off the shoulder and onto the expressway. It's out of sight much more quickly than I'd've expected, than I want. In the waves of heat rising from the road, the car seems to sink into the cement of the road.

The humidity seems to be growing by the second. I need to get walking. There's so much debris scattered along the shoulder, I have to keep my head down, watch every step.

I have no clear idea what to do now. But I'm happy. I really like having no clear idea what to do. I suppose I ought to go visit Mom and Harold, give old Dad a thrilling and sodden reunion, go swap tales with Emil.

So, what *can* I do? I can return to the city, get a job. Work hard all day, walk home through fields of dogshit, get frustrated, angry, unhappy, look up Lincoln Rockwell X and let him con me into a new set of wheels in just as bad shape as the last one. No, I don't think I'll do that. Maybe I'll stay on the road. Maybe I'll go destroy the Wheelers. That's worth thinking about anyway. Maybe I'll settle down in the Savarin, learn Emil's recipe for coffee. Maybe I'll go back to California, look for Kay and the kids. Maybe I'll go into business with Anton and Maria. Maybe I'll compose a symphony but leave it unfinished. Maybe I'll become chairman of the board of some revived carmaking firm and create the perfect set of wheels. Maybe I'll fix this ugly cracked highway all by myself. Maybe I'll find a way to get Cora to come back with me.

At least I've got options.